SHADOW OF SACRIFICE

SHADOW KNIGHTS
BOOK 5

MICHAEL WEBB

Copyright Page

Published by Whatup Publishing LLC 2024

Copyright © 2024 by Michael Webb

This novel is entirely a work of fiction. The names, characters, and incidents portrayed in it are the work of the author's imagination. Any resemblance to actual persons, living or dead, events, or localities is entirely coincidental.

Cover design by jeffbrowngraphics.com

ALSO BY MICHAEL WEBB

Get a FREE prequel novella to the Shadow Knights series - Shadow Knights: Origine - by signing up for my mailing list at www. subscribepage.com/michaelwebbnovels or scan this QR code

Did you forget what happened in the last book? I've got you covered!

Go to michaelwebbnovels.com/book-summaries to get short summaries of each of the previous books in the series.

CONTENTS

PART II
LOYALTY

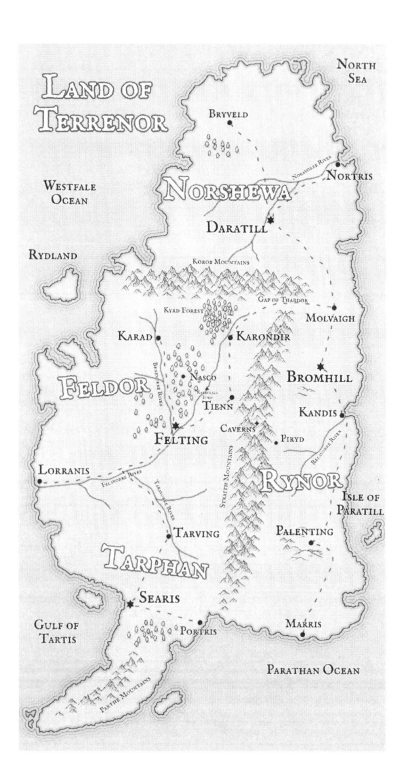

PART I

DESPERATION

1

DESPERATE ESCAPE

Labored breaths filled her ears as Chelci mounted the ridge. Her heart pounded. Sweat poured down her brow, stinging her eyes. She crouched and extended her hands. The metal chain connecting her manacled wrists jangled. "Come on. Hurry." Her voice was quiet but urgent. Their lives depended on speed.

Gavin followed behind, scrambling up the slope. His fingers clawed into the earth, ripping moss from rocks and staining his nails. Chelci pulled under his arm to help him up the final steps.

"Do you—" He paused to breathe. "Think that—" His chest heaved. "They're following?"

Chelci scanned the woods, her jaw tight. "I don't know." Fear and adrenaline coursed through her, bringing the early-morning scent of pine and evaporating dew into sharp clarity. "We need to keep moving."

Chelci led with Gavin running behind. Having crested a ridge, their path led along a rocky spine. The slope dropped precipitously on either side. The tops of the trees formed a blanket of green and yellow through the rolling hills of Eastern Feldor.

Boulders slowed their progress. They clambered up and down the stone obstacles, stumbling yet moving as fast as possible. The chains restraining their arms made balance difficult.

They ran down a short, flat trail until Chelci skidded to a stop. She gasped. A ravine blocked their path. Holding onto a tree, she leaned forward. A river rushed through a gully far below, frothing white where water tore around jagged rocks. Other than tumbling down a cliff, a fallen tree was the only escape from their dead end. The thick log spanned the ravine's gap with branches and limbs jutting in all directions.

"Do we cross?" Gavin asked.

Chelci sighed. "We have to."

"Gah!" Gavin yelled as he bent and tugged one of the metal shackles on his legs.

Chelci winced at the chafed, bright-red skin around his ankles. Hers looked just as bad.

The broken chains between his legs rattled as he pulled on the cuff. "I wish we could get these off!"

"Keep your voice down." Her words paled in comparison to the thundering river.

"If we could use the origine, we could leap over this."

"Or jump down the cliff," she added.

Gavin turned around. "Or rescue the others."

Chelci followed his gaze. She scanned the ridge they had run along and the forest floor below. *No sign of movement.* "Yes. At least we'd have a chance to save them."

"What's our plan?"

Chelci raised her eyebrows.

"If we get away, what do we do next?"

"I say we head back to Felting. We need Veron and Lia. With all of us together, without these shackles . . . maybe we can . . ."

"Do you, uh . . . think Veron is . . . ?" Gavin didn't finish his question.

"No!" she snapped, unwilling to entertain hopeless thoughts. "He's all right. I know he is." A memory of Veron's collapsed body turned her stomach.

Gavin nodded then glanced down the trail. "Do you think some-one's coming after us?"

Chelci shook her head. "I don't know. They have the other five knights still. Maybe they won't care about us."

A branch moved along the ridge. Chelci ducked behind a tree, her muscles tensed.

"Did you see something?" Gavin whispered, joining her.

She didn't answer. Peering around the trunk, she scanned for any sign of pursuers. The river roared in the ravine. Wind blew across the ridge, ruffling her clothes. Her fingers pressed against the bark while her eyes focused. A gasp escaped her lips. Two marked ones in gray clothing dashed around a bush, heading their way—Gralow and Heathine.

With stringy hair and a gray beard, Gralow's massive arms and broad shoulders knocked branches aside with ease. Heathine was shorter with bare, toned arms. Her long hair faded from brown to a hazy gray. Black marks stained their throats, and red crystals hung from their necks. Despite looking well along in age, they moved with the agility of young warriors, leaping from rock to rock with ease.

"They're here," Chelci whispered, backing away from the tree. She turned to the fallen log and took a deep breath. "We must cross." She pointed at the tree. "Go, quickly!"

Gavin nodded. He touched a hand to an askew branch and stepped onto the log. His steps appeared confident as he moved steadily across. The chain dangling from his foot rattled against branches.

Chelci set her foot on the tree and turned. The pursuers in gray sped along the ridge, approaching quickly. She turned back. Gavin was only halfway across. *I can't wait any longer.* She mounted the log, using a branch to steady herself.

The fallen trunk began broader than her shoulders but narrowed considerably by the time it reached the far side. Some of the bark had been stripped, and a smooth surface remained. Mist rising from the churning river coated the log, creating a slick and treacherous bridge. She shuffled her feet, moving only a bit at a time.

Between branches, she had nothing to grab. Chelci held her shackled arms up, adjusting them side to side to keep her balance—difficult with the limited range of movement. She kept her eyes glued on the log, but the jagged rocks of the distant river below caught her attention. Sweat beaded on her forehead, but she didn't dare wipe it. She released her breath when she grabbed the next solid branch.

Gavin leaped to the ground on the far side.

Chelci glanced up. *Halfway. I can do this.*

"There's a tricky part in a bit," Gavin said, "but if you—"

His words cut off mid-sentence. The look on his face chilled her bones. Holding onto the sturdy limb, she turned carefully, pivoting her feet on the slick log. The two marked ones dressed in gray stood on the other side of the chasm. Both faces held an intrigued expression—curiosity, not worry.

"Where do you think you're going?" Gralow asked, his head cocked with a half-grin.

Chelci clenched her jaw and turned toward Gavin.

"Keep going, Chelci." Gavin urged.

"What are you going to do over there?" Heathine taunted.

"Run!" she shouted at Gavin.

"Not without you! Come on!"

"You think you can outrun us?" Gralow asked. The laugh that followed sent a chill through Chelci's body.

Chelci stepped forward. The log narrowed and glistened with mist. She held her arms ahead as she moved steadily to the next branch. Below, the roar of water and rocks teased her, begging her to slip.

A whoosh of air shook her cloak, forcing her to clutch the branch. At the edge of her vision, Heathine's body flew through the air, landing gracefully on the far side of the ravine.

Gavin took a step back, glancing between Chelci and the marked one.

"We can track you anywhere," Heathine said, sauntering toward Gavin. "Running is pointless."

"Gavin!" Chelci yelled. "Get out of—" Her leg caught. The

dangling chain pulled against a limb, caught on a knob. She extended her leg and shook it. *Come on. Get free!*

"Be careful," Gavin called.

Chelci's other foot turned, sliding on the wet log. Her weight shifted, sending her foot off the side. Her stomach dropped. She flailed her arms as she fell. Sharp pain registered in her leg as her fall was arrested. The chain link hooked onto the branch, leaving her dangling upside down over the rapids.

"Chelci!" Gavin yelled.

Swaying in the air, Chelci watched as Gavin scurried back onto the log. "No!" she cried. "Leave me! Go!"

He didn't listen.

The pain from her ankle seared through her mind. Gavin's muscular form crossed the log and crouched above her.

"Give me your hand!" a faint voice called.

Her vision spun, dimming. She flailed her arm. The pain in her leg diminished. Her mind begged her to let it fade to black. Just before she gave in, her arm found resistance. Another hand closed around her forearm, and her head lifted.

When she blinked her eyes open, she lay across the log. Feeling in her leg had returned, and a blazing pain shuddered through her body. Gavin crouched next to her. She looked down. The river waited.

"Are you all right?" he asked.

She nodded, grimacing. A glance behind revealed Gralow still on his side and looking ahead showed Heathine waiting at the opposite end. Both held swords resting casually against their sides.

"Where do you want to go now?" Gralow taunted.

Chelci cringed and looked at Gavin. His shoulders slumped. "What should we do?" he whispered.

With his help, Chelci managed to stand. Holding on tightly to a branch, she positioned her feet firmly on the log. Her ankle throbbed with piercing pain.

"Feel free to jump," Gralow said. "That will make two less people for us to keep track of."

Chelci sighed. "Come on." She headed back toward Gralow. "They're right. We can't outrun them."

Gavin helped steady her as they progressed across the fallen tree. Chelci winced when she finally hopped back to the ground. Heathine had already leaped across the ravine again, and both marked ones held swords out.

"Are you going to try that again?" Heathine asked.

Chelci shook her drooping head. She twirled her foot. It hurt but wasn't broken.

After sheathing his sword, Gralow grabbed the back of her shirt and pushed her ahead. Heathine did the same to Gavin. Walking side by side, the two shadow knights trudged back along the ridge, returning to the others they had left not long before.

2

THE GLADE

A pricker pulled at Lia's shirt. "Ouch!" She extricated herself then looked ahead.

Veron tromped forward, paying no attention to the thick undergrowth of the forest.

Raiyn paused next to her. "You all right?"

A faint smile grew. She hitched her heavy pack higher on her shoulders. "I'm fine. Thanks. Just a scratch."

"Does your father know where he's going? Or do you think he's going crazy, grieving the loss of the other knights?"

"He's not going crazy," Lia said. "Plus, the knights aren't lost. They're just . . . gone for a bit. We'll get them back." She pictured her mother slung over the man's back as he ran off with her. She fought against the thought that they might never see her or the other knights again. *We were all so helpless without the origine.* Her stomach turned. *And now Father can't use it at all after whatever they did to him.*

"You don't think he's still trying to track them, do you?"

Lia frowned, glancing at her father. "I don't think so." They had spent the previous two days scouring the roads, woods, and the banks of the Felavorre River. Despite the Marked Ones' numbers and the hostages they transported, they couldn't find a trace of their path.

"If we hadn't forced him to stop, I think he'd still be out there," Raiyn said.

"And I'd be with him," she said with a sigh, "but . . . it didn't make sense anymore. If we hadn't found a trail by that point, we weren't going to."

"So, where do you think we're heading?"

She shook her head. "I have no idea, but it seems like he knows where he's going. Either way . . . with Danik and those goons in control of Feldor, we can't stay in the city. It's best they believe the Marked Ones killed or captured us."

"Yeah," Raiyn admitted. "And we can't keep sleeping on the ground like we have the last couple of nights."

"Agreed. Someone might find and identify us."

Raiyn chuckled. "I was referring to my back. I'm hurting all over and have barely slept."

A short distance ahead, Veron stopped and looked back. The pack on his back swung to the side, knocking morning dew off a branch. He waved. "Come on, you two."

Lia and Raiyn caught up. "Sir, can you share where you're taking us?" Raiyn asked. "We're well away from the city, and there's no one around to hear."

"Tell you?" Veron said. "Where's the fun in that?"

The bit of vigor infusing him encouraged Lia. He'd been sullen and overwrought for days.

Veron continued forward. "We're almost there."

"You said it was a . . . shelter of sorts? Like a cave or a hidden place to pitch tents?"

"It's a place we can stay that should keep us from getting discovered."

A jumble of rocks as tall as Veron grew out of the forest floor, piling atop each other. A ray of morning light fell through the leaves, giving the ground a glowing look. Trees surrounded them, creating a shady haven of stone, wood, and earth. Past the pile of rocks, a stone cliff emerged from the woods.

"Whoa! Where'd that come from?" Raiyn's eyebrows lifted as he stared ahead.

Veron continued toward the wall.

"You ever been here?" Raiyn asked.

Lia shook her head. "I've been through these woods plenty. I've always known there were cliffs here, but we steered clear because they made travel difficult."

The cliff grew clearer as they passed more trees. Before long, they stood at its base, staring up. Lia's jaw hung loose. She craned her neck. The top soared above, easily ten times as tall as her. Most of the rock was sheer with nothing more than a few sparse ledges decorating the side. Shadowed crevices contained moss, and a trickle of water ran down a depression, disappearing into a damp circle on the ground. High up, a small tree clung to a crack, growing out then up. Its roots twisted around the rock wall like a serpent.

"Are we climbing this?" Lia asked, a twinge of excitement fluttered inside.

Veron laughed. "You're so much like your mother."

Lia's insides turned. Guilt over neglecting her guard duties and her mother almost dying rushed through her.

His warm smile softened the tension in her shoulders. "Chelci loved climbing anything and everything. Remember that time she fought a valcor in a tree?"

Raiyn jerked his head. "Wait. What?"

"I remember you *telling* me about it," Lia said, shifting.

"A valcor?" Raiyn said. "As in . . . monster of the night with massive teeth and claws that flies, shoots fire, and turns people to stone?"

"Lia." As if he sensed her remorse, Veron rested a reassuring hand on her shoulder. "It's all right. Guilt creates nothing but regret."

"She almost died because of me."

"Don't worry about what happened in the past. You remember the other day? When you saved my life and defeated Valdok without use of the origine?"

"Yeah, that was awesome!" Raiyn added.

A smile grew on Lia's face.

"We'll get all of them back. Now, come on." Veron turned along the base of the wall. "We're almost there."

Leaves crunched under Lia's feet as she followed.

"Valcor?" Raiyn whispered, springing a few steps to walk next to her. "He's kidding, isn't he? Those are just stories, right?"

Lia grinned. "For part of her life, my mother grew up in the village of Nasco"—she pointed ahead—"a couple days' walk in that direction. They *say* a valcor was slaughtering villagers, and she, uh . . . killed it in a tree."

"She *fought* it in the tree the first time," Veron corrected. "She didn't kill it until a while later, and that was on the ground."

"On the ground," Raiyn said matter-of-factly, "as most people are when they kill valcor."

Lia chuckled.

"Laugh if you like." Veron pushed a branch aside. "But I watched as she chopped off its head."

Lia stopped laughing.

Raiyn glanced at her with wide eyes.

She leaned toward him and whispered, "I still don't think they're real."

"Here it is." Veron stopped at a crack in the rock. The cliff split halfway down, creating a tunnel the width of a person. An uneven path of roots and stones curved up and around, disappearing into darkness.

"What is this?" Lia asked.

Veron smiled and slid the pack off his back. "I'll show you." He turned sideways and stepped into the dark crevice.

Lia glanced at Raiyn.

"You want me to go next?" he asked. "Clear out any spiderwebs he misses?"

"I'm not afraid." Lia removed her pack and stepped into the darkness. The temperature dropped and dampness filled the air. She scooted sideways, following her father, who shuffled ahead. The walls were slick, damp from trickling water and covered in moss. A musty smell filled the passage.

"Phew!" Raiyn whistled. "This is tight."

She glanced his way. His broad shoulders scraped against the mossy stone. The pack dangling from his hand bounced between the walls, but his feet shuffled along.

"Watch out for this wire," Veron said.

Lia looked ahead to where her father crouched, pointing at a thin line she would never have noticed in the darkness.

"What does it do?" Raiyn asked.

Veron pointed up into the yawning darkness of the crack. "You see that?"

Lia craned her neck to look up. "The blackness?"

"Hidden in that blackness is a ledge containing twenty boulders. The wire connects to a trigger that drops them."

Lia gulped.

"Not only would they kill you, but it would block this passage for quite a while."

"So . . . don't touch the wire," Raiyn said. "Got it."

Lia stepped over the line, pointing to make sure Raiyn saw it as well.

"Keep moving," Veron called as he disappeared around a corner.

Lia shuffled to catch up. An invisible object tickled her face. She ducked, swatting with her hand to knock away the spiderweb. When she rounded the corner, light returned. Down another tight passage, her father's body posed in silhouette at the end of the crack. A dozen steps brought her to the end. She stepped out of the passage and arched her back, blinking away the slanted sunbeams that blinded her. She set a hand against the rock and took a few steps forward.

Her eyes adjusted and grew wide. "Whoa!"

"Watch it." Veron pressed a hand against her shoulder, then pointed down.

Another wire ran across the path, nearly invisible against the forest floor.

"More death?" Raiyn asked, his eyes on the wire as he emerged from the crack in the rock.

Veron shook his head. "No boulders, just music." He pointed to the closest tree.

Hidden among its leaves, Lia spied a dangling cluster of chimes.

"What is this place?" Raiyn gasped when he finally turned his attention outward.

The high cliffs created a large circle, stretching out into the distance. Rather than making a plateau, the center of the area was hollowed out, forming a bowl, hidden from the world. Trees spread out and green grass formed a small field. Orange and yellow butterflies flitted through the meadow, dancing between the wildflowers growing there. A stream poured from one of the cliffs, cascading in a waterfall to a pool at its feet. The far side of the pool flowed over rocks and created a serpentine path of water that disappeared into the cliff on the far side of the area.

Veron waved his hand forward with a proud smile. "This is the Glade."

Lia's jaw hung loose. It wasn't the meadow or the waterfall or the fact that it was hidden from the world that left her in wonder—it was the buildings. A half-dozen small homes filled the Glade, weaving around trees and connected by crushed-stone paths.

Each home had wooden walls with glass windows. A few included covered porches, while others contained decks above the living quarters, perched as high as the tree branches. All contained stone chimneys peeking through wooden-tile roofs. In one, a hammock swayed off the deck, rocking gently in the breeze.

In the center of the Glade, a larger building stood out from the others. Three windows lined the wall Lia could see, and a chimney poked out of each side of the vaulted roof. Beside the larger building, a small bridge crossed the stream to a flat, cleared area the size of the courtyard back in their old training facility.

"Who lives here?" Lia asked, her mouth dangling and her eyes scanning.

Veron's smile grew larger. He inhaled, his chest puffing out. "We do."

THE STONE CRUNCHED under Lia's feet as they walked the path toward the center of the Glade. "This is amazing!" she said. "How did you . . . Where did . . . ?" Unsure of what she wanted to ask, her words faded.

Veron laughed. "We've been working on this for years."

"We?"

"Gavin, Bradley, Dayna, Ruby, Salina, Chelci and I."

"Wha—" Her words wouldn't work again. "When?" Lia pointed and tilted her head. "Those missions you kept taking to Karad? The ones you wouldn't let any of us go on . . . ?"

A guilty look swept over her father.

"You were here, working?"

"Sometimes."

"Why didn't you tell us? We could have helped, too!"

"We wanted to keep the circle of people who knew as small as possible."

"So . . ." Lia paused, scanning her brain. "You knew we would need to leave the city?"

Veron nodded. "We've been too well known since we defeated Bale. I worried about the fame, knowing it could lead to problems. We needed a new home—someplace no one knew about where we wouldn't be discovered." His face fell. "I only wished we would have moved sooner." After a forced smile, he crossed the short bridge and pointed to the cleared area ahead. "This is the training yard."

Lia craned her neck, looking for piles of boulders. She laughed to herself. *I'm sure we'll find some to use, eventually.*

"And this is the main hall." Veron opened the door to the larger building.

Lia entered the hall first, and her smile grew. A kitchen with large counters rested against one side of the room. Barren shelves and a clean stone hearth appeared to have barely been used. Tables and benches identical to the ones in Felting filled the room. Lia ran her hand along the sanded surface. "Much cleaner than the old ones."

Veron laughed and set his pack on the countertop. "I should hope so. Some of those were over one hundred years old."

Lia and Raiyn both followed suit in dropping their packs. Her shoulders thanked her for the relief. "So this is why we loaded up all those supplies."

"I wondered what use this was all going to have in the woods," Raiyn added.

Along the back wall, a sitting area held padded chairs and another stone hearth. The roof of the main hall vaulted up with one long wooden beam running the length and three smaller ones crossing the width. What gave Lia the most pleasure were the large windows on each side that allowed the morning light to fill the room with a glowing cheer. The view from each direction showed the verdant hidden valley.

"Check this out," Veron said, bouncing with excitement. He approached a basin set in the middle of the kitchen counter.

A straight length of bamboo stretched over the basin with something covering the end. Lia cocked her head. "What's that?"

Veron pulled the covering off the end, and a stream of water poured through and into the basin.

"Whoa!" Raiyn cried.

Lia's jaw fell. "Ugh! All those trips to gather water in Felting! We could have had this all this time?"

Veron laughed. "I'm glad you approve."

Raiyn leaned out the window. "How does it work?"

"The bamboo picks up water from the stream as it runs through the Glade. If the stopper is on, it continues along its way, back into the stream. But when the covering is removed . . ." He wiggled his fingers in the gathering water. "It was your mother's idea."

"I love it," Lia said.

Veron unfastened the straps on his pack and began pulling supplies out. Lia and Raiyn joined in. Soon bowls, plates, utensils, and cups piled on the counter. Lia's pack held blankets, paper, and writing supplies. And Raiyn's contained candles and more kitchen equipment.

"After a brief rest, we'll head back to get another load."

Lia stepped to the door, looking out to the rest of the Glade. "What are the other buildings? Are those homes?"

"Living quarters. Two people to a building. We were building enough for twelve knights, but the last one isn't finished yet."

Lia counted the five similar homes with trails between them. A partly finished one had a frame and portions of a roof, but that appeared to be it.

"At least we needed space for twelve at one point. We talked about making the move as soon as we learned about the Marked Ones. But then Chelci was injured, so we waited." Veron's head fell. "Too long, apparently."

Lia looked to the ground, fighting to keep her guilt away.

"Go." Veron cleared his throat then motioned to the Glade. "Choose a home—any you like."

Her head lifted as did her spirits. The one with the hammock caught her eye, and she made a beeline for it.

After ascending the short rise, the cliff walls cast her in shadow. She stopped and peered up at the building as Raiyn came alongside. "Would you like this one?" Lia asked, her breath held, hoping he would decline.

Raiyn shook his head and pointed to the side. "I like this one." The home he gestured toward had a front porch that faced the waterfall.

"That looks nice, too." She walked up the last few steps to the structure she had her eye on. The small house nestled against the base of the cliff with trees growing thick on both sides. She pulled on the handle, and the door to the building opened easily. She stepped inside.

The room was pristine. Despite having been built a while and not maintained, it remained clean with the fresh smell of hewn wood and hay. The main room was cozy but not cramped. Beds of straw covered with fabric sat on either side of the room with rudimentary tables next to each. A clean stone hearth lay between the beds, and a window looked out to the Glade from the center of the opposite wall. In the far corner, a wash basin tucked away with a familiar-looking bamboo spout. She grinned.

That's going to be nice.

In the center of the room, a wooden ladder stretched up, ending at a loft. She climbed the rungs. Small spaces to each side could be used to store things, but the door was what interested her. She opened it, and a grin spread across her face.

The deck had enough space for two chairs with a railing against the end. Tree limbs flanked either side of the small house, providing a bit of privacy. While the stone cliff continued higher, standing on the deck brought her close to the top. She peered down into the Glade. The stream babbled from the nearby waterfall. The grassy meadow lay just beyond, and the main hall with its adjacent training yard was only a stone's throw away. The sweet smell of spruce trees mixed with the fresh air and the faint mist.

Part of the railing cut away, and the hammock she'd eagerly spied dangled in the air. One end tied to the house while the other fastened to a spruce limb. Lia grasped the fabric and tested the tension. *It seems sturdy.* Her heart jumped as she leaped, feet first. The canvas caught her. She bounced gently as the tree limb gave before straightening to its original position.

"It's just your size."

Her father's voice startled her. She grabbed the sides of the hammock then laughed, turning back toward him. "You scared me."

"Sorry." Veron stood on the deck and nodded toward the hammock. "How do you like it?"

She grinned. "I love it. The hammock. The view. The cliffs. It's beautiful."

"You know . . . this is the house Chelci pictured for you."

Lia's face fell, weighed down by her sense of responsibility for the kidnapping. "How are we going to get them back?"

Her father's jaw extended, clenched. "I'm not sure yet. With their trail dried up, we can't just scour Terrenor." He inhaled and blew out a long breath. "We'll get the supplies we need first. Then, once we're ready, we'll figure it out."

"What do you think the Marked Ones want us for?"

"Labor, I assume." Veron shrugged. "A shadow knight could do work that would be impossible for a regular slave. They took people from that village in Rynor. Maybe they're trying to upgrade their worker population."

"How do we stop them?" Raiyn ascended the ladder and stepped onto the deck. "If we can't use the origine around them, what do we do?"

"I killed one." Lia raised a finger in the air as the hammock swayed back and forth.

"Yes. It will be difficult, but . . . it's possible," Veron said.

"Origine or not, I'm with you both," Raiyn said. "If we have to tromp across Terrenor to find them, I'm in."

Veron smiled. "Thank you, Raiyn. We'll need you." He looked back to Lia and clapped. "What do you think? Ready for another trip?"

3

SUPPLIES

The dusty, brown hood smelled of sweat and dirt, but Lia didn't dare lower it. She kept her head down, following Raiyn and leading her father—the most likely to be recognized. The guards at Felting's gate talked amongst themselves, bantering about their ability to hold down ale. Lia didn't even draw a look as she shuffled through the arched opening.

Her heart settled as the guards faded behind them and the street opened. Her father stepped beside her, and Raiyn waited.

"That wasn't bad," Raiyn said. "They didn't even look at us."

"We must assume that Danik infiltrated the army and all extensions of the government," Veron said. "That means, anyone could recognize us. Fortunately, he will assume the Marked Ones captured us, so he's probably not looking."

"I can't believe Danik would turn like that." Lia's anger toward him bubbled to the surface.

"Can you not?" Veron asked. The question didn't contain judgment, only sorrow.

Lia sighed. "I guess I can. Still, he changed so fast . . . and killing Grandfather . . ."

"King Darcius was a great leader and a great man. He will be missed. I expect things will change around Felting." Veron glanced at Lia. "Tell me more about the group he's with."

Lia wrinkled her nose. "They want power and money, and they'll do anything to get it."

"I counted six of them plus Danik. Is that all?"

Lia nodded. "At least for now, but it seems the devion is a quick and easy study. He taught them in about a week. I imagine he'll build his ranks."

"Agreed. Before long, he could have an army of soldiers powered by the devion."

"Can we stop that?" Raiyn asked. No one answered. "Of course finding Chelci and the others is our top priority, but . . . if Danik's going to build up his crew, might it make more sense to go after him first?"

Lia's stomach churned. She didn't want to answer, and her father's silence indicated he didn't either.

"I fought him in the castle before I lost the origine," Veron finally said. "I couldn't beat him. The devion is powerful."

"If we can rescue the other knights, that will improve our odds," Lia suggested.

Veron nodded. "Let's focus on the Marked Ones for now."

Traffic was light on Rampart Way. No familiar faces turned their way or noticed who they were under the hoods.

Veron checked each direction before opening the door to the training center. He held a finger to his lips as they padded inside. "Move quietly. They could be waiting for us."

"Who?" Raiyn asked. "Danik's men or the Marked Ones?"

"Either."

Lia gulped and followed her father down the hall. The common room was empty, both of people and supplies. Raiyn grabbed a small sack of beef jerky from the counter, the only food item that remained, and tucked it in his bag.

Veron continued toward the courtyard. He stopped at the edge and peered around the corner. The afternoon light lit up the space, warm with an orange glow. After a moment, his shoulders relaxed.

"Looks clear. Let's check upstairs. Grab anything useful, then we'll load up on weapons before we head back."

Lia bounded up the stairs and entered the sleeping quarters. Normally marked by conversation and laughter, an eerie quiet filled the passageway. Doors hung ajar. Rooms were empty, left in the same state as the night everyone was taken.

She stopped at the third door on the left and paused in the threshold. The small room had been hers all her life. Drawings of animals still decorated the walls. A chip in the stone by the window marked the time she was angry with her Mother and threw a knife at the wall. She laughed.

A stuffed cow caught her attention on the desk, its two button eyes staring back at her. *Mr. Butters.* She smiled and picked up her friend. He was on his third tail and looked like he'd been dragged through the mud dozens of times. Despite the grime, her stuffed companion always helped her feel better.

"Hey there, little cow," Raiyn said, interrupting her thoughts from the doorway.

She smiled then held the animal up for him to see. "His name is Mr. Butters."

Raiyn held up his hands in mock apology. "I'm so sorry, Mr. Butters. I didn't realize. It's nice to meet you."

They both laughed.

"I've had him as long as I've been alive," Lia said, rubbing her finger along his matted back. "Mother always reminded me I could keep him as long as I wanted."

"You gonna bring him to the Glade?"

Lia stared at the animal for a long moment. Her fixed smile widened. "Yes, I will." She opened her pack and set the stuffed animal inside. "You find anything?"

Raiyn shook his head. "I don't have anything here. I'll save space for the weapons."

Lia opened her drawers. Some of her clothes were left in Tienn, but she still had a few outfits. "I know I told you the other day, but . . . thank you for coming for me—in Tienn."

A blush swept over Raiyn's face.

"I would have died if it weren't for you."

"It was nothing. The Dream told me where you were, so I came to find you."

"And rescue me from a fiery death."

He smiled then nodded toward the hall. "It seems your father trusts me now."

Lia laughed, stuffing clothes into her bag. "Saving his daughter's life tends to help."

Raiyn's face fell. "Even if my father happens to have been his mortal enemy."

Lia reached out and touched his arm. "You are who you are, and who you are *now* matters. You can't control where you come from. I see that, and Veron does, too, even if it took him a while."

"Yeah, but . . . Raiyn Bale . . ." He shuddered. "I've avoided using the name most of my life."

"You can stick with Crabtree, if you prefer."

"Yeah," he smiled, "I think I might."

Her mind told her to take her hand off his arm, but the touch of his skin sent a warm flush through her body. She returned his smile.

Footsteps in the hall turned both of their heads. Veron appeared through the door. "You ready?"

Lia dropped her hand, and they both nodded.

"Let's load up in the armory."

Sunlight blinded Lia as she stepped through the doorway at the top of the stairs. She descended the steps and noticed the blackened item her father held. "What's that?" she asked.

Veron glanced over his shoulder then down at his hand. He lifted the object. Charred pages ruffled.

"Is that . . . ?" Her heart sank.

"The Shadow Knights' book?" Veron nodded. "Yes—well . . . it was. Talioth burned it." He tossed it to the dirt of the courtyard when he reached the bottom step.

"All that knowledge and history, lost. Should we . . . write a new one or something?"

"Possibly. After we get the others back and deal with the Marked Ones and Danik, we'll start a new era of Shadow Knights."

Veron shrugged the empty pack off his back and tossed it on the dirt. "Now . . . We can pile the weapons together and roll them up in the packs."

Lia's eyes flicked up, and the hairs on her neck prickled.

Something feels out of place.

She glanced around but saw nothing out of the ordinary.

Raiyn joined in a vigilant scan of the courtyard. "What is it?"

She shook her head. "I'm not sure. It's like something doesn't belong."

Veron continued, "Set your packs down. We should be able to—" He stopped as he looked at them, tensing. He pulled Farrathan from its sheath over his shoulder.

Lia and Raiyn pulled their swords, the grate of hard steel echoing in the space.

Raiyn breathed, "What do you think it—"

"Shh!" Lia held up a finger.

They stood silent, heads turning and eyes shifting. Lia began to think her intuition had been wrong. She lowered her blade.

A yell drew their attention to the armory. From the back corner, a boy with dark skin ran at them, shouting and waving a short sword. The savage look on his face could have sent an attack dog running in fear.

Veron was the closest to the boy and deflected a round of his ferocious strikes. "Whoa there."

Lia stepped clear of the action but could immediately tell the boy was experienced beyond his age. Her father—without the use of the origine—barely managed to stay ahead of him. Lia pulled from her power inside and swooped in. She grabbed the boy's hand, knocked his sword away, then held his arms behind his back.

"Let me go!" the boy shouted, tugging and yanking his arms.

A backward kick glanced off her shin, causing Lia to groan. "Hold still!"

She dodged a reverse headbutt. *All right. That's it!* Lia pulled against his chest and slammed him on his back against the dirt. She held her hand against his body, keeping him pinned.

Unkempt, thick black hair covered his ears. A brown tunic hung off his body with holes and loose threads. Despite the gaunt look of his face, the black skin of his arms rippled with muscles. He looked young but tall—that in-between age where boys shoot up overnight. Lia guessed he was thirteen or fourteen.

The boy coughed and writhed but gradually calmed. "Where are they?" he wheezed, his eyes pinched and chest heaving.

Her father and Raiyn shared equally confused expressions.

"Where are who?" she asked.

"The Shadow Knights!"

Lia's pressure against his chest lightened.

"I heard there was an attack, and I saw the blood." He pointed to the end of the courtyard where Lia had killed Valdok and a dark bloodstain still covered the ground.

Veron stepped forward and kept his sword up. "Why are you looking for them?"

The boy paused. His eyes darted between them, but he clammed up.

"What business do you have with the Knights?" Veron's demeanor softened as did his voice. "And why did you attack us?"

The boy's voice was weak. "You're pillaging from them. I thought . . . maybe you were the ones who—" He stopped.

Veron let his sword droop. "You thought we came here to steal from them?"

The boy nodded.

Veron lifted his sword and slid it into his scabbard before he lowered his hood. "We're not stealing from the Knights. We *are* the Shadow Knights . . . what's left of them, at least."

The boy's eyes widened. "You're Veron Stormbridge! I'm so sorry. I didn't mean to—I wouldn't have—"

Veron lowered a hand and helped the boy to his feet. "It's all right. No harm done. You put up quite a fight. How old are you?"

"I'm thirteen, sir."

"Where'd you learn how to use that sword?"

A proud smile replaced the embarrassed look on the boy's face. "My father taught me."

"Who's your father?" Lia asked.

The smile faltered, and the boy's eyes widened. "My father . . . ? He, uh . . ."

Veron pressed closer, his eyes narrowing. "Why are you here?"

The boy took two steps backward until the wall stopped him. "I wanted to see if my father was all right." A tear pooled at the corner of his eye. "I-I needed to know if he was okay, but—"

"Who's your father?" Lia repeated.

The boy paused, glancing between them. "I-I'm not supposed to—"

"Who?" Veron asked.

"Gavin," the boy said finally. "Gavin Hamblin. I'm Marcus . . . his son."

Lia's eyes grew. She glanced at Veron, who raised his chin and leaned backward.

"Gavin doesn't have any children," Veron said.

The boy hung his head. "My mother met him in a tavern when they were both young." He smiled. "She called me a 'beautiful accident.' Father only found out about me when I turned eight. My mother and he decided not to tell anyone, but he visited me regularly. He brought me gifts. We explored together. When I was strong enough, he taught me the sword."

"Who's your mother?" Veron asked.

"Harmony Garnett." Marcus' head fell. "She died last week—blue fever."

"I'm so sorry," Lia said.

"Did Gavin know?" Veron asked. "About your mother."

Marcus nodded. "He was going to speak with someone about seeing if I could stay at the center. He pointed out this building—that it was your base. In the meantime, he brought me food, but . . . Then I heard about the attack." A moment of silence fell. Marcus looked between them. "Do you know where he is?"

Lia took a deep breath and glanced at her father, noticing his pursed lips and wrinkled brow.

Veron lifted his chin. "Gavin was taken."

Marcus' eye flickered. "Where? Who took him?"

"A group attacked and took seven of our knights. Your father was one of them. We don't know where they went, but we're working on it."

"I don't understand. You are all shadow knights. You can stop anyone." He glanced between the three. "Right?"

"I wish that were the case," Veron said. "We'll be going after your father soon, but—" He glanced around the center. "We can't stay here anymore. It's too dangerous."

Marcus' shoulders slumped. "I understand." He shuffled, walking toward the exit. "If you find him, can you tell him to look for me?"

"What do you mean?" Veron asked.

Marcus pointed over his shoulder. "I'm going to ask around the docks—see if anyone has work I can do. Can you tell my father to check there?"

Lia frowned, leaning toward her father. "Can we . . . invite him with us?"

Marcus paused.

"We could use all the help we could get, and if he's really Gavin's son . . ."

Veron pursed his lips. "We can't," he whispered. "Not considering the risk it would be for us to invite in a stranger, it's too dangerous for him." He stood taller and looked at Marcus. "When we find him, we'll make sure he looks you up."

Marcus nodded and continued his shuffle out the door.

"Wait!" Raiyn called. Marcus turned as Raiyn jogged across the courtyard, sloughing his pack off his shoulder. "Take this." He handed the jerky over.

The boy smiled as he took it. "Thank you. This is great. It will help a lot." He nodded again to Lia and Veron before he ducked into the hall to leave.

The door down the hall clicked shut, and Lia sighed.

"I wish we could take him," Veron said, "but we can't risk it, Lia. Even if he's related to Gavin, we don't know him. We must protect that location from everyone."

"I know," she said. "It's the right call . . . but I still hate it."

"Come on." Veron turned back to the armory. "Let's pack what we can of these weapons and head back to the Glade."

4

CORONATION

Danik looked down at the crowd before him. His tight doublet dazzled with shining silver buttons and gold embroidery. The collar stood stiffly, itching his neck. Nicolar told him it looked regal, so he had stopped tugging at it. He worried the velvet cape was too much, but the sight of himself in the mirror convinced him to keep it on.

The high lords who had served the late King Darcius stood in a line at one side. Herman Miligan frowned, slumping, with a red face and thinning gray hair. A cough made him look weak. Past him, the high lords of Commerce, Trade, and City Affairs looked no better than him. They all frowned, staring at the crowd.

Old, frail, and bitter, Danik thought. *I'd love to replace them all.*

On the opposite side of Miligan, the High Lord of Treasury, Magnus Hampton, stood tall with his chin up. In his late-thirties, the youngest high lord held a satisfied grin as if he were happy to be there.

Danik smirked. *I'll bet he's someone I can use.*

Geoffrey Bilton stood at the end of the line. The High Lord of Defense held his shoulders back and his chest out. A ceremonial sword hung in a scabbard on his hip, and a measured smile showed on his face. Bilton was the one man Danik *needed* on his side in order to keep order in the kingdom.

At least until I can build an army of my own.

Opposite the high lords, Danik's ragged team of thieves stood and watched. Their clothes were sloppy. Their hair and beards needed attention. Their casual stances suggested a lack of discipline. Even Nicolar's appearance left much to be desired. The leader of the crew sported a mop of shaggy black hair. The scar on his lip remained visible through his messy goatee. Despite their unkempt appearances, the devion flowing through their veins made his crew powerful.

Danik pulled from the energy even while he stood. The tingling flow pulsed through his body, fueling his muscles. He marveled at how the strength and endurance far surpassed that of the origine.

I can't believe I spent so many years following the Shadow Knights. I missed out on so much.

The crowd filling the Hall of the King contained the aristocracy of the city and the leaders of the kingdom. Bankers, guild leaders, and wealthy merchants of Felting mixed with the barons and lords of Lorranis, Karad, Tienn, and Karondir. Officers in the army looked on, turning to High Lord Bilton to take their cues. The onlookers fidgeted, mumbling to each other.

Danik grew antsy as well. He glanced at Bilton and raised his eyebrows in question.

Bilton shrugged with a look of apology. "He should be here. I'm not sure where he is."

Danik clenched his jaw. *I can't believe this. All these people together, waiting. This is supposed to show my authority, not—*

A door burst open, and Quentin Cotterell, advisor to the late king, hurried through. His face was flushed, and his breath labored. "I'm so sorry. Darcius never wore it. I thought I knew where it was, but . . . It took time." The crown of Feldor rested on a red velvet pillow with golden tassels. Twelve curved spikes pointed up, each with its own embedded jewel.

Danik's frustration faded at the sight of the crown. *Power. Author-*

ity. Wealth. It was all his to do with as he pleased. He looked at Nicolar and the thief grinned back.

Danik turned to Bilton. "You can proceed."

High Lord Bilton stepped to the front of the dais and raised his hands. The muttering in the crowd stopped. "Citizens of Felting!" His sonorous voice boomed through the room. "Yesterday, we buried the previous King of Feldor, and today, we crown a new one. Darcius Marlow ruled Feldor for seventeen years. Although the kingdom saw an extended time of peace during his reign, his life is not to be celebrated, and his reign will not be glorified."

Curious looks covered the faces in the crowd.

"As you know, the Shadow Knights were killed the same night the king died. What you do not know is that Darcius was the one who colluded with foreign mercenaries to eliminate them, revealing their secrets and their weaknesses. The otherwise invincible knights were killed in their sleep, betrayed by the king they faithfully served."

Grumbles filled the space.

"Liar!" a man in the back shouted.

Danik tensed. His eyes traced two guards who swooped in from the sides to grab the man by the arms. They covered his mouth and restrained his thrashing limbs as they pulled him down the nearest hallway.

Bilton lifted a hand again. "King Darcius grew paranoid and feared an uprising. To him, the Knights represented a threat to his rule. Yesterday, it was stated that the king died of his heart giving out." Bilton shook his head. "That wasn't true. He died by the sword from the same men he summoned to betray the Knights."

More mumbles filled the room. A lone cry of, "Down with Darcius," called from the crowd.

Danik fought to keep from smiling. He gave a subtle nod to the man who had shouted—the man Nicolar had bribed to do so.

Bilton continued, "Veron Stormbridge and nearly all his knights have been killed. Their bodies were taken by the rogue warriors, but their legacy will live on in this great kingdom." The words settled into silence. "Despite Darcius' betrayal, one knight survived, having been away as a guard at the Felting Orphanage that very night."

Danik cringed. *Orphanage. It sounded good when I wrote it, but hearing it out loud . . . It might have been too much.*

"He studied under Stormbridge and grew to be a leader in their ranks. He led missions to serve both Feldor and our neighboring kingdoms. Highly respected, the other knights looked to him for guidance and wisdom." He glanced at the line of high lords as he continued, "Per tradition . . . when a king dies, the high lords of Feldor convene to determine a successor. We have met and debated potential candidates for the crown. The decision was unanimous."

The other high lords watched with grimaces. Danik bit his tongue. *Keep going, Bilton. You're doing great—just as I ordered.*

"As the next King of Feldor, the High Lords of Felting are happy to introduce Danik Bannister!"

The crowd filled with lukewarm applause. Danik stepped forward, waving as his velvet cape rustled against the stone floor.

"Long live the Shadow Knights!" the bribed man yelled.

"King Danik!" another person cried.

Aside from the planted responses, the crowd seemed hesitant. Danik accepted the lackluster cheers with a raised hand and a winning smile.

Bilton crossed to Quentin and removed the crown from its pillow. Danik tightened his jaw to keep from grinning. He inclined his head forward but refused to bend his knees. Bilton raised his arms, lifting the crown and setting it on Danik's head. It rested heavily, pressing his hair down and sliding lower. The object continued to drop—to his ears, then past.

"Sorry," Bilton mumbled, lifting the crown and tilting it.

Again, it fell past his ears.

Danik flushed. "Let me." He pushed Bilton's hands out of the way and adjusted the jeweled object, himself. It slid and ruffled his hair, but he couldn't find a position that worked.

"We'll have it adjusted, Your Majesty," Quentin said, bowing.

Danik tilted it back. Finally balanced, he removed his hands and exhaled.

Bilton took a step back and pulled the decorative sword. The crowd was silent as the High Lord of Defense touched the sword to his lips then bowed to the new king. "My king in life and in death," Bilton recited. The phrase echoed from the captains and army officials throughout the room.

The booming cadence resonated in Danik's head. The moment didn't feel real. He lifted his eyes and took in the scene. Everyone with power in all of Feldor deferred to him as their king. His chest rose as he stood taller and inhaled.

Bilton gestured to him and stepped backward. "I present to you, His Majesty, the ruler of Feldor, King Danik!"

The applause barely registered. Danik's head felt thick, like he swam underwater but floated in the air at the same time. His smile stuck on his face as he scanned the hall. He hardly knew any of them, but they were now his subjects.

"Thank you!" he called with a wave. "Thank you all!" The loosening of his tongue helped his head to clear, and gradually, the crowd settled. "I accept this honor with a heavy heart. The other shadow knights were brothers and sisters to me. Their loss is immeasurable, and I cannot forgive Darcius Marlow for what he did."

Bilton's eye twitched, but the high lord didn't drop his supportive smile.

"I pledge that I will rule this kingdom with a fair mind and a just hand. Crime will not be tolerated and poverty will not be overlooked. Yes, I am the last of the Shadow Knights, but do not let fear take hold. The Feldorian army is strong. The constables in Felting are the finest around. And this group, here—" He gestured to Nicolar and his team. "Darcius wasn't aware that we had already begun training for a new class. Selected by Veron Stormbridge himself, these new recruits will soon usher in a new era for the Shadow Knights."

An excited rumble grew in the crowd.

"In a matter of days, they have already learned what it took most knights years to accomplish. We will be more active and more visible. Feldor will be the most prosperous, the safest, and the most powerful kingdom." He raised a fist. "Long live the Knights! And long live Feldor!"

Applause returned, stronger than before, and Danik basked in its glow. A year before, he had been a lowly knight, still in training and barely trusted. *And now I'm the most powerful man in Terrenor.*

DANIK PACED the balcony off the Advisors Council chamber. Men and women gathered inside, but he had no desire for small talk. Nicolar, Jade, and Cedric guarded the three arched openings to the room. He touched his neck where flesh-colored powder covered the hint of a dark mark that had recently shown up.

"Nicolar," Danik said, beckoning the older man to join him.

"Your Majesty," Nicolar said, bowing with a bemused smile.

"That's so strange," Danik muttered at the salutation then shook his head. "I'm concerned about the Feldorian army."

"How so?"

"Bilton seems loyal, but will the army follow us blindly? They have far more numbers, and if someone grew ambitious—" He glanced over the man's shoulder then lowered his voice. "It would not be difficult to overthrow us."

"What do you suggest?"

"I want to build an elite force—like our group but larger—trained and disciplined. I want them loyal to me and capable of using the devion. Can you recruit?"

Nicolar flashed an evil grin. "How many?"

Danik pursed his lips. "Twenty-five to start . . . maybe more. We can grow from there."

"Any place in particular you'd like me to begin looking?"

"Felting's Red Quarter. It's filled with poverty, but there are plenty of fighters. If we can pull recruits out of that forsaken hole, we can win their loyalty."

Nicolar nodded. "I'll see to it. What do you think about the rest of the high lords?"

"What do you mean?"

"They've sworn allegiance to you, and the bribes will help. But do you think we can trust them?"

"We *could* replace them all," Danik said, "but there's no guarantee the next ones would be any better. What these high lords care about is money and power. As long as I ensure they keep it, they'll stay in line. Plus, with the loss of the Shadow Knights and their king in one day, Feldor needs all the stability it can get."

"Yes, that's a good point."

"But I'll be keeping a close eye on them. If someone steps a toe out of line, I won't hesitate to eliminate them."

Cedric cleared his throat and took a step closer. "They should be ready now, sir."

Danik took a deep breath, straightened his collar, then lifted his chin toward the closest archway. When he entered the chamber, the talking ceased. The high lords and city barons sat around the oval table, staring at him with tight lips and narrowed eyes. The other three of Nicolar's men paced behind the seated guests.

"Thank you for coming," Danik said. "I'll keep this brief—"

"What really happened to the King?" Rodrick Devenish, the baron of Karondir, interrupted.

A hushed gasp preceded a tense silence. Danik extended an open hand toward Bilton.

"As I mentioned," Bilton said, "he hired men to kill the Shadow Knights, and the group turned on him."

"Lies!" Devenish stood, his chair scraping the floor. "King Darcius would no more have turned on the Knights than I would on my own mother."

The city barons nodded, mumbling in agreement.

Bilton glanced at the other high lords, his mouth frozen.

"He speaks the truth," Magnus Hampton interjected, his voice thin and wavering. "We, uh . . . the high lords were here when it happened." Hampton's eyes flicked to Danik.

Baron Brice Shepley from Tienn spoke up. "The death of the Shadow Knights is a tragedy. We will mourn them and wish you success in rebuilding, Your Majesty. I must ask the high lords though .

. . Explain the reasoning behind appointing the last remaining knight to the throne of Feldor. I intend no disrespect to you, King Danik, but in the past, the Knights were always kept separate."

"And why was that?" Danik asked, his back bristling.

"To free them up to impact other kingdoms. Also, to, uh . . ." Shepley squirmed. ". . . make sure there was no abuse of power."

Danik laughed. "Miligan."

The High Lord of Justice coughed as he straightened.

"Was abuse of power something you worried about?"

The sickly man shook his head while clearing his throat. "No. Never."

"Stokes." Danik turned to the High Lord of Commerce. "Did you have reservations about selecting me as king?"

Kennith Stokes's eyes flicked to each side. His jaw trembled. "No . . . Your Majesty. We, uh . . . never, uh . . . We thought you were the best."

Shepley leaned forward. "Again, I mean no disrespect, but . . . 'the best' . . . out of all the experienced people in Feldor?"

"That's what he said!" Danik shouted, his patience gone. "Feldor needs power and strength! Do you, Brice, want to try your hand against mine?"

The baron raised his hands. "Of course not, I—"

"Don't forget who appoints you . . . Baron." Danik stared daggers at the man.

Shepley swallowed.

"All of you—" Danik swept his gaze around the room. "You're appointed by *me*, so if you have any doubt about your ability to serve under my rule, let me know, now."

The room was silent. The high lords and barons averted their eyes, looking at the table.

"I thought not. So . . . as I was saying, I aim to make a few changes around here."

Heads perked up.

"This castle was once the glorious symbol of Feldor, but it's been neglected for years." Danik ran his hand along the back of one of the chairs, cringing at the rough wood and trace of dust. "The luster is gone. The grandeur we need to remain the envy of the other kingdoms faded long ago. King Darcius was irresponsible and Wesley before him."

"Sir." High Lord Windridge raised her hand. A hesitant lilt replaced her typical commanding voice. "That was a conscious choice by both men. They invested in the people rather than displaying wealth."

"And see how well that worked for them? They were weak and cowardly. The other three kingdoms laughed at us. That's why Norshewa builds an army again. There's only one purpose for one of that size—invasion. Do you think King Darian would have been thinking about conquering if Darcius Marlow had displayed a spine?"

Windridge opened her mouth but refrained from answering.

"The other kingdoms have no respect for us," Danik continued. "We will change that, starting here at the castle. The stones are old and dingy. Some areas crumble and need to be repaired. I want new furniture. I want gold and silver decorating the halls and rooms. Visitors should be in awe over what we've achieved. I want every person across Terrenor to be filled with reverence when they hear the name Danik Bannister. They will know that I brought Feldor back from a run-down kingdom to one that is worthy of respect."

With a wrinkled brow, Magnus Hampton raised his hand. "Your Majesty, we don't have the resources for a renovation to the castle."

"Then find them." Danik turned to Windridge. "City Affairs, where are we spending money? What can we cut?"

The stout woman's eyes grew wide. Her mouth opened but only stuttering sounds came out.

"Roads? Drainage?"

"Y-Your Majesty," she stuttered. "We—"

Danik snapped his fingers. "The Felting Orphanage."

Her jaw dropped. "It does have a decent cost, but we can't—"

"Shut it down." Danik turned back to Magnus Hampton. "See? Finding money is easy."

"But, sir," Hampton protested. "The funds from an orphanage don't match what it would require to—"

"Raise taxes, then! You're the High Lord of Treasury, right?"

Magnus inclined his head. "You want us to take more money from the people? They may not appreciate it when they hear you're raising taxes on your first day as king."

Danik's jaw hardened. He stepped toward Magnus, forcing the high lord to lean back in his chair. "First . . . I don't care if the people 'appreciate it.' The job of a king is to rule his kingdom effectively, not make everyone happy."

"But sir—"

"And secondly . . . *I* am not the one raising taxes. If *your* treasury department is raising taxes, the decree comes from you, not me. It's your job to find the money I need. How you do that is on you." Danik turned to the barons. "Men, I require support from your cities as well."

The barons squirmed but didn't argue.

"In addition to returning this castle to the glory it deserves, I need money to rebuild the Shadow Knights."

Eyes squinted and heads cocked around the table.

"The Knights won't be a paltry group to handle sporadic, secretive missions. I plan to elevate them to the position they've always deserved. There will be hundreds of trained, powerful warriors, the likes of which Terrenor has never seen. They won't cower behind walls but will lead Feldor. They will be the first on the battlefield. Our enemies will turn and flee out of fear."

Danik caught a wicked grin from Nicolar and Dayna.

"What enemies?" Logan Marshall, Baron of Karad, asked. "We all felt the impact Edmund Bale had during his brief, chaotic rule. Since then . . . we've been at peace."

"Peace doesn't mean you have no enemies," Danik said. "It means you've forgotten they're there. Feldor will be ready if Norshewa marches through the Gap of Thardor, and the Shadow Knights will ensure we remain victorious."

Silence surrounded the table, exactly the effect he had hoped for.

5

REPURPOSED TRAINING

"Y ou trained in this place?" Cedric said, the scorn in his voice palpable as they approached the Shadow Knights' training center.

Danik cringed, feeling a possessive inclination to defend the building. "We did. It's not much, but it worked."

The aged wall left no indication of anything special beyond the barrier. Dark streaks ran down the side where rain had trickled for years. The weathered wooden door hung askew, leaving a slanted gap between the door and the frame. Danik pushed. The hinges creaked as the door pivoted. He led the way down the familiar halls where he'd spent the last several years of his life.

"Why are we here again?" Broderick's thick brown beard muffled his voice.

Danik arrived at the end of the hall and reemerged into the light of the courtyard. He held his arms out and came to a stop. "This is why."

"It's decent," Nicolar said. "Not much, but . . . it will work."

"So, we'll train here?" Broderick's contempt was unmistakable. "Isn't there someplace nicer in the castle?"

Danik shrugged. "There may be." He scanned the courtyard.

Memories of sweat and steel filled his head. He smiled, remembering the grueling workouts that formed him into the man he'd become. Bloody stains in the dirt served as a grim reminder of what took place only days before. "Training isn't meant to be *nice* though. You need a private place with space to spread out. Plus, we have all the gear we need—over there." He nodded toward the armory. "And with the Shadow Knights gone, you'll have free reign of the place."

High Lord Bilton stepped forward, his jaw forming a sharp line. "The Shadow Knights used it for one hundred and forty years. It should work for you."

"I thought they'd been around longer than that," Nicolar said.

"They didn't always live here," Danik said. "They began in Karondir after they defeated Vitrion, but then they moved after killing Talon Shadow, when he turned on them."

"Why do we need to train at all?" Cedric flexed his arms. "I could pound anyone with this devion power."

"We will train because you're undisciplined, lazy, and unskilled," Jade said. "I could defeat you in my sleep without breaking a sweat."

Cedric's face flared red. He pulled a sword from his hip. "You wanna see what 'lazy' can do to you?"

Jade dropped into a crouch, daggers appearing in each hand. "Let's find out."

"Stop it!" Danik stepped between them. "You're here to become a cohesive unit—to fight alongside each other, not against."

Jade's eyes narrowed, but her muscles visibly relaxed. She stood, the daggers disappearing with a flick of her wrists.

Nicolar broke the tension. "How often should we train?"

"Every day," Danik said. "Jade's right. You need discipline and to refine your skills. The devion amplifies your power, but you need to be elite fighters without it."

He chuckled after playing his words over in his mind. *As frustrating as Veron's training was, there was wisdom to it.*

"Do you intend to have hundreds?" Nicolar asked.

Danik nodded. "The devion seems quick and easy to learn, unlike the origine. We should be able to grow a sizable force."

"Where do you intend to enlist from?" Bilton asked. "The army?"

Danik paused, looking at the high lord. A bird cawed from the wall, accenting the silence. "We're working on that."

"The army is filled with strong and disciplined fighters. They could make formidable warriors with your . . . devion . . . thing."

"Are you suggesting we should train you?"

Bilton startled. "No, Your Majesty, I—" He paused, his head cocked and his eyes growing distant. "No, I'm not sure I would want that."

Danik narrowed his eyes. "Not sure you would want ultimate power? The ability to defeat any enemy?"

"I mean—I guess I would. It's just that—" He blew out a breath. "I've lived by the strength of my arm and my blade all my life. It's difficult to imagine relying on something I don't understand. But if you would train me, I would be honored to join your force."

Danik's eyes roamed up and down the high lord while the man waited. "No, I don't think I would use you. I need you where you are."

A flinch registered on the older man's face, but he offered a short bow. "Of course, Your Majesty. I'm happy to serve in whatever capacity you require."

Danik pulled Nicolar to the side while the others talked amongst themselves. "I prefer to avoid the army," Danik whispered. "There are hierarchies and allegiances already. If we give them access to this power, they could easily disseminate it to others. They could prove more difficult to control. I don't want Bilton for the same reasons."

Nicolar nodded. "He has connections already. If he had power to match, he could take the throne. I agree; we find new recruits."

"Fighters—people who can handle themselves but have no current loyalties. We can treat them well and make sure they value what we provide."

"Of course, Your Majesty."

"What are we using out of here?" Alton called, standing at the entry to the armory.

"The weapons," Danik said. "You need to become experts at swords, knives, bows, clubs, axes, shields . . . everything."

"And . . . this room will help with that?"

"You'll drill on each discipline until you're comfortable with them all. We'll mix in physical training on stamina, balance, and—" The confusion on Alton's face made him pause. "What is it?"

Alton gestured toward the armory. "Are those supposed to be in here?"

Danik stomped across the courtyard. "Are you blind? I'm talking about the—" Danik stopped, dust kicking up.

Bare wall hooks filled the room. The shelf of supplies was empty. A few wooden swords, clubs, and a heavy sledge remained, but the majority of the weapons were gone.

"Did the Marked Ones take them?" Jade asked.

Danik spun toward Nicolar "Were these missing the other night when you moved the bodies?"

Nicolar shook his head. "No, it was filled."

Danik's stomach churned. He took in a deep breath, trying to settle his unease.

"It could have been anyone, right?" Cedric suggested. "Thieves. Citizens angry at the Knights."

"Could some of them still be alive?" Alton asked.

Danik's chest tightened. He ran his finger over a bare hook, narrowing his eyes as a hush settled over the group around him. He turned and walked purposefully across the courtyard.

Light slanted in from the high windows of the common room. The furniture hadn't been touched but the shelves were bare. No food was to be found. *That means nothing. Any thieves would have taken food.* His eye twitched. *And . . . cooking supplies. It doesn't mean . . .*

He left the common room with his heart thumping. He took the steps to the second floor, two at a time. The upstairs hall was quiet and empty. Some doors were shut, but several hung open. Danik pushed open the first one—Veron and Chelci's room.

The sheets on the bed lay rumpled but nothing appeared out of the ordinary. Danik placed his hand on the door and moved to pull it when something caught his eye. A small wooden frame sat on the end table next to the bed—one that had been there for as long as

he'd been with the Knights. But it was wrong. The picture inside—
the one Lia made for her parents—was gone. Danik's teeth clenched
as his pulse raced.

Veron is alive.

He exited the second floor and walked down the steps while
heads craned up at him.

"What is it?" Jade asked. "Is everything all right?"

"Veron—Lia's father, the leader of the Shadow Knights—is alive."

"How do you know?" Nicolar asked.

Cedric's hand moved to the sword at his hip. "Are there others?"

Danik reached the ground. "Somehow, he survived Talioth's
attack. Maybe he stayed back and let the others be taken. He must
have come back and scavenged what supplies he could. There could
be others. I don't know."

"Where would he be?" Nicolar asked.

Danik glanced at Bilton, who raised his hands in surrender. "I
have no idea," the high lord said. "He had history with the Marlow
family, but they're all dead. There was a friend, Brixton, but he's been
gone for years. I'm sure he has other friends, but I don't know who."

"Maybe he fled?" Jade suggested.

Danik mulled the idea over. "He's probably hiding in the city."

Nicolar stepped closer. "What do we do about it?"

*I had hoped Talioth would take care of them all so I didn't have to. The
Knights were my home for years, but . . .*

He breathed in, then exhaled a heavy breath. "They could put a
stop to everything. We need to find them, and we need to kill them."

His group of recently empowered thieves straightened their
postures. Cedric wore a wicked grin and Jade narrowed her eyes.

"Bilton," Danik said. "Are you with us?"

The High Lord's chest puffed. His eyes reflected an eagerness to
retain power. "Absolutely."

6

UNCERTAIN PLANS

A vague thunk registered in Veron's mind. He opened his eyes and stared at the ceiling of his small home.

Thunk.

He blinked. *There it is again.*

He sat up and looked out the window. Light had only just begun to spill over the cliff wall into the Glade, illuminating the morning fog like a glowing blanket. Movement caught his eye next to the main hall.

Thunk.

Veron chuckled, a smile coming to his face.

He grabbed a cloak to fend off the morning chill and stepped outside. His breath hung in the air as a thin cloud. He dodged the trees beside his house and crunched down the rocky path, causing a nearby group of birds to take flight. He crossed the training area and slowed.

Thunk.

"Good morning, Raiyn," Veron said.

The young man looked up from his pile of logs. Sweat dripped off his forehead, and a grin covered his face. "Good morning, sir!"

"Chopping logs, huh?"

Raiyn scanned the pile. "Yeah. It feels good. It's been a while." He turned with a concerned look. "I didn't wake you, did I?"

Veron chuckled. "It was time to be up. Nice work here."

"Thanks. I worked as a logger in Searis for a while. Now that I understand how this origine works, it's *much* easier. I'm just chopping firewood, but if you need any wooden beams for building, I can do that, too."

"Have you seen Lia?"

Raiyn nodded. "She's checking the traps outside the Glade."

Veron nodded. "You want some water?"

"Sure, that would be great."

Veron entered the meeting hall and selected two cups from the shelf. He filled them under the bamboo pipe, smiling at the simplicity of the process.

Thunk. The chopping resumed.

He exited the building and handed a cup to Raiyn, who wiped his forehead and took a long drink.

"So . . ." Raiyn began, appearing to search for something to talk about. "What'd you do before you led the Shadow Knights?"

Veron smiled at the attempt to get to know him better. "I actually did a variety of things. I worked for a grocer for a while, then I ran my own market for a couple of years. After I was betrayed by a friend, I ended up a slave in Chelci's family's home."

"Was that Brixton?"

Veron raised an eyebrow.

"Lia told me about him and how you eventually reconciled."

Veron nodded. "Brixton helped us defeat—" He stopped, realizing who he spoke with.

"Defeat Bale?" Raiyn finished. "It's all right. You can talk about it. Don't forget, I despise my father as much or more than everyone else."

Veron flashed a weak smile. "Brixton was a good man, deep down, but it took him a while to grow into that. As a slave, I gathered water, washed floors, waited on people—all sorts of things."

"And that's where you fell in love with Chelci?"

"That's right. Eventually the king purchased my freedom and made me one of his advisors."

"King Darcius?"

"No, King Wesley."

"That's right. I remember hearing of him."

"Wesley died not long after, and just after that, we killed—" He hesitated, "We . . . stopped your father, then we formed the new Shadow Knights."

Raiyn nodded, gazing intently as he spoke. "What was King Darcius like?"

A stab of pain twisted in Veron's gut. "Darcius was a great man."

"Lia's grandfather, right?"

Veron nodded. "All he wanted was to make life better for the citizens of Feldor. He was fair and kind."

"I wish I had known him. I'm sorry for your loss."

"Few people knew it, but he was actually dying."

Raiyn's brows pinched together.

"The doctors said he only had a couple seasons to live. He was about to step down from the throne."

"Wow! I didn't realize."

"Still, I hate that he had to go like that."

A genuine look showing both concern and eagerness covered Raiyn's face. "Sir, I realize I'm new here, but I know you've been through a lot. I want to thank you for allowing me to stay. I've searched for a place to fit in all my life. Having people who understand who I am means the world to me. It's very freeing, so . . . Thank you."

Veron nodded. "You're welcome."

"Also, I'm eager to help. My skills are still fresh, but whatever you need from me, I'm in with both feet. I'll do whatever I can."

Veron's chest felt tight. The young man's genuine nature was exactly what he looked for in shadow knights. *I judged him wrong earlier.*

"I had some ideas while walking around the Glade this morning."

"Really?" Veron gestured toward him. "Please share."

"Once we rescue your wife and the other knights, this is meant to be our hidden base, right?"

Veron nodded.

"If we're living here, I thought there were a few things we might need to do. First, what would happen if people stumbled across this place." He pointed toward the area of the Glade where they had entered. "They'd get crushed by those boulders, right?"

Another nod.

"That's good if they're enemies, but what if it's a hunter in the woods, or some kids out exploring?"

"You think we should take the boulder trap down?"

Raiyn shook his head. "Then we could be in a spot of what to do with someone who randomly finds us. We need to hide the entrance."

"More than it is?"

"We disguise the crack in the cliff. Pile up brush and grow a wall of vines. We need to prevent someone from stumbling in and finding it. But if someone is tracking us to find the Shadow Knights, the boulder trap will do its job."

Veron nodded. "Yeah, I see your point."

Raiyn moved on. "Second. Firewood. You'll need wood year round for cooking but a lot more during wiether for heating. There are a lot of trees in the Glade. Even after harvesting what you did to build the houses, there are plenty left, but you need to plan ahead. Years down the road, your supply will grow lean, and it's going to be a lot more difficult to carry wood through that narrow cliff entrance, not to mention the suspicion that could come from harvesting trees outside the cliffs."

"So we need to cut back?"

"No, you need to plant." Raiyn pointed toward a clearing. "New trees will need at least ten years before they are large enough to produce decent fuel. Then moving forward, whenever you cut a tree down, plant another in its place, preferably with a few fruit trees mixed in."

"Yeah," Veron agreed. "Another good point."

"And last . . . once we're settled in, we should raise our own food instead of hunting and scavenging for it."

Veron raised a finger. "I *had* thought of that." He pointed across the training area. "I figured that field would be good for a large garden. We can get a plow and some tools. The knights can rotate duties to keep it up. Maybe one day, we'll even have families who can help.

Footsteps sounded on the bridge. Veron turned as Lia approached with two limp rabbits hanging from her hip.

"We've got some meat," she said with a smile.

Raiyn pointed at the animals. "Rabbits—another example. They'd be easy to raise. Chickens, too."

Veron took the carcasses from Lia. "Nice work." He entered the hall and set them on the counter. "Great ideas, Raiyn. As soon as we know we'll be here for a bit, we should start on those."

The young man bounced to a table in the hall and scooped up a bundle of loose wildflowers. When Lia entered next, he extended the bunch toward her. "For you. I-I thought you might like them."

Lia's eyebrows lifted. She accepted the colorful bouquet and blushed. "Thank you."

"The, uh, the yellow ones reminded me of you because I know how you enjoy the sunrise. Then the red and orange ones, they are— um . . . they're just pretty."

She brushed a strand of hair behind her ear as her mouth quirked up at the corner. The shade of her cheeks nearly matched the red petals of the petunias. "Thanks."

Veron wanted to glare at the young man's advances toward his daughter but restrained himself. The gesture of kindness was a refreshing change of pace.

Lia cleared her throat and moved toward the shelves where an empty glass jar sat. "Speaking of how long we'll be here . . . What do we do next, Father?"

Veron took in a deep breath.

She set the flowers in the jar then used the bamboo spout to fill it with water. "We need to find Mother, right?"

"I know." His shoulders slumped. "We do."

Raiyn crossed the hall and leaned the wood-chopping axe up against the wall, next to the pile of weapons they'd brought from the city. He selected a battle-axe from the swords and knives and tossed it back and forth between his hands. "This just feels right," he said, sliding it in a hook on his belt. "I'm ready."

"We can't just . . . walk into the woods," Veron said.

Lia walked to the weapons. She picked up a hilt with a ruby embedded at the guard. The steel blade of Farrathan caught the early-morning light slanting through the window. She turned it around and extended the handle toward Veron. "We have to do something, Father."

Veron took the handle. The familiar grip balanced in his hand, but the sensation felt strange. His heart sank as he realized what was different. *I no longer have the origine.* He ran his finger down the length of the blade and sighed. He turned it back around, extending the handle toward Lia. "You should carry it."

Lia's forehead wrinkled. "What?"

"Farrathan is the sword of the Shadow Knights."

"And you're the Shadow Master. You—"

". . . are no longer a shadow knight," Veron finished.

Lia's mouth hung open, and she blinked several times.

"Without the origine, I'm a regular person."

"Sir," Raiyn started, "you're the definition of what it means to be a shadow knight."

"Yeah," Lia added. "It's your blade, and you're still one of the greatest swordsmen in Terrenor, even without the origine."

Veron smiled. "That's kind of you to say. Still . . . My father insisted I have it when it was time for me to be a leader. Yes, I'm still here, and I'm still a knight, but . . . with your access to the origine and your strength, I need you to lead." He extended his arm farther. "Will you take it?"

Lia's eyes grew wider. She wrapped her hand around the hilt. The sword looked larger than normal in her hand, but she could use it as well as any man.

"It's not too heavy, is it?" Veron asked.

Her look of wonder turned into a scowl. "What are you suggesting?" Her toned arms flexed.

Veron laughed and shook his head. "Nothing."

Lia's unsure look morphed to one of confidence and strength as she examined the blade. She swung it a few times, smiling as it wooshed through the air. Finally, she nodded. "All right. I'll use it for now." She picked up the scabbard that it paired with and adjusted it on her back. The sword fit, peeking diagonally over her shoulder with the ruby shining at her.

"Father?"

Veron's eyebrows raised.

"You *are* a great fighter." Lia pointed between herself and Raiyn. "And we can use the origine. But—" She paused. "Do you think it's enough?"

The question sat heavily on him. "To fight Talioth and his group?" He thought about the Marked Ones, their crystals, and their incredible powers. The idea of fighting them again twisted his stomach. *But we have no other choice.* He lifted his chin and set his jaw. "Yes," he said firmly. "We will get them back."

Lia's eyes narrowed. Her frown told him she didn't believe it. "What about the 'pure connection?'"

"What about it?"

She shrugged. "I don't know. Just wondering if there could be any advantage there."

His mouth curled up. "I thought you didn't believe it was real?"

"I don't." Her eyes flicked to Raiyn and back. "But on the chance that it is . . . I'm curious."

"I haven't figured anything out. When I found it, I was desperate and almost dead. I shouldn't have had any power left, but I was suddenly bursting with it. I needed it to save Chelci. I thought that may have been the trick—the urgency of need and the fact that I was spent—but I've never replicated it. I'm sure that could be a great advantage, but it's only a wish at this point."

"What about the other kingdoms?" Raiyn asked. "Should we reach out to them for assistance?"

"I don't think large armies will be effective. We could tie the marked ones up, but . . ." Veron shook his head. "Rynor's army would be slaughtered." The memory of Ambassador Dane's visit came to mind. "Bravian Fire," he breathed.

Lia raised her eyebrows.

"What's that?" Raiyn asked.

"There was a rumor Norshewa had discovered Bravian Fire."

"Are you serious?" Lia asked.

Veron waved a hand to dismiss it. "It was only a rumor. Plus . . . I'm not sure what good that would do for us without knowing anything about where they are."

"I'm sorry," Raiyn lifted a finger. "What's Bravian Fire?"

"It's a legend," Lia said. "All-consuming flames."

"Like a blast furnace?"

"No," Veron said. "It consumes everything, even stone. It burns so fast and hot that it destroys anything around it. Supposedly, it can demolish a city gate or even burst the wall of a castle."

Raiyn whistled. "That would be . . ."

"Dangerous."

"I was going to say incredible."

"Incredibly dangerous," Veron said. "Still . . . I don't know if it's real or how we would use it."

A peel of chimes floated through the window, faint but clear. Veron snapped his head in the direction of their alert system. Adrenaline surged through him.

Running with the origine's power, Lia and Raiyn were out the door before Veron even moved. He sprinted through the hall. Once outside, he crossed the footbridge and ran up the path as fast as he could. After a few pounding steps, his feet slowed.

At the end of the trail, Lia and Raiyn held out their sword and axe, but the weapons drooped. Marcus, the boy from the city, stood between them with wide eyes. His dark-skinned arms lifted in the air, shaking.

"Marcus?" The tension in Veron's limbs relaxed as he arrived.

"What are you doing here?" Lia asked.

The boy looked between them, keeping his hands up. "I'm so sorry. Don't hurt me!"

Lia lowered her sword. "We're not going to hurt you. How did you get here?"

"I-I waited outside the city gates yesterday, then I followed you."

"You—" Veron's mouth hung open, not finishing his sentence. *I'm getting careless.*

"I lost you yesterday when you got to these cliffs, and I ending up sleeping in the woods. I saw Lia out again this morning."

"You came through the tunnel?" Lia asked.

He nodded.

"What about the wire in the passage?"

"I saw you step over it when you walked through, but I didn't know about this second one."

"You can't be here," Veron said.

Marcus dropped his head and slowly lowered his arms. "With my mother gone, I don't have anyone or anyplace to live. I thought, perhaps, you were going to a village or something." He looked at the trees and houses. "I didn't realize you were coming here. It's like a secret Shadow Knights base!"

Veron's nerves rattled. *We can't afford for others to find out about this place.*

"Would it be possible for me to stay with you?" Marcus asked.

Lia turned to Veron with compassion in her eyes. "Father . . . we do have all these empty homes."

With his heart torn, Veron shook his head. "We need to keep this place a secret."

Lia held her hands open. "But he's here. You're not suggesting we . . ." She leaned in, raising both eyebrows, ". . . silence him, are you?"

"No! Of course not! It's just—"

"He could help out around the Glade. The garden will take work. We'll need help with cooking and cleaning, not to mention hunting."

Raiyn stood quietly to the side. Veron remembered kicking him out from an abundance of caution not long before, and that decision turned out to be the wrong one.

Marcus raised a tentative hand. "Sir, I realize I'm not an elite warrior like the Shadow Knights, but I'm willing to help in any way I can. Plus, I can use a sword. If you're going to find my father, I can help. Please don't kick me out."

Veron sighed and nodded his head after a long pause. "We're not going to kick you out, Marcus. Any family of Gavin's is our family as well. You're welcome here."

Marcus rushed forward. Not holding a weapon, Veron tensed and made to strike with his hands, but the boy wrapped his arms around him and buried his head against his chest.

"Thank you, sir!" he said, muffled into his shirt.

Veron stood, awkwardly holding his hands out. They settled on the boy's back, and he pulled back, returning the hug. "You're welcome."

"Are you hungry?" Lia waved the group toward the meeting hall and began walking up the path. "We just caught a couple rabbits and were going to cook them."

"Actually, I'm all right." Marcus followed along the trail. He fished a crumpled sack from his pocket and handed it to Raiyn.

"The jerky," Raiyn said.

"Half of it's still there. I guess you all should have the rest, now."

The walk back only took a few moments, and soon, the group entered the hall.

Lia found a knife from a pile and grabbed the two rabbits by the hind legs. "I'll take these outside and start cleaning them."

Veron nodded and sat on one of the bench seats. He motioned to the spot next to him. "Marcus, come and sit."

The boy joined him. Tall for his age, he barely had to look up to meet Veron's eyes. His genuine smile and disarming eagerness helped Veron feel better about the decision to allow him to stay, despite his misgivings.

"How much has Gavin told you about what we do?"

"About the Shadow Knights?" Marcus asked. "Some. He talked

about how you go throughout Terrenor, helping people who need it and stopping bad guys. He talked about the training you do. *Lots* of training."

"Did he mention about . . . any abilities or anything?"

"The origine?" Marcus blurted. "Yeah. He didn't say much about it —only that it was what gave you special powers or something."

"Hmm. I see."

"He gave me some test last year—checking my balance and reflexes and stuff. I'm not sure what he was looking for, but he said I didn't have whatever it was I needed. That was fine with me . . ." His smile drooped. "I had him and Mother."

Veron rested a hand on his shoulder. "Don't worry, Marcus. We'll get him back."

"Speaking of which . . ." Raiyn said from where he leaned against the wall. "Do you have any thoughts of where to try next, sir?"

"It's too bad we don't have access to the library anymore." Lia's voice carried through the window, shouted from where she worked outside. "Weren't you wanting to research there?"

Veron sighed. "I tried that. I spent days poring through those books, but there was noth—" Lightning seemed to strike his brain as a memory jolted him. "Ah! I forgot!"

Raiyn leaped to attention, and Marcus sat alert. Lia appeared in the doorway with her hand on the sword hilt over her shoulder and rabbit blood on her sleeves.

"What is it?" Lia asked.

"The library!" Veron's breath came quickly as he jumped to his feet.

"What about it?"

Veron paced. "I-I was there. It completely slipped my mind after Danik and that night." He looked at Lia, and a grin formed. "I found a book."

She leaned forward with her brows raised.

"A book about the origine, the devion, their history . . . and a map."

"Whoa," Raiyn breathed.

"A map to what?" Lia asked. "Where they live?"

"I'm guessing so," Veron replied.

"That's what we need!" Lia shouted, her eyes lighting up. "Where did the map lead?"

"It pointed to a mountain range, but I don't know which one. I didn't have a chance to study it. We need that book."

"Where is it, now?" Lia asked.

Veron paused. His excitement tempered. He took in a deep breath then blew it out. "It's in the castle, in the king's library."

Lia pursed her lips then nodded. "That's all right. Danik's not going to be guarding the library. Shouldn't be too difficult for some shadow knights to get in."

Veron's mouth formed a thin line. "I wish I could use the origine."

Lia nodded toward Raiyn. "We both can. Between the three of us, I'm sure we can handle it."

Veron looked between them both. "Looks like we don't have any other choice."

Raiyn rested his hand on the axe at his hip. "When do we go?"

"Gather your things," Veron said. "We're breaking in tonight."

7

HOPE OF ESCAPE

Chelci paused at the top of the rise. Her heart pounded from the steady incline. Sweat dotted her forehead and made her tunic cling to her body. Despite the fresh mountain air, the scent of tired bodies filled her nose.

The marked ones, wearing gray and their crystal necklaces, didn't seem to strain. They split their group with a few walking in front and the others behind. Chelci and the six other shadow knights took up the middle.

Metal chains connected the manacles on their wrists. The ones on their legs had more slack, but not enough to run with. The links Chelci and Gavin broke the day before had been replaced with fresh connectors.

"Give them some water," Talioth ordered, bringing the entire group to a stop. The leader of the Marked Ones scanned up the slope as if he could peer through the mountains.

A surly looking man thrust a water skin into Chelci's hands. Despite her desire to throw the water on the ground in defiance, the pull of her parched throat won. She took a long drink, smacking her lips before passing the skin behind her to Dayna.

"Rosalik, you're up," the man named Centol called out.

Chelci looked over her shoulder as Rosalik's red crystal lit up. Centol's dimmed just after.

"Why do you do that?" Gavin asked, earning some scathing looks. "Taking turns glowing your crystals." He held up his arms and shook them to jangle the chains. "We can't use the origine with these, either way."

Gralow stepped in front of him, his broad shoulders equal in height with Gavin's eyes. "We do it because we can," he growled.

"But, if you—"

A punch in the gut doubled Gavin over.

Chelci winced as he coughed and wheezed. "You realize our friends will rescue us, don't you?" she asked.

Gralow chuckled. "I'd like to see them try to sneak into the caverns."

"Yeah," Rosalik said. "It's been a while since someone fell victim to the bears."

A laugh bubbled from the marked ones, twisting Chelci's gut. *What are the bears?* she thought.

"There's a village ahead," Talioth said. "Let's stop there for food."

A wicked grin formed on Gralow's face. "We've been stuck in that cave for too long."

Chelci pictured what they might do to a village, and her stomach turned. A shove at her back forced her forward, and the knights continued marching.

The path they followed wasn't the main road that ran north from Felting to Tienn. It was smaller, narrower, and rockier, leading them east. The path headed for the Straith Mountains, but before them, a collection of thatched roofs grew steadily closer.

A faint whisper reached her ears. "Chelci."

Trying not to draw their captors' attention, she turned, only enough to notice Dayna walking next to her, watching the ground.

"You have any ideas?"

Thirteen sets of feet traversing the rocky ground and clanking chains created a decent amount of noise. *Hopefully enough noise to cover a conversation.*

"Ideas about . . . escape?"

"Yeah. Like how you and Gavin broke your chains and ran."

"That didn't end up very well though."

"What if several of us ran at the same time . . . but in different directions."

Chelci's moment of hope faded. "There are seven of us and six of them, but . . . you didn't see them track us. It was—" She frowned. *I don't want to give up, but . . .* "I'm up for trying it, but we'd need to figure out how to break our leg chains at the same time."

"How'd you do it last time?"

"The clasps were corroded. We used leverage against a rock and they broke. But now—" She glanced down at the current chain, limiting her legs to short strides. The metal looked solid. "I'm not sure we could do that again."

Danya was quiet. The rattling chains filled the air, and the thatched roofs grew closer.

"We need to get this metal off. If we could do that, and if just one of us could get outside the reach of those crystals . . ." Chelci pulled at the clamp around her wrist. The thin, rectangular keyhole taunted her. *I wish I had my lock-picking tools.*

"Maybe we can do it," Dayna whispered.

Chelci's ears perked. "How?"

"That skinny one."

Chelci glanced ahead. The one named Centol had a ring of keys that issued a faint jangle from his hips. "You think you can get that?"

"I can try." Dayna shuffled forward, passing Bradley and moving close to the marked one with the keys.

Chelci's heart beat quicker, and her hands began to sweat.

Dayna made a half lunge but held herself back. Another stutter step moved her to the side. She leaned in until Centol glanced her way.

"What are you doing?" he barked, shooing her away with a hand. "Back off!"

Chelci sighed as Dayna slowed, The distance between her and the guard grew.

"We need a distraction or something," Dayna whispered.

The lead group came to a halt, and Talioth pointed to a gathering of rocks. "Rosalik, Centol, and Gralow, stay with the knights. The rest of us will see what we can get out of this village."

Three of their captors walked off, heading toward the thatched roofs. A glimmer of hope grew. *Only three guards. This could be our best chance*, Chelci thought. She gathered with the other knights, corralled into a circle of rocks where they were forced to sit. The three guards stood, spread out, blocking any thought of running away. Their hands rested on their swords, and their eyes scanned the seven knights.

"Any thoughts?" Dayna whispered next to her, leaning in.

"Quiet!" Gralow ordered.

Dayna startled then settled back into her seat.

Chelci frowned. *How can we distract them?* An idea formed in her mind. She wanted to grin but forced her mouth into a snarl. "You're a fool," she said to Dayna, her voice loud enough to be heard by all.

Dayna jerked her head toward her with her brows pinched together. "Huh?"

"I said, quiet!" Gralow barked again.

Chelci increased her volume. "Your ideas are worthless. You should have never even *been* a knight!"

A flicker of recognition reflected back from Dayna's eyes.

She gets it.

Her eyes hardened. "Well if *you* weren't married to him, you never would have been chosen either!" Dayna accented the insult with a shove.

Chelci and Dayna both leaped to their feet, their chains rattling.

"I was the head trainer!" Dayna continued. "Who were you? Nothing!"

Chelci hurtled herself back at Dayna, ramming her locked arms into the other woman's shoulders. Dayna stumbled backward, flailing her restrained arms for balance.

Chelci sneered, moving in a tight circle. "You were the trainer because we didn't want to have you around."

Gavin jumped up and held out his arms. "Chelci, Dayna, come on. We can't do this to each other."

The three guards looked between each other and shrugged. Gralow pulled a dagger and called for them to settle, but his order was drowned out by the yelling that ensued.

Dayna shouted, hurtling toward Chelci. The two knights collided in a fierce crash of limbs and knees. A punch to Chelci's gut knocked her breath away. She threw her elbow at Dayna, pressing her head away while the other woman tried to grapple her to the ground. Chelci groaned, her legs straining to keep her body upright.

Gavin pulled at Chelci's back. "Leave her be, Chelci! She's not the enemy!"

She sloughed him off and lunged at Dayna. Chelci's forearms collided into her chest, knocking her backward with considerable force. Dayna fell backward toward Centol, stumbling out of control and wrapping her arms around his waist to arrest her fall.

Chelci's heart pounded, less from the scuffle than from watching Dayna's deft hands at work.

"Get off me and cut it out!" Centol pushed Dayna up to her feet and back into the circle.

Gralow stepped forward and placed himself in Chelci's path, holding his menacing dagger forward with his head cocked. "Give me an excuse to use this."

Chelci sneered at the man but took a step backward.

"You! Sit at that end!" Centol turned and pointed at Chelci. "And you, over there!"

Chelci held her glare as she watched Dayna skulk to the far side. A sideways glance, safe from the marked ones' view, displayed a quick wink. Chelci's eyes drifted to Dayna's hands. They tucked into her clothes, folding a metal object into the folds of fabric. *She got it!*

"No more talking, or we'll start slitting throats!" Gralow yelled, looking at each shadow knight in turn. Chelci angled away as he gazed in her direction.

Gavin leaned closer. His brows pinched as he held her eyes.

Chelci pictured his confusion, but she couldn't explain to him.

Instead she nodded in an attempt to let him know things were all right. His furrowed brows eased.

Dayna sat on the far side of the rock. She faced away from the others, hunched over as if sulking. Her arms twitched. *She's working on the locks. What can she do if she gets them off, though?*

Now that everyone had settled, the guards' alertness dimmed. All weapons were sheathed again. Centol took a step away from the rocks and craned his neck in the direction of the village. "I hope they find something good."

"Yeah," Rosalik added. "I'm starving."

Chelci's breath caught as she watched Rosalik. The gleaming crystal around her neck continued its red glow, but the intensity had faded. *They're not worried because we're chained. How much does it need to dim for us to use the origine?* Her heart pounded.

A deep inhalation of breath sounded from Dayna. After filling her lungs, a round of coughs expelled into the air. Chelci heard a faint chink of metal buried in the cough.

Gralow took an interest. With his hand on the hilt of his sword, he took a step toward Dayna.

No! Chelci thought. *He can't catch her now!* She gulped in air then devolved into her own fit of coughing. She forced air out, trying to make it as loud and drawn out as possible, giving Dayna a chance to hide her work.

Gralow turned. "Stop that," he said, his steps angling in Chelci's direction.

"I'm sorry," Chelci muttered between coughs. "It's this dry air. Something's caught." She snuck a look at Dayna and caught a glimpse of her leg jerking. *She must be close.* Chelci redoubled her effort.

Gralow stomped toward her. "Cut it out!" He grabbed Chelci by the arm and shook her.

Chelci gradually settled, her coughs growing less frequent. Dayna glanced in her direction. Chelci raised her eyebrows as if to ask if she got them all. Dayna shook her head. She held up a finger to where only Chelci could see. *One more to unlock.* Chelci expanded her lungs and sucked in a full breath of air. Dayna turned back to her leg as Chelci readied herself. In a loud expulsion of air, she expelled a final salvo of coughs.

Gralow smacked her across the face.

The slap stung, spotting Chelci's vision with bright lights. A tingling feeling spread over her cheek. She pressed her hand against her skin.

Dayna's faint nod and hidden smile made the pain worth it. *She's free!* Chelci thought. She raised a hand toward Gralow in apology. "I'm good now. I'm so sorry."

The guard scowled then returned to his place in line with the other captors.

Chelci tried to appear calm but her pulse raced. Gavin looked at her with a quirked eyebrow, but she couldn't risk giving anything away. She turned her head. Her eyes grew wider at the sight of Rosa-lik's crystal. *It's nearly out!* Only a whisper of the glow remained. Possibilities spun through Chelci's head. Would Dayna pass the key around to free more of them? Would she try to take them out herself? Would she flee and go for help? *Whatever she does, it needs to be quick, before the others return.*

Dayna had turned. She faced the marked ones while keeping her body hunched forward with her hands in her lap. The guards paid no attention, but Chelci noticed her scooting steadily closer.

Nearby, a woman's scream rang through the air.

What's that?

Chelci turned toward the village, and her stomach twisted. She pictured some woman grieving over a murdered husband as the marked ones took what they wanted.

Gralow laughed, a deep, evil sound. "Sounds like something good will be here soon."

A metallic clink of dropped chains sounded. Chelci's ears perked, and her hope surged. *This is it!*

Dayna's form blurred as she exploded with movement. She lunged forward, colliding into Gralow and knocking him over. His dagger that had been in its sheath rang out as Dayna yanked it free.

During the flurry of action, the other knights jumped to their feet.

"Help her!" Chelci yelled. "Attack!" She ran, her teeth bared at Rosalik. Adrenaline surged inside her until it was doused nearly immediately. Even before Gralow's body hit the ground, the crystals hanging from the two standing guards glowed bright.

Dayna's speeding form slowed as the guards sped up. Centol pulled a sword and batted her newly acquired dagger away. Gralow sprang to his feet and buried his fist into her lower back. Dayna reeled. Her hands and legs were free, but access to the origine was gone. She stumbled then glanced at Chelci. Fear and disappointment filled her eyes.

Chelci reached Rosalik and swung her manacled fists with all the strength she could muster. Her punch never reached the marked one though. Rosalik's body seemed to disappear, dodging out of the way. Suddenly, her arm yanked behind her, pinning her forward as someone pushed her elbow back. Chelci yelled.

The other knights had similar results, lashing out at the captors but quickly finding themselves subdued or the recipients of a quick beating.

Dayna spun between the chaos until her eyes met Chelci's. "I'm sorry," she said. "I tried to—"

"Run!" Chelci cut her off. "Get help, then find us!"

Dayna nodded. With the marked ones occupied, she sprinted. She ran through the line of guards and away from the village, kicking dust into the air.

"I've got her," Gralow said, the crystal around his neck glowing brightly.

"Come on, Dayna," Chelci muttered, looking sideways as Rosalik continued to pin her arm backward. "Get outside of its reach."

Dayna's body grew smaller, sprinting as fast as she could to get away.

Gralow grabbed Bradley and lifted his body off the ground. He tossed him into the crowd, sending Ruby and Bridgette sprawling against the rocks. He casually turned toward Dayna's fleeing form then ran. His body blurred, closing the gap between them in a mere second. With a distant cry, Dayna fell over, roughly knocked to the ground.

Chelci's shoulders fell. She stopped resisting and allowed Rosalik to push her back into the circle of rocks. Rubbing her bruised arm, she sat as Gralow returned, pulling a fighting Dayna along by her hair.

"Gah!" Dayna yelled, her head craning backward.

"Centol, where's your key?" Gralow asked.

With a red ring of embarrassment growing around his neck, Centol searched the discarded manacles on the far side of the rock. Chains clinked as he rummaged through them and picked up the thin metal object. He glanced at Gralow with a look of apology.

Chelci sighed. *How can we possibly escape? Running didn't work. Even getting out of these chains doesn't help.*

Centol worked to refasten Dayna's chains while Gralow held his dagger to her throat. At the final click of the key, Gralow spun her around to face him. "One attempted escape we could forgive, but this . . . this deserves a consequence. Which of your ears would you like to lose?"

Chelci gasped, and Dayna's body stiffened. She didn't answer.

"I'll only take one, and I'll even let you choose," Gralow said. "What more do you want?"

Dayna spit, sending a wad of phlegm into his face. The guard's body went rigid. A trail of spit dripped down his cheek and the side of his nose. With a sickly smile, he wiped the saliva away. "Fine." He turned to the other guards. "Exact the punishment on one of the others."

"What?" Dayna blurted. "No!"

Chelci's insides felt watery. Rosalik's eyes locked on hers, her face glowing red from the crystal. The marked one pulled a knife from a sheath up her sleeve and closed the distance in the blink of an eye.

Chelci's hair was pulled up, held in the firm grip of the devion-infused woman. She struggled, but it was like her hair was caught in a vise. She tried to punch or kick, but her chains rendered attack impossible. "No!" she yelled.

Rosalik pulled Chelci's head against a rock, leaning her ear awkwardly to the side. Her pulse thundered in her ears. Sweat beaded on her forehead. Rosalik's knife flashed the sun as it lifted in the air.

"No! No! No!" Dayna yelled. "I was the one who tried to escape! Here . . . Take this one!"

Chelci strained to see. Dayna extended one side of her head, pulling her hair back to reveal her ear.

A strained silence filled the rocky circle. Chelci's breathing stopped, every muscle in her body tense.

Gralow grabbed the extended ear while Centol held Dayna's head in place. "Having second thoughts?" Gralow lifted the knife and held it next to her ear. He teased the blade back and forth in the crook between her ear and her head. "You'd rather sacrifice your own than that of your friend. How noble."

He glanced back at Rosalik and sneered, "Let's take them both."

Chelci gasped.

Gralow's dagger sliced down in a rapid flick. Dayna screamed then lifted her restrained hands to where her ear used to be. When Centol released his grip, she dropped to the ground.

The pressure on Chelci's scalp increased as Rosalik leaned against her body and laughed. The knife drew close, angling at the side of her head.

"What is this?" A smooth, commanding voice called.

The pressure on her scalp loosened. Chelci lifted her head to see Talioth and the others returning. Splatters of red stained both Talioth's and Heathine's gray outfits. Chelci swallowed hard, picturing the poor villagers who had been involved.

"What happened?" Talioth asked.

Dayna groaned on the ground, pressing against the side of her head with blood dripping down her arm.

The three captors guarding them glanced between each other.

"This one tried to escape," Gralow said, pointing to Dayna. "She —" he looked at Centol and hesitated.

Centol sighed. "She got my keys and unlocked her chains. Then, she tried to attack us and flee."

"But we stopped them," Gralow added. "It was nothing."

Talioth's eyes narrowed. "So . . . what are you doing, now?"

Rosalik looked at the knife in her hand and straightened, backing off Chelci. "We were, uh . . ."

"We were cutting an ear off each of these two," Gralow said, "as punishment."

Talioth walked into the middle, between the three guards. "They take your keys, attack you, and try to run off while you three are on watch."

Centol adjusted his stance and looked at the ground.

"I should be cutting *your* ears off!" Talioth stood in Gralow's face and shook a finger at him. "If this happens again, I won't hesitate."

"Yes, sir." Gralow nodded, standing straight.

Talioth pointed to Dayna. "Bandage her up!"

Gralow snapped into action and rummaged through his bag.

The leader turned to the knights. "And you all . . . that's twice. If any of you attempt something like this again, we won't just cut ears off. We'll kill all the others you left behind. Understood?"

Chelci swallowed. No one replied, but everyone heard. *No more escape attempts.*

"Not that you three deserve it, but . . . here." Talioth motioned, and the others passed out bread, smoked meat, and fresh skins of drink to the guards. They took what was offered with eager eyes and relieved expressions.

Chelci settled on a rock, her heart slowly calming from the close call. Bridgette sat next to her while their captors focused on the food.

"Hey," Bridgette whispered. She opened her cupped hands to show a stylus and a scrap of paper. "I had these in my pockets. Can you think of anything we can do with them?"

Chelci looked up at the thatched roofs peeking over the trees. Her pulse spiked again. "Let me have them."

She took the items and turned her body away from the captors. While trying to look inconspicuous, she scribbled onto the paper, writing as much as she could fit. When the space ran out, she glanced up to make sure none of the marked ones had noticed.

"Pass me that rock." She nodded toward a small stone at Bridgette's feet.

The young knight leaned forward and scooped the object up. She passed it to Chelci without looking in her direction.

The paper surrounded the rock, and Chelci crumbled it against the smooth surface. It fit in her palm, easily hidden from sight.

"Now we hope we get an opportunity," she said.

When the marked ones had gorged themselves and a bandage was wrapped around Dayna's head, the leftovers finally made their way to the knights. They ate with shackled hands and passed the food between each other until it was gone.

"Drink up," Talioth said. "I hope you enjoyed your rest, because now the difficult part begins."

Chelci followed his gaze to the mountains towering in their path. Peaks of snow blanketed the higher regions, and jagged spires shot up everywhere she looked. She took a deep breath then exhaled.

The marked ones prodded the knights into a line and resumed their travel toward the looming peaks.

Before they left the area, movement caught Chelci's eye. Along the path to the village, a boy's head peeked out from behind a tree. A glimmer of hope surged through her. She checked over her shoulder to where Centol and Rosalik brought up the rear of the line. Their eyes drifted toward the mountains—*away from me.*

With a flick of her wrist, Chelci tossed the paper-covered rock down the path. It hit the dirt, bounced, and rolled until it stopped close to the boy's tree.

The peeking head disappeared when the rock arrived.

Come on! Get it!

She waited, staring down the path.

"Move!" Centol shouted, pushing against her back with a strong arm.

She stumbled forward, struggling to keep her feet under her. Soon, she caught up with Gavin. After a few more paces, the trail turned. She glanced behind as the path was about to move out of sight.

The boy's head was visible once again. His eyes stared in their direction.

Get it! Get it!

She took another step. As her body moved around a bend, the last thing she saw was the boy's eyes turn. He looked into the path, directly at the rock.

8

DINNER PLANNING

The thick aroma of smoked meat filled Danik's nose as he entered the royal dining hall. He inhaled, savoring the sensation. A portion of the large rectangular table was filled with platters of food: roasted vegetables, piles of assorted cheese, and steaming bread. In the center, a full smoked chicken sat, waiting with a carving knife stuck in it.

"This is what I've been waiting for," he said with his arms out. A servant pulled out the chair at the end, and Danik sat, his stomach rumbling with anticipation.

Another servant approached with a glass decanter of swirling dark liquid and poured it into the royal goblet. "The Palenting red you requested, Your Majesty."

Danik allowed a smile. Veron would have never permitted the Knights to purchase such a rare vintage, but the castle's wine cellar had crates of them collecting dust.

The silver chalice contained a wide rim curving down like half of a ball. The stem sparkled with sapphires and emeralds in the base. Danik tipped the cup at his lips and allowed the earthy wine to trickle down his throat. He smacked his lips, savoring the expensive drink.

Danik pulled on a leg of the chicken and used the knife to cut it free. He sank his teeth into the juicy meat and closed his eyes while he chewed. The sound of footsteps preceded the entrance of Nicolar and the previous king's advisor, Quentin Cotterell.

"Any luck, Nicolar?" Danik wiped his mouth while chewing.

The thief with the shaggy black hair grinned, revealing the tight scar on his bottom lip normally hidden behind his goatee. "Indeed. We already have five promising subjects from the Red Quarter, and I have a team assembled to locate more. Soon, we'll visit other cities to recruit."

"Excellent. In a matter of weeks, the Shadow Knights should be larger than what Veron could produce in years. What about his whereabouts?"

Nicolar shook his head. "Nothing yet, but we continue to search. The army is helping." He chuckled. "I have them asking around about shadow knight impersonators—seeing if anyone has seen or heard anything."

Danik tilted his head. "You know what? I don't think the name Shadow Knights is fitting anymore."

"Oh?"

"It's archaic—representative of the old regime. We're going to be different—more powerful, more visible. We need a new name."

Nicolar scrunched his face while his eyes grew distant. "Maybe . . . Day Knights or Knights of the Light?"

"Something stronger."

"Knights of Strength?"

It came to him, and Danik grinned. "No . . . Knights of Power."

Nicolar nodded, smiling back. "I like it. It conveys a message of force and also that we're not cowering in the shadows."

"Plus, we're more powerful than the Shadow Knights ever were."

"What do you think it is that makes the devion so much easier to learn? You said the origine takes a while?"

"Most people can't learn the origine at all," Danik said. "And the ones who can, take weeks or months of practice. I think it's the raw power that makes the devion easier to access."

Nicolar pursed his lips. "It's strange."

"What is?"

"If it's easy to learn and more powerful . . . why have the Shadow Knights avoided it?"

Danik thought of the hidden black mark on his neck that grew more prominent every day. He bit back the fear gnawing at him that it was related to his use of the devion, but he didn't know what it meant.

More footsteps approached, and Nicolar turned toward the door. "This must be . . . Yes, the companions you requested. This is Lisette and Dawn."

Danik's heart pounded as two women entered the room. Appearing in their early twenties, the young women radiated a fierce beauty that took his breath away. Lisette's pale skin paired well with the shocking-red hair that flowed down to rest in front, disappearing into the matching red dress. Her face contained a warm glow that ended with smooth cheeks and a sharp jawline. Her slender waist gave way to full hips that hugged the tight curve of the gown.

Contrasting Lisette's light pigment, Dawn's skin contained a rich chestnut hue. Her short black hair curled just under her chin. The neckline of the obsidian-colored dress plunged into a deep V. Her full lips curved into a hesitant smile. She flicked her eyes at Lisette, who looked just as uncomfortable.

"They've agreed to provide company while you eat," Nicolar finished.

Danik stood. He took each woman by hand in turn and kissed them. "It's my honor for you to join me. Please, have a seat." His gaze lingered while each of them moved to the seats on either side of his. Before he returned to his chair, he raised his eyebrows toward Nicolar who wore a smug look of satisfaction. "Well done."

His right-hand-man nodded in return.

"Please, ladies," Danik said, gesturing toward the food. "Join me. Eat as much as you like."

The ladies appraised the food with wide eyes as if they'd not eaten in a while. Dawn made the first move for some bread, and

Lisette quickly followed. Danik watched while they ate. Lisette's hand trembled as she moved the bread to her mouth.

"Where are you ladies from?"

Dawn lowered her bread and looked at the table. "I live near Turba Square."

"And I'm in the Red Quarter." Lisette's voice shook.

Danik leaned forward, ignoring the chicken leg sitting on his plate. He extended his arms under the table and rested his hands on each of the ladies' bare legs. They tensed. "As king, I have the entire kingdom at my command. Anything I say will be done." He rubbed his hands over the tops of their knees. "Would you like to get out of the Red Quarter? I can provide rooms for each of you here in the castle. Every luxury would be provided. You'd have food, clothing . . . whatever you desire."

"Keep in mind, His Highness doesn't like to be disappointed."

"Nicolar, please." Danik held up his hand toward the black-haired man and laughed. "Why would they *not* want to stay?" The ladies looked at the table, giving him pause.

"Your families will never forgive you if you displease the king," Nicolar added.

Watching the women's hesitant expressions, Danik didn't correct him. "What do you say?"

Dawn turned first, her weak smile drawing his attention away from the glisten at the corner of her eyes. "Of course, Your Majesty. I would be happy to stay. You are very generous."

Lisette followed by nodding. "As would I," she breathed with a catch in her voice.

A moment of regret at having to kill Lia washed through Danik. *Why did she have to turn me away? We were perfect together. We could have been king and queen.* Dawn and Lisette were a welcome distraction though, and he was content to keep them around. For a while.

Quentin cleared his throat.

Danik sighed and turned as the young women devoted their attention to the food. "Ah, yes, Quentin. What news do you have of the city?"

The advisor took a half step forward. "The people are . . . less than enthusiastic."

Danik's eye twitched. "What do you mean?"

"Your tax increase is—" He stopped. "I'm sorry . . . High Lord Hampton's tax increase is causing unrest."

"In what way?"

"King Darcius dropped taxes at the beginning of the season, so the increase—let's just say . . . it hasn't been well received."

Danik frowned. "What do you mean? What are they doing?"

"Nothing has been . . . done, but there's talk—grumbling."

He waved a hand. "I can deal with grumbling."

"The guilds are meeting," Quentin added. "All of them. They're pushing for a retraction of the tax. There's talk that your—" The advisor's mouth shut as he glanced at the ladies.

"That what, Quentin?"

The older man swallowed hard. "That your rule isn't legitimate."

Danik bristled. "Is that what they say?"

"I've heard it too," Nicolar added, "in the taverns."

Danik leaned back and blew out the air from his lungs. "What do they want?"

"They, uh . . ." Quentin glanced at Nicolar. "They want King Darcius back."

Danik pounded his fist on the table, causing the ladies to jump. "That's not going to happen."

"Of course not, Your Majesty."

"They need time," Nicolar said. "Time to forget Darcius and adjust to a new way."

An idea formed, and a grin grew on Danik's face. "I know what they need. They need a distraction. Something exciting. Something they've not seen in a while."

Nicolar's head tilted. "What do you have in mind?"

Danik noticed Lisette staring at him and hesitated. "Later. We'll discuss it when delicate ears aren't around. Gather Bilton and—who's the justice lord again?"

"Herman Miligan," Quentin answered.

Danik sneered. "That's right." He sighed. "Yes, gather him, too. Let's meet tomorrow after breakfast. In the meantime . . . Keep focusing on—" He stopped, remembering the women's presence. "On the man we seek."

"What if he's fled the city?" Nicolar asked. "You know him better than most. Where might he have gone?"

Danik sighed. "A number of places. He has history in Karad. He has friends in Tienn, Karondir, even Lorranis. But if he *is* alive, he'll be trying to figure out where—"

The memory returned in a flash. Moments after Danik killed the king, Veron had arrived in the Advisors Council Chamber, announcing he saw something in the library. *Maybe he found something.*

Danik stood in a rush, his chair scraping the floor. "Quentin, where is the library?"

The advisor's face scrunched. "The library?"

"Yes, the royal library—the one Ver—" He caught himself. "The one people sometimes use for research."

"It's in the south tower, at the top. Would you like me to take you there?"

"Yes, immediately." Danik turned to the young ladies. "I apologize to have to leave. Nicolar here will ensure you're made comfortable, and I'll be back soon."

He leaned toward Nicolar. "Keep them away from Cedric."

"Of course, Your Majesty. I will cut off his arm if he touches them."

Danik laughed then nodded to Quentin. "Let's go."

Royal guards snapped to attention as he exited the dining room. They followed as he and Quentin proceeded down the hall. Danik looked over his shoulder at the men with gray-and-blue tunics and metal breastplates. "You don't need to follow me. If there is a threat I'm not able to handle on my own, trust me . . . you wouldn't stand a chance."

The guards glanced at each other and faltered. Despite the insult to their abilities, they continued forward, fulfilling their duty to protect the king.

A narrow opening cut into the curved wall of the south tower. Stone steps circled counter-clockwise up, disappearing into darkness. Quentin grabbed a lantern from a wall post and led the way.

The steps seemed endless. A musty scent filled the stairwell. The echo of four pairs of feet bounced off the walls. Quentin's breath grew labored as they continued the upward march, but Danik's legs felt strong.

The stairs ended in a large circular room filled with books. "This is," Quentin paused to breathe, "the first floor."

Cases lined the walls with a few spaces for windows. Short shelves rested back to back in the center of the room alongside an empty table. Danik stepped forward, gaping at the overwhelming amount of books. "Where would I even begin?"

Quentin didn't answer. Danik ran his fingers along a shelf, touching the spines. The old, cracked leather tickled his fingers. Doubt and disappointment ran through him. *What did I expect to find up here?*

A separate short staircase led up, and Danik took the flight, hoping his curiosity would be rewarded by some revelation. The second level was just as stark as the first—nothing but stacks of shelves. "This is pointless," he muttered as the advisor topped the last stair behind him. He eyed the next flight that led another floor up. "What's up there?"

"More of the same."

Danik rested his hand on the railing, wavering between leaving and continuing the pointless search. With a *humpf*, he took the next flight up.

The third level looked similar to the others. The roof curved inward, and a loft perched above the floor with a small spiral staircase leading to it. The castle tower came to point above the room, signaling the end of the line. The shelves looked just like the other floors.

"And this is it," Quentin said.

Danik's shoulders fell. He examined a shelf, hoping something might jump out at him, but the titles he scanned looked dry and uninteresting.

Through an open window, a shutter rattled against the stone while a breeze seeped into the library. He stepped to it and peered outside.

Felting lay far below with the setting sun reflecting off the Benevorre River. Danik sighed. *He could be out there anywhere—in the city, in the woods, even in another kingdom by now. We must keep looking, though. He could ruin everything.*

He pulled the shutter closed, throwing the latch over it to keep it closed. As he turned, the table caught his eye. It wasn't empty like the other floors. An empty cup and a half-filled glass pitcher rested next to three books in a careless pile. A faded green book and a cracked brown-leather one lay on the bottom while a small red leather book covered them. He picked up the red one. It was light, and the blank cover was smooth. When he flipped back the cover, he gasped.

"What is it?" Quentin asked.

Danik looked up at the advisor while his lips curled.

9

VISIT TO THE LIBRARY

Raiyn kept his head down as he walked the Felting streets. Ahead, the castle projected its silhouette into the darkening sky with its spires jutting into the air. A handful of windows gleamed yellow, but most remained black.

He wore a plain brown cloak with its hood pulled up. The smell of sweat and dirt reached his nose. His pulse thumped steadily, and his heavy breathing sounded abnormally loud. Lia walked beside him, covered by a hooded cloak of her own.

In the street ahead, a steady hum of conversation trickled out of a tavern. The windows glowed with a warm light, and a peel of laughter rang through the air.

Leading the way, Veron stopped outside of the tavern door. "We should wait a few hours to give everyone a chance to turn in. We can bide our time in here."

Raiyn had spent little time in taverns, and inside was a shock to his senses. The low ceiling contributed to a cramped feeling, and the humid air made his skin feel sticky. Lanterns hung on the walls, sending flickering light in all directions. A low, wooden bar stretched along one wall, and tables filled with men and women occupied the rest of the room. Veron led them to a lone booth in the back corner where little light reached.

"Why get here so early if we just have to wait?" Raiyn asked as he slid into the booth.

Lia joined him in his seat, and Veron sat opposite, keeping his hood up.

"For starters," Veron said, "the city gate closes in thirty minutes. We got here when we did to avoid unwanted questions and attention."

"I didn't realize that. Good call."

"Also," Veron raised his nose and sniffed, "I'm hungry, and a warm meal sounds delicious."

A pair of drunk men in the booth next to them argued about their wives. Raiyn tried to block out the noise when the scent of roasted meat reached him. His mouth watered.

A gruff-looking man arrived at the head of the table and scowled at them. His sleeves rolled up over bulging forearms, and stains of food and drink dotted his pants. "Ale?" he asked.

"Please," Veron said answering for them all. "Also, what food do you have?"

"Tonight's meal is roasted boar with potatoes and greens. Food and drink makes one tid per person."

"Give us three orders." Veron pulled out coins from a pouch and set them on the table.

The man slid the coins off the table and into his pocket then walked away without replying.

"Friendly fellow," Raiyn said.

Lia leaned forward, lowering her voice. "Any ideas about how we get this book? I doubt they're going to welcome us through the front door."

"They probably would if we tried." Veron took a deep breath then exhaled. "The guards would likely be happy to see us, but . . . we can't risk that exposure. I'm sure Danik has bribed their loyalty in any way he can."

"So, how do we get up to the library in the tower if we can't—" Lia paused at her father's knowing look. "We climb the outside."

Raiyn's eyebrows raised. "The . . . outside? You mean the outside of the castle?"

Veron nodded. "It's the best way."

"But without the origine, you can't—" Lia stopped again. "Oh. You're not going."

"I can tell you where it is, but I can't get up there."

Raiyn lowered his voice even more, his pulse increasing. "So . . . Lia and I will climb the outside of the castle, all the way to the top of the tower. Then we'll grab the book and come back."

"That's it."

A nervous laugh rumbled from his throat.

"I know it's a lot to ask," Veron said. "I hate putting you in that position, but the book is our only lead. And every day we delay puts Chelci and the other knights in more danger."

A round of laughter bounced over the booth from the nearby patrons.

"It's all right," Lia said. "Climbing is fun. It should keep us far away from Danik and his crew, and there should be little risk."

"Except for the risk of falling," Raiyn added.

"If anything goes wrong while you're up there, you get out." Veron looked intently at his daughter. "Do you understand?"

She nodded.

"So what else do you know about the book?" Raiyn asked. "It explains the origine and the devion?"

Veron shrugged. "I'm not sure."

"But that's what it's about, right?"

"According to the title, it seems so."

Lia leaned in. "Was it written by Talon Shadow?"

"I have no idea."

"Does it talk about him and when he turned to the devion?"

"It did look around three hundred years old, but I don't know either way."

Lia scoffed. "What *do* you know about it?"

Veron turned his hands up. "Like I told you . . . I know it has a map, and that's about it."

Lia groaned, turning her eyes toward the ceiling.

"I had all of about five seconds with it before I spotted the marked ones arriving."

"Don't worry," Raiyn said. "We'll get the book, then we'll all be able to dig into it more."

The gruff-looking server arrived with three pints of ale and set them down. Foam jostled over the lip and ran down the sides to wet the wooden table.

"Thank you," Veron said to the man's back.

Raiyn and Veron grabbed the handle of their mugs but Lia's finger danced on the table while a smirk teased her mouth. "What's this, Father? We're drinking on the job, now?"

"There's a difference between throwing back a bunch of drinks and sipping on one." Veron took a short drink. His finger made a furtive circle to indicate the rest of the tavern. "What's more helpful in this situation is for us to blend in with our surroundings without drawing attention. Sitting *without* a drink could raise questions."

Raiyn tilted the mug, allowing the ale to trickle down his throat. It smelled like an old book. He swallowed then puckered at the sour taste—like drinking cooked cabbage.

"Well, I don't care what they say," a slurred voice said from the other side of a high-backed wooden divider. "I don't believe the Shadow Knights could have all been killed."

Lia and Veron tensed, and Raiyn's ears perked, suddenly attuned to the men.

"Then what do you think happened?" another man in the same booth asked.

"I don't know, but think about it . . . The king betrays the knights by summoning someone to kill them, and *all* of them killed or captured? *Pfff.* I don't believe it. They can take out anyone!"

"Then where are they?"

"What do you mean?"

"If they didn't get killed or captured, where did they go?"

"Maybe they're in hiding?"

"Hiding? Doing nothing while Danik—" The man's voice dropped low before he continued. "If the Knights were around, they would be doing something."

"Maybe they are."

The other voice grumbled. "It's not enough, if they are."

"What do you want them to do? Stop taxes? It's within the king's right to issue them—as much as I hate it."

"But the city, it's . . ." A sigh reached over the booth wall. "We need something to be done. He's going to run the city into the ground if this is how he's going to lead."

"That's what the high lords are for. If things are bad, they can step in."

Raiyn's attention turned to their server, who arrived with three plates of food. Steam curled off the boar meat, teasing his nose with its peppery scent.

When the man left, Veron held a finger to his lips, and Raiyn understood. *No talking about the Knights or Danik.* They dug into the food. Raiyn closed his eyes, savoring the tender boar and salty potatoes. He sipped his drink, enjoying the moment of peace while they waited for the time to pass.

RAIYN'S FINGERS pinched onto a sliver of a jutting-out stone. One boot rested on what could barely be called a hold, and the other pressed against the wall for friction. The origine simmered inside him, fueling his arms and legs with unnatural strength, but nothing assisted with his nerves.

Holding the crimp with one hand, he leaned back and shook out his other arm as he looked up. Lia was a body length above him, steadily moving up the wall.

"Almost there," Lia said, her foot scraping the stone. With a sudden burst of movement, she rolled up and over a lip of a roof. Her arm appeared a moment later. "Give me your hand."

Raiyn extended his legs and reached for another hold. With the origine, it was just enough to grasp. He glanced down to find where to move his feet, and his eyes focused on the drop. Hundreds of feet below, the roofs and spires of the castle spilled in all directions. A swooping feeling turned his stomach. His pulse thudded and his hands grew clammy.

His foot found purchase, and he pulled his body toward the wall. Another few moves, and Lia's hand was in reach. When his hand grasped hers, the worry fled. She pulled him up, his feet and other hand coming off the wall as he sailed over the edge then rolled onto the roof next to her.

"Whew!" he whistled. "Thanks."

The short roof they lay on stuck out only a body-length from the main tower. Several windows extended up from where they rested, not too much farther to the top.

Lia pointed up. "The second window should get us in. But let's take a moment to recover."

Raiyn looked toward the city, and his mouth fell open. The buildings below looked built in miniature. Lanterns burned in the main streets, providing a faint outline of the neighborhoods of Felting. A shimmer of moonlight reflected off the river, and a deep blackness waited beyond, where the forest took over.

"Amazing," he breathed.

"Yes, it is. And Danik is going to ruin it all."

"What's his deal, by the way?" Raiyn turned to her.

She pursed her lips. "I'm not sure. The desire to be king—sure, I can see that. He can do whatever he wants and have all the money. Who wouldn't want that?" Her face fell. "But I don't understand his willingness to take it at others' expense. He killed my grandfather. He betrayed the Knights. He *tried* to kill me. We used to be close—always getting into trouble together, but . . . I can barely remember what I saw in all of it, anymore."

"People change over time."

"I know I've changed," Lia said. "I like to think it's been for the better, but Danik seems to have grown worse. Did you know that when he was young, his parents died—killed by a thief?"

"No, I didn't."

"I think that event shaped him a great deal. Ever since then, he's wanted more power—the ability to stop things like that from happening."

Raiyn took a deep breath. His pulse had settled. The energy inside him felt primed. Steadying himself against the slant in the roof, he stood. A light breeze fluttered the hem of his shirt, and he bent his knees to remain low.

"Careful," Lia warned. "Don't want to fall from here. All the origine in the world wouldn't help your legs absorb that fall." She rose and ran her hands along the surface of the tower. "Holds are good. This last part should be easy. You ready?"

Raiyn nodded.

Lia moved first, climbing up the wall as easily as if she ascended a ladder. Raiyn waited while she paused at the second window. Clicks and scrapes sounded from above.

"Everything all right?" Raiyn asked.

"Give me a second." More scrapes preceded a solid thunk. "Got it!" A glass and metal frame pivoted outward, and Lia slunk inside the tower. A moment later, her shadowy head popped out. "Come on."

He took a deep breath then grasped onto the wall. The stone holds were no better than the previous section they had climbed, but using the origine, it didn't prove to be a challenge. After several moves upward, he grabbed the sill of the oval-shaped window. Lia lifted under his arm and helped him inside.

"Thanks again." He dusted off his hands on his pants. The presence of books caught his attention. Despite the dim light, a packed shelf stared back at him. "Looks like we found the library."

"Yeah. I'm guessing there will be a lantern at the entrance." Lia walked across the wooden floor to the top of a set of stairs. A creak of metal filled the air. "Perfect."

Raiyn joined her as she pulled out a flint. A few scrapes later, the lantern roared to life. "That's better," he said.

Shelves of books packed the circular room, pressed against each wall. Tables and chairs dotted the center, leaving space to move between the shelves. A sweet, musty smell filled the room, and the flickering flame of the lantern was the only noise.

"This is a lot of books," Raiyn said.

Lia pointed up a staircase. "There are two more floors."

He whistled. "So, what are we looking for?"

Lia snapped into action. "It should be on a table. There should be three books: brown, green, and red."

"That's assuming they're still sitting out."

"Right. Let's hope they are." She moved to the stairs. "Come on. It was on the third floor."

Raiyn followed her up. The next level looked identical to the first, but Lia didn't stop to inspect. When they arrived at the third floor, she gasped.

"You see it?" Raiyn asked as he mounted the last step.

Her face held a grin as she stared at a table by the window. The table held a pitcher and three books—brown, green, and red. "Nice!"

They crossed the room, and Lia picked up the red one. "That's lucky." She flipped open the cover, and her smile faltered.

"What's wrong?"

She shook her head and flipped more pages.

"Is it not the right one?"

"This is where Father said it was, but . . ."

"But, what?"

She turned the book around, holding it open.

Raiyn leaned in and squinted. Nothing appears on the pages. "It's blank." His forehead pinched. "This is the book that's supposed to help us find the knights? I don't get it."

Lia's gaze fixed on the window while she stood, unmoving. "Something's wrong."

The hair along his arms prickled. Lia was normally confident and sure. Seeing her hesitate troubled him.

"Not what you hoped it would be?" A strange voice interrupted the silence.

Raiyn spun. Across the room, an unfamiliar man stood at the base of a spiral staircase while another descended the last few steps from the loft above.

"Cedric! Donte!" Lia gasped. "What are you—?"

"Danik had a feeling someone would turn up, but none of us expected it would be you." The man with the scruffy beard leered at Lia before shifting his eyes toward Raiyn and angling his sword. "Who's this?"

Lia didn't answer. She glanced at the book before tossing it back to the table.

Raiyn moved his hand to the axe at his hip.

"Careful," the man on the left said, stepping closer and pointing his sword at Raiyn. "I'll run you through before you move a finger."

Raiyn's arm tensed. He inhaled but didn't draw the weapon.

"Where's the book?" Lia asked.

"What's it to you? Danik will want to talk with you. He's going to be surprised to see you alive." He flicked his sword toward the stairs. "Come on, both of you."

Raiyn looked at Lia. Her eyes remained wide, but she didn't budge. "What do we do?" he whispered.

"Head down the stairs." The man's voice grew louder.

Lia's jaw formed a hard line. She stared back at Raiyn. A flick of her eyes toward the window told Raiyn what he needed to know.

His heart pounded. He tensed his muscles to spring into action. A warm tingle shook his insides.

Moving in a blur, one of the men lunged first. Raiyn wasn't prepared for his speed. Before he could jump to the window, the man arrived there, flung the shutters closed, then spun to face them.

The bookcase closest to Lia exploded at the same moment. She hurled the wooden object forward, sending shelves of books flying through the air. The ripple of paper sounded like a flock of birds taking flight. With a boom, the shelf crashed into the table, cracking the legs and knocking it to the floor. The books seemed to hover in the air.

Lia and Raiyn sped toward the stairs, but the man with the messy beard stepped forward to intercept. Lia swung her sword to drive him away, but his speed was even faster. They traded blows, so fast the books still hadn't fallen to the ground.

Blocked from the exit, Raiyn turned and gasped. The man who guarded the window had approached. He held his sword up, ready to strike. Raiyn leaped out of the way at the last moment, and the man's weapon cut though the aged wood of the bookshelf. The blade caught. Using the split-second, Raiyn kicked, sending all the power he had into his leg. His boot caught the man in his chest. A cracking sound filled the room. Raiyn winced as the man flew backward, striking the shutters of the window. The wood splintered, bursting outward. The man disappeared through the oval window into the night, yelling as his body faded.

"Raiyn, go!" Lia shouted.

He spun. She pointed toward the window before returning both hands to her sword. She parried a quick succession of strikes, the clang of metal filling the air. His legs felt like lead weighed them down.

Lia shoved the man she fought, and he fell partly down the stairs. "Out the window!" she yelled at Raiyn. "Come on!" She led the way, running toward the window with the burst shutters. A few steps away, she leaped. Her legs passed through the window first before her body slid against the frame. Her arm dragged against the stone casing, slowing her exit before she disappeared completely.

Raiyn gulped. His hands felt clammy as he stared at the oval-shaped blackness. The scuffling of feet and hands ascending the stairs behind him turned his head. The man with the messy beard mounted the stairs and ran toward him. The tip of his sword taunted as it rushed closer. Raiyn held his axe in hand, but the man's iron strength crashed into his feeble attempt to block. Raiyn's grip failed, and the weapon flew from his grip. He lunged toward the window but stopped when a thrown dagger sank into its stone casing.

"You step toward that window and this next one goes through your head," the knight of power threatened, holding another dagger along with his sword.

Raiyn's eyes flicked through the room. The window was too far, so were the stairs. He gulped, then glanced up. The loft was the only measure of protection he could find. Exploding with his powered legs, he leaped up and pulled his body over the railing.

Hidden from the bearded attacker, he surveyed the space. The bookshelves looked devoted to natural sciences. In addition to the rows of books, a variety of minerals, powders, and jars of scientific specimens filled the shelves. Illustrations of animals, plants, and geologic charts covered the wall above the shelves. What held Raiyn's attention though was the poleaxe mounted over the books.

He grabbed it and spun toward the open loft. His hands clenched the shaft. He extended the head forward, straining his ears for any clue to where the man would pop up. His own labored breath was all he heard.

Footsteps reached his ears—not over the railing but coming up the spiral staircase. Step after step progressed slowly as if drawing out the tension. A malicious laugh mixed with the steps.

Raiyn turned toward the top of the stairs and pointed the axe. Only then did he notice the condition the ancient weapon was in. The head didn't have the shiny steel color he was familiar with. It was brown, riddled with bumps and nocks that came from years of rusting—*hundreds of years*. His heart sank. *One hit and it will crumble.*

He stepped away from the stairs and glanced at the shelves. Labels on the bottles of powder caught his eye: maglium, grellium, potannium. *Elements*, he thought. Memories of experiments with his mother rushed through his brain. He inhaled sharply and looked back at the rusted axe head. *Iron oxide!*

"Where are you going to go, now?" the knight of power taunted as he climbed the final steps. "My name's Cedric, by the way. We don't have to be enemies."

With his heart pounding, Raiyn lunged to his left and grabbed the jar of potannium. Blue powder filled half the clear glass container. He squinted as he smashed the jar into the axe, shattering the top half of the vessel.

Cedric chuckled. "A jagged jar or an ancient axe? Which do you think will give you better odds against me?"

Raiyn shook the cracked container onto the rusty axe head. The blue powder poured on the weapon, hissing and spitting flecks of sediment. Smoke rose.

"Is that supposed to intimidate me?"

Raiyn didn't bother to answer. He hopped over the railing, keeping the axe head pointed toward the man. He hit the floor of the main room next to the table, but a split second later, Cedric appeared, already down the stairs and blocking his path to the window.

"You're not gonna be faster than me," the knight of power sneered. "Give up."

The axe head continued to sizzle. A fleck of hot debris nicked Raiyn's face. He took in a deep breath then tossed the weapon to the floor. It landed with a *clunk* at Cedric's feet.

Cedric roared with laughter. "Nice move. What are you planning to do n—"

Raiyn lunged for the askew pitcher that had settled in the rubble. He grabbed the handle and flung the remaining stale water toward the discarded axe. Time stood still as the liquid sloshed through the air. A wrinkled line formed on Cedric's forehead.

When the water splashed onto the rusted, simmering head, a plume of smoke erupted. The thick, gushing cloud engulfed Cedric. He shouted and flailed his limbs, appearing as arms reaching out from a wall of blue fog.

Raiyn shouted as he charged. He lowered his shoulder and barreled into the center of the cloud, crashing into the chest of the knight of power and knocking him back. An acrid smell filled his nostrils. He saw nothing but blue. He backed out of the cloud, unable to make out the details of the crashing sound against the far wall.

Without hesitating, he sprinted toward the open window, using origine for speed and leaping headfirst through the oval opening. As he passed the sill, he grabbed at the stones to slow his progress and bring his body to the wall, but the rocks felt as smooth as glass. His fingers scrambled but failed to grasp onto anything. His body hurtled through the air. The wind buffeted him as he fell. His arms splayed, unsuccessfully attempting to grasp anything. His cloak wrapped around him, flapping upward, obscuring his view.

A solid thud reverberated through him as he hit a slanted roof. "Oof!"

His body bounced, rolling helplessly through the night, but he couldn't see. He flailed blindly. The tile of the roof passed the tips of his fingers.

He fell again. His mind struggled to remember the path they took while climbing. The mixture of walls and roofs became a blur. His cloak blew away from his face, and the route he was falling grew terrifyingly clear.

A banner flapped below him, stretched on a flagpole attached to the tower. He reached out and grasped at the fabric. His fingers clenched, filled with the strength of the origine. His falling slowed. His hand burned from the friction. When he thought he may be able to stop his dangerous descent, a hideous crack filled the air. The pole snapped, and he resumed his drop.

Another roof materialized and met his shoulder with a thud. Without time to gather himself, he again bounced over the lip. But, as the edge of the roof disappeared, a hand wrapped around his wrist. He jerked to a stop. His arm screamed, threatening to separate from his body.

"I've got you!" Lia gritted through her teeth.

The billowing cloak settled, and Raiyn's sight returned. He dangled from the side of the short roof. Lia leaned over the edge, her hair framing her face while the muscles in her arm rippled. Raiyn's helpless feeling gave way to relief as she pulled him up.

He collapsed with his back against the cool tile of the roof. His shoulder and limbs ached from the beating they took.

"Use the origine," Lia said, breathing heavily with her eyes closed.

Raiyn closed his eyes and focused on the power. He forced his breathing to calm and took a steady breath. A tingling sensation grew in his gut. The sharp pain in his arm and shoulder faded to a dull ache. The burn on his hand tingled before the sensation faded. He opened his eyes.

Two short drops remained between them and the surrounding buttress around the castle. Something caught his eye. Not far away, on the roof where they sat, a body lay crumped. A dark stain dripped down the roof tiles, running from the unmoving form.

"Donte's dead." Lia's voice was eerily calm. "Come on. We've got to keep moving." With control, she lowered her body over the edge, her fingers disappearing a moment later.

Raiyn risked a glance up. The window they had jumped through remained high above them. There were no signs of the other man following. He nodded to no one then dropped his body to the edge before he followed Lia.

10

FELDAN ARENA

The murmur of conversation grew as Danik ascended the steps. He ran his fingers along the stone walls, aged by centuries of wind and rain. A small crowd parted when he reached the top, and a freshly cleaned Feldan Arena spread before him.

Weeds had been removed from the cracks in the walls. Discoloration had been scrubbed away. The arena walls and seats gleamed as if they'd been newly constructed. Spectators filled the seats of the oval-shaped amphitheater, their excitement humming in all directions.

"Your Majesty." High Lord Bilton's arms opened with a smile on his face. "Welcome to the royal box. I trust this will suit?"

Padded chairs sat in the shade under a purple awning, and a platter of food rested on a table, untouched. Danik nodded, his eyes fixed on the tall young woman with red hair sitting in one of the chairs.

Lisette's smile didn't reach her eyes. "Welcome, Your Majesty."

Danik ignored the false front and returned a triumphant smile. "Thank you." He spun back toward Bilton as he sat in the nicest chair. "How long until we begin?"

"Very soon."

Cedric rounded a corner and hailed him. "Your Majesty."

A faint ring of red stained his nostrils. Danik cringed at the sign of borrell spice, but he waved the man forward and indicated to the seat next to him. "I heard about last night. You're sure it was Lia?"

Cedric nodded. "It was her, and she knew exactly where to look for the book."

Danik blew out his breath. His relief that she was alive warred with the complication it created for him. His voice dropped to a whisper. "Veron must be alive then, too. But he wasn't the one with her?"

"It was someone young—maybe twenty. Black hair, faint beard. She called him . . . Blaine? Brain?"

Danik's stomach turned, and his lip curled. "Raiyn."

Cedric's eyes jumped as he snapped his finger. "That's it. He's the one who killed Donte—blasted him out the window."

Danik turned his attention toward the arena floor. *I can't let them get that book. And I can't let them come out in public. They could tear down everything we've built.*

"What's in the red book?" Cedric sniffed then wiped at his nose. "Why do they want it so much?"

Danik set his jaw and inhaled. "We got where we are through a delicate peace between us and the Marked Ones. We needed them to take out the Shadow Knights, but that book threatens to tear it down."

"Destroy it then. Why do you hold onto it?"

"I may." Danik's lips formed a thin line while he stared at the stones on the floor. A trumpet blast raised his head.

Bilton gestured an arm forward to the front of the box. "Your Majesty, we're ready. Would you like to say a few words?"

Danik nodded then leaned toward Cedric. "They know the library is no longer helpful, but they won't give up. Double the guard in the castle. Bolt shut any unguarded windows, even if there's no way to access them."

Cedric dipped his head. "It will be done."

Danik stood. "And quit the spice. It's a disgusting habit. You need to remain focused."

Cedric jerked his head backward with his brows knit together. His jaw drooped, but he didn't reply.

Danik turned from the man to take in the scene. He approached the stone railing, where he rested his hands. Seats descended in rows, angling from where he stood down to the arena floor where grass and dirt spread flat in an open area made for combat. Four stone plinths stood freestanding, as tall as a man and evenly spaced in the arena. Spectators began to notice him. They hushed and prodded others until the entire gathering faced him, silently waiting on his word. At the railing, the mouthpiece to a curved brass horn opened before him.

"Citizens of Felting," he shouted into the horn, his booming voice tumbling through the instrument's curves and projecting into the arena. His greeting echoed off the far seats, and he raised his hands. "Welcome to the Feldan Arena!"

Cheers and clapping filled the air.

"To celebrate"—He paused to chuckle—"myself . . . along with our new Knights of Power, today we kick off one week of combat spectacles. This magnificent arena has laid dormant for nearly one hundred years. Kings Wesley and Darcius banned its use, but we hide from it no more! Today we gather to cheer on raw courage and skill."

He gestured with an arm toward a tunnel at the side of the arena. Hoots and claps filled the air as four men stepped into the sun.

The oldest was a pale man with thinning gray hair who looked to be around fifty. He carried a sword, held alert and ready. Two men with rich brown skin appeared to be in their late thirties. One sported a thick, black beard and carried a battle-axe, while the other—the largest of the four men—was clean shaven. His bulging neck and shoulders swiveled as he took in the crowd. He gripped a long spear tightly with both hands. The youngest of the men looked to be around twenty-five. Thin with tanned-skin, he held a sword awkwardly, as if he had no knowledge of how to use it.

"These men are criminals!" Danik shouted. "Held in the dungeon for theft and murder. They flaunted the rules of our city. They took advantage of good, honest people like you."

A rumble rolled through the crowd, and the men spun.

"But today, to kick off our string of events, we give them a sporting chance to earn their freedom. They will fight to the death, and whoever remains alive goes free."

The men snapped their attention from the crowd to each other. The weapons turned inward as the criminals stared each other down.

"They will not, however, fight themselves."

A metallic clank filled the air. A large, grated door against the far wall slowly rose. The criminals pointed their weapons toward the opening where a deep blackness yawned beyond the grate. When the spikes at the bottom raised high enough, Nicolar passed underneath, stepping into the arena. His shaggy black hair fell on either side of his face, and the corner of his goatee pulled up with his smirk. He wore a red vest with his rippling arms waving at his sides.

"Allow me to introduce you to Nicolar Gudrun, one of the founding members of the Knights of Power."

Nicolar raised his chin and spun, allowing the spectators to see him. He pulled a sword from a sheath, and a hush fell over the crowd.

"Nicolar represents a new era of defenders. He and the other knights of power will dedicate their lives to protecting our great kingdom. Today, he volunteered to join the entertainment for you." Danik looked over the five men on the arena floor. Nicolar nodded. "Last man alive wins!"

The four criminals instantly turned toward the new threat. They spread out, forming a semicircle. Mutters between the men drifted up to the box as they gestured in an attempt to work together.

Nicolar held his weapon loosely. It drooped toward the ground, while his face held a crooked smile.

Danik returned to his seat. Lisette's pinched expression caught his eye. "Does something trouble you?" he asked.

"A week of spectacles . . . why?" she asked.

He turned his eyes to the crowd. Around the stands, men and

women leaned forward, their eyes alight with excitement. "This is why. People love to be entertained."

"With killing?"

Danik shrugged. "What's more entertaining than watching a fight to the death? Men facing off under high stakes—kill or be killed. Anyone could be the winner. Nothing is more exciting."

A crescendo of noise drew all eyes to the arena floor. The bearded man with the battle-axe attacked first. His weapon rounded in an arc, but Nicolar stepped to the side, allowing the blade to bury into the ground. The knight waited while the dark-skinned man wrestled the axe out of the soft dirt.

The youngest criminal lunged with his sword. The attempt was weak and slow. Nicolar parried the blade away and kicked the young man, sending him falling backward. When he hit the ground, his grip gave out, and his sword bounced into the air. The hilt hit his own forehead. A peel of laughter spread through the stands, and a line of blood ran down his face. The young man scooted backward, grabbing his weapon from the ground and rising again to his feet.

The man with the axe was ready again. He used the end of the shaft to test Nicolar's reflexes then jabbed with the toe point at his stomach. The knight made a show of tucking in his stomach to barely dodge the weapon. Despite the close call, Danik caught the man's casual look.

He's barely even trying.

Lisette leaned closer. "Nicolar is one of your men . . . right? Why would you put him in danger?"

A wicked smile ran across Danik's face. "Oh, he's not in danger. Trust me."

"But he can die, right? Aren't they trying to kill him?"

"They're trying, but they will not succeed."

As if on cue, Nicolar's sword buried into the dark skin of the man's chest. The crowd cheered as the axe dropped to the ground, and the criminal fell backward. Blood ran from the wound while his body twitched in its death throes.

"Is entertainment supposed to distract the people from the ruin the city is falling into?" Lisette asked.

Danik's smile faded. Her words were curious rather than accusatory, but he still grew defensive. "They're also given bread when they come," he added.

On the arena floor, Nicolar danced between the two criminals with swords, taunting them. They both swung at his body, but he deftly ducked and rolled to safety. The crowd roared at the spectacle. He continued dodging and moving, just out of reach of the deadly blades, but he didn't appear tired.

The men with swords struggled. Their weapons drooped, and their swings slowed, but they kept their eyes on Nicolar while the man with the spear lagged behind them.

After ducking backward while a sword sliced a hair's width from his body, Nicolar brought his own blade down on the man's arm. The strike was as fast as a viper. The young man howled in pain. His sword tumbled toward the ground, but Nicolar followed up with a stab in the neck before the weapon had even hit the ground.

Another cheer filled the arena. Nicolar waved to the crowd then spun with a flourish to face the gray-haired man holding the sword.

The criminal stood in a crouch. He held his weapon with a comfortable ease that indicated years of experience. He stepped to his right, passing in front of one of the stone columns and beginning a circle without averting his eyes from Nicolar.

"This could be fun," Danik said to no one in particular. "He looks skilled."

Nicolar mimicked the man's crouch. He let the tip of his sword droop and sweep across the blades of grass. A chant of Nicolar's name swelled through the crowd.

The older man's body jerked. He clutched his side and issued a strangled yell.

Danik leaned forward. "What happened?"

The criminal with the bulging neck straightened as the older man fell. He pulled the shaft of his spear back. The tip shone red, and the crowd booed as the older fighter fell limp to the ground.

"Fool," Bilton muttered. "They should have worked together."

"I respect it," Danik said, nodding. "It may have been the wrong move, but he had to kill the man sometime."

Nicolar returned to his full height, and the final two men stared each other down. The prisoner towered a full head above the knight. He gripped the spear with both hands, holding it in a forward grip. Bellowing a sudden roar, he sprinted.

The crowd gasped. The spear jabbed forward in an attempt to skewer Nicolar, but he deflected it with his sword in the blink of an eye and spun as the man stumbled past him. The prisoner growled and used the butt of the spear to feint a side blow. Nicolar did not take the bait but remained cool with his sword held forward.

"It's like he knows what's about to happen before it does," Lisette said.

The corner of Danik's mouth turned up.

The massive fighter's movements grew frantic. He jabbed, struck, lunged, and whipped his spear through the air, but every attempt either found the whistle of air or a quick deflection. His chest heaved and his motions slowed. He took a step back and sucked in a deep breath.

Nicolar lifted his hand and opened his grip. The sword rolled from his hand, twisting as it dropped to the ground. A rumble grew in the stands. The challenger's chin lifted. Infused with new life, he yelled and sprang forward, jabbing the spear toward Nicolar's unguarded chest.

The knight of power didn't dodge or flinch. His sword remained on the ground as the weapon lunged for him.

Danik breathed in sharply, out of instinct rather than fear.

At the last moment, Nicolar's hand flew to intercept. His fist wrapped around the shaft below the tip, and the spear stopped just before it reached his body. The fighter and his lunging limbs came to an abrupt halt, as if he had hit a stone wall.

The thick-necked man cried out in shock, and the spectators gasped. In a deft movement, Nicolar held the spear head and chopped the shaft with his free hand. A loud crack filled the air. The criminal staggered, holding a wooden pole with a splintered end, but before he could move, the severed spear tip buried itself into the man's neck, driven by Nicolar's extended arm.

The man's mouth hung open. He fell to his knees then teetered onto his side.

The crowd erupted with applause.

Danik stood and clapped in a slow rhythm.

"That was marvelous," Bilton said, stepping closer to the king. "Is that your plan for this week?"

"Do you think it will be effective?"

Bilton looked out to the arena. The crowd roared. Nicolar held his hand up, waving in each direction as he stepped between the fallen bodies of the defeated criminals.

"They seem to love it," Bilton said. "A few more exhibits like this and no one will mess with the Knights of Power, that's for sure."

A grin grew on Danik's face. "That's the idea."

11

CAVERNOUS PRISON

The shivering didn't seem to help. Chelci's thin clothing did little to hold in what heat her body produced. Her fingers had lost sensation hours before. Her legs felt like stiff trunks, plodding up the snow-covered slope in the line of bowed-over knights.

They'd marched for days. Meager food and water kept them alive, but the higher they rose in the Straith Mountains, the more toil the elements took on them. The falling snow had stopped, but the air remained frigid.

The marked ones still looked fresh. The cold didn't seem to bother them. The pace they set was difficult to keep up with, but when the knights stumbled or slowed, they got a kick and a yell to motivate them forward.

"Do you have any warmer clothing you could lend us," Bridgette asked. Her lips held a blue shade as her teeth chattered.

Gralow, the closest guard to her, huffed but didn't reply or even turn his head.

"I guess that's a no," Ruby whispered.

"What about these chains?" Gavin asked, holding his bound wrists up. "You know we won't escape because none of us want to have you kill anyone left behind." He paused, but no one replied. "If the metal were removed, we could use the origine to warm ourselves. Plus, we could keep up better."

Talioth paused at the front of the line, causing the marked ones and knights to all come to a stop. "The chains stay on." He stared at the captives. "We're nearly there."

A wisp of wind picked up snow from the ground and whipped it across Chelci's face. She closed her eyes and turned out of the wind. The icy blast stung her exposed neck.

With a grunt from Gralow, the line of people resumed the ascent.

"Nice try, Gavin," Chelci whispered.

He looked at her with a frown. "We need to get out of these things."

"I agree, but I'm not sure what else to try."

"Where do you think they're taking us?"

Chelci looked ahead. Jagged peaks towered on either side of the white trail, and a gap marked what looked like the end of the rise with a curved arch spanning between the peaks. "Where they're from, I guess."

"You think they live up in these mountains? In these temperatures?"

"Could be. They don't seem bothered by the cold. That could explain why we've never heard of them until recently."

Chelci looked over her shoulder to ensure Dayna was still with them. The knight with the missing ear dragged a few steps behind. A rust color stained the bandage, where it pressed against the side of her head.

"How's it feeling?" she asked.

Dayna looked up, her face sagging. "It hasn't hurt at all today."

"That's good."

"Maybe, but I can't feel any of my face, so I'm not sure it's necessarily positive."

"Quiet!" Gralow shouted, appearing in front of her face.

The surge of adrenaline generated a flutter of warmth. Turning back around, Chelci closed her mouth and continued up the hill, her boots sinking into the powder.

At the front of the line, while approaching the arch, one of the marked ones emitted a barking, shrill cry.

Chelci's brows pinched. *That's odd.* She scanned the path, looking for any sign of other people. She squinted against the sunny reflection off the snow. Against the dark rocks of the cliff, a shadowy area waited ahead. *I wonder if that could—*

A red glow shone from the dark area, then a man stepped out from the rocks. Covered in gray furs, he carried a tall spear and wore a glowing crystal around his neck. On the opposite side of the trail, a woman in matching garb with a spear of her own stepped into view. Talioth and the fur-covered lookouts exchanged muddled words while the group waited.

Nearly at the top, the wind had picked up. Chelci stamped her feet, trying to hold on to any feeling. She strained to catch any clues about the mysterious group, but she was unable to make out anything. Finally, the lookouts tromped back toward their hideouts, and the marked ones they'd traveled with continued forward.

The uphill climb leveled directly under the stone arch, and they finally arrived at the saddle between the peaks. Chelci trudged the last few steps, and her jaw dropped at the sight over the edge.

The ridge formed a ring, connecting towering spires and sheer cliffs in an enormous circle. The gap they stood in seemed to be the only way through the circular wall. In the center of the ring, a valley sunk into the mountain range, hidden from the outside world by the rest of the peaks. A trail dropped steadily on the other side of the saddle. The snow that had been deep and plentiful on the march up began to melt only a few paces down the backside of the ridge. A verdant sight of trees and bushes took the place of the stark white scene. Plumes of steam rolled out of piles of rocks in several places throughout the valley. A lake shimmered with a fog rising from the surface. A flock of birds flew over the water and landed in the branches of a large tree on the shore.

"What is this place?" Gavin asked.

"It looks warm," Bridgette said. "That's all I care about."

A dark area caught Chelci's eye on the far side of the valley. A cave tunneled into the rock wall with a red glow emanating from its depths. "That's where we're heading," she said, pointing across the valley.

Gavin squinted his eyes. "That cave?"

"I'll bet that's where they live."

Dayna stepped next to her. "And it's glowing with those red crystals. Perfect."

Chelci gritted her teeth. She pulled on her arms, feeling the tension in the chains.

Talioth was the first to move, descending the path into the valley. The marked ones and captives followed. Their boots slid down the snowy path until the powder turned to slush. In a short distance, bare rock and mud revealed itself. The temperature warmed quickly, and soon their feet left the snow completely. A sulfurous odor filled the air, turning Chelci's nose as she passed a steam vent billowing from a pile of rocks. Her fingers tingled, and a pinkish hue returned.

The air cooled again when they passed through a grove of trees, barely taller than two men stacked together. Green tarrols budded at the end of serpentine limbs, a curious sight with the snowy rim above them in the background. Chelci scanned her surroundings, but no opportunity to escape presented itself.

After a twenty-minute walk across the valley, the glowing mouth of the cave yawned before them. The marked ones adopted smiles while they approached. A handful of men and women, clad in gray and sporting matching black stains on their necks, greeted them at the entrance. Some hugged, some clapped each other on the back, and they all cast a leery eye at the shadow knights.

"Well done," an old woman said, approaching Talioth. Long, gray hair fell past her shoulders. Her wrinkled skin suggested an advanced age, but her eyes looked young and her step was light.

Talioth grinned. "We did it, Meliand."

"You're missing three." The old woman's head scanned the crowd. "What happened?"

Talioth nodded. "We lost Albator, Raccult, and—" He paused, shifting his stance. "And Valdok."

The woman's eyebrows rose. "Valdok? What happened?"

"They had an alloshifter."

Meliand sucked in a breath. "Incredible." With a jerk of her head, she scanned the group of captives.

"Don't worry. He's not here," Talioth added.

"You killed him?"

Talioth paused, his eyes flicking toward the cliff walls. "Nearly, but ... no. We left him."

The woman nodded. "Probably for the best." She turned toward the group. "Is this the rest?"

He shook his head. "We left three in total."

While scanning the group, her eyes locked with Chelci's. Chelci straightened her back and stood as tall as her height allowed. Her chest puffed out, and she lifted her chin.

"Very well," Meliand said. "These seven will sustain us for years. And the reduction of the power drain should amplify everything."

Chelci caught eyes with Gavin. His forehead wrinkled. Her thoughts mirrored his expression. *How are we meant to sustain them?* she wondered.

"Is the new cell finished?" Talioth asked.

Meliand nodded. "Completed this morning."

Talioth turned to Gralow. "Take them to the hold."

CHELCI SQUINTED as she followed the line of heads. The red glow from the sporadic crystals set into the walls gave the passages a faint, eerie light. The cave system seemed to stretch in all directions. Some of the dark corridors splitting off appeared to be natural extensions of the cave, but others looked carved from the rock. The group kept to the main passage.

Her toe stubbed an unseen rock. Chelci groaned, the chains connecting her wrist manacles jingling. She stopped to grab her foot.

"Keep up!" an unseen man grumbled.

Something poked her in the back, and Chelci continued.

The passage steadily lightened. Rounding a corner, a gaping room opened before them. Stone columns ringing the room stretched to the ceiling, smooth and regal. A wide shaft of light poured in from a hole in the ceiling. Other marked ones filled the room, gathered in groups. All talking stopped when they entered. Some of the crew who had traveled with them spread through the room, greeting the others.

Against the wall, a statue of a man looked to burst from the rock. Obscured by wooden scaffolding, the gigantic form peered down, full of judgment and pride. *Is that . . . Talioth?* The carving held a close resemblance to the gray-haired man who appeared to be their leader. But the stain on the stone neck was conspicuously missing.

Chained workers in sweaty, torn clothing stopped chiseling at the sight of the new arrivals. A prisoner with a long beard and ragged hair stared at her. The deep lifeless void in his eyes held a mixture of loathing and hopelessness.

"Gralow!" shouted a man carrying a whip and watching the workers. A grin grew on his face.

The marked one who led the line of knights stopped to exchange an embrace and a few hushed words.

Chelci turned back to the man with the hopeless eyes, but he had already returned his chisel to the stone. His rhythmic strikes against it held an ominous cadence, each hit causing her eye to twitch.

Metal rattled. Gavin lurched forward as Gralow pulled on the chain to his restraints. "Move!" the man ordered.

The knights trudged forward. Chelci's neck grew hot. She stared straight ahead but felt dozens of sets of eyes boring into her. When they entered a narrow passage, the sunlight faded into the familiar, ominous red glow. The path descended, winding and dropping in a serpentine motion. Narrow passages caused her to shuffle sideways, and then an open space gave them enough room to walk two astride.

A cell door emerged from the gloom. A set of hands wrapped around the bars, and a faint red glow backlit the silhouette of a head.

"Keep moving," Gralow ordered. He blocked their path to the cell and pointed for them to continue forward.

After another few turns, the cavern expanded, and a gaping pit stopped them short. Chelci gasped. The rocky path ended abruptly, and a void blocked their way. Across a short chasm, an island with a barren, flat top rose from the pit. In the depths surrounding the stone platform, a red glow pulsed, lighting the room and leaving a faint hum in the air. The only object in the cavern was a wooden plank. Barely a foot wide, it spanned the gap from where they stood to the open-air cell.

Gralow smacked his foot against the wooden plank. "One at a time."

Chelci's eyes widened. The board barely looked strong enough to hold them, not to mention the precipitous drop if she lost her balance. "I'll go first," she said, her stomach turning.

She approached the edge, and Gralow held up a hand, forcing her to pause. Another marked one, a shorter man with a trimmed, black beard, held a mallet and a metal object. A few swift pounds from the tool resulted in jingling chains falling to the stone.

"Give me your arms," the shorter man said.

She held them out. After more pounding, the manacles fell free. She rubbed her aching wrists, celebrating the newfound freedom.

Free from the shackles, she instinctively reached for the origine. Her mind plotted the best leverage to surprise the three guards and knock them into the pit. She lunged, slow, as if her body remained asleep. The black-bearded man stood casually. She struck out, attempting to hit him in the back and fling him toward the pit. The sluggish attempt halted when Gralow's rock-hard arm blocked her path. The blow felt like she pounded against stone.

Chelci cried out. She didn't have her speed or her power. The glow in the pit intensified.

"Fool! Your powers are useless here!" Gralow shoved her back to the plank. "Walk!"

She looked across the pit. Her arm throbbed from where she had struck him. A body stood close, the warm breath causing her to cringe. "All right! I'm going!"

She took a step. The bounce in the board unnerved her. She held out both arms for balance then took another step, watching her feet. Suspended above the chasm, the glowing nothingness below gave a floating sensation. Tendrils of mist swirled below, painting a cloud of red. She kept her steps smooth and moved steadily. Her next breath only came when she stepped on the solid stone island.

The open-air cell was square shaped, roughly the length of two people end to end. The backside dropped off in the same way the front had. Chelci squinted as she peered down but couldn't see a thing.

Two feet landed behind her. Gavin had arrived.

"Nice place you have here," he said with a half grin.

The other shadow knights crossed the plank one at a time, and soon, all seven gathered, trapped by the pit.

The bearded man pulled a rope attached to the wall, and the wooden plank lifted. Chelci grabbed for it but let go as it passed her head. Fully raised, the plank rested nearly vertical, attached to the other side. The guard tied the rope off, leaving their only hope of escape dangling well out of reach.

"What are you going to do with us?" Gavin asked, his question echoing through the cavern. "What did that woman mean that we would sustain you?"

Gralow grinned. His shoulders bounced as his throaty chuckle ricocheted off the walls. The other two guards moved first, disappearing back through the passage. The large guard's gaze lingered. Finally, he turned and left, leaving the knights alone.

12

DANGEROUS MEETING

"I don't like it." Raiyn lowered a branch that blocked their view.

Lia sighed. "I don't either, but what choice do we have?" Her skin tingled with anticipation, heightened by her simmering use of the origine.

Wind whispered through the forest, rustling the leaves above. Tendrils of cold seeped through Lia's cloak, but she ignored the discomfort. Her knees rested on the soft ground, and her body remained still.

"No choice," Veron said over her shoulder, his quiet voice unwavering. "We need that book. It's our only hope to find the knights."

"And Mother," Lia breathed.

Past the leaves, the eastern bridge of Felting arced over the Felavorre River. Water gurgled below, and a full moon shone above, radiating a glow across the span.

"I think they're late," Raiyn said.

Veron glanced at the moon and squinted. Lia imagined the wheels turning in his head as he estimated the distance. "Not by much," her father said.

"What if he didn't get the message—or ignores it?"

"He'll get it," Lia said. "And he'll come."

"What if he tries to kill us?" Raiyn asked.

Veron brushed another branch aside. "He will."

"Wait. What?"

"I agree," Lia said. "He needs us dead. We are the only ones who can stop him and his gang. We need to keep alert."

Veron shook his head. "Knights of Power." He scoffed. "Ridiculous."

Motion drew their attention to the bridge. Lia traced an owl with her eyes as it swooped low and snatched a rat from the path.

"Father," Lia began. "When they arrive, Raiyn and I should meet them alone."

The muscles in his neck tensed. "I'm not going to let you—"

"You can't use the origine," she interrupted. "They'll kill you before you lift a sword."

"*They* don't know that." Veron's reply sat heavily in the air.

"What do you mean?"

"Danik and his men don't know my power is gone. With three of us standing together, they'll be less likely to try anything."

Lia pursed her lips. She turned to Raiyn, who shrugged.

"I'm not asking for your permission, Lia," Veron said. "I know I can't fight them without my power. If it comes to it, I'll run."

"Fine." She pointed at her father. "Stay behind me though."

"Fine." He mimicked her same tone. The corner of his mouth curled up.

"What should I do?" Raiyn asked.

Lia turned to him. "Stand beside Veron and let me handle the talking."

"I could tell him I'm a fully-trained shadow knight, now."

"No. Don't say anything. I know Danik best. We need to focus on getting the book, and that's it. Above all . . . we can't engage them in a fight."

"Agreed," Veron added. "The devion is powerful. Their strength is significant, and they don't tire as quickly. With even numbers, we'd be at a disadvantage, but I'm guessing we'll be outnumbered."

"The note said to only bring three people, right?" Raiyn asked.

"They'll have more than three," Veron said as if relating a fact. "Like Lia said, we need to keep alert."

Lia looked at Raiyn. "If we *do* have to fight. Stay next to me. We'll hold them off together while we give Father a chance to run."

"No problem," Raiyn confirmed.

Lia turned to Veron. "Are you on board with that?"

After a pause, he eventually nodded.

Lia returned her focus to the bridge. She clenched then relaxed her hands, extending her fingers in a stretch. A swell of wind blew a handful of leaves over the bridge until they disappeared into the river. She took smooth, deep breaths, focusing on her pulse, trying to keep it down.

They'll arrive, and we'll talk. He'll listen to reason. It will be all right.

She wanted it to be simple, but a stitch in her side reminded her she didn't believe it would be.

"Did you hear that?" Raiyn whispered.

Lia held her breath and strained to hear. Despite her efforts to calm, her pulse thudded in her head. Her hands felt clammy. The clopping of hooves drifted through the night. She tensed, straining her eyes to pierce the gloom.

On the far side of the bridge, horses materialized. Danik sat tall on the one in front, wearing a crimson cloak that fell across the horse's flanks. He stopped at the far side of the bridge and dismounted.

"Should we go?" Raiyn whispered.

Lia set her hand on his arm. "Not yet."

"I only see three."

Lia nodded. Her eyes dug into the woods on either side of the bridge, but she noticed no other movement.

Danik arrived at the center of the bridge. Nicolar stood at his side, and Jade paced the span just behind them. Swords hung from each of their hips except Jade, who twirled daggers in each hand.

A rumble filled the air as Danik cleared his throat. "Come on out!" His head turned on a slow swivel.

Lia was the first to move. She stepped beyond the branch into the road, and the light of the moon hit her full in the face. Farrathan remained strapped on her back, and the flowing black cloak of the Shadow Knights waved behind as she walked. Veron and Raiyn followed.

Danik took in a deep breath and kept his hand at his hilt. His shoulders relaxed when Lia's feet hit the bridge. "So . . . it's true."

Lia stopped well out of reach.

"I was relieved when they told me you were alive."

Lia scoffed. "I'm sure."

Danik's brows pulled together. "I never wanted to hurt you, Lia." He gestured with outstretched hands. "I wanted us to do this together, but you refused."

"And then you tried to kill me."

He shrugged. "What was I supposed to do?"

"Maybe . . . give up? Stop stealing from people."

"The baltham? I only took back what was yours."

"It was Ben's."

Danik's eyes lit up. "Ahh. That's what you did with the rest of the money, isn't it?"

Lia's breath stopped. Her stomach churned.

A grin formed on Nicolar's face. "It should be no problem to get that back." The thief chuckled. "Not that we need it."

"It's not too late, Lia," Danik said. "Join us."

Lia clenched her fists.

"Think about living in a castle. Imagine all the riches you could have and people waiting on your every desire." He took a step closer. "I know you, Lia. I know how you love the thrill of the gambling hall and the hazy feeling of getting lost in a mug of ale." He held a fist in front of him. "Think of the power. The pure, raw energy of the devion. It's not something to fear. It's something to embrace! Join us!"

Lia's lips formed a tight line. She slowly shook her head. "I'll never join with you." Bitterness and contempt filled her words.

Danik's face turned dark.

Veron's deep voice cut through the night. "Where's the book, Danik?"

"Ah! The book. The one with the red leather cover. *History of the Origine: Rise of the Devion.*"

"Give it to us."

Danik's hearty laugh cut through the night. Nicolar and Jade joined in, and the combined sound covered the gurgle of the river. "Why do you want it?"

"We need to find the Marked Ones."

Danik nodded. "You need the map."

Lia took a step in. "They have the rest of the knights. Gavin, Bridgette . . . my mother."

Danik's eyes dropped to the bridge. He shifted his weight. "I'm sorry about your mother."

"Danik. Please." She tried to plead with her eyes, but he wouldn't look at her.

"What are you offering for it?" Danik finally raised his head.

"Offering?" Veron asked. "These are your fellow knights. You lived and trained with them for years. They're going to die! My wife—" He stopped mid-sentence. "You brought the Marked Ones here, so their blood will be on your head. Give us the book and let us have a chance to rescue them."

Danik paused. Every moment he waited made Lia's heart raced. "No," he said, finally.

Her stomach dropped. The breath in her lungs felt caught.

"The time of the Shadow Knights is past. The Knights of Power are now in control, and we don't need you messing things up. The book stays with us."

"Why did you come here, then?" Lia asked.

Danik shrugged. "I wanted to hear you out. And I didn't want to give up hope that you'd change your mind. Plus . . ."

A tingle ran up Lia's neck at the pause.

"We need to get you off the streets where you can cause trouble."

In a flash, Lia pulled her sword from over her shoulder. Metal rang from Veron and Raiyn behind her. The origine rushed through her body, tingling and warm, ready to be used. She dropped into a crouch, her weapon poised and ready to strike.

Danik and the knights of power followed suit. Light from the moon flashed off his exposed blade. He held up a hand. "Whoa! Hold on. Don't act rashly and end up dead. There are civil ways we can do this."

Lia's eyes flashed to the woods. She backed away from Danik while scanning both banks of the river.

"I still don't see anything," Veron said.

Raiyn's voice shook. "Me neither."

Three sets of metal restraints clattered on the bridge. "Put those on," Danik said.

"Never!" Lia shouted.

"Put them on, or we'll have to use force."

"Then we use force!" Veron shouted.

"Father," Lia whispered over her shoulder. "Let me handle this."

The two parties stared at each other, frozen in battle positions, ready to engage at a moment's notice. Sweat made Lia's grip on her sword slick. The smell of dirt and trees wafted on the air.

"Why did you send them for the book?" Danik asked.

Lia glanced at her father, whose eyebrow quirked.

"You were the one who found it, right?" Danik asked. "Why wouldn't you have been there to retrieve it?"

Lia gripped her weapon tighter.

"Our business is our own," Veron replied.

Danik's eyes narrowed. "But this book is what you need to save your wife? As the one who knew where it was, why would you not have come, yourself?"

"Let's go," Veron whispered.

Lia half turned. "But we need the book."

"He's not going to hand it over. We'll have to find another way to get it."

Feet shuffled behind her. Keeping her sword up, she backed away with her father and Raiyn.

"Where do you think you're going?" Danik moved forward, along with Nicolar and Jade.

Lia turned, her legs moving rapidly off the bridge. She eyed the tree line where they came from, longing to get lost in its depths. Veron jogged toward the darkness. "Run, Father," she whispered.

Veron skidded to a stop. Lia gasped as she saw the subject of his hesitation. Cedric emerged from the woods with Broderick, and Alton. The three new knights of power spread out, blocking any hope of an easy escape.

"Danik, you don't want to do this," Veron said.

Lia and Raiyn stood back-to-back.

"Why not?" Danik said. He sauntered across the bridge. "There are six of us and only three of you. Do you really want to try your steel against ours? Do you remember how it went in the Advisors Council chamber?"

Even in the faint light, Veron's face looked pale. The three from the bridge completed the circle around the shadow knights. There was nowhere to go.

"Are you sure you don't want to take the easy route with these?" Danik asked, pointing to the restraints Nicolar had picked up. "We *will* kill you if we have to."

"He's going to kill us anyway," Lia whispered. "We *cannot* turn ourselves in."

"Take me," Veron said, lowering his sword. "If you allow them to leave, I'll go willingly with you."

"Father, no!"

"Ha!" Danik laughed. "The one who can wield origine through metal volunteers to be shackled. Do you take me for a fool?"

"It's not like that," Veron said. "I'll go with you and won't fight. I promise—"

"I want *all* of you!" Danik yelled. "Alive or dead."

"Raiyn, we need to act," Lia whispered. "Move together. Force a hole on Veron's side so he can run."

"Lia, it's pointless," Veron said. "You can't—"

"We have to try."

"I'm following you, Lia," Raiyn said.

Danik dragged his sword against the dirt. "No? You want to make a futile stand then?"

Jade rubbed her daggers together, creating a hiss of steel.

Lia's heart pounded. Jade's steely gaze bored into her. Raiyn's heavy breathing raised an alarm. *I hope he has enough energy to fight.* Power waited inside her, begging to be used. "Now," she breathed, barely loud enough to penetrate the darkness.

Raiyn and Lia moved in unison. Using the speed of the origine, they raced around Veron to engage with Cedric and Alton on his side of the circle. The sudden rush of movement caught the men by surprise. Lia got a blade on Cedric's arm before his instincts kicked in and he spun away.

"Argh!" the man shouted, stumbling backward.

Raiyn heaved his battle-axe toward Alton, narrowly missing the man. His flurry of swings that followed created a wind that blew Lia's hair back. She raised her sword to Broderick, who stepped forward to take Cedric's place.

"Father, run!" she shouted.

Veron didn't hesitate. He sprinted between Lia and Raiyn, heading toward the inky woods.

"Stop him!" Danik shouted.

Jade crouched then exploded in a leap over the circle.

Lia jumped in response. As Jade was about to clear the others, Lia grabbed her leg in midair. Strengthening her muscles with her inner power, she flung the dagger-wielding woman back toward the rest in the circle. With a crash, her body collided with the ground then tumbled down the bank into the river.

Lia smiled at her father as he disappeared into the edge of the forest.

"Go after him!" Danik yelled.

Broderick lunged forward, but Lia spun Farrathan to deflect his crashing sword. The world blurred as the two exchanged blows. He landed a punch to her gut, knocking the air out of her lungs. She leaned over, sucking in air, but the attacker was back. She pulled more origine, whirling out of the way of an overhead attack. As quick as a viper's strike, she jabbed her blade. It found flesh in his side. He yelled and dropped his weapon.

While Broderick stumbled, Nicolar tried to run past Lia, but her extended sword stopped him from pursuing Veron. Raiyn backed up, forming a wall next to her, blocking Veron's escape from the others.

"Stay by me," Lia said.

Cedric and Broderick nursed their wounds, allowing the devion to do its healing work. Jade floundered in the shallows as she tried to escape the river. Nicolar and Alton stood before them until Danik pushed past them.

"You can't defeat us, Lia," Danik said.

She raised her sword higher, her chest heaving as she tried to recover her spent energy.

Danik turned to Raiyn and gestured. "And you! Look at you! Running and fighting. Well done. I'd almost think you were a shadow knight."

Raiyn's jaw formed a sharp line. He didn't reply.

"How long are you going to follow Veron until you try to kill him . . . like your *father* attempted?"

Raiyn shuffled his feet.

"You can't escape blood," Danik taunted. "It's who you are."

"Don't let him get to you, Raiyn," Lia said. "Stay with me."

Nicolar lunged at her with a sudden thrust. Time slowed as she met his speed, barely deflecting his sword away from her stomach. A swift origine-fueled kick to his chest sent him sprawling backward.

"Does Lia know about your feelings for her?" Danik asked.

Lia's eyes flicked to Raiyn, whose eyes had grown wide.

"Come now, it's obvious. You've followed her around like a puppy since you arrived. Would you like to know what she thinks about you, Raiyn?"

"What are you doing, Danik?" Lia asked.

"She told me how much she despises you."

"He's lying."

Danik laughed. "She said you had no talent and that training you was a bore. After you were kicked out, she told me how relieved she was."

"You can say whatever you want, Danik," Raiyn replied. "You can't get to me." His words seemed confident and strong, but his arms trembled.

"But don't let me discourage you from trying with her though. If you have hopes of bedding her, don't give up. I've slept with her over a dozen times." He leaned forward with a wicked grin. "Trust me . . . she's easy."

Raiyn ran at Danik, yelling and lifting his axe.

"Raiyn, no!" Lia shouted, but her words were lost in the tumult.

Danik backed up, drawing Raiyn forward until Nicolar and Alton penned him from behind.

Lia started to run after him until Cedric arrived, blocking her path. His arm had healed, and he looked eager for revenge. Lia ran to either side, but his incredible speed kept her back.

Steel clashed as Raiyn and Danik exchanged blows. Through the bodies, she caught a smirk on Danik's face while he defended against the greener and less-experienced knight.

"Is that all you have?" Danik asked.

Another roar from Raiyn led to a flurry of crashes, but he made no progress.

Danik jumped out of reach and held up a hand. "Raiyn, I have something for you."

Raiyn gulped deep breaths as he walked, his axe up and ready. "What?"

Nicolar and Alton grabbed him from behind, pinning his arms against his side. His axe dropped to the ground, and a set of metal restraints clinked around his wrists.

"That," Danik said.

Lia yelled, "No!"

"Take him to the castle," Danik ordered. "We might need him."

The men pulled Raiyn forward, his feet dragging on the ground.

"Lia, I'm sorry!" he called over his shoulder. "Get out of here!"

Jade had finally made it back to dry ground. She approached with Danik, twirling swords and daggers. Cedric and Broderick blocked Lia's path on the other side.

I can't get to him. The thought left a sinking feeling in her gut.

Imagining her father fleeing through the woods behind her brought clarity to what she needed to do.

"Raiyn! Don't worry. We'll rescue you!" she called.

She raised her sword and paused, glancing between each of the knights of power. Finally, her eyes rested on Danik. His impassive face and steady breath turned her stomach.

We'll meet again soon.

Pulling all the origine she could summon, she turned and ran.

13

PRISON CHAINS

The air grew musty as they descended the stairs. Raiyn wrinkled his nose. A sheen of mildew coated the stones, damp from water seeping through the ground.

"Keep moving," Alton said, pushing him from behind.

Raiyn's foot slipped. His bound hands shot up to touch the wall. A boot found purchase on the next step, and he avoided tumbling.

A hand grabbed his tunic against his back and bunched it up. The pressure moved him forward.

The stairs ended in a seedy, gray dungeon. A lone torch flickered on the wall. Black pitch dripped from the wooden handle, pooling on the stone below. A row of cells with heavy metal doors formed one side of the room.

Despair clutched at Raiyn. *Not another dungeon.*

Near the torch, a guard tipped a chair against a wall on its back two legs. He sat up at the sight of the new arrivals. The legs crashed on the floor, and he jumped to his feet. "Sir!" he fumbled. "I-I didn't expect visitors this late."

"You should always be ready and alert," Alton said, "no matter the time."

"Who is this?" The guard nodded toward Raiyn. "A new guest?"

Alton's grip tightened on the bunched fabric. "He needs the isolation cell."

The guard raised his eyebrows and looked Raiyn up and down. "He doesn't look that dangerous."

"Trust me."

"I won't cause any trouble," Raiyn lied.

The guard shrugged then pulled a key ring from his pocket. "Fine with me." He waved them forward. "This way."

The guard took the dripping torch off the wall and proceeded down a far hall. With nowhere else to go, Raiyn followed without being pushed. The stone walls pressed close as they left the room of cells behind. The route turned twice before a lone metal door waited at the end. Keys jangled as the guard sifted through his ring. With his key chosen, he set it in the lock and turned. A *clank* filled the hall, and the door swung open.

A rough shove threw him forward. He tried to use the origine to help keep his feet under him, but the well of energy remained inaccessible. He rolled as he fell, letting his shoulder take the brunt of the impact against the hard floor.

"Keep his chains on, always," Alton ordered.

The guard pulled on the door. The hinges creaked, loud and grating, until the crash of the metal silenced them.

Raiyn scrambled to his feet. He ran to the door and placed his face against the bars of the small window. The men turned the corner at the end of the hall, the light from the torch soon disappearing. His shoulders slumped, and he exhaled.

I shouldn't have let him taunt me. Lia will be furious. She'll wind up caught herself if she tries to break me out of here.

He pounded his fist against the door. The metal shook, but the impact sent a shiver of pain up his arm. He pulled his arms apart, straining against the chain links. He flexed his muscles and grasped fruitlessly for origine. His head shook, and his hands quivered. With a gasp, he dropped his arms.

I hope Lia and Veron escaped. A quivering sensation rushed through his gut. *I wonder what she thinks about what Danik said. Did she already know how I feel?*

He turned his back to the door to inspect the cramped cell. A high, barred window let in a faint bit of light from the moon. A wooden bed lay flush to the wall, but it contained no blankets or a pillow.

He sat on the cold, hard surface. He leaned his head against the wall and closed his eyes. *I hope they escaped.*

Footsteps in the hall jolted him awake. Raiyn's eyes shot open. He lay on the bench, his back twisted uncomfortably. A beam of light poured through the window and splashed across the floor. He blinked and sat up, his heart pounding with anticipation of whoever approached.

Rather than the door opening, a small hatch at the base lifted, and a bowl slid through, scraping along the stone floor. The hatch dropped behind the bowl with a slam.

"Hey! Wait!" Raiyn shouted, jumping up. He grabbed the bars in the door's window.

A new guard walked down the hallway, away from his cell.

"Don't go!" he shouted. "Do you know who I am?"

The guard hesitated then turned. Wisps of thin brown hair rested on his head, and a long beard fell the length of his neck. His eyes paused on Raiyn. "I don't care who you are."

He started to turn away until Raiyn stopped him by pounding against the bars. "I hear Danik is running the city into the ground. Did you know he's the one who killed King Darcius?"

The man's eyes narrowed.

"It's true! And he told you the Shadow Knights were all dead because he wanted everyone to trust him and his crew, but it's a lie. The Shadow Knights aren't dead. I'm one of them!"

The guard took slow steps in his direction. "You're a shadow knight?"

"Yes, well . . . I was training to be one. My name's Raiyn. I've been in hiding with Veron Stormbridge and his daughter."

The guard's eyes flared. "Stormbridge is alive?"

Raiyn's heart pounded. Hope surged in his chest. "He is. I was with him last night. We can stop Danik. I just need out. Can you help me?"

The guard stopped just out of reach. He cocked his head. "King Danik promised double my wages from last year. Why would I want to stop him?"

Raiyn's stomach dropped. "Please. Where do you think that money comes from? Think of everyone else."

The guard's shoulders loosened. He pursed his lips. "My mother had her taxes raised. She doesn't have any income and can barely afford the collector's demands."

"See! Think of your mother and everyone else's mothers. What's your name?"

The guard lifted his chin. "Brannon."

"Brannon, you want her to be all right, don't you?"

He nodded. "I do . . . and with my increased wage to help, she'll be fine."

Raiyn groaned, gripping the bars tighter. "Don't just think of you and your mother. Think of—" He stopped and shook his head, unsure of how to get through.

"I do miss King Darcius."

"Yes! I heard he was a great man. And Danik murdered him."

Brannon stood silently, staring at the wall.

"Help me out of here, Brannon. I'll make sure you're taken care of, and we'll stop Danik from destroying this kingdom."

The guard continued staring at the wall. Movement at his hip caught Danik's eye. He touched a ring of keys that dangled from his belt.

Raiyn held his breath, hoping the man would take the chance on him.

Brannon turned. His eyes dropped to the door where the lock would be. The keys jangled as he fingered them.

Come on. Do it!

The guard took a step closer. "What will you do?"

"If you let me out?"

Brannon nodded.

Raiyn's heart pounded. "I'll meet up with the other shadow knights, and we'll confront Danik. The high lords will be loyal to the kingdom again once he's gone. They'll select a new king, someone true to Feldor and what it stands for."

The nodding continued. "How do I know you're not lying? Prisoners say anything to get out."

"I promise I'm telling the truth."

"Prove it."

Raiyn's forehead wrinkled. "What?"

"You say Stormbridge is alive. Prove it."

Raiyn scoffed. "I'm in a dungeon. I can't just—"

"Tell me where he is. I'll find him and verify it."

Raiyn breathed deep and paused in thought. After a moment, he shook his head. "I can't take that chance."

"All right then. You say you're a shadow knight. Prove that."

Hope flared again, and Raiyn raised his bound hands. "I can! Take off my restraints."

"Pfff!" Brannon took his hand away from the keys and waved toward him. "I'm not falling for that."

"No! I'm serious. Without the metal restraints I can show you."

"Without the restraints, you can knock me over the head and run out of here. Then, instead of double wages, I get a knife in the neck." The guard stepped away, chuckling to himself. "Sorry, Raiyn. Nice try."

"Brannon, no! Wait!" He kicked the door and knocked over the forgotten bowl at his feet. A lukewarm, thin soup spilled across his boots and ran across the floor. He strained, clenching the bars and pulling with all his strength. "Gah!"

The guard disappeared around the corner, and Raiyn hung his head. Footsteps faded in the distance. The upturned bowl caught his eye, and his stomach rumbled. *He sounded willing to help. How can I prove Veron is still alive?*

Footsteps returned. Raiyn's nostrils cleared. He looked back through the window.

Brannon rounded the corner, his gait firm but head down as he walked.

Raiyn frowned. *What's wrong?* His answer came when Danik came into view behind him.

The king wore a thick robe of red velvet, and a sword hung on his hip. Between the bars, they locked eyes, even from down the long hallway.

Raiyn stepped away from the door. The lock turning filled him with dread. The creaking hinges did not signal the rescue he'd hoped for.

"Leave us," Danik ordered as he stepped into the room.

Brannon's footsteps retreated, and Raiyn's back pressed against the wall.

Taller by a hand, and older by a few years, Danik made an impressive-looking king. After shutting the door shut behind him, he turned to stare.

Raiyn fidgeted under the piercing gaze, his chains rattling. "Whatever happened to 'my secret being safe with you?' Back at the training center?"

Danik's stern face broke into a mirthless laugh. "It no longer suited my purpose."

"And what was your purpose? Eliminating competition for Lia?"

"You were never competition."

"Then why didn't you like me?"

Danik looked to the side and shrugged. "Lia and I used to be tight —aligned in our views and desires. She was changing."

"You didn't like that she was growing kinder and more responsible?"

"I liked her as she was!" His shout filled the cramped cell.

"Then, in Tienn, when she wouldn't change back, you decided to kill her."

Danik pointed a finger, his lip curled at the edge. "That was on her. She had a choice, and she chose wrong. Betraying me is unforgivable."

"Like you betrayed me? With my secret?"

"I don't ask for your forgiveness."

"What *do* you want with me?"

Danik inhaled deeply before speaking. "I need the Shadow Knights silenced. Clearly, Talioth didn't finish the job."

Raiyn nodded at the sword. "Go ahead then. Stab me."

Danik chuckled. "I'm not going to stab you. I'm going to execute you."

Raiyn's heart dropped.

"Tomorrow, in the square. We don't kill in back rooms. We do it in public, where our justice is on full display."

"Justice? Ha! Is that a joke?"

Danik shrugged again. "We could avoid all of this, you know."

Raiyn's forehead pinched. "What do you mean?"

"I'm not interested in your *death*. I just need you three out of the way."

"I'd say this is pretty out of the way, already."

"Where are they hiding?"

Raiyn shut his mouth.

"You know where they are, and if you want to live, you need to tell me."

He pressed his lips tighter as if the words might slip out.

"Think this through with me." Danik paced in the tight room. "You are going to die tomorrow. After that, Veron and Lia will attempt something crazy and get killed in a futile skirmish. One way or another, their path ends with my sword. I have what they want, I'm stronger, I have more men behind me, and Veron's noble, brainless heart won't let him stop trying."

"What do you suggest?" Raiyn asked.

Danik's face softened. "I lived with them for years. Despite our differences, I still love both Veron and Lia. The last thing I want is for them to die."

"Then don't kill them."

"They're forcing my hand." He held up a finger. "However, if we can bring them in peacefully, all three of you can live. We can find a more comfortable cell than this, and you can all live long lives."

"In the dungeon."

"Which is better than in the ground."

Raiyn hung his head, bobbing it slightly. "I've learned a lot since arriving in Felting. I learned how to sharpen my skills. I learned more about putting others first." He raised his head to look the king in the eyes. "And I learned very well how Danik Bannister cannot be trusted to keep his word."

Danik's friendly face turned down into a scowl. His chest rose and fell while breath seethed between his teeth. "Why did Veron run?"

Raiyn cocked his head and raised an eyebrow.

"At the bridge, he ran, leaving you two. Why?"

"He was late for another appointment."

Danik lunged forward and grabbed Raiyn by the neck. His fingers clenched, cutting off the airway. Raiyn grasped his forearms and tried to pull the king's hands back, but it felt like trying to move a stone wall.

"What's wrong with Veron?"

Raiyn sputtered, desperately trying to breathe. His neck strained. He felt a pull upward and held onto Danik's arms while his feet lifted from the ground. He attempted to kick, but it had no effect.

"Was he tired and unable to fight? Was there a crystal nearby cutting off the origine?"

After more sputtering, Raiyn's feet hit the ground again. The pressure around his neck loosened only a bit.

"Tell me!"

He struggled to push out the words, "If you're going to kill me, then kill me."

After a pause, Danik released his grip.

Raiyn doubled over, coughing and wheezing. He sucked in air, desperate to relieve his aching lungs.

Danik opened the door and left. Metal slammed as the barrier pulled closed again.

When Raiyn's breath settled, he looked up.

Danik stared at him through the barred window. His sharp jaw cut a firm line. "You die tomorrow." He let the words sit for a moment. "Let me know if you change your mind."

14

SEPARATED

"You want more?" Marcus asked.

Lia stared at the table's wood grain. Her eyes felt sluggish and puffy. Out of a desire to not be rude, she forced herself to look. The boy held up a plate of rolls. She shook her head.

"You should eat more." He grabbed one for himself.

"I'm fine."

Marcus slathered some jelly on the bread before putting it in his mouth. "You don't sound fine," he said, his mouth filled with food. After a pause, he swallowed and set down the uneaten portion. "I'm sure he's all right. I'm sure they're *both* all right."

Lia laughed. "Sure. I bet Raiyn is enjoying a fine breakfast in the king's dining hall right now." She scratched her nails across the table. "If he's even alive."

"Surely your father's safe though."

"Then why couldn't I find him? I scoured the woods for hours."

"If you couldn't find him, then I'll bet those other guys couldn't either."

Lia frowned. "I thought he would have made it back here to the Glade, but now I'm just waiting."

Marcus put the rest of the roll in his mouth. He stood and waved her forward. "While we wait, spar with me."

"Marcus, I'm not—"

"Come on! It will help me, and it will take your mind off waiting." Marcus crossed the room and grabbed a sword from the pile of weapons.

Lia sighed. "At least get the training swords."

"My father always used steel. It's fine."

She mumbled while following him through the door to the training yard. Without having to think, her hand wandered over her shoulder and worked Farrathan out of the back scabbard. The grip of the hilt felt good. Worried thoughts about her father drifted away with the wind.

Marcus turned to face her. A nervous grin on his face showed his excitement. Toned curves formed in his dark-brown arms as he lifted his weapon above his head and settled into a slight crouch.

"Dragon stance?" Lia remarked

His eyebrows raised and sword dropped. "Is that all right?"

She smiled. "Of course." She leaned in and tapped under his arm. "Keep your elbows up though. The old style dropped the arms, but you'll get better leverage by keeping them up."

He raised his elbows. "Like this?"

"Perfect." She nodded, then settled into horn stance. "Come at me."

Marcus hesitated then stepped forward. His sword swung in an arc. His face scrunched in a focused display.

Without using any origine, Lia deflected his blade and slid to the side. Another blow came for her, fast and strong. Her block left her arm reverberating from the impact.

He's surprisingly strong!

She pushed off, throwing his light body backward. Before he prepared again, she came at him. Marcus' eyes widened while he fended off quick strikes on alternating sides of his body. His steps shuffled backward. He held his sword with both hands, barely managing to keep up with her.

As Lia prepared to tap him on his upper arm with the flat of her blade, he ducked. She missed, her weapon continuing its momentum above his body.

She inhaled. His blade came for her unprotected side. From habit, the origine surged in her, allowing her weapon to return to her side. The defending blade stopped the boy's strike with a loud clank.

Lia stepped back. Both fighters lowered their swords while they sucked in lungsful of air.

"I wasn't going to hit you," Marcus said quickly. "I was going to stop it."

Lia puffed air from her nose while a smile pulled at her mouth. "That was really good. How long did you say you've been training?"

"Around three years—whenever father visited. He also gave me a daily regimen to work on."

"You're fast . . . and strong."

Marcus beamed. "How does the origine work . . . if I were able to use it? Would it make me faster and stronger?"

Lia froze. "Um . . . I'm not sure it's my place to teach you about it."

He waved his hand. "I'm sorry. I didn't mean to pry."

"No, you're fine. It's just that . . . the Knights are very particular about who and when people are trained." Her eyes flicked toward the walls of the Glade. "My father and mother usually have a say in that."

She bit the inside of her cheek while she stared. *Will I ever see either of them again?*

"Tell me about your mother," Marcus said. "What was she like?"

"She's . . ." Lia paused for a long moment. Her frustration and resentment mixed with a familial longing. She chuckled. "She was a good mother—*is* a good mother. We fight sometimes, but she means well. The times when I get the angriest—once things blow over, I can usually see her side. I made a mistake a while ago. I left my post, making her vulnerable, and she nearly died. It was my fault. For all I know, she may be dead now, but . . . I have to believe she's alive. I need to rescue her."

"To make up for not being there for her earlier?"

"Yeah, I guess so." Lia nodded then wiped at her eyes. She took a step back then lifted her sword. "Let's try it again. This time, be aware of your eyes. Don't let them telegraph your next move."

The boy nodded then resumed his stance.

"Elbows up!"

Marcus raised his elbows higher.

Stone crunched, turning Lia's head. A man in a black cloak crossed over the small bridge at the stream.

"Father!" Lia ran, tucking her weapon into its sheath as she hurried to greet him.

Veron's eyes sagged. His hair was matted from sweat and his shoulders drooped.

Meeting him as he crossed the bridge, she threw her arms around him and pulled him into an embrace. "I couldn't find you. I searched the woods for most of the night before I came back here. What happened? Where'd you go?"

They pulled away, and he entered the main hall. "I found a break in some rocks." He raised his limp water skin to the spout to fill it. "I knew I wouldn't be able to outrun them, so I hid."

"All night?"

He shook his head. "For a few hours. I heard Danik's men for a while, but it was too dark to find me. When I came out, I figured you would come here, but I wanted to see about Raiyn. I heard when he was taken."

"You went into Felting?"

Veron took a long drink of water, smacking his lips as he lowered the container. He nodded. His mouth was tight and formed a thin line.

A watery feeling churned inside Lia. "You found something?"

He reached into his cloak and pulled out a folded sheet of paper. It crinkled as he smoothed it. He paused before placing it on the counter.

Lia gasped as she read:

Son of Edmund Bale Captured
Convicted of Theft, Murder, and Treason

Execution by Crossbow Line - Finday at Noon in Turba Square

"A public execution? Why doesn't Danik just—" Lia stopped as the reason made sense. "He doesn't *just* want to kill Raiyn."

"He wants all three of us," Veron finished.

"And he knows we'll go after him. It's a trap."

Lia continued to stare at the paper, wishing the message would change. *Could we break him out beforehand? Could he escape himself, like he did in Searis?* Every one of Danik's men would be there, looking for them.

"Father," she started. "I know what you would say."

Veron raised an eyebrow and met Lia's gaze.

"It doesn't make sense to try to save him. They'll be looking for us. We won't be able to rescue him, and we'll likely end up captured ourselves. I know how it looks. But . . ." She looked back at the paper, and moisture formed at the corner of her eye. "He came for me—in Tienn. I would have died. And he came for you too—for all the knights. Then he put his life on the line to try and get that book so we can find the others."

Veron opened his mouth to speak.

"I know we should stay away," Lia blurted. "But we can't. We owe it to him. He came for us time and time again. We can't just leave him to die!"

Tears blurred Lia's vision. Her chest rose and fell.

Veron's eyebrows raised while he paused. "Are you finished?"

She nodded and wiped at her face.

A smile came to her father's face. "He *did* come for us, and we will *not* leave him to die."

Lia's eyes grew. A tentative smile formed.

"Danik's men *will* be there . . . and so will we."

15

SPRINGING THE TRAP

Danik peeked through the crack of the castle door. A mob of people waited at the bottom of the steps, and a general roar built in the crowd. He pulled back. Each of his knights of power waited around him, fully armed and ready. Raiyn stood in the middle, wrists shackled together with his head down, a gag over his mouth, and two palace guards on either side.

"Do you see them?" Nicolar asked.

"Not yet," Danik replied. "But they'll be here."

"Should we go?"

Danik inhaled then breathed out long and slow. "Yes. It's time."

A palace guard opened the door, and the jeers of the crowd rose. The group proceeded through the door and descended the grand palace steps.

The ire and insults of the crowd were directed toward the prisoner. Raiyn hung his head.

Danik, on the other hand, scoured the crowd. His eyes jumped from face to face, searching for familiarity.

The crowd pressed in at the bottom of the steps, shouting.

"Your father deserved to die, and so do you!"

"We should have been rid of your kind long ago!"

Carriages waited for them, but the mass of people blocked the path.

"Get through them," Nicolar ordered.

The guards pushed ahead. A man with a wild look in his eyes swung his fist at Raiyn, hitting him on the shoulder.

"Push them back!" Nicolar yelled.

Two more from the crowd pressed close, shoving the prisoner. A woman on the opposite side got in his face and yelled.

"Guards!" Danik yelled. "Control them!"

A young boy with dark skin ducked around the pushing arms of the guards. He pressed close to Raiyn, leaned into his ear, and muttered something with vitriol on his face. A shove from a guard sent the boy stumbling backward.

"Get in," a guard yelled, holding the door to a carriage open.

Raiyn entered, pushed by Nicolar. Jade and Danik followed. The king took the cushioned seat facing the prisoner. He looked out the window as the vehicle began to roll. His mind whirred. The sword and two daggers he wore comforted him, but his palms still felt clammy. He rubbed them against his knees.

A mumble came from the opposite seat. Raiyn's head bobbed, the gag vibrating with a mutter.

Danik nodded to Jade. She worked her fingers through the fabric then pulled the gag down.

"What were you saying?" Danik asked.

Raiyn stretched his jaw, flexing his lips at their newfound freedom. "I said . . . you're nervous."

Danik scowled but didn't answer.

"You're worried they'll be here."

"Ha!" He leaned forward, his scowl turning into a forced smile. "I'm counting on them being here."

It was Raiyn's turn for his confident look to falter.

"What? You think I don't know Lia and Veron? That my years with them haven't given me insight into their every predictable move? For instance . . . right now, they're probably waiting in Turba Square in disguise. And they hope to use the origine to free you from my clutches in a noble display of loyalty."

"And you're not worried?"

Danik's rapid pulse thudded. His cheeks ached from keeping the smile. "No."

Raiyn raised his eyebrows. "No?"

"No!" Nicolar and Jade turned at Danik's shout. "They're used to what they know—what they can control. The Knights of Power are something they know little about. They're outnumbered and outclassed. We *will* capture them. Then you and your friends will die."

A MAN JOSTLED AGAINST LIA, pushing her as he squeezed his way past. "Excuse you!" she said.

The man glanced back. He wrinkled his nose then continued pushing farther into the square.

"Ignore him," Veron said beside her, his face barely showing from inside the brown hood. "The less attention we draw the better."

"I still think the smell from these clothes might do more harm than good."

"Trust me. When your cloaks stink as much as these do, people want to spend as little time around you as possible. It will keep any guards or knights of power from checking us too closely."

I believe it, she thought. The rank scent of body odor and manure assaulted her nose, although the impact lessened the longer she wore them. She fought the urge to lower the hood and put the fabric as far away from her face as possible. "Where did you even find these?"

"A stable near the north gate," Veron replied. "I rubbed them through the old hay to help."

"I don't think *help* is the word you're looking for."

A clock on the side of a building showed two minutes past noon. Turba Square was packed with people. Vendor carts had been cleared, and men and women, young and old filled the space. Next to the familiar statue of Veron, a platform raised above the crowd. On the stage, a wooden backdrop formed a wall against the far side.

Nothing unified Felting more than their hatred for the short-lived rule of Edmund Bale, who had ruined and killed many of the citizens. Time may have passed, but feelings for the voracious conqueror were slow to die. The chance to execute one of his descendants whipped the crowd into a fury.

"Are you sure we shouldn't be closer?" Lia asked.

Veron craned his neck higher and looked around. "This should be good. We don't want to be too close where we will be more likely to be spotted."

"But we're going to need to move quickly."

"Which we can do. Getting spotted before we're ready will be a death sentence for all three of us."

A murmur grew in the crowd. Lia turned her head and saw the source of the commotion. A line of four carriages entered the square. The crowds parted, creating space for them to approach the platform. Jeers sounded from every corner of the square. A purple verquash hit the side of the carriage, splatting vegetable guts across the vehicle. A palace guard opened the door and scanned the crowd. No more objects hit the carriages.

One by one, the vehicles emptied. Lia's gaze jumped back and forth.

"There," Veron said.

Lia followed where he looked and found Raiyn cringing under the barrage of boos. Palace guards pulled on his arms, leading him toward the stage. "This is too familiar," she said.

Veron tensed next to her.

"What is it?" She spotted the subject of concern. Knights of power fanned in each direction, inspecting the crowd. Her heart raced. "What if they get here?"

"Let's hope they don't."

A young boy with dark skin squeezed between them.

Lia flinched until she realized who it was. "Marcus! Did you get it to him?"

The boy grinned. "No problem. The guards tried to push me away, but I made it."

"Did he know it was you?" Veron asked.

Marcus nodded. "He saw me. See, I told you I could help."

Veron clapped him on the shoulder. "Great work, Marcus."

The tension in Lia's shoulders loosened. She turned back to the stage. Raiyn's hands fidgeted, busy at work, unseen by the guards.

"This is just like in Searis," Lia said. "Hopefully, he can make quick work of the cuffs. Have you seen your guys?"

"The dock workers from the Red Quarter?" Veron raised onto his toes. "They're on the far side, by the shops. They look ready."

"You're sure they'll follow through?"

"I paid them four argen, and they're getting six more after. All they have to do is cause a disturbance just before they shoot him." He nodded. "You should have seen their living conditions. Yeah, they'll come through."

"What if he doesn't get his shackles free in time?"

Veron didn't answer for a moment.

"If he can't undo them, should we—"

"No," Veron said, quiet but firm. "We can't show ourselves. Raiyn will make it."

Jitters filled Lia's stomach. The plan had plenty of holes, but she couldn't think of anything else to do.

Cedric came into view, between the heads of the crowd. The closest of Danik's men, he weaved through the people, jerking back hoods and inspecting faces. Lia pulled her hood farther.

"Citizens of Felting!" Danik's voice rang out. He stood on the stage with Raiyn and four palace guards.

The people of the square hushed, turning their attention to the king.

"Thank you for joining us to commemorate this justice. Edmund Bale, the former king of Norshewa conquered Feldor over sixteen years ago. The foreigner nearly ran this kingdom into the ground during his brief reign. After his defeat, all traces of his lineage were supposedly wiped out."

Cries of approval rang through the crowd.

"My new elite force, the Knights of Power, tracked down and captured one of his descendants. A son who slipped by—Raiyn Bale."

Shouts filled the square, and a few objects flung through the air.

"This spitting image of the late ruler picked up where his father left off. He wanted to subdue Feldor once more and bend this kingdom to his whims. He sought followers wherever he went, deceiving those he met. While I rule, this land will *not* fall into the hands of foreign conquerors!"

"Kill the heir!" a voice yelled from the masses.

"Shoot him!"

Danik nodded. "We will."

"Hey! Watch it!" a man called from the side.

Lia turned her head and stifled a gasp. Cedric pushed past a man, too close for comfort. She faced forward, keeping the fabric of the hood between them.

"They're moving," Veron whispered.

Lia thought he meant the knights of power until she caught sight of the dock workers. They had left their place at the edge of the square and drew closer to the stage.

A jerk from Raiyn's hand brought her eyes back to him. She leaned forward, narrowing her eyes. *Was that . . . ?* The metal shackle on his left hand twisted. "He's got one," she whispered.

"Really?" Marcus said, raising on his toes.

"Keep it down," Lia said. "You don't want to—"

"You!" Cedric's voice cut through the crowd to her left. "Have you seen a young woman in her late teens with long brown hair. She'll be with a man in his late thirties." Mumbled non-committal replies didn't seem to help him.

"He's getting closer," she whispered.

On the stage, Danik stepped to the edge of the platform, his eyes looking out and panning through the people.

"Move to your right." Veron lightly pulled on her arm.

She stepped, her hood blocking most of the view when her father's arm turned from a pull to a hard stop. "What is it?"

"Jade." His voice was barely audible. "Coming this way."

Eight soldiers with crossbows, wearing all black, approached Raiyn. They positioned him against the back wall then stood only a few paces away.

Lia's pulse raced. The familiar sight of Raiyn about to be executed turned her stomach into knots. Held in front of him, a hand covered his frantic work on the remaining cuff. The turns of his wrists and flicks of his fingers would go unnoticed by the rest of the crowd.

Come on, Raiyn. You can do it!

The soldiers raised their crossbows, pointing the projectiles at his chest and head.

The dock workers came to the end of their path, stopped on the far side of the stage.

"They're ready," Veron whispered.

"He's not though," Lia breathed.

Raiyn's hands clenched. They had turned red as he pulled and twisted them.

So close!

Danik held up a hand, stopping Lia's breath. He pointed at one of the guards.

"What are they doing?" she whispered.

"I don't know," Veron replied.

Two guards approached Raiyn with a pile of chains.

Lia's heart sank. "Oh no!"

The guards worked together to wrap the metal links around his torso. The three loops of chains pinned his arms against his body.

"No, no, no." Her mutters echoed hollow in her ears.

A small object dropped from Raiyn's hand. He was too far away for Lia to hear it hit the wooden stage, but the widening of his eyes told her all she needed to know.

"Father, what do we do?" Her voice was quiet, but it still wavered.

A rumbling noise grew around the dock workers on the far side of the stage. Yelling voices, thudding punches, and shouts tried to distract her. She could only stare at Raiyn, stunned.

Two of the palace guards from the stage descended the steps to deal with the men. The knights of power in that vicinity moved to help, but the distraction failed.

Raiyn fought against the chains. The one loose wrist shackle fell free, but the act accomplished nothing. He was trapped beyond hope.

"Father." She grabbed Veron's arm. "We have to go after him. It didn't work." She turned to him. "I know you said we couldn't—" Her father's focused expression stopped her. "What is it?"

Veron's eyes were narrowed, locked on the stage. "It's Danik."

She looked at the king, her heart pounding. "What about him?"

Danik kept his eyes out, panning back and forth.

Lia's pounding heart prevented any thoughts from forming.

"He's not going to kill him," Veron whispered.

It took a moment for his words to register. "What? How do you—"

"He's sweating."

"So?"

"He's worried he won't find us. He needs us, and he needs Raiyn to get us."

The origine buzzed inside her. Her limbs begged to explode into action. "We can't risk it. I'm going."

Veron's hand held her arm back as she pulled.

"Lia," he hissed. His eyes indicated to her other side.

She slowly turned her hood until she caught sight of Cedric, even closer than before.

"I've got to go, Father." Thick and laced with emotion, the words struggled to make it past her lips.

"If you go, you will die . . . as will he. But, if you wait, Danik won't kill him. Wait, and you'll see."

Tears pooled in her eyes. "I can't chance it." She could break her father's grip with very little effort, but the pull held her there. She stared at the stage, and Raiyn's eyes found her.

He stopped struggling. The metal clinking of the chain links ceased. His chest inflated as he sucked in a breath. He lowered his chin with a resigned look of acceptance.

Her breath caught. Her chin trembled, and her mouth hung half open. "He saved me." Her words barely even reached her own ears. "I have to save him."

Her own words failed to prompt her to move. Tears streamed down her cheeks, hidden under the hood.

Danik continued searching the crowd. He locked eyes with Nicolar who stood near the stage. Nicolar raised his eyebrows then Danik turned away.

Lia's heart thudded in her chest. Her feet remained rooted in place. Her father's grip softened, turning tender. Her shoulders shook.

Abandoning the crowd, Danik turned to Raiyn.

No! Lia thought, the unspoken words yelled in her mind. *Don't do it!* She pulled again, Veron's hand tightening.

Out of the corner of her eye, Cedric stepped closer.

She no longer cared.

Danik took a step closer toward Raiyn. He held a hand up, his finger ready to signal the men with crossbows.

The men stood still with stocks against their shoulders and bolts pointed forward.

Lia heard only the thump of her pulse in her head as she stared at Raiyn. Her lungs ached, craving a breath, but her body wouldn't cooperate.

His shoulders were slumped, his head drooped.

"Wait!" A call came from the steps, and Nicolar ran up them.

Lia managed half a breath. Her father's hand jerked in response, tightening.

A murmur grew in the crowd as Nicolar passed a sheet of paper to Danik.

A smile creeped across Lia's face.

Veron's grip softened. "He needs him," he whispered.

Appearing to be finished reading, Danik turned to the crowd. "New information has come to light," he called, less forcefully than before. "You came here to see justice delivered, and I'm sorry to have to disappoint you. It seems the prisoner may be useful still. We will delay his execution for the time being."

Boos erupted from the crowd. Hands lifted in the air, shaking in Raiyn's direction.

Lia exhaled. A weight tumbled from her shoulders.

"You were right," Marcus said.

"Come on," Veron said. "We must get out of here . . . quickly."

He pulled them both backward toward the exit of the square.

Lia kept her head down and noticed Jade's leather pants and hands filled with daggers pass just behind them.

Veron pushed forward, bumping into onlookers.

"Hey!" a man shouted. "Watch where you're going!"

"I'm sorry," Veron replied, softly. He held a finger to his lips, but the man didn't seem to notice.

"If I smelled as badly as you, I would keep clear of anyone else."

"You're right," Veron said. "We're leaving."

They made it to the end of the square. Before passing the stone arch that marked the exit onto Castlewood Street, Lia chanced a glance over her shoulder. The chains were being removed from around Raiyn. Danik paced the platform looking all through the square. She chuckled, reveling in the angry look he wore.

With the event aborted, grumbling people shuffled through the square in all directions. For a split second, a path parted. Lia's gaze fell along the path until she spied what lay at the end. She gasped. Jade stared at her, daggers in hand.

The woman's posture changed. Her eyes bored into Lia's, and her jaw fixed shut. Then, she moved—a walk at first until she started shoving people out of the way.

"Go!" Lia yelled, turning back to her father. All pretense of secrecy was gone. "Jade's coming! Run!"

Veron didn't look. He grabbed Marcus' hand and ran.

Filled with the origine, Lia had the ability to fly past them, but her father and Marcus remained vulnerable. The people of the square would buy them time before Jade or any other knights of power arrived on Castlewood, but once they did, there would be no escape.

"We need to get off the road!" she yelled.

"I've got it!" Veron shouted back, his feet slowing. "In here!" He threw open the door to a nearby shop and waved them in.

The street remained clear by the time Lia ducked through the door. She panted, breathing heavily under the hood. The shop was a grocery, filled with fruits and vegetables. The smell of soup filled the room.

Lia furrowed her brow. *I know this shop.*

"If you're in trouble, I'm going to have to ask you to leave," a familiar male voice said.

Lia turned and lowered her hood. A portly man in his fifties stood by the back wall with a broom in hand. He held it like a staff, as if he were ready to attack. When the man got a better look, his eyes widened. The broom dropped from his hands, clattering to the floor. A woman behind him held her hand to her mouth.

"It can't be!" the man breathed. "I thought you were dead!"

Veron stepped forward. "Hello, Morgan. Hi, Jeanette. It's good to see you both. We're alive, and if you can hide us, maybe we'll be able to stay that way."

16

TRAPPED

The embrace with his old friend felt good, but the proximity of the knights of power made Veron pull away quickly. "I'd love to reminisce, but we really need to hide. Do you have any—"

"Come," Morgan waved a hand, the smile on his face hardening in an instant.

Jeanette walked to the front door. "I'll keep watch."

Veron followed through the doorway, past the narrow stairs to the back storage room. Crates stacked with food. The scent of freshly picked produce hit his nose. A door with a glass window pane led to an alley along the back of the building.

Morgan knelt by a wooden plank on the wall. He pulled at the board, wiggling a bit at a time. After a struggle, the plank came free. The board beside it came easier, leaving a black hole leading to a space under the stairs. "Get in. Quickly!"

Veron entered first, crouching and squeezing through the narrow slit in the boards. He shuffled as far as he could until a wall met his side and back. Lia came next, squeezing beside him. Marcus was the last to enter the cramped space. Thankfully, his slight body didn't take up much room.

"Someone's coming!" Jeanette's urgent voice called through the wall.

"You three, be quiet." Morgan placed the first board back. When the second board slid into place, darkness engulfed them. Morgan's footsteps sounded muffled as he left the back room.

The heavy breathing from Lia and Marcus matched that of his own. Instinctively, Veron tried to pull from the origine to settle his nerves. The feeling of the empty well still felt foreign. The shop bell rang, causing him to tense. The three of them held their collective breaths.

"Where are they?" a muffled male voice yelled.

"Excuse me," Jeanette said. "Watch where you're swinging that. This is our shop."

A woman chimed in, "Where did they go?" Her voice held a threatening edge.

Lia leaned in and whispered, "It's Cedric and Jade."

"Whoa!" Morgan said. "There's no need for daggers here. Who are you looking for?"

A pounding noise against a wooden surface shook the wall of their hideout. "Don't play with us!" Jade said. "The man and young woman who entered here moments ago. Where are they?"

"We heard them, but we were upstairs when they arrived." Footsteps drew closer, and Morgan's voice grew loud. "When we came down, they had just burst out the back door, here. I spotted them sprinting down the alley. That direction—away from the square."

"The man was around forty?" Cedric asked. "And the girl was in her late teens with brown hair and light skin?"

"Yes." A creak announced the back door opening. "That was them. They can't be far."

A moment passed, but the footsteps didn't exit the shop. Veron's heart thumped. He pressed against his chest to try and keep his breathing steady.

"What's up those stairs?" Jade asked.

"That's where we live," Jeanette said. "With our family."

"No one else is here?"

"Our boys are at school. It's just us for now."

The floor creaked in the direction of the stairs. Another pause.

"You're welcome to look up there if you like," Morgan added, "but that's not where the people went."

"Come on," Jade said.

Cedric mumbled something, and their footsteps faded. After a moment, the door closed.

Veron didn't dare speak. He barely breathed. Seconds turned into minutes, and the minutes stacked up. *What if Danik's goons didn't actually leave?*

He nearly jumped when the boards in the wall jostled again. Light poured in, forcing him to shade his eyes.

"They're gone," Morgan said. "You can come out."

Veron stumbled out last. He stood straight and stretched, arching his back.

"I'm so relieved to find you alive." Morgan glanced at his wife before turning back to Veron. "Do we get to find out the truth behind King Danik's lies, now?"

VERON SAVORED the last spoonful as it slid down his throat. The rich, meaty soup warmed his stomach as well as his heart. Lia, Marcus, and he sat around the Fenster table in the upstairs room.

"Would you like more?" Jeanette asked, her eyes bright, and her smile genuine.

Veron shook his head as he set down his spoon. "Thank you, but this was just right."

Marcus' eyes jumped from Veron to their hostess.

Jeanette locked her sights on the boy. "Are you still hungry?"

His head retreated to his shoulders, and a sheepish grin formed on his face. After a beat, he nodded.

Jeanette laughed and picked up his empty bowl. "Lia? How about you?"

"No, thanks," Lia held up a hand. "This was excellent."

Jeanette returned to a large pot on their kitchen counter. With a wooden ladle, she scooped a generous portion into the boy's bowl. His eyes sparkled as she set the dish before him.

The kitchen was plain but equipped enough to meet the needs of a family of four. Shelves with cookware, spice containers, and food stacked vertically over a short counter with a deep-set washbasin. Past the table, two seats with faded cushions and torn fabric faced each other in the middle of the room. They sat next to a hearth. Cold ash filled the bottom, and black soot marked its walls.

Two open doorways led off opposite ends of the humble kitchen. One room displayed a blanket, pulled taut across a double bed, while the other showed two smaller beds.

A click at the door caused Veron to snap his head in the direction of the stairs.

Morgan entered the room. Deep lines marked his face as he closed the door and threw the latch behind him.

Veron breathed out, his nerves settling. "Anything?"

"Nothing outside," Morgan said. "But I checked down the street." His face fell further.

"What'd you see?"

"A checkpoint where Castlewood meets Rampart Way. They're inspecting everyone."

"Regular soldiers?" Lia asked.

"Yes, but two of the knights of power as well."

Veron sighed. "I guess we return to the square. From there, we could—"

Morgan's shaking head caused him to stop.

"They're there, too?"

Morgan nodded. "Every side street. Every alley. Swords. Crossbows. Danik himself is even searching." Morgan exhaled heavily. "You're trapped, and they know you're somewhere in this area."

A sinking feeling grew in Veron's gut. He looked at Jeanette. Her face held a firm display of support and a desire to be hospitable, but he sensed fear behind it.

Veron stood, his chair scraping the wooden floor. "It's time for us to leave."

Lia's eyebrow raised, and Marcus lifted his spoon to his mouth faster.

"You can't leave," Morgan said. "The area is blocked, and there's nowhere to go. If you still had your origine, you could leap over buildings or something, but . . . it's too dangerous for you to go out now."

"Danik knows where you live." Veron's words caused a silence to fill the room.

Morgan's jaw set. He glanced at his wife and drew in a deep breath.

"He knows who you are," Veron continued. "He knows where you are, and it's only a matter of time before he comes here."

"You're right." Lia's chair scraped as she stood. "We're putting you in danger. We need to leave."

"Hold on." Morgan extended his arms with palms pointing out. "You are our friends. Even more than that, you're family. We will take whatever risks we have to, for you to be safe.

Jeanette stepped at his side and ran her arm through his. "I agree. We can hide you back in the storeroom."

Veron shook his head. "Danik will tear this place apart. And when he finds us, he'll kill you as well as us. You may be willing to sacrifice for us, but I won't accept it." He turned to Lia and Marcus. "Come on. We're leaving."

"Where will you go?" Jeanette asked. "Can you fight your way past them?"

"Not with my power gone, but there is one place we can sneak out."

A smile grew on Morgan's face. "Of course. Why didn't I think of it."

"The cistern?" Jeanette asked. "I thought that tunnel was built over."

"It was," Veron said, ". . . sort of. Masons covered it up, but Darcius had them build in a backup plan."

He stepped to the window and pressed against it. Three buildings down, the bubbling spout of the cistern poured water into the basin below. A woman gathered water into a jar, but the area looked clear.

"We need to get into the castle, but escaping the city is our best play at the moment." Veron turned to Morgan. "Can you keep an eye on Marcus?"

"What?" Marcus said, his spoon clattering to the empty bowl.

Morgan and Jeanette both nodded. "Of course," Morgan said. "We'll take care of him."

"No!" Marcus shouted. "I'm going with you."

Veron pointed at him. "You are not. You're staying here. They're not looking for you because they don't know you're with us. But if you're caught with us while trying to escape, then they'll kill you too."

Marcus' mouth hung open as if poised to argue, but he said nothing.

"We'll be back in a day or so, once the attention dies down." Lia said. She rested her hand on the boy's shoulder. "You want to rescue your father from the Marked Ones. So do we. In order to make that happen, we need all of us to stay safe. Will you wait here with Morgan and Jeanette?"

After a moment, Marcus nodded.

"Good," Veron confirmed. "Let's move."

Veron led the way down to the shop with Lia and the others behind. The room of groceries was dark. A "closed" sign hung on the glass window, keeping any shoppers away. Veron rested his hand on the doorknob and looked in each direction through the pane.

"Looks clear." He glanced at Lia. "You ready?"

She lifted her hood to cover her brown hair and nodded.

Veron raised his own hood and turned his head to the others. "Thank you both. And Marcus . . . In case you must run, go to the Glade." A click sounded, and he pushed the door open.

An electric energy seemed to fill the street. People walked in each direction, but no one spoke. Their eyes darted around.

"Keep your head down," Veron said.

He turned up the street and adopted a casual shuffle to his step.

One leg dragged slightly, and he watched the ground in front of his feet. Lia's steps matched his, walking at his side.

Despite a burning desire to scout the area, he didn't dare look up. A building passed to his side, then another. He nearly ran into a man leading a horse but dodged out of the way. A bubbling sound reached his ears. He chanced a look, his heart thudding in his chest. The cistern was empty of people. Arcs of water fell through holes in a stone wall. The basins below caught the streams, creating a shallow pool to drink from. Veron stopped at the wall and pressed his hand against it.

"Is this where the passage was?" Lia asked.

Veron nodded. "This portion of the wall was added."

"How do we get there, then?"

Veron looked up, sighting the top of the wall. Holding his hands up, he jumped and grasped the edge. His boots pressed into the wall, scooting his feet higher as he pulled. His arms strained. The stone edge of the wall scraped against his forearms as he flung them over, pulling with his elbows. Higher. Higher. His hip hinged over the lip. He turned to the side and swung his legs up, rolling onto the top. Sweat dotted his forehead. His breath was heavy, and he wiped at his face. *This would be much easier with the origine.*

As if proving his thought, Lia seemed to float as she mounted the wall, landing lightly on her feet.

Veron chuckled. "I sure miss that."

He turned his attention to the top of the wall. The flat area covered what used to be the metal door that led to the escape passage. He rubbed his hand across the stones. "It should be here somewhere."

Lia joined in, pressing her hand into the stones inset into the top of the wall.

Veron's fingers slid across an exceptionally smooth rock. His mouth curled up. He pushed in, and a faint click sounded. "Found it."

He turned around and lowered his legs down the backside of the wall. When he reached his hips, he dropped the rest of the way, landing lightly in the narrow area hidden from the street. A rounded stone structure indicated where the hidden passage lay buried. Veron found the seam. He pressed a leg against the wall and pulled to the side. A stone barrier pivoted, leaving a space just wide enough to squeeze through.

"Let's go," he said.

Veron entered first. The damp, cool air enveloped his skin. He ducked slightly to not bump his head on the ceiling of the tight passage. Narrow shafts allowed sunlight to permeate the tunnel, providing just enough to see from. Something felt off. The hairs on the back of his neck prickled. He took a step forward, his boot splashing gently in a puddle. His eyes narrowed.

Lia stepped into the passage. "What is it?"

"I'm not sure." His words were slow in contrast to his racing mind. "Something's wrong."

"When's the last time you were here?"

"Years ago." He sniffed, the moldy scent of earth dominating the air.

"Are we good to go?"

Veron paused, his ear straining for anything out of the ordinary. Drips of water were the only sounds. Finally, he nodded. "I'll get the door."

He braced his feet and pushed on the stone barrier. The wall slid to the side, and the gap closed. When the light had all but disappeared, Broderick's bearded face appeared in the thin crack, and his hand slammed into the rock.

Veron jumped and yelled, "Lia! Help!"

He pushed against the stone, but the man on the other side was far stronger. The stone barrier opened rapidly. Veron strained, pushing with all his might.

Like a battering ram slamming into a gate, Lia arrived. Her origine-infused body pushed along with Veron, and the door reversed direction.

"They're in here!" Broderick shouted. "Help me!"

Veron groaned, leaning all his weight against it. Lia roared as she pushed.

"Just. Need. Latch," Veron said through clenched teeth.

The door crept closer. The light from the crack disappeared.

"Aaaargh!" Lia yelled, her arms quivering.

A click reverberated through the stone barrier. Veron sighed and collapsed to the ground, panting. Lia bent over her knees, breathing heavily as well.

"Come on," she said, waving a hand. "We've got to move before they figure out the switch."

Veron groaned as he struggled to his feet.

"Can you run?" Lia asked.

Veron nodded but saved his words. With his back bent and his head angled down, he set a jogging pace. Lia followed behind, but after only a dozen strides, a new noise stopped him in his tracks.

"You think they can't open the door again?" a man with a thick, Norshewan accent said.

"Nicolar!" Lia shouted, sliding around Veron to put herself between them.

Veron cringed at needing his daughter to protect him. "How did you get here?" he asked.

Nicolar laughed. "You're so predictable, and now we have you both."

A click in the passage behind indicated the stone door had unlocked.

"Fight past him," Veron whispered to Lia. "Clear the way. I'm with you."

Lia didn't hesitate. She blasted forward, the sudden movement creating a vacuum in the tunnel that pulled Veron forward. He braced himself to sprint after her. With Nicolar knocked aside, they could run through the passage and get lost in the woods on the other side.

Nicolar cried out as Lia caught him in the stomach. His body crumpled into the side of the tunnel. Lia continued forward, the wide open space in her wake inviting Veron to follow. He longed to run with her. He wished he could keep up with her speed and strength. He desired to call out to her.

He couldn't do any of it.

An unbreakable hand covered his mouth, and another wrapped around his chest in an iron grip. His body was being dragged backward, his heels digging fruitlessly into the floor of the tunnel. He braced to yell, but only a muffled sound escaped. Rounding a corner backward, he lost sight of his daughter just before a black shroud covered his head, taking away what little sight he had left.

His heart dropped. Hope of escape trickled away. Tired of fighting, he let his body go limp.

17

INCREASING PRESSURE

Danik's carriage traveled for barely more than a few seconds before it rolled to a stop. He didn't even wait for assistance before he opened the door and stepped to the street himself. A frown pulled on his face, and he didn't hide it.

"Your Majesty," a guard fumbled, hurrying to the door.

Danik waved him away without a look. He stared ahead at the familiar shop. *Fenster Foods.* He'd never been in, but he knew the person who owned it. The sign in the window indicated the business was closed.

Broderick opened the shop door, the friendly bell sounding out of place. "He and his wife are here," Broderick said, "and Jade will be back soon."

"Did you have any trouble?"

"There was a kid in the shop when we arrived—a young teen with dark skin. He pitched a fit when we kicked him out, but no issues since then."

Danik nodded then entered the shop.

The curtains had been drawn. What would have been a light and airy store felt solemn and foreboding. The scent of ripe fruit clung to the air laced with tendrils of fear.

Rope bound the shopkeeper's and his wife's arms. They stood against the wall with two guards holding crossbows on either side. Morgan's fierce eyes pierced the king, forcing Danik to look away.

"Has he said anything?" Danik asked.

Broderick shook his head. "Nothing yet."

"It's good to see you again, Morgan," Danik said, raising his eyes to meet the shopkeeper's. "I understand Veron and Lia Stormbridge were here only a bit ago."

"And I understand you sold out your own Shadow Knights and murdered King Darcius." Morgan raised his chin. "It seems we're both caught up, now."

Danik's eye twitched. He paused, then forced himself to pace. "You wanted to help your friends escape, so you hid them until they could make it to the cistern tunnel."

It was Morgan's turn to flinch.

Danik formed a half smile. "It might surprise you to know we were waiting."

"So, you have them?"

Danik didn't reply.

"You don't have them?"

"Veron is with us, and Lia will be soon."

Morgan's face fell. "What do you want from me?"

"It's not about what I *want* from you. It's about what I can do *for* you. Legally, I should have you executed."

"For what?"

"Treason." The words sounded heavy even to Danik's own ears. "You deceived the Knights of Power to harbor enemies of Feldor."

"By which you mean . . . protecting those who fought for Feldor with their lives and were the kingdom's closest allies and defenders?"

Danik ignored the barb. "Treason is an offense punishable by death."

"I know what treason is. Do you?" Morgan glared, his usual smile nowhere to be found. "Why are you here?"

"I have a soft heart," Danik said. "I don't want to execute anyone, and I'd love to have a reason to pardon you."

"Then do it."

"I need something in return."

"I have some perfectly ripe verquash—produce fit for a king. Or maybe some carrots?"

Danik narrowed his eyes.

Morgan pursed his lips. "You want Lia . . . and you think I know where she is."

"I do."

Morgan's smile returned. His shoulders bounced as he chuckled. "Well, you couldn't be more wrong about that."

"I could march you to Turba Square right now and fill you with crossbow bolts."

Morgan shrugged. "I don't know what to tell you. You want something I don't have."

"Then get it."

The grocer's head cocked, one eyebrow raising.

"Reach out to her. Find where she is and bring her in."

The man chuckled. "I have no way to reach her. I don't know where she hides. You're grasping at straws."

Danik's teeth clenched. Morgan's refusal to assist was not unexpected, but the casual manner in which he defied a king boiled his blood. The grocer's wife caught his attention. Where Morgan was defiant and bold, his wife looked hesitant.

"How about you?" Danik asked. "Jeanette, was it?"

Her eyes flared, and she swallowed hard. "I just make the soup for the shop." She glanced at Morgan then back to the king. "I don't know anything about the girl."

Danik stepped closer and smelled her cheap rosewater perfume. "And what if we took your husband to be executed. Would that jog your memory?"

Beads of sweat popped onto her brow. Her head shook, short and tight. "I'm-I'm sorry, but I don't know anything."

Danik bit his tongue, trying to keep the frustration from showing. "Maybe I should point the crossbows at *you* instead." His eyes flicked to Morgan to gauge the man's reaction.

The grocer tensed. The muscles in his neck bulged.

Danik waited, letting the silence do the heavy lifting, hoping their resolve would crumble.

Behind him, the bell over the door rang, snapping him out of the moment. From the terror in Morgan and Jeanette's eyes, Danik had an idea of who had arrived. He spun.

"Jade, you're back." His eyes dropped to the boy and girl whose arms she clutched. "And I see you have new friends."

The door closed behind them, and the kids squirmed in her grip.

"You leave them alone!" Jeanette warned.

"Mother . . . Father," the girl said. "What's going on?"

"Everything's going to be fine, Suzy."

"Don't lie to them." Danik turned to the mother. "Don't promise her something you can't back up. Unless . . . you *can* back it up." He paused before turning back to the kids and bending down to their level. "It's Suzy and Beckham, right?"

"Suzanne," the girl said, leaning away.

"Are you the king?" Beckham asked.

A smile grew on Danik's face. "I am. We've met before but you were younger. It's an honor to meet you again."

"Weren't you one of the shadow knights?" Beckham asked. "I remember you being one of the trainees."

Danik's smile hardened. "I used to be. Now, I rule Feldor. Times change."

The children stared back with suspicion. He stood and smoothed the front of his doublet. His stomach churned, making his insides watery. Life was simpler when he drank, played dice, and sparred. He turned back to Morgan, attempting to portray confidence.

"Morgan, you have a decision to make."

"I thought we already went over my options."

"Those were only to warm you up. This is where things get interesting."

Danik stepped forward. He let the man sweat, pondering what might come.

"I need Lia Stormbridge. I believe you either have the information

I need or are able to get it. You've shown you're not interested in preserving your own life in exchange for this, so let's raise the stakes."

Morgan stared back, not blinking or even appearing to breathe.

"While you may not value your own life, do you value your wife, your son, and your daughter?"

Jeanette muttered, "You despicable—"

"Quiet!" Danik cut her off.

"Father?" Suzanne cried. "What does he mean?"

Morgan still hadn't moved.

Danik turned to the children. "What do you think, Beckham? Will your father choose for you to die?"

A tear trickled down the boy's face.

"Is he going to kill your sister and your mother, too, in order to save someone he barely knows?"

The girl sobbed, filling the room with choking cries.

Danik turned back to Morgan. He expected to find a broken man, cowering and repentant. Instead, he discovered a firm jaw and a confident stance.

"How dare you?" Morgan's strong voice projected through the shop.

Danik's stomach churned.

"Sixteen years ago, another throne usurper stood before me and threatened my family. He wanted something I didn't have. When I didn't give it to him, my wife and two children were murdered in front of my eyes." A tear rolled down his cheek, but his voice didn't waver. "That was the darkest day of my life, something I hope no one—including you—will ever have to experience."

Morgan took a step forward. The guard's crossbow pressed against his chest.

"The irony isn't lost on me that once again my family's life is threatened, and again, the ask is for me to betray the Stormbridge family. Like before, I don't have what you seek, so I can't help you. But even if I *did* know . . . I wouldn't tell you." He looked to his wife and flashed a pained smile before turning back to the king. "Not because I value their lives less than someone else's, but because turning in people who have done nothing wrong is not what I do. It's not the type of person I am."

Danik fought to keep his legs from shaking. The grocer's piercing gaze pinned him back and nearly took the breath from his lungs.

"The decision is up to you, King Danik, and you must decide what type of leader you will be. Are you a man who follows in the footsteps of Edmund Bale? Will you kill a person's family in order to prove a point? Or are you someone who can admit when he's wrong—someone who can leave a family be when there's nothing to be gained by hurting them. Personally, I think you're the latter."

The room was silent, and all eyes looked at Danik. His heart pounded. Inside, he raged—*I can't believe he would speak to a king that way. I can't believe he would endanger his family.*

His chest rose and fell. He swallowed hard.

I can't believe he's right.

LIA PEEKED from around the corner of the building. The shadows hid her well. The cloudy night covered much of the moon, making skulking through the city a breeze. She had discarded the pungent cloak, but its rancid scent remained. No longer hiding in a crowd, she still needed to remain unseen.

Guilt ate at her for losing her father. By the time she had realized he was gone, she was too far down the tunnel to have done anything about it. At least that's what she told herself. Her heart had begged her to return. She could have flown down the tunnel, fueled by origine with fists blazing, but she didn't. She hesitated. Logic pricked her mind, saying she would only end up caught as well. Sacrificing herself with no guarantee of results would be pointless. She gave in to the survival instinct.

I'm still alive.

Her stomach turned at the thought.

It's what Father would have wanted . . . Now, I need to find them both, plus the book.

Morgan's shop and the room above it looked dark. The street was quiet—as still as she could hope for. Lia stepped out from her hiding place, barely any more visible in the exposed street.

Her head was on a swivel as she crossed the road. Her eyes darted to each potential ambush point. She reached the door to Fenster Foods without issue. As expected, the door was locked. She pulled out her lock-picking tool, glanced over each shoulder, then went to work. In a few moments, a solid click rewarded her efforts, and the door swung inward with a slight creak.

Lia only allowed a narrow crack. She kept an eye on the bell above, stopping the door's movement before the device announced her presence. Safely inside, she closed the door behind her.

The shop was empty—dark and silent. Walking amongst the quiet produce felt eerie. Her confidence grew as she ascended the stairs. The door at the top opened smoothly, and Lia leaned her head inside the Fenster living quarters. Again, all was quiet.

"Morgan? Jeanette?" she whispered.

No snoring greeted her. No heavy breathing. Tendrils of fear crept into her mind. She passed the kitchen and peered in the bedroom. The blanket lay flat. Her shoulders fell.

"Hello?" Her voice grew bolder. "Is anyone here?"

She crossed the living area and checked the children's room— empty. Her limbs trembled. *Were they taken? If Danik knew they harbored us, what would he do?*

Something caught her eye on the table. A scrap of paper was out of place. Lia approached to inspect it. She leaned forward to read it in the dim light.

LIA,

We heard about Veron's capture. We're so sorry. Men came and questioned us, but thankfully, we didn't have any information to divulge, so they left us alone. To be cautious, Morgan wants us to go into hiding for a couple of days until things settle down.

When Danik's men were here, we overheard something about what their plans were for Raiyn and Veron. I hesitate to write it down, but if you read this, come and meet me.

Around two years ago, we joined you for dinner, and you mentioned a place you hated when you were young. Do you remember where it was? I'll be at that location this Finday and Marketday, an hour till midnight.

IN HOPE,

    Jeanette

LIA SMILED. *They're all right.*

She exhaled a held breath. From the moment they stepped into the shop earlier that day, she'd been worried about what might happen to Morgan's family. Hearing they were safe relieved her.

Not only are they safe, but she has information.

She glanced out the window to look down the street at the clock hanging off the nearby bank. *Thirty minutes. Perfect. Plenty of time to get there.*

A whiff of her own hair drifted across her nose.

And I could use it.

18

THE BATHHOUSE

During the day, people packed River Street. The road connected the docks and the warehouse district to the rest of the city. Markets, shops, and homes lined the way, making it one of the busiest roads to walk. As night fell in Felting, people either grabbed a seat at a tavern or settled into their homes, so the normally bustling street became quiet.

Lia ambled past the Felavorre Bathhouse twice. No lurkers waited with an eye on the building. No ambushes waited in the dark corners of the surrounding street.

After first reading the note from Jeanette, she'd been relieved to have any sort of lead, but in the time since, she'd grown suspicious. *There's no way Jeanette and Morgan would betray me,* she told herself. *But I can't know it was written by her. What if they forced her to write it? What if Danik and his men are waiting inside?* The sobering possibility was too real to ignore.

Her nerves kept her outside the building, walking past and scouting instead of going in. Her arms trembled.

But what if it is really Jeanette? I can't miss this chance.

She looked across the street to where lanterns burned on either side of the bathhouse entrance, inviting her inside. With her chest up and shoulders back, she crossed the road and pushed against the heavy, wooden door.

Thick, wet air greeted her inside. The dampness crawled down her throat. Her skin felt sticky, enveloped by the blanket of humidity.

A woman behind a counter read a book. After a half glance in Lia's direction, she extended a hand while continuing to read. "Three pintid," the lady droned, wrinkling her nose.

Lia dropped the copper coins into the woman's hand. "Have you recently seen a group of men come in here?"

"I've seen lots of men."

"Scary-looking ones. Probably with swords or some sort of weapons. They would have arrived in the last hour or two."

The woman shook her head. "No one like that." She turned back to her book. "Women are to the right. Don't forget soap and a towel."

The lump in her throat lessened its pressure. Lia grabbed a sliver of soap and a threadbare towel from the pile on a table. She passed the counter then turned to the right down a stone corridor. A dim lantern lit the way. The temperature rose as she proceeded down the hall. The stones under her feet were slick. The walls carried a sheen of reflective moisture.

The end of the hall opened to a larger room. Shelves lined the walls, and three backless wooden benches sat in the center of the room. One shelf contained two piles of folded clothes, but the rest of the room was bare.

She sat on a bench and removed her shoes and stockings. It had been a while since her feet had felt the air, and the smell that wafted up confirmed the fact. It felt odd disrobing in an empty room where anyone could enter at any time. It seemed more normal when the bathhouse was full. Then, she was invisible, lost in the crowd.

When the last of her clothes had been removed, she wrapped the short towel around her body. Not a moment later, feet shuffled around the corner. Lia glanced up, hoping to find Jeanette and terrified it could be Danik. It was another worker.

The woman wore a faded blue robe. Her gray hair was tied up in a bun, but loose strands fell on either side of her face. She walked with a hunch and tucked a pile of towels under one arm. She didn't even spare a glance or a greeting before she shuffled out the other end of the room.

Lia folded her clothes and set them on a shelf. She left her shoes on the ground, tucked against the wall. After taking a deep breath, she stepped through the opposite doorway.

The grand bathing room always left an impression on her. The expansive open space was the largest room she knew of in Felting, outside of the castle. Four lanterns spread through the room, giving a dim but flickering light. The stone walls around the perimeter were twice her height. From there, a curved vaulted area passed over the water, meeting at a sharp angle where the roof of the building ran across the room like a spine. The pool was nearly as large as the courtyard of the Shadow Knights training facility. Six stone columns spread through the water, emerging from the surface and rising to the vaulted ceiling.

Steam hovered over the surface of the water like a thick fog. Heads of two women peeked through the haze. They soaked in the water, engaged in low conversation. Lia stepped closer, squinting. Her shoulders fell. *Not Jeanette.*

The worker shuffled between benches around the edge of the pool. She picked up towels and straightened a few seats that seemed askew.

Lia crossed the room on the opposite side, taking her farther from the worker as well as the two bathing ladies. Glancing over her shoulder, she confirmed no one else was around. The women were busy talking. The worker was far away, partially blocked by one of the large columns.

Lia pulled the edge of her towel and dropped it onto a chair. Her bare feet made faint slapping noises as they padded through puddles toward the steps that led into the pool. Her exposed skin felt warm in the humid air. Despite the confident front she adopted, and even though no one watched, her cheeks grew warm as she walked.

The first step into the water shocked her foot. Even in the warm room, the heat of the water stood in sharp contrast to the air. After a brief moment to allow her lower legs to adjust, Lia submerged to her neck. She waved her arms, letting the magic of the hot water dance along her skin. A smile covered her face. Finally, she dunked her head.

Weightless in the water, she floated, eyes closed. The comforting sensation enveloped her. She ran her hands through her hair. Crusty patches loosened. Tangles parted for her fingers to work through them. Tossing the strands behind her, she lifted her head and wiped at her eyes. A moan escaped her, the sound of satisfaction echoing through the room.

The women on the far side stopped speaking then smiled in her direction.

Lia waved a dripping hand. "Sorry. It's been a while." Her voice bounced across the water.

The women nodded.

While she waited, she made use of the soap. The level of grit and grime coating her skin only became apparent when it was attacked with the cleansing bar. She scrubbed using her hand and the soap's scratchy texture. The already dark water surrounding her grew cloudier with a tinge of brown.

Once her skin was sufficiently cleansed, she worked up a lather then ran her hands through her hair, massaging it into her scalp and pulling through the length of the strands. Rinsing it left an even darker cloud in the water.

The two women at the far end chatted as they exited the water using the opposite steps. They picked up their towels and dried before heading to the changing room.

Lia leaned back and rested her head against the stone edge of the pool. She allowed herself to float, her toes barely touching the bottom. Her eyes drifted to the ceiling where mosaic images of mountains and flowers stared down in bright colors.

The emptiness felt odd. During the day, the bathhouse could be filled with dozens of women. They came to clean, but the social time was what kept them there. Late at night, visits were rare.

A noise drew her attention toward the changing room. The

worker in blue shuffled out of the large room, leaving Lia completely alone.

She frowned. *Jeanette should have been here by now.*

Despite the warm water, a chill crept up her spine. Bumps formed on her arms.

Maybe it really was Danik. She spun. Water splashed from her turning arms, but no one waited behind her. She glanced around the room. Her pulse increased its rate. Bouncing to her left, Lia peered around the opposite sides of the stone columns. *Empty.*

She shook her head and chuckled lightly, hoping the lighthearted sound would help her feel more settled. *She's probably just running late.*

What do I do if any knights of power show up?

The thought made her breath quicken. Her eyes remained fixed on the doorway to the changing room—the only way into the pool area.

They may have the devion, but I have the origine. I would be fine.

They would be strong, but so would she. Their speed wasn't appreciably faster than hers. She could heal. She could think quickly. She could jump, fight, block, and dodge.

If needed I could—

She paused mid thought, not wanting to consider the implications.

I could hold my breath as long as them.

Her eyes skimmed the water. The lanterns didn't penetrate the surface.

Surely no one could—

Her heart pounded. An irrational fear told her to check.

No, it's silly.

She glanced toward the changing room. Nothing.

Her limbs trembled. Naked, soaking in an enormous pool, the unseen world below the surface suddenly had become a source of terror. She was exposed, raw, and vulnerable.

Jeanette will be here soon. I don't need to—

Her jaw dropped, cutting off her thought. Passing the closest column, a faint ripple rolled across the surface, moving in her direction. Her gut twisted in a knot. She took a deep breath then dropped below the water, keeping her eyes open.

At first, she saw nothing, only the deep hue of dark-blue water, but gradually, something took shape. At first, it was only a glint that caught her eye—light reflecting off something metallic. Soon, the arm that held it was unmistakable. A moment later, the whites of eyes emerged from the gloom—eyes staring at hers with wicked intent. In the dim light, the woman's body was visible. Dark olive skin from head to toe, jet black hair, and a dagger in each hand.

Jade.

Air escaped Lia's mouth, the shock of the woman's presence taking her by surprise. She readied to leap from the water, but by the time her feet planted on the bottom of the pool, the other woman had already propelled toward her. Rather than jump out of the way, Lia was forced to engage.

Moving through water normally felt like running in slow motion, but the origine allowed her to react in impossible ways. Jade thrust a dagger at her chest. Lia batted the devion-fueled strike away with her bare arm, catching the attacker's hand just past the danger of the blade.

The other knife came at her from the opposite side, and Lia ducked. The woman's arm grazed off her back, the rush of water nearly knocking her off balance.

Still underwater, Lia kicked, striking Jade in the chest and knocking her head above the surface. Lia pushed off the stone wall behind her and exploded. She grabbed both of the woman's wrists and pushed her backward. Her feet flew up. Her arms thrashed. Lia slammed the older woman into the nearest stone column, a crack of bones reverberating through the water.

One of the daggers fell from her limp grip, and Lia scooped it up before it had even fallen to the bottom of the pool.

Lia raised her head above the water and sucked in air. While she could hold her breath almost indefinitely, moving with the origine used a lot of energy. She pushed her body back through the water then settled into a crouch, her lone dagger held just above the surface.

Jade winced. She bent over, pressing against her injured body while a hideous grimace covered her face.

Attack! Lia thought. *While she's distracted, go for her! Don't let her heal!*

She hesitated long enough for Jade to lift her eyes. Her look of pain had vanished, and a smirk replaced it. The other dagger lifted, tip first from the water until her entire bare arm floated above the surface.

"What happened to Jeanette?" Lia asked.

Jade chuckled, low and menacing.

Lia understood. *She was never going to be here.*

"We turned them over to the city constables, but I had to step in because they were too timid. It took some persuasion to get her to talk."

"What do you want from me?"

"I'll show you."

Lia's eyes grew until the water of the pool erupted. Jade lunged for her but Lia fought back. Their knives clashed, blocking and striking. Arms punched at faces and chests. Legs kicked at anything they could reach.

The water did little to hamper the fight. The power from the origine and devion resulted in waves cascading in all directions. A spray filled the air. Lia moved so quickly, she dodged the water droplets.

Fueled by the devion, Jade's speed and stamina never seemed to wane. Lia pulled as much origine as she could. She moved as fast as possible, but the other woman was faster. A sinking feeling crept into Lia's gut as the origine depleted.

A lightning-fast swing of an arm sent a splash of water high into the air. Lia jumped back, the dagger barely missing her neck. With a flick of her wrist, she sliced the olive skin of Jade's arm.

A yell echoed in the chamber. Jade stepped back, pulling her arm to her chest. Drops of red plinked into the water. The woman breathed quickly while keeping her eyes on Lia. A shudder and a quick blink of her eyes ended with releasing the injured arm. The cut had already healed. A faint pink line marked the area that should have been an angry red color.

Attack now while she's weak!

Despite her fatigue, Lia lunged. Waves rushed across the pool as her arms scrambled to find a target for her knife. But Jade didn't appear weak. The healing energy she'd used only seemed to have made her faster. Lia's offense quickly turned into a retreat. She edged backward until the stone wall stopped her progress.

Jade sneered then attacked with a fierce abandon. Lia twisted side to side, narrowly glancing away the woman's dagger with her own. A punch landed in her side, knocking her wind out. Lia hunched over. Her lungs screamed for relief. Her heart thumped with a crazed speed. She needed rest. She needed help.

Jade's dagger found her.

"Aargh!" Lia screamed. The knife buried to the hilt just below her shoulder. Searing pain like white fire pierced her nerve endings. Her left arm went limp.

She jabbed frantically with her good arm, which chased away Jade's grip on her weapon. The other woman left it buried in Lia's skin and backed up a step. Lia held her good arm out, keeping the knight of power at bay.

"Good luck fighting me now," Jade taunted.

Lia swung the knife, pushing the woman back another step. She tried to pull the weapon stuck in her shoulder with the other hand, but the arm wouldn't move. She groaned.

"You'll want to heal that wound, won't you?" Jade said. "You'll be dead without the use of both arms."

The origine tried to divert itself to heal her injury, but Lia fought against it. Using it to heal would wipe her out. She'd be helpless.

I could use that pure connection about now. The need was urgent. She was nearly spent. She strained as if squeezing a rock. *Come on!* No surge of power rushed into her. Instead, she cocked the knife in her hand, readying to throw it.

Jade tensed. Her eyes focused on the weapon, ready to dodge or even catch it in midair. She took another step back.

Rather than toss it at the woman, Lia extended her arm up as she threw it. The dagger flung end over end, over the pool to the opposite side of the room. It clattered as it settled on the stones.

"Nice toss." Jade smirked. "Now, what are you going to do?"

Lia narrowed her eyes and grabbed the hilt of the knife stuck in her shoulder with her good hand. She gritted her teeth and growled as she pulled. A wave of nausea washed over her. Her head felt light. When the blade was free, she bared it toward Jade. Her flick of the wrist flung drops of blood that splattered across the woman's face.

Jade cringed and ducked her head in the water to wash it away.

With all the power and speed she could muster, Lia flung the knife.

The sharp blade flipped through the air, turning over as if in slow motion. Jade lifted her head from the water. Her hands tossed back her black hair, but water dripped over her eyes while the knife continued to turn. Jade rubbed the water away, blinked, then jerked to a sudden halt as her own dagger embedded itself in the flesh of her neck.

Her eyes bugged, forming a distant stare. She moved a hand to the weapon and paused, teetering in the pool. Blood ran down her chest, staining the water.

Lia surged forward. Before Jade could act, Lia grasped the handle of the dagger. She gritted her teeth and turned her head away. Her guttural yell covered any sound as she turned the knife.

Jade's body went limp and dropped with a splash. A red stain spread through the water.

Lia gasped for breath. She scanned the room, looking for others.

She jumped from the pool in one motion. Water splashed across the ground, and waves rocked the pool. She extended her arms, using them to keep her balance as the room seemed to shift. She grabbed her towel, pressed it against her wound, then sprinted toward the changing room. A glance back showed Jade's lifeless body bobbing in the pool, face down.

In the changing room, she cradled her pile of clothes and shoes with her weak arm. She didn't bother to put them on but turned up the hallway and ran as fast as she could. She flew through the lobby. The woman at the front desk yelled as a wind rushed through the room, rustling a pile of papers.

Lia flung open the door and entered the dark street. Her pale skin was more visible in the night, but she moved so fast that no one would be able to see her. A glance behind at the first turn showed the door to the bathhouse remained closed. Turning down a side alley, she ducked behind a crate into the shadows and bent over with her hands on her knees. She allowed herself a moment to rest until the blood dripping down the side of her body elevated her nausea.

With the small amount of origine left in her body, she directed the energy to healing her wound. Her body tingled. A warm ball spread from her gut, and her shoulder prickled as the cut and the internal damage healed.

Lia shook, pulling all the energy she could. Her arms trembled. Her teeth clenched. With a gasp, she released the energy and panted anew. The cut had sealed, forming a tight pink line where it had previously dripped blood.

Fighting to stay on her feet, she wiped the blood away with the towel. The cleanup wasn't perfect, but it was better than nothing. Her vision spun. The opposite wall of the alley moved up and down.

Clothes. Must. Get. Them. On.

She rifled through her garments, pulling them on one at a time. Her hand pressed against the alley wall to keep from falling. She paused to lean over her knees, her chest heaving while she gulped for air. She pulled on her shirt then leaned against the wall. Her well of energy was empty. Weak and depleted, she allowed her body to slide down.

Lia blinked, trying to steady what she saw, but the exhaustion took over. Before she knew it, her head hit the ground, and her eyes closed.

19

JAILBREAK

Lia's body was stiff, her eyes heavy.

Where am I?

A nudge brought her mind into focus. Through much effort, she blinked to clear away the cobwebs clouding her vision. A grizzled man with a long, scraggly beard bent over her, tugging at her pockets.

"Hey!"

The man jumped back, eyes wide. He muttered something unintelligible and stepped in the opposite direction. After a moment, he turned and ran.

Lia sat up and stared at the dirty, narrow alleyway. A waning light fell over the tops of the buildings. *Did I sleep through the day?*

It took a moment for the memories to return, and they arrived in a rush. The ambush by Jade. Almost dying. She looked under her shirt and winced at the aftermath of the bloody cleanup. *That man must have thought I was dead.* The cut under her shoulder looked good though—well healed.

Her head pounded with a deep throbbing ache. Her legs complained as she moved them. She wobbled her arms for balance as she stood. The wall spun until she touched it to steady herself.

What do I do now?

The hopeless thought brought a tear to her eye. Raiyn was in prison. Her father was taken. Morgan and his family were missing. She didn't even know what had happened to Marcus. An ache grew in her chest. She pressed against it, trying to relieve the heaviness, but it didn't help. Her sight grew blurry. All her life, something had pointed to what was next. The lack of plan left her empty.

Moving one foot in front of the other, she stumbled into the main street. Curious eyes gave her sidelong glances, but no one approached her. A thick fog hung in the air. Judging from the angle of hazy light, the sun would set soon.

A raindrop hit her head. *Great*, she thought sarcastically. More drops arrived and soon, a steady drizzle soaked her head and clothes. People in the streets threw up hoods, but she had none to wear.

I need to get the book. I need to rescue everyone. But I can't possibly do it on my own.

The sight of the Felting jail before her caused her feet to stop. She blinked as she stared at the windowless, stone structure. Discolored streaks ran down the walls.

Where the constables work, she thought. *I wonder if Morgan and his family are there?*

She pulled open the front door and entered the jail's cramped lobby. A second door stopped her from going farther, but a barred window revealed four cells lining the back wall of the building and several desks filling the rest of the open room.

Two of the cells were empty. One contained a hairy man with a long beard. He leaned against the bars of his cell, muttering and hitting his head against the metal.

She sucked in a breath when she viewed the last cell. Morgan sat on a bench. One arm draped around his wife, who leaned her head into him. The other arm wrapped around his children. His chin lifted up in a display that announced he was proud of his choices.

"What do you want?"

Lia jumped. A constable stared through the bars at her from his desk with a frown on his face. "I, um . . ."

Morgan head turned. His eyes grew wide as he caught sight of her.

"I'm here to see, uh . . ."

"The Fensters?" the constable offered. "Johnny Grizz?"

Her mind raced, considering the implications of announcing she was there for Morgan's family. *This was a stupid idea.*

"I'm here for Johnny. He's my, uh . . . uncle. Could I speak with him?"

The man's eyebrows raised. "Johnny Grizz is your uncle?"

She swallowed. "Yes."

His shrug eased her tension. The scraping of his chair filled the room when he stood.

Jeanette and Morgan both sat up straight and watched her silently while the constable approached the door to the lobby. A heavy click resonated before the door pulled open with a creak.

Lia passed through the door.

The uniformed man extended an arm toward the bearded man banging his head on the bars. "Knock yourself out but keep an arm's length from the bars."

Lia nodded. Her eyes danced around the room, looking for knights of power lurking in the corners. Lanterns hung on wall hooks of both ends of the room, giving a flickering light to the otherwise dim space. A ring of keys rested on a hook at the edge of the man's desk. Two other constables watched as she navigated between the furniture to approach the man's cell.

What do I do?

In the next enclosure, Morgan roused the kids. They remained seated on the bench but sat straight and alert.

Lia's path ended at Johnny's cell. His rhythmic banging stopped when she arrived. His chin lifted, and strands of hair parted to reveal two blood-shot eyes. He cocked his head.

"Um, hello." Lia's weak voice filled the otherwise quiet room. "How are you doing?"

Johnny's eyes narrowed. "Who are you?" His voice grated like a man who'd been yelling all day.

Her eyes flicked to either side. She sensed the constables watching. "I'm, uh, your niece, Bridgette. I came to check on you."

"I don't have a niece."

She chuckled and felt beads of sweat dotting her forehead. "Don't be silly. Of course you do. I'm your brother's daughter."

What am I doing? Should I just knock these guys out and grab the keys?

Johnny straightened. "I don't have a brother, either."

All three constables were standing. They each stepped closer to her.

A crooked smile washed over the hairy man's face. "But I'm happy to get to know you, Bridgette." Two missing teeth revealed a conspicuous gap on the right side of his mouth.

"What's your intention with Johnny Grizz?" the first constable asked. He stood closer than before and rested a hand on his sword.

"My intentions?" Lia asked. Her words failed her. She blanked at a plausible explanation, so she decided to take a different approach. She wrinkled her nose and sniffed. "Do you smell that?"

The constable's eyebrows quirked.

"Is something burning?"

"I don't smell anything."

Morgan's family gathered by the bars of their cell.

Lia exaggerated sniffing and turned toward the far corner. "I think something's burning. Do you all not smell it?"

The constables looked at each other then took tentative steps toward the indicated corner.

When their backs faced Lia, she pulled from the origine. Power flooded into her body, quickening her limbs and strengthening her muscles. She sprinted toward the opposite end of the room, moving faster than anyone would be able to see. Far from the other men, she grabbed a stack of papers off a desk, wadded them up, and stuffed them under a wooden chair. Finally, she grabbed the lantern off its hook and threw it against a chair leg. While the object hurtled toward the ground, she raced back into her position in front of Johnny's cell.

When she stopped using the origine to speed up, the glass from the lantern shattered, filling the room with a loud crash.

The men spun toward the noise. "What was that?"

Flames surged as the oil caught fire and splattered across the paper and wood. The room grew brighter, and a thick smoke puffed into the air.

"There!" Lia shouted. "It was on that end."

The three constables shouted in unison and ran toward the flames.

Lia didn't waste any time. She snatched the keys from the desk ring and flew to the Fensters' cell. Her fingers moved so fast, the door clicked open before the men even arrived at the fire. She pulled the barrier open then stopped using the origine.

"Go! Go!" She pointed toward the door to the lobby.

The Fensters took a moment to register what had happened, but soon, Morgan picked up his daughter and urged his wife and son forward. They ran toward the exit as Lia turned to the constables.

Two of the guards beat the flames with bundles of cloth. They kicked the chair over and pounded the fire, squelching the heat and light that fought to grow.

The third guard caught her movement over his shoulder. "Hey!" he shouted. "You can't—"

Lia interrupted his objection by whirling in and grabbing his arms from behind and pulling up. The man bent forward, immobilized by the awkward and painful position she put him in.

"Argh!" he yelled.

Lia yanked his arms, dragging him across the floor toward the open cell. When they reached the opening, she flung his form, twirling into the cell. His legs stumbled, keeping him upright only moments before his head slammed into the stone wall and he collapsed to the floor.

The bright light from the far side of the room dimmed as the men extinguished the last of the budding flames.

"Don't move!" a constable shouted toward Morgan's family.

"Go!" Lia urged. "I'll meet you out there."

The man pulled his sword and rushed her. "No, you won't."

He crossed the room and lunged the bare blade at Lia's stomach.

The blade never reached her. She stepped to the side and chopped his hand. His grip failed and the hilt fell into her hand. Gripping the fresh weapon, she slammed the pommel into the man's head. He cried out and stumbled backward. While he held his face, Lia shoved him through the open cell door.

"You!" Lia pointed the blade toward the final man.

"H-how did you do that?"

The man held his sword up, but his shaking arm gave Lia the confidence she needed. She pointed her weapon at him and prodded him toward the cell. He backpedaled until all three constables fit inside the enclosure. A rattling clang filled the room as she slammed the door.

"Come on!" Morgan urged. He held open the door to the lobby.

Lia dropped the ring of keys. After a glance to ensure the fire was out, she joined Morgan in running out the door.

Spitting rain hit her in the face as soon as she stepped outside.

"Walk calmly," Morgan said. He led the way, keeping his eyes down and feet shuffling.

Lia followed. She kept a look over her shoulder and around each corner. The Fensters flowed through the city without a halting cry or flash of sword stopping them. After turning down a narrow alley, a cry of "Jeanette!" called from an open second-story window.

"They're here," Jeanette breathed.

Thundering steps echoed through the building wall until a door with flaking red paint burst open. A man and woman appearing in their fifties wrapped both Morgan and Jeanette in brief but vigorous hugs.

"Are you all right?" the woman asked.

"We feared the worst!" the man added.

"We're safe." Morgan nodded toward Lia. "We had help escaping, but now we need to hide."

"Of course, of course." The man pulled the door wider and waved his hand to direct them through the opening. "Come in, quickly."

Jeanette held her children's hands as she followed the woman upstairs.

Lia swallowed around the lump in her throat. She blinked to clear her eyes of the rain.

Morgan passed through the doorway but stopped when he saw Lia wasn't moving. "They're friends," he said. "It's safe. Come on."

Lia's feet felt rooted.

His brows pinched. "Are you not coming?"

She managed a tight shake of her head. "I can't. Veron and Raiyn are still out there. They need me. Plus, I can't stay with you anymore. I put you in too much danger as it was."

Morgan's face fell. After a beat, he nodded. "I understand." He gazed up the stairs as if watching his family disappear up the passage. With a sigh he turned back to Lia and straightened. "How can I help?"

Lia smiled, a warmth filling her body from the displayed loyalty. "I see why my father likes you so much." She shook her head. "Thank you, but . . . no. You've done more than enough."

"Where are you going?" the man holding the door asked.

"She needs to find her father and a friend. They've been taken by the Knights of Power."

"I have no idea where they are," Lia added.

The man blanched.

She sucked in air. "What is it? What do you know?"

"I don't know it's them, but—" He shifted his hips. "There's something happening at the Feldan Arena tonight."

A sinking sensation ran through her gut.

"It's billed as the first night spectacle. Word is it will be something people have never seen before."

Morgan's shoulders fell. "It has to be them."

Lia nodded. She swallowed again, but the lump wouldn't go away. *What is Danik planning?*

20

A SPECIAL EXHIBITION

Raiyn stood when he heard footsteps. He walked to the barred window and peered out as the guard, Brannon, rounded the corner, carrying a torch. Hope spiked until he saw the man's expression.

"Did you see him?" Raiyn whispered. "They brought him in yesterday a few hours after the hanging. He passed by right there!"

Brannon pulled out his keys but didn't lift his face.

"You were about to free me the other day. All you wanted was for me to prove Veron Stormbridge was alive, and now I can. He's here in this dungeon! Brannon, come on!"

The keys jangled in the lock, and Raiyn stepped back. After a moment, the door pivoted on its hinges. The guard's mouth drooped, his eyes filled with sorrow.

Raiyn sighed. The tension in his shoulders faded. "You *did* see him . . . but you're not letting me go."

The guard grabbed Raiyn's shackled hands and inspected them. "I'm sorry Raiyn, but I have bills to pay. People like me can't afford to take up causes. It's out of my hands."

The flame from the torch flickered close to his face. "What are you doing with me?"

Brannon pulled his short sword and pointed down the passage. "To the end of the hall."

Raiyn swallowed hard. He didn't move until the sharp tip poked his back. He took shuffling steps forward. "Where am I going?"

The guard didn't answer.

At the intersection, Raiyn turned left to backtrack the path he'd taken each time he'd come or gone.

"No." Brannon pulled against his shoulder. "This way."

Raiyn turned around. The guard pointed in the opposite direction. The torch did little to penetrate the gloomy depths of the narrow passage. "Where does this go? Am I going to where Veron is?"

His only answer was the sword again pressing against his back.

The new passage was similar to all the others. A moldy smell filled the air. Unseen water dripped in the dark. When they rounded a corner, light from another torch danced ahead. Two guards waited with swords drawn. A hand held onto a prisoner's shoulder.

Veron?

Lia's father looked their way. His hair had been cropped short. He barely resembled himself, but the eyes were unmistakable. A mirthless smile formed on his face. "We tried to rescue you," Veron called when Raiyn drew closer.

"Quiet!" A guard hit the butt of his sword across Veron's neck.

Veron cringed and groaned.

"You see who that is?" Raiyn whispered over his shoulder. "We're the last of the Shadow Knights, and we're the only people who can stop Danik."

Brannon didn't answer.

When they arrived at the other guards, the men holding Veron took the lead and continued along the dark passage. No one spoke.

With the dungeons deep under the castle, Raiyn tried to imagine where they were headed. *Could we be outside the city walls? Surely we're well past the castle grounds.*

A stairwell with an iron grate emerged in the gloom. One of the guards unlocked it and took the lead. The steps wound up, higher and higher. Finally, the staircase opened to another metal gate.

Raiyn waited on the steps with Brannon at his back on the narrow staircase. A clank preceded the rusty groan of the gate opening. The party of five moved into a square room with a low ceiling. No windows adorned the walls. One other open doorway led down a passage with flanking torches set into the walls.

In the center of the room, a wooden stand contained dozens of weapons: swords, axes, staffs, knives, a mace, and spears.

Raiyn's eyes widened.

"Choose one and then wait here." The lead guard held up a hand before walking down the passage.

Raiyn glanced at Veron before stepping toward the weapons stand. He ran his hand across the swords and knives. The steel was old and dented. One sword contained a heavy amount of rust around the guard.

"What will we use these for?" Veron asked.

No one replied.

Raiyn settled on a battle-axe. It was shorter than what he had trained with, but the head was sharp, and the weight was balanced. Veron chose a two-handed sword.

While staring at the axe blade, Raiyn tilted his head. A dull roar seemed to fill the walls, coming from all directions. "What is that?"

A faint metallic smell filled the air, combined with the fresh scent of rain. Brannon kept his sword up, partially alert. His eyes rested anywhere but on Raiyn.

"What's going to happen, Brannon?" Raiyn asked.

The guard shuffled his feet and looked farther away. "Quiet," he said.

Boots on stone drew their attention along the passage. A new man returned with the other guard. Raiyn's stomach twisted. He recognized the man—one of the knights of power who had patrolled the square. *Broderick, I think.*

Broderick stood before Raiyn and grabbed his chains. His arms jerked forward. Broderick pulled at the clasps on his wrist and turned them over. Appearing satisfied, he dropped his arms and did the same to Veron. "Good."

He looked Veron in the eyes. "Several knights of power will have their eyes on you. If either of you raise your voice and say anything about the Shadow Knights or Danik, you'll both be gutted so fast, you won't even see us coming. Understood?"

Raiyn nodded along with Veron.

Broderick turned to the other guard. "They're ready. Send them out."

Raiyn's insides turned watery. "Out where?

All the guards avoided eye contact, but Veron returned his gaze. His face held a weary look. His shoulders drooped.

A sword pushed against his back. "Go on," Brannon said.

Raiyn and Veron walked side by side down the passage. With each torch they passed, the invisible roar grew.

"Is Lia safe?" Raiyn whispered.

"I think so," Veron answered. "We were escaping through the cistern tunnel when they caught me from behind and dragged me back. I'm pretty sure she got free."

"I got the pick from Marcus. Thanks for trying."

"We saw you almost had it, but the whole thing was a trap. Danik wants all three of us."

Raiyn nodded toward Veron's head. "Nice haircut, by the way."

Veron chuckled. "I think it's their effort to disguise me. Whatever's coming, Danik doesn't want people to recognize me."

"Speaking of which . . ." Raiyn glanced up at the flickering light playing across the low ceiling. "Do you have any idea what's coming?"

Their feet crunched the sand and pebbles of the stone floor, and the flames whipped. "I have an idea," Veron finally replied.

The passage ended at another metal gate. Two guards stood on either side of the barrier, holding it open. Raiyn passed through the gate first, and two sensations hit him at once.

First was the chanting. The dull roar was now oppressive and coming from all directions. It sounded like hundreds or thousands of people shouting in unison. Second was the rain. Beyond the gate, water fell from the sky, steady and thick, making visibility low.

The sky was dark, a potent combination of rain clouds and a lack of sun. He counted five covered lanterns. Set in elevated positions, the lights formed a circular shape and were shielded from the rain. In the stands, spectators crowded shoulder to shoulder. Most had hoods to cover their heads, but their moods weren't deterred by the weather.

Below the stands, separated by a tall stone wall, a field of grass and mud spread out. Puddles formed as the rain fell.

Raiyn walked forward. The unsettled feeling in his gut grew. "The Feldan Arena," he breathed.

Veron's voice cut through the rain. "If they make us fight each other, kill me quickly."

Raiyn spun. "What? No! I'm not going to kill you. They can't *make* us fight each other."

"We may not have a choice."

"Citizens of Felting!" a voice boomed through the downpour. It seemed unnaturally loud, as if amplified.

Raiyn turned and looked up. A covered patio held more lanterns, illuminating a gathering of men and women. At the front, barely protected from the rain, Danik's hand held the attention of the spectators.

"We return to the arena today with a special exhibition. I know you were disappointed yesterday by the canceled hanging of Bale's heir—the one who seeks to restore his father's tyrannical rule. We delayed his execution because new information indicated he could be useful. I'm happy to announce, the plan paid off. Not only will the Norshewan prisoner be killed today, but he will be joined by a new traitor."

A rumble grew in the crowd.

"Your Knights of Power captured this man last night. Not only was this man aiding the aspiring Norshewan leader, but we learned he was the man responsible for the murder of King Darcius . . . and for betraying the Shadow Knights."

Raiyn spotted Broderick in the front row of the stands with his hand on his sword. Although he longed to shout out, only a grumble made its way from his throat.

"I promised you all a special treat tonight," Danik continued, "and

I will not disappoint. These prisoners will receive their execution in a way none of you have ever seen before. Behold!"

Raiyn's pulse pounded. Nerves left him jittery. He gripped his axe with both hands and looked where the king pointed. A large, heavy grate stood twice as tall as a man. The entire crowd looked in its direction and waited.

"What do you think's going to happen?" Raiyn asked.

Veron turned, gazing at each section of the arena. "I don't think we're bait for Lia."

"No?"

"If that's what they wanted, they would pick something with better light, so she'd be easier to spot."

"You think she's here?" Raiyn asked.

"I hope not."

Several dozen more lit torches appeared around the circular arena. Soldiers carrying them descended the steps and stopped where the seats met the top of the wall. They placed the torches on mounted stands in alcoves, where the rain wouldn't snuff them out. When they were in place, a loose ring of fire blocked the fighting ring from the spectators.

"Do they expect us to jump that wall without the origine?" Raiyn asked. "That would be impossible."

A deep rumble filled the arena, and Veron and Raiyn spun to face the grate again. With a metallic clank and a shudder, the grate slowly lifted.

"Maybe it's not *us* the torches are meant to keep in place," Veron said.

The barrier continued up, and an inky blackness waited behind it. Raiyn squinted to see what was to come, but nothing emerged.

The rain increased its steady drumming. Raiyn's clothes were soaked through. His feet rested in puddles, but he didn't bother to move.

A loud clang filled the night, and the gate stopped its ascent. Veron lowered his hips and bent his knees. "Come on." He crossed the arena floor, moving to the center of the space.

Raiyn followed, his axe wavering.

"No matter what comes out of that hold, we need to work together," Veron said.

Raiyn nodded, his trembling lips unable to form a response.

A throaty growl rumbled from the darkness. A rotten smell of death drifted on the wind and turned Raiyn's insides to water. He fought to keep from gagging.

"What is that?" he whispered.

Veron lifted his sword above his head. He bent his knees and dropped into dragon stance.

The ground shook. The torches reflecting in the puddles bounced from the impact of something large. The growl grew more pronounced as a snout protruded past where the heavy gate hung suspended in the air. Long fangs curved down either side of the creature's massive mouth. It opened its jaws and unleashed a hideous roar. Two rows of jagged teeth shone in the torchlight.

"What. Is. That?" Raiyn repeated with a waver in his voice.

Veron didn't answer, but only tightened the grip on his sword. The beast moved forward, the ground shaking with each step. Spines stuck out of its head and ran down its neck.

"Is-is that a—" Raiyn's words left him. "Is that a . . . ?"

"Yes." Veron's voice finally shook. "That is a valcor."

"SPREAD OUT!" Veron's heart pounded as he pointed to his side.

Raiyn moved without hesitation. "I guess they are real, after all. You and Chelci fought one of these before, right?"

"Kind of." Veron remembered himself in Nasco, exhausted from having spent the origine. "Chelci did most of the work, though."

"Do they have any weaknesses?"

"Inside the mouth. It's soft and unprotected there."

"I-in-inside its mouth? How are we supposed to—"

Raiyn quieted when the beast turned its head in his direction.

I wish Chelci were here, Veron thought, fear coursing through his veins.

The animal stepped farther into the arena. The massive paws left imprints in the mud, its weight pushing into the soft ground. Water beat on its head then rolled down its neck and body. Steady drops dripped from the curved fangs protruding from its mouth. A guttural snuffle blasted from its nostrils.

Raiyn shifted his axe between hands, and Veron held his sword higher. With the valcor watching Raiyn, Veron's eyes shifted to the stone plinth at his side.

"Use the columns," Veron said. "We could never beat it on even ground."

Raiyn hurried to the nearest pedestal. Moving his body to the far side, he set his axe on the flat top then grabbed the edge. His jump wasn't enough. His feet slid down the side. "Give me a hand," he said. "I'll get on top."

Veron moved to his side. He kept his eyes on the valcor while forming a step with his hands.

Raiyn used the boost to clamber onto the plinth. He scooped up his weapon then bared it toward the animal. "I'm not sure how much this will help." His voice shook.

The valcor drew closer, and a rumbling growl filled the air. A fresh waft of decay turned Veron's nose. His chest vibrated. He kept his sword up with the plinth in front of him. He wiped across his face, pushing the water out of his eyes. With his hair and clothes soaked, there was no respite from the elements.

The animal lunged. It swiped with a front paw and snapped its jaws. Veron jumped to the side, glancing his sword against the animal's paw and moving around the pillar. A large chunk broke off the pillar from the beast's powerful blow. The front paws didn't concern Veron as much as the back ones did. Three enormous claws curved at the end of both back legs. Veron recalled the scene in Nasco and swallowed heavily. *I remember what those things can do.*

Despite the heavy rain, cheers from the crowd filled the air. Used to the people of Felting cheering for him and all the Shadow Knights, hearing cheers for him to be ripped apart by a monster was a strange feeling.

A fierce yell pierced the rain as an axe blade came down on the valcor's head. What should have killed most animals merely bounced off the thick hide and long spines that protected its head.

"Gah!" Raiyn yelled from above. "It didn't even make a scratch!"

The valcor turned its attention to the top of the column.

"Raiyn, look out!" Veron yelled.

The animal lifted its neck, ignoring Veron, to focus on the threat from above.

Raiyn held his axe in a forward grip. His feet were shoulder-width apart, planted on top of the plinth. With its neck extended, the beast nearly matched his eye level. He shouted as he jabbed, but the head of the axe never came close to hitting it.

The valcor lowered its head close to the ground and appeared to shrug its shoulders.

What's it doing? Veron wondered.

The ground shook as the animal pushed off the ground with its front feet. It reared up on its hind legs, standing taller than two men together. A bellowing roar filled the night.

Raiyn shrank back at the fierce blast of air. His axe wavered, and his jaw hung open. There was nowhere for him to go. He was unprotected and vulnerable. "Maybe getting up here wasn't the best idea."

Veron used the moment to strike. He rushed forward, within the valcor's striking range. He gripped his sword with both hands and yelled as he jabbed it at the beast's exposed underside. Trying by instinct to find the origine, no extra power supplemented him. His muscles were strong, his blow was ferocious, but the tip of his sword merely glanced off the thick skin of the animal's belly. Veron stumbled, his expected killing blow failing to do any damage.

The valcor glanced down and huffed.

"Here!" Veron stepped away from the pillar. "Come and get me!"

As if deciding between the two targets, the animal looked between Veron and Raiyn.

"Ha! Here!" Veron beat the flat of his blade against his chest, but his distraction did little good.

The monster's lips curled back, exposing the fullness of its rows of teeth. Its shoulders bulged before the massive right limb swiped in a blurred swat.

Raiyn had nowhere to hide. The front paw pounded his midsection, sending him flying off the plinth.

"Raiyn!"

His body slammed against the closest arena wall.

Veron ran to his side, splashing through puddles and keeping his sword pointed in the direction of the beast. The young man's eyes fluttered. He held his side, coughing while his face twisted in a grimace. "Are you all right?" Veron asked. "Can you get up?"

"I think it cracked my—" Raiyn's eyes widened. "Look out!"

Veron had a vague awareness of the ground rumbling as he spun. The valcor flew through the air with one of its back legs extended. Veron rolled to the side as claws as long as his hand reached for his stomach. His spin was fast, but not fast enough. A white-hot searing pain ripped down his arm, and his sword was knocked away.

After tearing across the flesh, the valcor's claws slammed into the stone wall, puncturing three holes in the ancient masonry. Its head was so tall, it nearly extended over the wall separating the arena from the crowd.

Spectators shouted, backing away from the monster, but the torch mounted on the top caused it to shrink back and return to the ground.

Veron yelled through clenched teeth, staggering away. He lifted his arm. An angry red slash ran across his tricep from back to front. Rain made the blood run swiftly, dripping down his arm and falling to the mud. He grabbed the wound and held it tight. Spots flashed at the corner of his vision from the pain.

Raiyn had rolled in the same direction. He groaned by Veron's feet, scooting across the ground, away from the monster.

Where's my sword? Veron's head jerked in each direction.

The valcor had turned to them, its eyes narrowed and teeth bared. The guttural growl grew.

Veron moved backward, but the valcor matched him step for step. His stomach dropped when his back ran into a wall. *Nowhere to go!*

Battered and bruised, Raiyn staggered to his feet. Weaponless, the two men stood tall, trapped.

The valcor's spines stood on end. Its fangs seemed to shake with anticipation. The massive legs flexed. Its body dipped, ready to pounce. Veron clenched his teeth and braced himself.

The shadowy form of a person dropped between Veron and the beast. He couldn't make out any features, but then a head raised. Soaking wet, shoulder-length, brown hair hung on either side of their face. Sopping clothes looked torn and dirty. Veron's heart pounded when the silhouette of a sword raised on their left and a long haft connected to the head of an axe raised on the right.

"Back off!" The shout carried over the rain.

Veron would recognize that voice anywhere.

Lia!

21

BATTLE IN THE NIGHT

L ia dug her feet into the soft ground. Both hands gripped the weapons Raiyn and Veron had lost, and she stretched them toward the face of the valcor. The smell was worse up close. Each grunt it exhaled sent a wave of rancid air into her face.

The animal looked perplexed, but the weapons didn't appear to frighten it. Its snout wriggled, as if sniffing the new arrival.

Origine flowed through Lia's body. Her limbs ached to move, to use the well of energy that waited inside. She had remained hidden in the stands as long as she could, but the sight of Raiyn and her father about to be killed became too much.

"Lia!" her father yelled from over her shoulder. "What are you doing? You're giving Danik what he wants!"

Her stomach twisted at his words, which she knew to be true. Rather than respond, she tuned him out, keeping her focus on the animal. The beast wasn't backing up. Its feet shook the ground as it neared. The deep gurgle in its throat grew louder.

She tightened her grip on the weapons. "I said . . . back!" She lunged forward, using the origine to bring speed and strength to her limbs while she attacked in a flurry of power.

Lia spun. The axe and sword became a whirling circle of steel.

The weapons struck the animal against its legs, on its snout, and on the side of the torso. She extended her arms in a dangerous display of ferocity.

A hideous shriek filled the air, and the valcor retreated several steps. Lia chased after it, driving it back, farther from the others.

Wielding one weapon per arm hampered the torque she wanted to achieve. Even with the origine, she struggled to get enough power behind each swing. When the axe bit into its flank and stuck, the wooden haft pulled from her grip.

The valcor twisted its head to look at the axe. It roared and snapped its jaws at the stuck weapon, grabbing the end of it with its teeth. Wood splintered as the handle ripped away. The axe head fell with a thud to the ground, and the animal spit out the splintered wooden shaft.

Lia moved both hands to the sword hilt.

Seeing she was down a weapon, the valcor appeared to regain some confidence. It lowered its head in a crouch and held its ground, stepping sideways. Lia matched its steps.

How did Mother kill one of these without the origine? A vague recollection of hearing she chopped off its head came to mind. A lighter-colored area on its neck showed in the dim light when it stretched its head forward. *That must be it.*

Pulling from her well of energy, she stepped forward and swung with both hands. Despite her lightning fast attack, the thick neck skin folded back over itself before she could get the sword to it. The blade struck true but didn't even break the surface.

"Go for the mouth!" Raiyn yelled, his voice nearly lost in the rain.

That's right, she remembered. *She stabbed it in its mouth!*

Rain pelted her head. She brushed her hair back and wiped the water from her face. The animal opened its mouth and unleashed a deafening roar. The terrifying sight would normally have frozen her in her tracks, but the view of its open mouth was what she waited for.

Lia rushed forward, sword up. Her heart pounded. She extended her arms, lunging to reach the soft inner pallet. Rows of jagged teeth stared back at her, shaking in the monster's roar. But as her sword arrived, the beast's jaw snapped shut around the end, its bellow cut short.

Lia stared, frozen. The valcor shook its head, ripping the sword from her grip and flinging it above the wall. The weapon clattered somewhere deep in the stands.

"Lia, get out of here!" Veron shouted.

She glanced back. Her father and Raiyn both sprawled against the wall, battered and bleeding. She drew in deep breaths, trying to settle her heart and allow her energy to recover.

"You can't defeat it with your bare hands. Get out of here while you still can."

It's got to have a weakness, she thought. She scanned its massive body looking for something that stood out. *Something I can—* Her eyes stopped, caught by one of the flickering torches mounted on top of the arena wall. *That's it!*

Lia crouched then exploded up, using the origine to propel her body in a leap to the top of the wall. Shocked spectators stared with wide eyes. She grabbed the torch from its alcove then ran along the top of the wall to the next one. With two torches, she dropped back to the arena floor. She bent her knees to soften the fall, and her feet sank into the soft mud.

The valcor stared at her, but its confident stance was gone. Its head ducked in a hesitant display. Lia walked forward, holding the torches ahead of her. The rain had lessened, but the danger of the fire going out was still very real.

"Back up!" she shouted, waving the flames in front of its face as she grew closer.

The animal snarled, baring its teeth. After a short show of defiance, it thudded backward, one step at a time.

Lia's heart leaped. She moved forward, slowly. Each arm extended as far as she could reach, penning the animal behind the fire. A half-hearted swipe of a paw showed its reluctance to engage the light. Lia quickened her pace, and the animal shuffled faster.

A spurt of water splashed onto one of the torches, dousing the light. Lia gasped. The monster paused its retreat and angled its head.

"Back!" she shouted anew, waving the remaining flame.

The beast continued its retreat.

Lia leaned to the side to see around the massive animal. *Almost there. Just a bit farther.*

The valcor bumped against the wall and slid to its side. Lia moved with it until its rear angled into the tunnel from where it originally came. A glance to its side made the animal stop. It snarled again and half-lunged. The snapping teeth made Lia step back, but she immediately pressed forward again. A yell and a thrust with the torch made the beast jump, backing into the darkness of the passage. Soon, its face, teeth, and a few spines were all she could make out in the dim light.

The rain stopped. She stood at the edge of the tunnel where the roof blocked the rain. She looked up. The gate hung above her, heavy iron lattice suspended in the air.

Lia checked the passage again, but the monster was gone. She held the torch out and saw nothing but the corridor fading to blackness.

Her eyes returned to the wall where a chain led above. She took a step toward the arena floor to follow its path.

Clear of the overhang, the rain returned, spitting against her face. She wiped her face and stared up. *There!* A lever stuck up from the top of the wall, manned by a guard.

Suddenly, her surroundings went dark. A hiss of steam permeated the air. Lia stared at her torch, wet and dark.

The guttural rumble returned. She peered into the darkness of the tunnel but couldn't see the animal. The ground shook, slow at first then speeding up. She tossed the torch down. No more weapons. No more fire.

The valcor's face appeared, faint but rapidly approaching.

Lia bent her knees then looked up, sighting the lever. With an explosive launch, she burst off the ground and flew into the air. Rain sprayed her face. Wind blew through her hair. She squinted to be able to see. At the apex of her leap, a slack-jawed guard, eye to eye with her, stared from on top of the wall. She stretched her arm to its fullest reach, then wrapped it around the lever and pulled. A heavy catch gave way. She released the lever as she plummeted back to the arena floor. Lia hit the muddy ground, again using the origine to absorb the impact.

Chains rattled and clanked. The ground shook. The immense form of the valcor had nearly arrived. It dug its claws into the ground, running at full speed. Its jaws thrashed. Its neck stretched forward.

Lia turned a shoulder in, bracing for a momentous impact. The beast was nearly to her. She closed her eyes and flexed her muscles.

Slam!

She flinched, her eyes still closed.

A horrendous sound shrieked through the night, deafening from steps away.

She opened her eyes. The iron gate had slammed down, digging into the soft ground with its massive bulk. The valcor thrashed against the metal lattice. Its teeth chewed at the holes. Its body pressed against the gate as if it could move the barrier.

Lia exhaled. She bent over, breathing deeply while her lungs sucked in air.

The crowd exploded into applause. Whistles and cheers filled the air. Clapping and stomping of feet grew to a deafening level, amplified by the circular shape of the arena.

The beast pounded one final time against the metal then shrank back into the darkness, its guttural rumble receding.

The applause faded—slow at first, then suddenly stopping.

Lia's ears prickled. The rain had stopped. The hairs on her neck stood on end. She spun.

Surrounding her, penning her against the entrance to the valcor's lair stood the four remaining knights of power—Cedric, Broderick, Nicolar, and Alton. Cedric held a crossbow, and the rest extended swords.

Lia looked past them to where two regular guards held swords against Veron's and Raiyn's chests. Her father's shoulders slumped. A hint of gratitude mixed with sorrow on his face.

"Kill them all!" Danik's voice boomed from somewhere in the arena.

Lia's blood ran hot. Her ex-best friend hid in the darkness and ordered her execution the first chance he had.

The warriors before her stepped in.

"No!" she shouted. "Think of the crowd!"

The fighters straightened and stopped moving.

"If you speak about who you are, your friends will be dead before you finish your sentence," Nicolar warned in an urgent whisper.

Lia paused for only a second. "King Danik!" She walked forward, toward the swords. Her stomach twisted in knots as she put on her most confident face and motioned for the men directly before her to part.

Slowly, Broderick and Nicolar moved back, giving her room to step away from the valcor's pen. They kept their swords up but allowed Lia to walk between them.

She held her breath and puffed out her chest. Her steps squished in the mud. She refused to glance at the sword tips a mere hand's breadth from her face.

Danik's robed form took shape above, illuminated by a torch next to his covered box where he watched.

"Your Majesty, you promised these people spectacles, did you not?"

Danik didn't reply. He held his hand to his chin and stared back at her.

A rumble grew in the stands.

Lia turned and gestured to the grate. "This . . . monster was entertaining, but is this how you reward the people of Felting? You kill off those who fight and defeat it? They don't want to see winners executed. They want to see epic battles between well-matched fighters."

Cries of assent dotted the crowd.

"This wasn't even your fight."

Lia spun.

Nicolar had taken a step and inclined his head forward. His voice was quiet, not projecting to the crowd. "You had your shot, Lia. You turned him down. Why would he keep you alive?"

"Because he wants to make the people happy."

Nicolar shrugged. "They're happy."

Lia turned her attention back to the crowd and projected from deep in her chest. "What could be more exciting than me—the Valcor Conqueror—fighting one of the knights of power? A chance for King Danik to show off his elite force."

Tentative cheers grew in the stands.

Nicolar sniffed and shifted his weight.

"What do you say, people of Felting? Do you want to see a battle of champions?" She paused to give the people a chance to cheer. "Or do you want to see us executed after giving the king a victory?"

The cheers turned into boos.

Lia turned to Nicolar and lowered her voice. "I'll fight any one of you if you're brave enough to face me."

"We want to see the Conqueror!" a voice called from the stands.

"Bracelets on or off?"

Lia spun.

A set of stairs had opened where Danik stepped from the stands down to the arena. His robe trailed behind him. A sword dangled at his hip, and four guards flanked him. Murmurs grew in the crowd.

Lia cocked her head. "You choose."

Knights of power surrounded her, pressing in with drawn swords as the king approached.

Danik paused, his eyes scanning her up and down. "You're looking . . . nice."

She smirked at his sarcastic remark then raised her voice to address the crowd. "The king can choose his greatest fighter. I will fight any of them with any combination of weapons. If I win . . ." She nodded to Raiyn and Veron. ". . . my friends and I go free. If I lose, we die."

She could read Danik's eyes. He wore a smile, but a frustrated anger simmered behind it.

The crowd began to chant, "Con-que-ror! Con-que-ror! Con-que-ror!"

Lia raised an eyebrow and pursed her lips, waiting.

Danik nodded. He glanced between his knights then up to the spectators. Finally, he held up his hands. The chant quieted. "A battle of champions between this . . . Valcor Conqueror and my greatest fighter."

Shouts of approval echoed from each direction.

"Tomorrow morning!" he bellowed. "Here in the arena at first light!"

"Who will fight me?" Lia asked.

Danik turned to her and squared his shoulders. "My greatest fighter, of course." He lifted his hands and raised his voice. "I accept the challenge!"

A roar exploded from the crowd.

Lia craned her neck, her brows pushed together. "You?"

Danik lowered his voice. "What? Are you worried?"

Lia narrowed her eyes.

He leaned forward and dropped his voice to a whisper. "Bracelets on."

Danik turned to Nicolar. "Put the prisoners back in the dungeon but leave her here." He pointed to the center of the arena between the four plinths. "Chain her, and guard her with eight men." He turned back to Lia. "Tomorrow, we battle."

22

ROYAL COMBAT

A shiver jolted Lia awake and her eyes flicked open. A breeze drifted through the arena. Her torn clothes left bare skin exposed to the air. The dampness of the garments sucked what little warmth her body retained. With her arms wrapped around her knees, she pulled them closer. She sat on the lone grassy spot while mud and puddles surrounded her. Unwilling to lay in the mud, Lia had sat up with her knees tucked the entire night. The brief moments of sleep were interrupted by balance checks and gusts of wind.

A thick fog covered the ground like a blanket. Gray morning light spilled over the top of the Feldan Arena, giving the ring a glowing, ethereal feeling. A red bird flitted across the ground, emerging from the haze. It dipped its beak into a puddle then pecked at a grassy section.

Lia stretched her neck and looked to the side. The disinterested guards had remained standing, surrounding her the entire night. The man closest to her yawned. He covered his mouth and squinted.

"When does it start?" Her unused voice cracked.

The guards flinched and straightened, but none of them replied.

A door opened on the arena wall, drawing Lia's gaze. A lone man with a thick beard and graying hair passed through the doorway. A dark-brown cloak hung off his shoulders and trailed behind him. When he grew closer, the familiar features came into focus.

Lia cleared her throat. "High Lord Bilton. What do you want?"

The ex-friend of her grandfather strode across the arena floor. His face held a hard line. His feet splashed through puddles without pause. The guards parted as the city leader approached.

The chains connected to Lia's wrists and ankles jangled as she struggled to her feet and stretched her cramped limbs.

"Lia," Bilton said, "I've come to wish you good luck in your upcoming fight."

Her eyes narrowed. "Are you serious? You betrayed my grandfather—your true king. You turned your back on my father, who spent his life bringing stability to Terrenor. And now you wish me luck?"

Bilton's face didn't falter.

"I thought you cared about Feldor?"

"I do!" Bilton's face flashed red. "The kingdom is best served by supporting the king."

"Danik *murdered* the king!"

"Danik *is* the king!"

Lia stared at the high lord until the older man began to squirm.

"Nothing can change that now. I support whomever I need, in order to get by."

"You mean whoever will keep you rich."

Bilton shrugged. "I'm sorry about your father and grandfather."

"Is that why you came? To clear your conscience?"

"You realize you may win today, don't you?"

"Like it matters," Lia said. "Danik will have a plan. He's not going to let all three of us go."

"You never know," Bilton said. "If you were to get a lucky jab, or a *hard hit* on the wrist—"

The way he emphasized his words then paused caused the hairs on her neck to prickle.

"Don't give up hope, Lia."

Bilton backed away and nodded at the guards. They reformed the circle around her, looking more alert.

Lia narrowed her eyes and watched as the high lord crossed the arena. *What is he up to?*

The spectators of the arena caught her eyes. Their blurry forms materialized in the fog. They sat in groups, talking between themselves and pointing in her direction. Everywhere she looked, eyes were on her.

Nicolar appeared. He walked past the tall iron grate where Lia had trapped the valcor the night before. The man cast a nervous glance over his shoulder at the dark passage before turning back to her. He motioned for the guards to disperse, leaving them alone in the center of the arena.

"Is Danik really going to fight me?" she asked.

Nicolar crouched, inspected her chains and the restraints that affixed to her limbs. He nodded. "I advised him against it, but he insists. I think you hit on his pride."

"Will he actually let me go if I win?"

Nicolar flinched. "He says he will."

Lia caught his lie. *So it's a fight to the death.*

The man stood. "Be ready. It should start soon, and like yesterday . . . say nothing to the crowd, or else." He walked off, leaving her alone.

Lia's breath caught. Her father and Raiyn emerged from the fog and stumbled forward. Their wrists were chained and clothes were torn. Bruises covered their faces and arms. A bandage wrapped around her father's arm where the valcor had slashed it the previous night. Guards pushed them from behind, leading them to metal rings set into the arena wall. They both looked at her with long faces. They clearly didn't feel hopeful for whatever spectacle Danik planned for the morning—a sentiment shared by Lia.

The murmur of the crowd grew as the minutes ticked by. The overcast sky kept the arena dim. A handful of torches had been lit around the space, but the fog remained thick. Lia scanned the seats.

She could only see a portion of the stands and noted how the empty seats were nearly gone.

A forced whisper reached her. "Lia."

She turned to find her father leaning against his chains.

"Danik's not going to let us free," Veron said, "even if you win. You'll need to—" An elbow to the face shut him up.

"Quiet!" the guard next to him barked.

The murmur grew to a roar. Lia turned to find the cause of the commotion and froze.

Danik strode across the arena, emerging from the gloom. His sword extended at his side, pointing toward the ground. His dark-red tunic looked spotless, and cuffed leggings showed off his polished boots. A thick gray cloak draped almost to the muddy ground.

Lia squared her shoulders to face him. She stood to her full height, raising her chin and throwing her shoulders back. She stepped forward. The chains attached to her wrists pulled her hands back. She flexed her muscles, keeping her arms taut. Her chest puffed forward. She wouldn't give Danik the satisfaction of thinking she was cowed.

A smirk danced on his face as he walked toward her. "Here we are, Lia," he said, quiet enough that only she could hear. "All three of you are in my grasp. I can finally put this all behind me."

"Did you think Jade was going to do all your work for you? You didn't think I warranted sending more than one of your goons?"

He laughed through his nose. "None of us actually thought you would be stupid enough to show. Having Jade there was a long shot, but I guess we should have paid it more attention. It's a pity. She was a good fighter." He raised his sword.

Lia tensed, acutely aware of the chains restraining her limbs. "Don't forget, you promised your people a show."

Danik frowned and stopped moving. "Yes. Yes, I did." He nodded toward the king's box.

"Citizens of Felting!" High Lord Bilton's voice boomed. "King Danik is unlike any leader we've seen before in Felting. He is willing to put his life on the line to provide you with entertainment and prove his bravery. Today he fights the Valcor Conqueror—a surprise arrival in last night's spectacle. Your king bravely accepted her challenge to duel."

Applause sounded through the crowd, pulsing with an eager energy.

A young assistant jogged out to meet Danik. After untying the clasp around his neck, the king sloughed off the cloak, tossing it to the young man.

Two guards arrived before Lia and bent to work on her hands and legs. Nicolar stood behind them, supervising as they worked.

Lia stared at the king while the guards pulled at her chains, making clicking sounds. After a moment, her ankles were completely free and one band remained affixed to her left wrist. Nicolar tossed a sword. It fell at her feet and splashed mud against her legs.

The guards retreated, and Danik stepped forward, his sword twirling in his hand.

Lia's heart jumped. "You said bracelets on." She glanced between Danik and Nicolar. "Are you going back on your word?"

The king pursed his lips and paused.

"Should I announce to the crowd about your cowardice?"

"Try it," Danik spat, "and we'll see how quickly your father dies." After a beat, he turned to Nicolar. "Give it to me."

Nicolar fished in his pocket. He pulled out a metal bracelet and passed it to the king.

Danik wrapped the object around his wrist. It clicked as it snapped fast. He held up his hand to show her. "Satisfied?"

"How do I know you'll keep it on?"

"I'll keep it on," he said, bitter and cold, "because I said I would."

"Fine," Lia said.

Nicolar backed away, leaving them alone in the center of the arena.

Lia squatted, not taking her eyes from the king. Her hand found the sword and lifted it. The mud sucked against the blade as it rose from the ground. She wiped the steel against her pants then gripped the hilt with both hands. The weapon was cold and hard. It felt off—unbalanced and top-heavy.

She raised her voice to the crowd. "If I win, my friends and I go free, correct?"

Danik nodded.

"Very well."

She sank into dragon stance, her sword poised above her head, pointing at him. The king mirrored her stance.

The wind was still, and the arena was silent.

Lia breathed slow and steady, her eyes locked on her opponent. She had fought him hundreds of times before. She knew how he moved and how he thought. She had won nearly every sparring match they had, but her stomach churned, nonetheless. She couldn't say why, but she felt like the one at the disadvantage.

Danik moved first, swinging for her shoulder. Lia, her instincts honed from a lifetime of training with her father, stepped forward, meeting the strike head on. Her blade pushed Danik's away, and her elbow jabbed at his face. A quick dodge left her hitting nothing but air.

He shuffled backward, but Lia didn't let him get away. She stepped with him, swinging her sword. Danik parried right, then left. Her weapon bounced from side to side until the king spun and pushed her back with a kick. Her upper leg stung from the blow, but she kept her eyes and sword up.

An overhead strike came at her head. Lia deflected the blow to her side and sent a kick of her own at his midsection. Expecting to reach a pile of flesh, his rapid block with the elbow threw her off balance.

He's fast. He must have been practicing.

Danik turned to the offensive. He stepped in and swung hard, strike after strike. Crashing steel filled the air. Lia retreated with each hit, shocked that each one seemed to grow stronger.

She tried to summon the origine, wishing for the extra reflexes and power the well of energy would provide. After all, if her father could find it through metal, maybe she could too. Hoping for a simmering feeling in her gut, nothing but tingling hands came as she blocked his advances.

At his last hit, Lia spun away, moving around the edge of a stone plinth. A missing chunk reminded her of the night before when the valcor attempted to take a piece out of her father.

Danik lunged to his side, and Lia stepped in the opposite direction, keeping the obstacle between them. "You can't hide here," he said.

Lia adjusted, keeping out of his reach. "Hiding and resting aren't the same thing."

"So you need rest, do you?"

His taunt brought a warm creeping feeling up her neck. She imagined her face turning red. "Have you been practicing?" she asked.

"Every day. I've been waiting for this chance."

Lia swung her weapon at his face, but he ducked behind the column. The blade bit into the stone, breaking off a sizable chip. She gasped as he appeared suddenly on the opposite side, lunging at her. She narrowly dodged the extended sword.

A wave of disappointment rolled through the crowd. "Get her!" someone yelled.

Lia abandoned the plinth and pivoted around the king, keeping her sword up. Her pulse raced. Her breath came fast and heavy. She glanced to her side to ensure her father and Raiyn were still all right, but a flash of movement brought her eyes back.

Danik flew at her. His sword danced through the air, bringing unexpected dangers faster than she could block.

Her eyes grew. Her arms ached, jerking and moving as fast as possible. *How is he this good?*

Her sword was caught out of position, and Danik's elbow found an opening. It struck her chest, hard and solid.

"Oof!" she groaned, stumbling backward. Her lashing arm jammed the hilt of her sword into his wrist.

Danik shook his hand as if the blow stung.

Cheers from the crowd turned his attention toward them. While they seemed to be rooting for an exciting fight, he raised a hand to accept the applause.

Lia gasped. The bracelet around his wrist contained a sharp line where a crack formed. White powder leaked from the break, floating to the ground.

It's not metal.

Danik's cocky grin faltered. He followed her gaze toward his wrist, then his body grew rigid.

"Cheater," Lia hissed.

Danik's face hardened. He stepped forward, shouting as he unleashed a ferocious attack.

23

A DESPERATE FIGHT

Lia backpedaled. Her sword flew from side to side, desperately blocking the devion-powered strikes. Her feet sank into a thicker section of mud. She slogged backward. Her mouth felt dry and sticky. The smell of sweat mixed with the earthy scent of the damp arena.

Danik pounded against her again and again until she ducked behind another plinth.

Lia took the moment to breathe. Her sword was up. Her feet stepped sideways, keeping the obstacle between them, but her eyes never left his. "That's the only way you're brave enough to face me, huh?" she said.

Danik shrugged. "I'm the king. I do what I want." He sucked in deep breaths but seemed to be trying to hide the effort.

Lia chuckled. "Tiring?"

His eyes narrowed. "I have plenty of energy—something you could have experienced yourself had you not turned me down."

Lia gestured to the crowd but kept her voice down. "Are you going to show these spectators your full ability? Will you let them see how it was never actually a fair fight—that you're too much of a coward for that?"

Danik didn't reply.

I can't beat him like this, Lia thought. The hopeless feeling sank in her gut. Her eyes darted around the arena, desperate for any idea to cling to. Her father and Raiyn remained at the wall. They both stared back, trapped. The wall of the arena was too high to escape without the origine. The stone plinths didn't get her anywhere.

The heavy iron grate caught her attention. Behind it, the valcor lay hidden somewhere in the darkness. An idea shot into her mind.

"What?" Danik moved from behind the pillar. "You have some crazy idea to get out of this?"

Lia turned and ran toward the far corner of the arena, near neither Raiyn nor the valcor's lair.

"Where do you think you're going?" Danik's lip pulled up in a sneer as he ran around and stopped her in her tracks.

She turned and ran the opposite way, dirty water splashing in all directions. Again, Danik popped in front of her, his sword up.

She angled to the right, toward the cage, putting the plinth between them. Danik didn't stop her but allowed her to halt in front of the iron lattice.

"Dead end," Danik said.

Lia stepped to the grate and set her hands on the open iron rungs. She stared through one of the openings. Past the grate, deep breathing reverberated from somewhere in the dark.

"If you want to get in there, I'm sure it can be arranged."

She raised an arm and banged the metal circlet against the gate. The resounding clank bounced down the dark tunnel. "You awake?" Lia shouted into the gloom. She banged her wrist several more times.

"I'm not sure that's the best idea," Danik said.

She tuned out Danik's remark and looked up. The grate stretched to the top of the wall like rungs on a ladder. She craned her neck back and spied the object she sought—the lever that controlled the grate, situated atop the arena wall, next to a flickering torch.

The steady breathing had stopped, and a rumbling growl replaced it.

"What are you planning, Lia?" Danik's boasting tone was gone. The question trembled.

"This." She dropped her sword.

Lia stepped on the rungs of the grate and climbed as fast as possible. Hand over hand. Foot over foot. Her body flew up the barrier, rising toward the top and scooting toward the side.

Danik scoffed. "Trying to run, huh? You can't get away from us."

I'm not trying to run, you idiot.

The top of the grate was well off the ground. A drop from there with the power of the origine would be nothing, but a fall without it would break a leg.

Lia didn't hesitate when she reached the top. As soon as Danik realized her intent, he would pluck her off and throw her back to the arena. She couldn't give him the chance. She leaped.

Her foot pushed off the metal rung. One hand pulled her body up while the other stretched. She passed the edge of the grate and flew toward the lever.

Her body stretched high in the air with nothing but space between her and the ground far below. Rushing air blew her hair back. Her opposite hand scraped the stone wall. The lever approached, closer and closer.

Got it!

She grasped her hand around the lever and held on, her body dangling over the drop. Her palm ached. Her arm strained. Her other hand flung itself and joined in pulling on the round object extending from the wall.

Lia grunted as she lifted a foot over the edge. Her muscles screamed. Her knees scraped against the top of the wall as she scrambled to her feet. Spectators with seats nearby leaned away, their eyes wide.

Without a pause, Lia grabbed the lever, set her feet, and pulled. Chains hidden deep in the stone wall clanked to life. The weight of the grate rose below her.

"What are you—" Danik's words cut short, his inflection rising.

The crowd roared. The deep growl grew louder. The sound drew closer.

Lia reset the lever and pulled again. As soon as it clicked as far as it would allow, she reset it again.

"Stop that!" Danik yelled. He leaped, rising to meet her.

Lia grabbed the lever with one hand and flung herself over the brink. Her weight carried past the lip. Danik's eyes grew as she planted her feet against his chest. Using the devion, he responded and batted against her legs, but there was nothing he could do to change his trajectory.

She kicked against him. The impact returned her back to the safety of the wall where she kept her hold on the lever. She watched as Danik fell backward. His arms flailed. His legs kicked air until his back collided into the ground.

The crowd gasped at the king's fall, but Lia had stopped watching. She managed two more full pulls on the lever.

Keep going. Keep going.

She had no idea how many pulls it would take to give it the height it would need, but she intended to pull at it as long as she could.

The tension of the lever evaporated. A metallic scraping sound filled the air, shrill and piercing. A second later, a crash shook the wall.

Lia's balance shifted. She lost her grip on the lever and waved her arms, teetering. A glance down revealed the arena floor far below. Danik lay sprawled on the ground, staring toward the dark tunnel. Her breath caught. The valcor's head already pressed into the arena. The animal shook the ground with each step.

Ignoring the lever, her attention turned to the nearest torch. She wrapped a hand around it moments before her body dropped. The torch yanked off its holder, tight in her grip. She flung her free arm toward the suspended metal grate. Her hand grasped the lowest rung, and her arm yanked at her body.

Lia shouted, but her grip held. Pointed metal ends stuck out from the bottom of the grate. Her legs swung freely, her body like a pendulum. She glanced down.

The valcor had stopped under the portcullis. Tall spines stuck up from the beast's neck. It winced at the light, pawing at the air.

"Back! Back!" Danik yelled.

Lia's fingers ached. As soon as one digit lost its grip, the others followed suit. When she hit the ground, she rolled, tucking her body against the side of the tunnel. The torch remained lit. She looked up.

Danik had backed up to the center of the arena with his sword held high. The four knights of power had dropped onto the floor and stood with the king. The guards with Veron and Raiyn had abandoned their posts. The valcor stared toward the arena, oblivious to her presence beside it. Her eyes scanned the ground. She gulped when she found her sword, trapped under the beast's taloned foot.

She snuck farther into the dark passage, scanning the space for any weapons or useful tools. The smell turned her nose. The rank scent of death and decay grew stronger the farther she traveled. The passage ended in a large square space, where they kept the animal. A door set into the back wall. She ran to it, her hopes high, and pulled on the handle. It rattled, but the solid barrier stayed firm.

She cringed at the grisly sight of bones—some white and bare, some still containing portions of dried flesh. A glint of metal caught her eye. She rushed to one of the piles of bones and sifted through the carcass. A scrap of clothing contained a royal guard symbol. Her pulse sped when the hilt of a sword materialized.

"Ha!" she laughed. But when she pulled the weapon out from the rubble, her hope sank. The blade was broken just above the hilt.

A roar behind her made her spin. The silhouette of the valcor remained at the exit of the tunnel. It hadn't left the comfort of the dark passage, stopped by the light.

Lia tossed the broken weapon down, and a metallic clink perked her ears. *What was that?* She dug through the disintegrating pile and a metal ring materialized. She pulled it out and stared. Four keys hung on a ring. Lia fell to her knees. *Keys like those that could unlock a restraint.*

She held the torch in her left hand while she used her right to work. The hole in the shackle around her wrist looked shallow. She dismissed the first two keys due to their length. Holding her breath, she pressed the next one into the hole. It fit, but when she tried to turn, nothing happened. She twisted harder, but the key didn't fit the space.

She sighed. *One more.*

The final key looked similar. It slid into the hole, fitting snugly. She paused to take a deep breath. Her heart pounded. Her hand trembled. She twisted. The key turned. A click filled the passage, and the pressure around her wrist loosened. She gasped.

The shackle fell free.

A nervous laugh bubbled from her chest.

I'm free!

The comforting presence of the origine hummed inside her, warming her gut. She ran to the door and tried one of the longer keys. The teeth slid through the hole and turned with a creak. The hinges groaned as the door pivoted a crack.

She thought of rushing out of the arena and disappearing into the city or the woods, but the image in her head of Raiyn and Veron trapped in the arena stopped her.

She spun. Past the outline of the monster, past Danik's men cowering in fear, her father and Raiyn remained stuck against the arena wall with shackles holding them in place—shackles that looked just like hers. Veron stood, poised and ready despite having no weapon or ability to move. Raiyn pulled at his chains as if hoping they may have suddenly weakened.

Lia gripped the key ring tightly with one hand and the torch with the other. After blowing out a breath, she jogged down the passage toward the dark outline of the valcor. *Now, if I can just keep Danik and his men occupied . . .*

"Hey!" she shouted as she drew close.

The animal didn't seem to hear her. It continued to roar, swatting at the soldiers in the arena but refusing to go closer to them.

She stood directly behind its hind legs, close enough to reach out and grab one of its long claws. "Hey!" she kicked its hind leg.

The animal bellowed a guttural roar as it turned.

Lia held the torch higher, as far away from her body as she could. "Back up!"

Faced with the new light source, the animal cringed. It stepped backward, toward the arena.

The torch crackled as she waved it through the air. Her arm danced, the fire forcing the beast away from the comfort of its lair.

Behind the animal, the knights of power and royal guards continued to move back. Their weapons were held up, but they neither attacked nor ran.

Lia caught Danik's eyes looking at her. His lips formed a snarl, his eyes darting between her and the monster.

It just needs to move a bit farther. She stepped forward and lunged with the flame.

The valcor shrank from the torch, its body nearly past the first plinth. It opened its mouth and bared fangs at her.

Lia crouched and jammed the butt of the torch into the mud. The flame remained steady, blocking off the entrance to the tunnel.

"Kill it!" Danik shouted.

Fully in the arena, the valcor turned in the direction of Danik and his men, cringing against the light. The soldiers held up their swords, jabbing and thrusting the blades. Several attacks bounced off its flank, but none seemed to penetrate the skin. The knights of power moved and darted with speed provided by the devion.

The valcor swiped with its front paw. While Danik's men were able to dodge, several of the regular guards tumbled into the mud. A furious roar shook the arena.

Lia ignored the fracas. Keeping to the arena wall, she ran with a burst of speed around the exterior until she stopped at her father.

Veron held up his wrists when he saw her ring of keys. "Well done."

Lia jiggled the key into the holes of each restraint until they fell loose. "I figured we could use a distraction."

"That thing qualifies." Raiyn nodded toward the massive animal then held up his irons. "Any thoughts on how we can get out of here?"

"Most of the guards are occupied," Veron said. "If you two can help me over this wall, we should be able to run out of the arena."

"Couldn't Danik just follow us though?" Raiyn asked.

A thud drew their attention to the wall next to them where a royal guard's body collided into the stone wall. A slash ran down his torso from where the valcor had eviscerated him.

Veron blinked and opened his hands. "We have to try something."

Raiyn's chains fell with a crumpled clank to the ground.

"Come with me," Lia said. "I've got a better idea."

Her run was slower than she would have liked, but her father wouldn't be able to keep up, otherwise. The tunnel seemed to take forever to return to. As soon as they arrived and ducked under the portcullis, another flying guard landed directly under the gate. Lia jumped to the side but was still splashed by the wet mud the body flung into the air.

A hiss turned her blood cold as the light in the passage dimmed. She turned to the torch and gasped. A twirl of smoke rose from the top. The flame was out.

Lia glanced toward the arena floor, and her stomach dropped. The valcor stared into the tunnel, directly at her. A rumbling growl echoed down the passage. She turned and squinted through the darkness. The door left cracked at the far end waited. Far away. Too far.

"Run!" she yelled.

Veron and Raiyn followed, sprinting down the tunnel.

A deafening roar filled the air, and hot air warmed the back of her neck. The ground shook with thundering footsteps. Lia pulled from her well of energy, pumping her legs.

She arrived at the door in seconds and pulled. It was heavy, and the hinges were stiff. Without the origine, opening it may not have been possible. She used what energy she needed and strained as the crack widened.

"Through here!" she shouted.

Raiyn arrived a moment later, pausing just inside the doorway. "Veron! Come on!" he shouted.

Her father wore a pained expression on his face. He ran down the tunnel, hampered by his inability to use the origine.

The massive head of the beast loomed over his shoulder. Its teeth opened as it lunged forward. With a sudden jerk, Veron's body collapsed into the dirt floor.

Lia screamed.

Her father looked up. For a long moment, his eyes found hers, pleading. Anguish filled them. "Run!" he shouted. As his shout cut off, he was jerked backward, dragged along the ground by the beast until he was flung into the light, tumbling past the iron grate.

"No!" Lia lunged forward, but Raiyn's arms wrapped around her. "Let me go!" She pushed against his hold.

In the light of the arena, several knights of power surrounded her father with swords held to him.

"Stop it, Lia!" Raiyn's arms strained against her.

"I can't leave him again!" Tears streamed down her face. She pulled against the steel door, but Raiyn's origine-powered grip was too much.

"You can't save him!"

A metallic banging sound caused the portcullis at the end of the passage to shudder. After a loud creak, it dropped, slamming to the ground.

Lia stopped pulling and blinked away the tears. Her father was gone. The passage had grown dark again, and a rumble shook the walls. Trapped in the same tunnel, the valcor raced toward her.

Raiyn pulled at her. "Lia. Get. Back!" He dragged her past the doorway then pulled on the door.

Lia could only stare as the animal roared in attack.

Slam!

A dent pressed into the door after the animal collided into it. Once again, a metal door saved her from the snarling teeth.

A choking sob filled the air. Her chest heaved, not from exhaustion but from sorrow. She leaned into Raiyn and wrapped her arms around him. He held her in return. His body was warm. His head leaned against hers. The tang of sweat and mud filled the narrow, dark passage. She had rescued him, but her father—although still alive—was not as fortunate.

She squeezed harder until he winced. "I'm sorry." Lia released her hold and stood back.

"It's all right." He pointed to his chest. "I think my ribs are still broken." He slid his other hand down her arm, squeezing tenderly. He waved farther into the blackness. "Come on. Let's see where this goes."

24

THE CHAMBER ROOM

Chelci sat on a rock, staring across the pit at the ledge against the far wall. A marked one strolled along the short walkway, casually watching them. Chelci attempted to look calm, but her tense body was ready for action.

"Get ready," she whispered out of the side of her mouth.

Adjusting bodies rustled on the small island behind her.

Looking content at the prisoners' docile nature, the guard moved on through the opening into the glowing-red passage.

The knights all jumped to their feet as soon as the man left their sight.

"I still insist this is a bad idea," Gavin whispered. "We don't know what they want us for, yet."

Dayna joined Chelci at the edge. "'To sustain them.' That sounds pleasant. You want to just sit here and die?"

"We talked this through," Chelci said. "This is our best shot. We only have around five minutes until he's back. Let's go."

"They did bring us food and water," Bradley said. "That shows that they want us alive."

"You think they're fattening us up?" Dayna asked. "No. Chelci is right. We need to do something, and this is our time."

"They may just want us for labor," Gavin suggested.

"Labor for what?" Bradley asked.

Gavin shrugged. "Carve statues. Dig tunnels. Remember those other prisoners up the passage and the workers carving that statue? If we keep our heads down, a chance to escape might present itself. Maybe Veron will show."

A hush washed over the group.

"I'm sure he'll try to find us," Chelci said. "But . . . honestly, I don't know how he would find this place, or get us out without being caught himself. We need to try something."

Bridgette stepped forward. The youngest and lightest knight inhaled a deep breath and dropped her shoulders back. "I'm ready. Let's do it."

"How is this throw less dangerous than climbing?" Gavin asked.

"We can see where we're going, for one thing." Chelci pointed to the vertical plank on the far side of the pit. "And that board is just waiting for us."

Dayna gestured over the side of the cliff. "Climbing down would be impossible. The pit wall is sheer, and without the origine, we wouldn't have a chance. I doubt there's a bed of straw waiting at the bottom, either."

Gavin sighed. "I still think we should be patient."

"And wait to die?" Dayna asked.

"We don't know we're going to die."

Dayna set her hands on her hips. "Then where is Shawn?"

The others grew silent.

"Veron said they took him away. He would be here, right? He's 'sustaining them' somehow, and I don't imagine that's a positive outcome. If he were alive, why wouldn't he be with us?"

"I'm sure Shawn is dead," Chelci said. "And I'm guessing we will follow suit unless we find a way to escape. And the clock is ticking on that guard returning. Let's go."

Bridgette set her hand on Gavin's shoulder. "If we do nothing, we're all going to end up dead. This way, if I die, at least I tried something."

Gavin shook his head and frowned. "Fine."

Chelci's chest tightened with a stressed anticipation. Salina and Ruby joined them.

Chelci turned to Bridgette. "Chances are, you're going to fall short and hit that wall."

"And you'll hit it hard," Dayna added. "Keep your head back, so you don't smack it with your face."

Bridgette nodded then pointed. "I'll reach for that hold—the horn sticking up at the edge."

"When you pull yourself up, lower the bridge," Chelci said. "Our only hope is to get all of us over there before the guard returns."

Bradley stood at the edge of the pit then leaned forward. He glanced down and shook his head. "Please don't fall."

Bridgette's laugh sounded grim. "Throw me far enough and I won't have to."

Gavin stepped forward, facing Bradley. They extended their arms and locked them together in a square shaped grip.

Chelci joined Dayna, standing closely behind Bridgette. "We'll give as much boost as we can," she said. "Make sure to jump as they lift."

Bridgette stared ahead, across the pit, and nodded. She lifted one foot and placed it on the brace the men had created. Her other arm gripped Gavin's shoulder, and the men lowered their arms. She jumped up, lifting her other foot. Raised off the ground, Bridgette squatted with her hands on both men's shoulders.

Chelci set her hands behind Bridgette's upper-left leg, and Dayna did the same with the right.

"Can you get any closer?" Bridgette's voice shook.

The men scooted closer, stopping at the edge of the drop off.

"We'll bounce three times to get the timing," Gavin said. "On the third, we'll lift as hard as we can."

Bridget inhaled and nodded.

Chelci glanced past her body and sighted the far edge. *That's a long way.* Her pulse quickened. "Push hard, Dayna," she whispered.

The other woman nodded.

The men lowered their bodies, then rose.

"One."

Chelci adjusted her hands and flexed, ready for action.

They lowered again and lifted.

"Two."

She held her breath and braced as they lowered one last time.

Bridgette's legs tensed, ready to spring. The men gulped air and puffed their chests.

Chelci counted in her head, her mind anticipating the next number. Her muscles ached to explode. But as she was ready to exhale and push, the tension in Bridgette's legs vanished. Her body became off balance as if the two men lost sync of their timing.

"What are you doing?" Chelci shouted.

Bridgette's feet stepped to the ground, and Dayna backed off.

"We were ready," Chelci said. She spun between the group. "What happened?"

Gavin held up his hands and looked her in the eyes. "Chelci," he whispered.

"No, Gavin! We have to try something! And this is our best shot!" She grabbed his shoulders.

He tensed his muscles and shook her. "Chelci!"

The way he shouted gave her pause.

What's going on?

Gavin raised his eyebrows and motioned for her to calm.

She looked at the others who stared across the pit.

Chelci's eyes panned across the glowing-red nothingness, and her stomach dropped. The massive form of Gralow stood on the far side with his hand resting on the hilt of his sword.

"Having fun, are we?" Gralow's words echoed in the cavern.

Chelci's teeth clamped together. She backed away from the edge.

"You two—" the man pointed at Chelci and Gavin. "Come with me. The rest of you stay put."

Chelci gulped, but the catch in her throat wouldn't go away. Bridgette, Bradley, and the rest looked at her with fear in their eyes.

The wooden plank landed with a soft clatter, spanning the drop. Gavin's mouth formed a thin line. "This isn't good," he whispered.

Chelci moved first. She kept an eye on the wooden board, trying not to focus on the pit below as she crossed.

Gralow glared when she stepped off on the far side. His sword was out, and his crystal glowed bright red. Gavin stepped off moments later.

Gralow made eye contact with Chelci and nodded up the passage. "Walk slowly. You first."

Chelci stepped into the tunnel, searching for more guards. *Is he the only one?* Her mind raced. *We could overpower him, or maybe I can run ahead?*

A pained wince from Gavin behind her stopped her thoughts.

"And in case you think of trying anything stupid," Gralow said, "your friend will receive a slash through the back, then I'll run you down, all in a matter of seconds. So don't be rash."

Chelci's shoulders drooped. She walked forward, following the serpentine passage.

"Turn right," Gralow barked.

Chelci nearly missed the passage branching off on her right. It wasn't the path they had followed to get there. "Where does this go?" She turned sideways to slide through the narrow opening.

"Quiet!"

Gavin hissed and groaned through gritted teeth.

Chelci imagined what sort of injury would cause that reaction. She turned. "Stop it!"

The two men followed closely but were merely silhouettes.

"Behave, then I won't have to hurt him."

Her jaw tightened and fist clenched.

"Move!"

She continued. The narrow corridor spilled into a larger one, which eventually turned down another path. Chelci was turned around. The passages all looked the same, as if they walked in a circle.

A new light warmed the path ahead with a yellow, earthy glow.

Her blood pumped faster. Her eyes hungered to look on anything but the red light, and when she turned a corner, she nearly gasped.

A massive oval-shaped chamber lay before her. The floor was mostly smooth and flat with a handful of stalagmites rising up. A carved-stone column rose from the center of the room to the ceiling. Shafts cut through the roof, tunneling through what looked to be a sizable amount of rock to allow in natural light. Against the far end of the chamber, three stone seats sat on a raised area with a rectangular-shaped box before them. The old woman they had met outside the caves sat in one of the seats while Talioth paced the raised area.

Gralow pushed against her back. "Move!"

Chelci crossed the chamber, reminding herself to lift her jaw.

Talioth stopped pacing as they approached. "I see we have visitors." His crystal hummed to life.

"I caught them attempting to escape," Gralow said.

Talioth chuckled. "Let me guess, jumping the pit?"

Chelci swallowed and lifted her chin, but she didn't reply.

"They were about to, but I stopped them."

Talioth looked at Chelci. "Do you know how deep that pit is?"

She narrowed her eyes.

"Do you know what happens when you fall from that high?"

Gavin stepped forward. "If you want us to stick around and not kill ourselves, maybe we need to discuss an arrangement."

A smile grew across Talioth's face until he burst into laughter. The old woman's smile formed wrinkles at the corners of her eyes.

"Do you see this chamber?" Talioth gestured with his hand. "This was built by axes and chisels. That column there was hand carved by dozens of laborers."

"So, that's what you want us for," Chelci said. "Labor?"

Talioth shook his head. "We have plenty of labor. The villages on the outskirts of these mountains provide the supply we need. What we want with you . . . is power."

Chelci wrinkled her forehead. "The origine? You use the devion, right?"

"Oh, Chelci, there's so much you don't know." His eyes fell on the large rectangular box. "So much."

Chelci's eyes traced his sight to the object. "What's in there? Is that the source of the devion?"

Talioth turned back to her and ignored the question. "We're happy to keep you alive for a while, if you behave. But if you're foolish enough to throw your life away so soon . . ." He shrugged. "That works as well. So, be my guest. Fling yourselves into the pit. Try to run. Your death will be quick, but we won't mourn you."

The woman sat forward in her seat. "Should we siphon one?"

The way she pronounced the word 'siphon' set Chelci's hair on edge.

"The young one was great," the woman continued, "but that man looks like he would sustain us for quite some time."

Talioth pursed his lips and stared. After a long pause, he shook his head. "Not yet."

Gavin's sigh was audible.

"What did you do to Veron?" Chelci asked.

Talioth raised an eyebrow. "He was your husband. Yes?"

"*Is* my husband," she corrected. "Did you—" She choked up, straining to voice the words. "Did you kill him?"

"Veron requires a special touch. His case is different."

"What makes someone an alloshifter?" Gavin asked. "What does that mean?"

"I grow weary of their ignorance." Talioth turned and waving his hand. "Take them back, Gralow. Three days without food for the whole group as punishment."

"It will be done," the guard grunted.

He prodded her and Gavin back in the direction they had come. Chelci followed at Gavin's heels as they left the light behind and disappeared into the glowing red halls.

25

EARNING RESPECT

Breath hissed through Danik's teeth as he paced the balcony outside the council chamber. He played the events of the morning over in his head, growing angrier by the minute. The dried mud on his boots left a brown trail across the balcony. The morning clouds had burned away. His view stretched to the mountain range, but the scenery did not improve his mood.

"Your Majesty, this is what we wanted." Nicolar leaned against the wall, picking mud out of his nails with a dagger.

Quentin Cotterell stood quietly by the doorway with his hands folded in front of him.

"It's not what I wanted," Danik said. "I wanted a definitive victory. I wanted the people of Felting to see my strength and know Danik Bannister could defeat anyone. They should see me as a warrior, capable of anything!"

"Which is, uh . . . what happened." Nicolar said.

"It's not!" Danik yelled. "She ran circles around me, teasing me with that . . . monster. I thought that thing would be the ultimate death sentence—an executioner the people would fear. Instead, Lia and her friends have bested it twice, making a mockery of it. I should never have had it brought here."

"I think you're giving her too much credit. She barely lived—twice, surviving by dumb luck and fortuitous timing. Now, she and that other boy are dead."

Danik's head whipped toward him. "You confirmed it?"

Nicolar shrank back. "Well . . . not yet." He glanced at Quentin.

"I have heard nothing either," the advisor added.

"The men should be back at any time. But Lia and Raiyn were trapped in there with that monster. I think it's a fair assumption that they're dead."

Danik narrowed his eyes. "Never assume with them."

"Once we confirm, then we'll kill Veron. Then, this will all be behind us."

Danik stopped pacing. He closed his eyes and breathed out. "Yes. That will be nice."

"With the prisoners dealt with, you can focus your attention back on Feldor. What do you want to do?"

"What do you mean?"

"As king. You have the increased income coming in. The spectacles at the arena have been a hit. What comes next? Build a monument? Conquer another kingdom?"

Danik raised his eyebrows. "Another kingdom? That would be something." He turned toward the edge of the balcony and stared to the horizon, rubbing his chin. "With a Knights of Power army, we would be unstoppable. Rynor would be a nice jewel to add to our crown. Half of Terrenor would be under my rule."

"Lots of fertile farmland," Nicolar said.

"And the eastern slope of the Straith Mountains is supposed to be teeming with baltham." Danik stared at the mountains, imagining the cities and people on the other side. "Maybe soon. We'll need to build up our team first."

While he stared at the mountains, a pull tugged on his chest. He adjusted his arms for balance but then realized he had not actually moved. *What was that?* He spun around, seeing if something around him had caused the sensation. He stood alone.

"Sir?" Nicolar prompted.

Danik looked toward the mountains, and a drawing power built once more, as if luring him. His heart rate increased, but as quickly as it had arrived, the feeling disappeared.

"Is everything all right?"

Danik stood motionless. The pull was gone. *What was that?* Eventually, he turned his gaze away and found the other men staring at him. "Everything is fine," he said. "How is the training going?"

Nicolar cleared his throat and straightened. "The five we started are learning quickly. We're beginning with some basic combat work then giving them a taste of the devion to make sure they can access it before we go too far. They don't need a great deal of fighting skill in order to become an elite warrior with the devion, but some will help."

"Agreed," Danik said.

"We have another dozen starting next week, and I had some ideas of where we could find more."

Danik raised his eyebrows.

"I know plenty of people in Tienn who would jump at the chance to become an elite warrior—people with no current allegiance to anyone else. Also, there's a group in Lorranis called the Black Lanterns."

Danik's eye twitched at the name. *The group the Shadow Knights stopped.*

"They experienced a setback a while ago, but there are still plenty of members. I know several of them personally—good people."

Danik nodded.

"For now, the new trainees could use some time with you, if you can spare it. We all learned from you, but our training is no substitute for the original."

"That would be fine."

Boots clunked across the floor, growing closer. Danik turned as Cedric stepped onto the balcony.

"Hey, Danik." Cedric corrected himself. "I'm sorry—Your Majesty." He offered a quick bow then pointed with a thumb over his shoulder. "Some guy wants to see you."

"Some guy?" Danik huffed. "You don't simply let in anyone who wants to see me."

"His name's Athrian Dane. Says he's authorized to speak with the king or something like that."

"That's correct," Quentin chimed in. "Athrian is our ambassador to Rynor. He had regular audience with the Advisors Council whenever issues arose."

Danik sniffed, then nodded. "Fine. Show him in."

Cedric hurried toward the door, and Danik strolled inside from the balcony with Nicolar and Quentin following. The unlit space of the Advisors Council chamber looked gloomy without people in it. The empty table and chairs reminded him of the night he killed the previous king.

When Cedric opened the door, a plump man entered with sharply pressed and spotless clothing. His trim beard and neat hair gave a fastidious look that contrasted with the unsure expression covering his face.

Danik stopped moving, letting the short man cross the room to him. He folded his hands in front of his body and raised his eyebrows. Cedric hovered over his shoulder.

"Your Majesty." Athrian Dane offered a quick bow, puffing from his red cheeks. His eyes flicked to Nicolar and Quentin then returned to Danik. "I apologize for not having visited sooner to congratulate you on your crown."

Danik lifted his chin. "No apology needed. What kept you?"

"I wasn't sure how King Tomas wanted to respond, given the situation, so I needed to check with him."

Danik leaned forward. "Given, what?"

"The . . . situation with—You know. How you came to be king."

"I'm sorry, but what *situation* do you speak of?"

Athrian's mouth opened but closed again without answering.

"King Darcius died—a most tragic event, but not unprecedented. Feldor followed their standard plan of succession, which was for the high lords to choose the next king, and they chose me."

"You're right. I didn't mean 'situation.' It was more of—It was just unusual to happen like it did, and with you being, um—"

Danik leaned forward. "Me being . . . ?"

"Young. Younger than usual, at least."

"The high lords followed standard protocol. Choosing me wasn't unusual given my status as a shadow knight and a well-known servant of the kingdom."

Athrian choked on a laugh.

Danik's blood heated up. "Is something funny?"

The short man struggled to regain his serious face. "No, sir. Not at all."

"Then why are you laughing?"

"It's just the term 'well-known.' Typically kings were lords or leaders of the kingdom—respected and popular people. I'd simply never heard of you."

Danik ground his teeth together, his breath hissing through his nostrils. "Why did you say you were here, again?"

"I'm sorry." Athrian's eyes flicked to his hands where he clutched a letter. His weight shifted to his other hip. "I, uh, finally received a message back from King Tomas."

The man's hesitance gave Danik a sinking feeling in his stomach.

"I think it's best if I simply read his words."

Danik gestured with an open hand for him to proceed.

"Keep in mind, these words are from King Tomas, not from me." The ambassador cleared his throat twice, pressing on his chest as he did so. He shifted again as he stared at the letter.

"Danik," Athrian read, "I want to express my sympathy to Feldor for the loss of King Darcius. He was a great man and will be dearly missed. I'm sorry your kingdom has required so much from you, and I can only imagine how overwhelming it all must be for a boy of your age."

Danik stiffened.

"If you have any questions or need help, please send a message through my ambassador. Would you like me to send any of my advisors? I'd be happy to lend a couple to assist with any questions you may have, until they . . ." Athrian paused to clear a catch in his throat. ". . . until they choose an actual replacement for Darcius."

The ambassador lowered the paper and kept his eyes on the floor. "How should I respond, Your Majesty?"

Danik seethed. "Actual replacement?" His arms shook as he stepped closer. "A *boy* of my age?"

"I'm sorry, sir." Athrian backpedaled. "The king clearly didn't understand—"

"Get out." Danik pointed at the door.

"But what should I tell him about the—"

"Get out!" His yell bounced off the stone walls of the room.

The ambassador flinched, then ran to the door and disappeared beyond, chased off by Cedric.

Danik took in deep breaths and blew them out. A dull throb beat against his temple.

"He's a fool," Nicolar said when the man's footsteps had faded down the hallway. "Pay him no attention."

"Is that what people think of me?" Danik asked, his voice sounding weaker than he intended. "Do they see me as a boy?"

"Surely not," Quentin said. "Perhaps people haven't had enough of a chance to see you and interact with you yet, though."

Danik tapped his chin as he stared toward the hallway. *How do I win their approval? How do I earn their respect?* An idea came to him. "That's what I need."

"What's that?" Nicolar asked.

"They need to see me. Talk with me. Celebrate me." A smile formed on Danik's face. He looked away from the main entrance and began across the room. "I've had enough scheming and trapping for the moment. I'd like to appreciate something more . . . refined."

"Refined?" Nicolar followed, along with Quentin.

Danik began up the stairs. "That's right. I've been king for, what . . . two weeks?"

"That's right."

"And we have yet to celebrate."

It was quiet as the footsteps continued. "What sort of celebration did you have in mind?" Quentin asked from the back of the line.

Danik stopped in the hallway on the next floor. Guards flanked either side of a set of double doors at the end. At his presence, they snapped to attention and pulled open the doors. The king turned back to his assistants as they arrived at the top of the stairs. "A ball." He raised a finger. "In *my* honor. Food and dancing."

Quentin nodded. "Who should we invite?"

Danik shrugged. "Whoever is normally invited to these things. I don't know. Do you have a list?"

The advisor pursed his lips. "I'll see what I can find out. When would you like to have this ball?"

"As soon as possible. How long do you need?"

Quentin's eyes widened. "How long do *I* need?"

Danik felt his face redden. "Well, *I'm* surely not going to plan it. Are you not up to the task?"

The advisor's face jumped between Danik and Nicolar. "I guess I can make it happen. It will take some time to arrange food, invitations, musicians, servants. Attendees may want to get new dresses made." He swallowed hard. "I'll see what I can do and get back with you."

Two shapes caught Danik's attention in the doorway at the end of the hall. The guards remained frozen with the doors held open, but Lisette and Dawn now stood in the opening.

A broad smile grew across his face. He held his hands open. "Girls! I've missed you."

Lisette managed a timid smile, but Dawn didn't appear to bother.

Danik walked toward them. "I'm sorry this morning's activities didn't play out as I anticipated. I hope it was thrilling for you all the same. Now . . . I could use a bath." Danik turned to address the men as he walked backward. "Make it happen, Quentin." He pointed at the man. "As soon as possible!"

The advisor nodded.

"And Nicolar, I want to hear as soon as you get confirmation on the bodies."

"Of course, Your Majesty. May I ask what might be a foolish question?"

Danik raised an eyebrow.

"Do you know how to dance?"

26

SEEKING HELP

L ia held the scrap of fabric she used as a shawl to keep the wind from blowing it away. She peered across the street, staring at the shop window.

"Anything yet?" Raiyn asked. He faced the opposite direction, pretending to lace his boots over and over.

"Someone is sweeping, but there are still customers inside. Should be soon."

Two women exited Westcott Bakery, carrying long loaves of bread under their arms.

"How long did you say it's been?" Raiyn asked.

"A few years."

"And you're sure Danik won't have this place watched?"

Lia glanced for the hundredth time up and down the street. "*Pretty* sure. I don't think he would know them."

Inside the shop, the woman with the broom moved toward the door.

Lia jerked to attention. "It's time. Let's go."

She stepped to cross the road. The shawl draped over her face, cutting off her peripheral vision. Raiyn's footsteps followed.

At the bakery, she pulled open the door just as a woman turned around a sign that indicated the store was closed.

"I'm sorry." The woman's voice was pleasant and apologetic. "We just sold the last of our loaves, so we were closing. If you're looking for pastries, we still have a few."

Despite being around Lia's mother's age, Emma Barton kept a youthful look. Her curly blonde hair bounced as she leaned against her broom. A genuine smile showed on her face with only a hint of wrinkles at the edges of her eyes.

Lia pulled her shawl off.

"Are you interested in some—" Emma stopped, her eyes widening. Her hand jumped to cover a gasp.

"What is it, dear?" Matthew asked from behind a counter. He balanced an armload of loaf pans precariously. A matching gasp sounded from his side of the shop before a loud clattering of pans bounced and echoed in the room.

Emma beckoned urgently with her hand, allowing Lia and Raiyn to enter before she closed the door behind them. She then proceeded to pull curtains across each of the windows.

"Lia Stormbridge!" Matthew breathed. "I thought all the knights were—" He cut himself off.

"Dead? Yes, that's what Danik told everyone."

"Your parents? Are they safe, too?" Emma asked.

Lia frowned and shook her head. "Father's in the castle dungeon, and Mother's been taken."

Emma rested a hand on Lia's shoulder. "I'm so sorry."

Matthew walked around the counter. "What can we do? What do you need?"

Lia glanced at Raiyn before looking back at the bakers. "I hate to ask it of you, but . . ."

"Anything," Emma said.

"Do you have a place we could hide out for a bit?"

"Ouch," Raiyn said.

Lia turned and glared, her hair brushing against a branch.

"Sorry," he whispered. "A pricker got me."

"Don't move, and nothing will get you."

"I know. It's just that . . . we've been crouching here for a while, and my legs . . ." He faded out.

Lia turned back to the house, peering into the night. "Use some origine."

The ground floor windows lit up with lanterns. Bodies crossed the rooms occasionally, but she hadn't found what she waited for.

"So this is your parents' old house? It's huge."

Lia shook her head. "Just my mother. She grew up here."

"Ah, King Darcius lived here then."

"That's right, until he moved into the castle. Veron met my mother here when he was a servant."

"It's crazy how that all worked out."

"Yeah. My father saved my mother's life, or something like that. They fell in love, defeated Bale, and got married."

"And this is where it all began." Raiyn laughed. "That's wild."

The wind picked up, rustling the leaves.

"Lia?"

She held her breath. His eyes were soft and earnest.

"I haven't had a chance to thank you."

"For what?"

"Trying to rescue me in the square, and then actually doing so in the arena."

A half smile tugged at her face.

"Other than my mother, I've never had anyone stand up for or worry about me." He inclined his head forward. "Never. My life has been a lonely one filled with secrets and hiding. I've never had true friends. I've never"—he paused—"cared about anyone before."

A warm feeling creeped up Lia's neck.

"I expected to die from the moment I was captured, but when I got the pick from Marcus, I felt . . . loved—known."

Lia dropped her head. "When they wrapped the chains around you, I thought it was over. I tried to run for you. Well . . . I wanted to. Father held me back. He was sure it was a bluff, but I needed to try. I couldn't let you—" She choked up, her words caught in her throat. "I didn't move."

"Hey." Raiyn rested his hand on her arm.

The touch sent a tingle through her body. A flush filled her cheeks.

"Your father was right. I'm glad you didn't do anything. They probably would have caught all three of us."

She looked up. Shaggy, black hair dangled over part of his face while his mouth formed a tender smile. Her pulse quickened.

"You cared, and that's what mattered the most."

She stared at his lips while she processed his words. *I do care*, she thought.

Raiyn sat, frozen, watching her. The moment drew out, and her face felt even redder.

Turning away, she cleared her throat softly then rose, shuffling the branches. "I'm worried we're going to miss him. Let's get closer."

Leaving the cover of the low brush, Lia crossed through the moonlit, open space. She hurried in a crouch until stopping behind a well. Raiyn squatted next to her.

"What makes you think he's going to come out?" Raiyn whispered.

Lia peered over the stacked stones of the well, keeping an eye on the back patio door. "I don't know him well . . . but this is our best shot."

A bird chirped. Another echoed the call as if passing the intruder warning along. The clothing Matthew and Emma gave them smelled better than their old outfits. The lack of odor would help them stay unnoticed, but it was difficult to avoid the sharp eyes of birds.

"Should we go up to the house?" Raiyn asked.

Lia considered the suggestion. "Maybe. I'd rather not involve anyone else though—for his sake as well as ours."

"What if—"

Lia stopped him by setting her hand on his arm.

A man exited the door of the house. He promptly descended the steps to the plant garden and headed toward the smaller building at the far end of the property.

"You were right," Raiyn whispered. "He's going to train."

The man disappeared into the building.

"Let's go," Lia breathed.

She led the way, hunched over as she soundlessly padded through the night. A vegetable garden looked ready to harvest on her left. She kept to the trees on the right, ducking into the shadows. After a moment, she found herself on a meandering path of manicured plants.

The square, wooden building at the end of the path was well preserved. A glow flickered in the glass window. Eaves of a sloped roof hung out over the sides, and a tree grew beside it.

"Should we just walk in?" Raiyn whispered then pointed at the roof. "Maybe we should enter up there. We could climb the tree and sneak in through the window."

Lia shook her head. "I don't need to spy. I just need to talk. You stay here. I'll speak with him alone." She stepped forward. "Keep to the shadows and look sharp."

Raiyn snuck off the path and hid under the low branches of a tree.

Lia faced the building. She took a deep breath then approached the door. It opened silently.

Heavy breathing greeted her as she entered. Dark, wooden flooring led down a short hall to an open room with a vaulted ceiling. A lantern hung on a stand, casting light around the space. In the center of the room, High Lord Bilton worked through sword forms, huffing and panting. He wore a flowing, white robe as he swung his weapon with powerful, controlled motions. At sixty years of age, he moved surprisingly well.

"What's your game, Bilton?" she asked from the shadows.

The high lord jumped then spun, his eyes wide and sword raised. After a moment, he lowered the blade, craned his neck forward and squinted. "Lia Stormbridge? I—How—You're alive?"

Her planted feet were ready for action. "Yes, I am."

Bilton looked past her, toward the door.

"Don't even think about calling for anyone," she warned. "I'll be gone before you could even finish the word 'Help.'"

He held up a hand. "I'm not. I just—It's dangerous for you to be here, for you as well as me. Did anyone see you?"

She stared but didn't answer.

"What about the boy . . . Raiyn? Is he with you?"

"You'd like to know, wouldn't you?"

"No, I-I'm not—" Bilton paused and pursed his lips. "Why *are* you here, Lia?"

She took a step forward, letting the lantern light fall on her face. "Why did you tell me to hit his wrist?"

His concerned look morphed into a hesitant smile. "The bracelet, of course."

"It wasn't metal. Fabricated to look like it."

He nodded.

"He cheated, making me think his abilities would be muffled like mine. Why did you warn me?"

"To give you a chance." Bilton's shoulders relaxed. His smile looked genuine. "I've *never* supported Danik."

Lia's brows pinched.

"That's right. I was there when your grandfather was killed. I *saw* Danik assassinate him, but I didn't want it."

"Why didn't you stop him?"

"I couldn't!" Bilton's eyes darted outside before he lowered his voice. "You know the abilities he has. Now, he has those Knights of Power behind him, too. I was powerless."

"But you support him, now?"

Bilton sighed. He walked to the wall and set his sword on its mount. "I'm in a difficult spot, Lia. Before Danik arrived and killed the king, the other high lords were about to name me as the next king. Did you know that?"

She stared for a beat before replying, "Father mentioned that Grandfather was stepping down and you were likely to be crowned. Does Danik know that?"

Bilton scoffed. "I wouldn't be standing here if he did. He'd kill me as a threat. But Danik needs people around him—people who know how to run this kingdom."

Lia nodded, the pieces coming together. "And as long as he thinks you're on his side, he'll keep you around."

"Exactly," Bilton confirmed. "I have no loyalty to him. Not only did he kill a great leader, but he took the crown from me. If I can act like I'm with him, I'll remain in his confidence."

"Have you learned anything helpful?"

"He thinks you and your friend are dead."

Lia chuckled. "That could be good." Bilton's head shake caused her to frown. "No?"

"He gave the order for your father to be killed."

"What?" Lia yelled in a hushed voice. Her heart pounded. "He can't. He should keep him around in case he could use him as leverage for—" Her mouth froze, hanging open as the truth hit her. "If he thinks we're dead, then he's free to execute him."

"Correct." Bilton held up a hand. "Don't worry. He's waiting on confirmation of your death. He sent some guards into the valcor's lair to check."

Lia tilted her head. "And . . . what did they find?"

"Sharp teeth, I'm guessing." Bilton laughed. "I heard the order and followed the guards who were sent to check."

"You killed them?"

"No, but I heard the screaming. They never came out."

"And Danik doesn't know?"

"Not yet—that I'm aware of. He'll send more men soon, and eventually, someone will confirm your and Raiyn's bodies aren't there. In the meantime, he's not going to kill Veron, and the longer he thinks you're dead, the safer you are."

Lia nodded. "That makes sense."

"What do you need, Lia?" Bilton's hands clasped together, folded in front of him. "What can I do to help you?"

"Can you get my father out?"

"Impossible."

Lia folded her arms and raised an eyebrow. "Aren't you the High Lord of Defense?"

Bilton sucked in a deep breath and blew it out slowly. "Your father has a slew of guards around him. Anything I might try would draw a lot of suspicion, and it would mean my neck at the gallows for treason next time."

"Treason against a usurper king is simply loyalty to your realm."

Bilton stared for a long moment. He ran a hand through his thinning, gray hair and sighed. "When we first met, I thought Veron was a troublesome young man poking his nose where he didn't belong. Soon I learned he had wisdom beyond his years, and I should listen. He ended up saving not just Feldor but all of Terrenor."

"You owe him."

Bilton pursed his lips in a pause. "I'll see what I can do, but I make no promises."

A grin creeped onto Lia's face.

"Is there anything else you need?"

"Yes, a book. Danik knows we want it and is probably protecting it."

"The red one? Thin?"

Her eyes grew. "You know it?"

He nodded. "He keeps it on him all the time." He pointed to his chest. "In his jacket pocket."

She frowned. "Any chance he'd give it to you?"

"Ha! Beyond impossible. He's not letting that go."

"When might he set it aside? How about when he sleeps?"

Bilton shook his head. "Guarded, heavily."

Lia nodded. "What about bathing time?"

"I heard he bathed earlier today—after the fight. It will probably be a while until he does again."

"Hmm . . ." Lia propped her foot on a ladder that stretched to a loft. "We need a way to get close to him."

"There is the Coronation Ball, tomorrow night," Bilton suggested. "I could get you in."

Lia froze. "A ball?" Her legs grew shaky.

"You know . . . Food. Drinks. Dancing."

"I know what a ball is," she snapped. "And then I . . . what . . . take it out of his pocket?"

"How quick are your hands?" Bilton asked. "Pretty fast, right?"

An unsettled feeling rumbled in her gut. "That might work." She wrung her hands together. "How would I get in?"

"You'd need an invitation. They went out this evening, but I could get you one."

She nodded then sighed. "So you'll get me an invitation, I'll snatch the book, and you'll break Veron out."

Bilton held up a hand. "I didn't say I would be able to do it."

Lia stepped forward, her posture straight. "You want to get rid of Danik, right? Then we need Veron free."

Bilton nodded after a pause. "I'll work on it."

Lia moved to leave.

"Lia," Bilton said, turning her back around. "There will be plenty of people who could recognize you there. Get a wig. Disguise yourself."

She nodded.

"When you're there, you'll want to blend in as much as possible—not stand out in any way. To do that, there's one more thing you'll need."

She frowned. "What?"

He chuckled and indicated to her body. "A gown."

27

REFINED PREPARATION

Raiyn stuck by Lia's side as she led the way through Turba Square. Portable stands formed the early morning market where citizens of Felting packed the aisles, buying food and bartering with the vendors.

The empty execution stage next to the statue caught Raiyn's eye. He tried to pull his head away, but the memory of standing there, staring down the crossbows seared into his mind.

"I can't believe I'm doing this." Lia's words pulled his gaze back. With her head hidden under a hood, her frown was barely visible.

Raiyn chuckled. "I still can't believe you've never been fitted for a dress."

"Why would I need to? I've spent all my time with swords and sneaking through shadows."

"I figured all girls wore dresses at some point."

"I've worn dresses."

Her defensive tone made him regret the comment.

"But they've never been fancy enough for me to visit a place like this. I'd prefer a loose pair of comfortable pants any day."

He spotted the sign for Rosalie's Dress Shop at the edge of the square. "Is that the one?"

Lia nodded. "Mother's been there. Let's just hope she has something already made that will work."

Raiyn opened the door first, the bell above the door announcing their presence. He held it open while Lia entered.

Instantly, he felt out of place. A handful of completed dresses hung on rods, but much of what covered the store was fabric in various colors.

"Welcome!" a portly woman of around sixty years called from across the shop. "This fine morning is now made better with yer arrival. I'm Rosalie, but I don't believe I've met either of ye."

Lia froze until her uncertainty melted into a smile. "I'm Kate, and this is . . . Benjamin, my friend."

"Kate and Benjamin, it's so good to have met. Now, what can I help ye with?"

"I need a dress."

Rosalie pinched her brows together and cocked her head. "Fer . . . ?"

"The Coronation Ball."

Raiyn added, "Something nice, but not too showy where it would stand out."

The shopkeeper's mouth turned down.

"Is that a problem?" Raiyn asked.

"It takes me a full day to make a ball gown, and that's if I don't have any other work. I'm backed up through the end of the week as it is."

"But . . . the ball is tonight. How does the king expect anyone to—"

"Because the king is a fool." Rosalie flinched after she spoke. She glanced around the shop, craning her neck as if looking for people hiding in the corners.

Raiyn hid a laugh.

"Sorry fer being blunt. I'd send ye to another shop, but ye won't find anyone in Felting who could make one that quickly."

Lia turned to Raiyn. The concern etched into the lines on her face made his stomach turn.

"What should we do?" Raiyn asked.

"Emma said she didn't have anything. Not like what I'll need." She turned to the dresses on display in the shop. "You have several dresses here. What about these?"

Rosalie waved her hand back and forth. "No, no, no. These won't do." She lifted the sleeve of a brown dress. "They're quality dresses, but fer a ball, ye need a gown. Ye said ye didn't want to stand out. This would make ye stand out fer all the wrong reasons."

Lia rubbed her forehead. "All right. Well . . . thanks for your time." She turned toward the door.

Rosalie's eyes grew. "Oh, wait!" She hurried to a back room and rounded a corner.

Raiyn leaned in and whispered, "You don't think she recognizes you, do you? That she's sneaking out back to alert someone?"

Lia shook her head. "It doesn't seem like it."

A squeal carried through the doorway.

"I'm guessing that's good," Raiyn said.

Rosalie turned the corner with a crimson silk dress draped across her arms. Fabric cascaded to the floor with layers upon layers of fine fabric.

Lia gasped, and Raiyn felt his eyes widening. "That is *not* a blending-in dress," he said.

The shopkeeper's beaming smile hesitated. "No, it's not, *but* . . . I think it's the right size."

Lia stood straight while Rosalie held it up to her body. "Where did it come from?" Lia asked.

"It's a sad story, really. Suzanne Quigley ordered it weeks ago."

The name was foreign to Raiyn.

"That's a shame," Lia said.

"I'm sorry," Raiyn said. "Who is that?"

"She was one of Grand—" Lia stopped mid-word, her eyes flashing between the two people. "She was an advisor to King Darcius."

Rosalie nodded. "She died the same night as the king. It's awful. She was a good woman." She stared at the dress and paused for a beat. "And . . . she was around yer size. If ye need a ball gown today, this might be yer only option."

"I'd look ridiculous in this," Lia muttered. She turned to Raiyn. "What do you think?"

Raiyn turned up his hands. "I don't think we have much choice. How much is it?"

"This fabric's not cheap. The cost to Suzanne was eight argen."

Raiyn whistled. "How much did he give you?"

"Only four." Lia's face fell. "He didn't think something subdued would cost more than that."

"And he's right," Rosalie said. "This, unfortunately, isn't that sort of gown."

Both Lia and Raiyn blew out a long breath.

The shopkeeper gathered the dress. "Ye know . . . I'll help ye try it on. It's not doing me any good sitting in the back room. If it fits . . . I can let it go fer four."

LIA ENTERED the bakery then held the door open. Raiyn followed with the gown draped over his arms. His eyes scanned the shop, breathing in relief at the lack of customers.

"What is *that*?" Emma yelled from behind the counter. She scurried around the end, holding her dough-covered hands upturned, away from her body. "You said you were getting a *plain* gown."

Lia pulled down her hood, and a sheepish look formed on her face. "It's all she had."

Emma shook her head. "That's a work of art! You're going to turn every head in the castle."

"I know, but it's this or nothing."

Raiyn turned to Matthew. "Any luck at the theater?"

The baker nodded. "They didn't *want* to let me borrow them, but . . ."

"He took 'em," Emma interrupted, smiling. "I still can't believe it. My honorable baker husband *stealing*."

"I'm going to give them back." He nodded to the far end. "Under the counter."

Lia followed his nod and rounded the corner. She ducked, disappearing below the counter.

"Did you get lost down there?" Raiyn asked after a moment.

When her head popped up, her hair had transformed. Instead of the usual straight brown hair, a wig of wavy blonde locks fell just past her shoulders.

"Wow!" he said. "That's a change."

"Good or bad?" Lia asked.

"You don't look like you," Raiyn said. "That makes it good."

Emma passed behind her to return to her dough. "You look great," she whispered.

"But not as good as before," Raiyn added.

Lia cocked her head. "Not as good, huh?"

His eyes grew. "I mean—Yes, you look good. I'm just saying—I mean—I don't want you to think that *I* think you didn't look good before, because you did."

"You're saying the *normal* Lia looks good?" Emma said with a mischievous grin.

"Emma!" Lia scolded in a whisper.

Raiyn wanted to run his hands across the back of his neck, but the armload of fabric prevented it. "I—uh . . ."

"This is for you." Lia changed the subject by raising a black, fuzzy object.

"Yes." Matthew pointed. "I thought the beard color matched."

Raiyn stepped closer and allowed her to set it against his face. "How does it look?"

Lia grinned. "Not as good as before."

"Ha ha," he laughed.

"I spoke with my friend," Matthew said. "He said we can borrow his carriage for the night."

Lia brightened. "Great. I was going to regret walking all the way to the castle in that thing."

"And my suit is clean, Raiyn. With that, my hat, and this beard, you should be unrecognizable as her wardman."

Lia pulled the wig off. "Let's take all this upstairs."

Raiyn followed her up the back stairs.

The living quarters above the shop was tighter than Morgan and Jeanette's place. A small table and sitting area filled the kitchen and common room, and a doorway led to a single bedroom.

Raiyn draped the gown across the quilt top of the bed, taking care not to wrinkle it. He returned to the main room. "Any thoughts about how to get the book from Danik?"

Lia tossed the wig and fake beard on the table as she sat. "Ideally, we'd think of a way to have him remove his outer jacket."

"It is still suether. Maybe the room will get too hot, and he'll take it off?"

"We can't count on that though."

"What about a smash and grab?"

"What do you mean?"

Raiyn pounded his hand into a fist. "I smash him, and you grab it."

Lia chuckled. "I'm not sure how well that would go. Remember, he and his goons can use the devion."

"Do you know what I'm supposed to do as your wardman? I don't have much experience with it, and I'd rather not stand out."

"My mother had one growing up. Basically, just do anything I ask. They'll probably have a separate area for you at the ball. If I need something, I can call you over."

"All right. Stand around then do whatever you say." Raiyn nodded perfunctorily. "Got it."

"I just hope I'm able to not look like a fool."

"What do you mean?"

"Danik's the king. He may not be there for a while. I'm going to have to fit in with a bunch of dressed-up sycophants."

"Are you ready to dance?"

Lia scoffed and shook her head. "I'm not dancing."

His face tensed. "If . . . you don't want to stand out, you're probably going to have to dance."

"No!"

Her emphatic tone made Raiyn lean back. "That's what people do at these things."

Her neck pulsed as she took in rapid breaths. She glanced at the window but didn't reply.

Raiyn adopted the kindest tone he could manage. "You don't know how, do you?"

"Why would I?" Flustered, she threw up her hands. "It doesn't matter. I can do whatever I want there."

"If you're trying to avoid attention, standing conspicuously on the side while everyone else participates is not going to help."

Lia crossed her arms. "Let's trade places then. You wear the wig and the gown. Let's see how you do with it."

Raiyn pursed his lips and stared back. He sighed. "Lia . . . I—"

"You know how, don't you?" Her expression softened to one of curiosity.

Raiyn nodded. "My mother taught me. She knew all the court dances from every kingdom. She would hum out a tune while we danced through our tiny home." He smiled at the memory. "We never attended balls or danced for anyone else, but it created moments of joy in an otherwise dreary life."

"My mother taught me how to wield a rapier."

They laughed.

"I can teach you," Raiyn said.

Lia raised her eyebrows, a nervous energy emanating from her body.

"Dancing, not stabbing people," he clarified.

"I figured." She nodded. "Sure. I guess I should learn."

Raiyn smiled then stood, his pulse suddenly speeding up. He moved the two sitting chairs to the edge of the room and pushed the table out of the way to create floor space.

"Feldor is known to prefer the Lendlion," Raiyn said.

"I've heard of it. There are a lot of dances though, aren't there?"

"There are others, but you can't learn them all. You don't need to dance every song, but you'll stand out if you skip them all. The Lendlion is the most common, and they're sure to play it. Plus, the steps are easy."

Raiyn stood in the center of the cleared space and motioned for Lia to stand next to him. "It starts in a circle, alternating men and women." He put his hand in hers, an excited spark shooting through his body. Her hand was as rough as his, but her touch was tender. "Step four counts to the left, then back to the right. One, two, three, four. One, two, three, four." He moved slowly, letting her mimic the pattern of his feet. "Good. Then forward four and spin."

Lia laughed as she twirled. They caught hands on the opposite sides and stepped four beats back across the floor. They made the best use of their space to mimic turning in large circles.

Raiyn counted beats as they danced through six rounds. After some initial missteps and wrong turns, Lia moved like a natural. Her steps were precise, and her twirls grew more and more exaggerated as her confidence increased.

Raiyn stopped counting and they released hands. "How do you feel?"

Her smile bounced with her heavy breathing. "Good. It's actually fun. What else?"

He raised his eyebrows. "You want to learn another?"

She shrugged. "Why not?"

Raiyn's eyes wandered to the ceiling while he pursed his lips. "Hmm . . . The next most common is probably the Rose."

Her head cocked. "I don't think I've heard of that one."

"It will likely come up, but you don't need to learn much. At some point, a male guest of honor will initiate the dance. He hands a rose to his spouse or date or whoever, and that signifies the beginning. That couple dances a round of the song on their own. When the music repeats, the other women at the ball are to ask any man to dance with them."

"Do I have to?"

Raiyn turned his hands up and shrugged. "You don't *have* to, but it would be poor form to skip out."

"Who should I ask?"

"Find someone." He chuckled. "Probably not your wardman."

"All right. So how does that one go?"

"It's, um—It's a more . . . personal dance."

"What do you mean?"

His hands felt suddenly sweaty. "You'll see when the lead couple demonstrates, but the goal is to . . . connect." He stepped closer and held his left hand out. "Hold up your hand like this."

Facing him, she extended her hand on the opposite side.

"No, sorry, be a mirror to me. Other hand."

She changed hands and stepped forward.

"That's it." Raiyn placed his hand in hers, moving closer. "My other arm, uh, wraps around your back." He placed his hand on her lower back, pressing into a slight curve.

She straightened, her eyes darting around the room as she cleared her throat.

"Sorry," Raiyn said. "I know it's close."

"No," she said quickly, keeping her head to the side. "It's fine. What do I do with my hand?"

"Rest it on my arm."

She set her hand against his upper arm, near his shoulder.

With his hand on her back, he felt her breathe in and out.

"What do we do next?" she asked.

It took him a second to register the question. His head jerked. "I'm sorry. Next. Right. You, uh . . . move with the music."

"What sort of beat?"

"It will be slow. Follow as he leads, stepping with him. There's no planned movement." Raiyn swayed in a slow, steady rhythm.

Lia moved with him, mirroring his actions. "Like this?"

"Yes, that's good, but—" He swallowed the lump in his throat. "We, uh . . ." He released her hand and patted his chest. "We have to be, um"—he pulled against her until their bodies pressed close—"touching."

"Oh." Lia lowered her chin and angled her face to the side. "That is . . . close."

Raiyn's forehead itched where drops of perspiration formed. He resumed moving his feet. "Like I said, it's . . . personal."

They danced. Other than the creaking floorboards, the room was silent. Raiyn's heart pounded in his chest. With their bodies pressed together, he imagined she could feel the intensity, too.

Gradually, the tension in her back softened. The grip in her hand relaxed, and her free arm shifted position, casually laying against his.

"This isn't too hard," she said.

"No, it's—" He cleared a catch in his throat. "It's not."

Raiyn angled his head toward hers. Her natural, brown hair brushed against his cheek. The scent of her body, so close, made him feel warm all over.

"Thank you for being here, Raiyn," she whispered, her breath tickling his neck.

"There's nowhere else I'd be."

"What you're doing for my father . . . and my mother, it's—"

"I do it for you."

His response cut her off. She turned, and their eyes locked.

Raiyn opened his mouth to say more, but nothing came out. No words did justice to describe how he felt.

Her gaze dropped to his lips, where she lingered, breath shallow and rapid.

His heart felt like it would pound out of his chest. Dryness creeped up his throat, and his hands felt clammy.

She gently released his hand.

Raiyn sucked in air and followed her hand with his eyes. It dropped, slowly and purposely until it touched his hip. She pulled gently against him, but there was nowhere for their bodies to go. His chest pressed against hers, a tingle running through his body.

Their eyes found each other again, and he repeated his unsuccessful attempt to speak.

Her hand on his arm grew firm. She leaned closer, her lips parting as she took in a faint breath.

He leaned toward her. His pulse raced and his hand on her back trembled. He tried to make it stop, but the effort only resulted in shaking her.

Lia's eyes flitted to the side.

No! Raiyn thought. *Get it together!*

She leaned away, the pressure on his arm and hip lessening. "I'm sorry." She lowered her gaze.

"No," he said. "It's all right. It was stupid of me to think—"

"That's not it." Lia's eyes lifted again. A tender gaze contained smile lines at the corners. "You're great, Raiyn. *Amazing* even. I wish —" She sighed, blowing her breath out slowly. "I just need to focus on getting my father and mother back."

He nodded, swallowing a lump in his throat. "Of course. I get it. It's fine."

Her face contained a flush and her lips pressed together in a rueful smile. "Thank you—for understanding."

He smiled back, his face lying about the disappointment he truly felt.

Footsteps preceded the door opening, and Matthew and Emma entered.

Emma paused. "Are we interrupting anything?"

Raiyn stepped away from Lia and cleared his throat. "No, of course not." The calm note of his voice belied the continued pounding of his heart.

Matthew held the door open and looked behind him. "We found a friend."

Morgan Fenster passed through the door with a nervous smile.

"Morgan!" Lia said. "Is everything all right? Is your family safe?"

He nodded. "Jeanette and the kids are fine."

"What are you doing here?"

"I had to find you, and I figured you might remember Matthew and Emma."

"What happened?"

"I went by the grocery to make sure everything was all right."

Lia raised her eyebrows.

"It's fine—just as we left it with a 'Closed' sign on the door. But two people sat against the wall, waiting."

"Waiting for the store to open?" Raiyn asked.

"It seemed unlikely so late in the day," Morgan said, "so I approached them—a man and a young boy. Their clothes were coarse, and it looked like they hadn't bathed in weeks. They didn't look like they were from Felting."

Lia stepped closer.

"I greeted them and asked what they were up to. They said they were waiting for Fenster Foods to open. I asked why, and they said they needed to speak with Morgan Fenster."

"Sounds like a trap," Raiyn said.

Morgan nodded. "I thought so, too, but there was something about these two—an earnest look. I told them I was Morgan. It took a moment to get past their skepticism, but they opened up."

"Who were they?" Lia asked.

"They're from a village in the foothills of the Straith Mountains. Two weeks ago, they ran into chained men and women being marched into the mountains by a group dressed in gray."

Lia's eyes widened. "The knights?"

Morgan nodded and held out a crumpled piece of paper. "One of them tossed this."

"A note?" Lia's words breathed with hope. She took it with a trembling hand and read aloud. Raiyn looked over her shoulder.

Give note to Morgan Fenster in Felting.

Knights captured. Heading into mountains toward caverns. If Veron or Lia follow, have them watch out for bears.

Chelci

"They're still alive," Raiyn breathed.

Lia turned to him, her eyes bright with a hopeful smile. "At least they were two weeks ago."

"'Watch out for bears?'" Raiyn quoted. "What does that mean?"

"Bears shouldn't pose too much of a problem, especially with our use of the origine. She knows this. It's odd." Lia cocked her head to the side.

"The man and boy didn't know anything else," Morgan said. "But they thought it important enough to seek me out."

"I wonder what caverns she's talking about?" Raiyn asked.

Lia sucked in a breath. "Where are they now?" Her voice held a nervous energy that brimmed with hope. She craned her neck as if hoping to see them down the stairwell. "If they can take us to their village . . ."

Morgan's sagging shoulders and frown cut her off. "When we were talking, I kept looking over my shoulder, looking for knights. They grew skittish when they learned people were looking for me. After they gave me the note, I asked them to wait. I ran upstairs to grab a map so they could show me where it was. By the time I arrived back at the road, they were gone."

"No!"

"I jogged the streets, but I couldn't find them. I'm sorry."

Raiyn set his hand on Lia's shoulders. Disappointment radiated from her skin. "Hey," he said, getting her to turn his way. "At least we know what direction they're traveling. That's something. Plus, we know to look out for bears."

She nodded. "Yeah, that's better than nothing. Thank you, Morgan, for finding us." She shook the paper. "This helps."

"Despite the new information, we still have a pressing matter to deal with," Raiyn said. "We still need to prepare for a ball."

28

BALLROOM BLENDING

Raiyn stood motionless as his gaze traced along the street out the window. A leather shop led to a butcher, followed by a tax office. A clock on the side of the office caught Raiyn's eye. *We need to hurry.* He tapped his foot, trying to be patient.

"Almost done," Matthew said, standing before him, focusing on the tie tugging at Raiyn's neck.

Matthew's suit fit him well. The dark-gray, wool coat was a bit warm and the pants were a tad short, but the waist and shoulders were near perfect matches. It was nicer than anything Raiyn had ever owned, and he could put up with the temperature for one night.

The only thing that bothered Raiyn was the beard stuck to his face with a clear adhesive. He repeatedly tried to scratch it, but the older man kept batting his hand away.

"There!" Matthew announced, standing straight. "One last piece . . ." He turned to the table and picked up a matching, round hat.

Raiyn took the hat then whispered, "How long do you think they've been at it?"

Matthew glanced at the closed door to the bedroom and whistled. "Hours."

Raiyn set the hat on his head and pushed down the thick, black hair.

"Wow," Matthew said. "You look good."

"Hold on," Emma called from behind the bedroom door. "We want to see, too."

"Hurry up, then." Matthew glanced out the window at the street clock and frowned. "The carriage will be here soon."

"We're almost done."

Raiyn moved to stand in front of the small mirror on their wall, and a laugh escaped. "I can't believe that's me."

Matthew stood next to him. "You look just like a proper wardman. Remember . . . act like you belong and be attentive. When you're not needed, you're expected to be out of the way."

Raiyn nodded. "Got it."

The older man lowered his voice. "A word of advice."

Raiyn turned to him and straightened.

"She's gonna look different—clothes she doesn't normally wear, a wig, makeup—she'll probably feel a little foolish. No matter how she looks, make sure to say something nice."

"Sure," Raiyn whispered back.

"Trust me on this. It seems like there may be a few sparks between you two. Kind words will—" Matthew's eyes flicked over Raiyn's shoulder, and he stopped mid-sentence.

"What is it?"

Raiyn spun, and his jaw dropped. He tried to speak, but nothing came out. The most beautiful person he'd ever seen stood in the doorway—a woman in a scarlet red gown with wavy, blonde hair.

"Lia?" His mouth continued to hang open.

Her smile gave her away. "What do you think?"

He half-laughed, but the sound cut out. He managed a few more incoherent noises, but nothing that formed actual words.

Her crimson dress cascaded in luxurious folds, tumbling to the floor. The fine silk swished gently with the movement of her body. The neckline cut in a striking V shape, low across her chest. She lifted a hand to cover the pale skin. Spotless white gloves covered her hands and extended to her elbows. Her face looked shockingly different from what he was used to. Dusky eyes smoldered, and her lips popped with a sensuous shade of deep red.

The blonde hair threw him off the most. He imagined it brown, and a smile came to him.

"Do I look all right?" she asked, her forehead wrinkling.

Raiyn tried to answer. He opened his mouth, but his words had yet to return. A nudge from Matthew forced him to take a step forward. "You're more beautiful than anyone I've ever met," he croaked.

Lia looked to the ground, her smile puffing out cheeks that ran red.

"I think she's ready," Emma said, hands on her hips. "How about you, Raiyn?"

It took effort for Raiyn to tear his eyes from Lia. "Yes. I'm ready, but I just had an idea." He turned to Matthew and nodded toward the window. "That store across the street—Felting Tax Accounting & Research. Do they have books on taxes?"

Matthew frowned. "Um . . . I think so."

"Can you do me a quick favor?" A mischievous smile pulled at his face. "I have an idea."

THE CARRIAGE BUMPED along the street, jostling Lia's dress. She pulled the fabric, making sure it didn't catch and tear. *This thing is ridiculous,* she thought. *It's going to be tough to hide in the crowd.*

The dress spilled across the floor of the vehicle, leaving little room for Raiyn's legs. "Sorry it's so big," she said.

Sitting across from her, he laughed softly, covering his mouth with a hand.

"What?"

"Nothing." He continued to smile. "It's a side of you I've never seen before."

"And you never will again." She dropped her arms into her lap with a huff. "Is my face disguised enough?"

He nodded. "The shade around the eyes really helps. I wouldn't be able to tell."

She pointed to his face. "Are you going to grow a beard like that after this?"

"Not likely." He scratched at it. "It's so annoying."

"Don't do that!" Lia waved her hand. "You don't want to mess it up. Come on. Let's go over the plan, again."

Raiyn sighed. "We've gone over it so many times."

"Well, excuse me for wanting to get it right. Plus, I'm stressed about being late. I need to put my mind on something. You have the invitation?"

Raiyn opened the jacket and pulled the corner of a piece of paper from a pocket. "Got it."

"Tell me again what he said."

"Bilton convinced Nicolar that the guards checking on us had died, so Bilton selected a team to follow up. He's set it up so they'll return partway through the ball."

Lia nodded. "Then, after Danik realizes the threat, he'll move Veron, but instead of going to a new cell, he'll be intercepted and released."

"That's the plan," Raiyn said. "As for the book . . ."

Lia lowered her chin and swallowed. "I'll get close to Danik. You'll create a distraction, then I'll swipe it from his jacket."

"What if it's not in his jacket pocket?"

"Then I give you the signal, and you sneak off to his bedroom." Lia pointed at him. "You have the map?"

Raiyn nodded, patting his pocket. "And if he has it on him but catches you taking it?"

She smiled. "Smash and grab."

"That's right. You sure you're able to get to everything?" He nodded toward her dress.

"I'll be fine," Lia said, a strain of petulance coming through. Her hand wriggled through the slit on the side of her dress. Raiyn averted his eyes while her hand rooted around. "Ugh, these garters are tight.

There!" She pulled her hand out, a silver dagger coming with it. "See? Easy."

He chuckled. "I'll be there to back you up, and we'll get out as soon as possible."

"What are we going to do if Bilton doesn't come through?"

After sighing, Raiyn shrugged. "He seemed confident a few hours ago."

Lia's stomach felt tied in knots. She wrestled under her dress to put the dagger back in its place. "I hope this works."

The carriage slowed. Lia glanced out the window and recognized the circular drive that ran in front of the castle.

"Here we go."

The rolling stopped. After a moment, footsteps approached, and the door opened. Raiyn exited first, hopping to the ground. He turned and raised his hand.

Lia smiled as she took it. "Thank you, Benjamin."

Raiyn nodded, standing to the side for her to pass.

Two other carriages unloaded on either side of theirs. Men and women exited the vehicles in suits and gowns. They held their noses up, ignoring their servants as they ascended the castle steps.

"I'm following you," Raiyn said over her shoulder.

Lia took a deep breath then nodded. She lifted her dress slightly as she walked, taking care not to step on the fringe. Two guards posted at the door, at the top of the steps.

"Invitation?" one asked.

Lia looked over her shoulder as Raiyn scurried forward. "Of course." He extended the card.

The guard ran his eyes down it before waving them forward. "Show it at the end of the hall."

Raiyn handed the card to Lia as they entered. "How are you doing?" he asked when they were out of earshot of the guards.

"We haven't done anything yet." Her insides jumped. "I'm fine."

Her gown swayed as they walked the familiar hall. She'd been down it many times before, but never under the same pressure. A deep breath helped soothe the jitters.

At the end of the hall, the line of previous arrivals backed up at the columned entrance to the ballroom. A man in formal attire took the invitations while two more guards past stone pillars ran their eyes over the guests.

Lia's breath caught. Broderick and Alton stood beyond the guards with swords dangling at their hips. The knights of power watched the line of people, glancing from face to face as they whispered between each other.

"Stay natural," Raiyn whispered. "They're not looking for us. They think we're dead."

Lia swallowed and gave a faint nod. "Unless word has already gotten back."

Over the shoulders of the people in line, past two lion statues and down a short grouping of steps, men in suits and women in gowns filled the ballroom. Some held small plates with food and most held a glass. Musicians sat on a raised platform, performing music that drifted through the doorway, mixed with the dull hum of conversation.

"Edgar and Ellen Waterford," the man at the doors announced in a booming voice.

The man and woman at the front of the line entered the ballroom. Lia eyed the lady's gown with jealousy. Light-blue in color, it was elegant but not flashy, stretching to the floor. *Just like I wanted.* Their attendant followed into the room unannounced.

The crowd in the ballroom glanced their way while conversations continued.

Lia and Raiyn stepped forward, waiting on one more couple. Her peripheral vision showed Danik's men leaning together.

She strained her ears, the origine tingling in her gut as she tried to hear their conversation.

"Killed?" Alton said.

"Apparently," Broderick answered. "The animal ate them, or something."

"Which is why they took so long to report back. And Bilton sent more men?"

"Six of them. Danik wants it confirmed tonight. He's—"

The men stopped their conversation. At the edge of her sight, Lia felt the men looking her way. She fixed her jaw, fighting the creeping redness that seemed to climb up her neck. *Don't recognize me. Don't recognize me.*

"Marcus and Hellory Stanton," the man at the door announced.

The next man and woman entered the ballroom with a male and female attendant following. Again, a few heads glanced briefly in their direction.

Broderick continued, "He's eager to be rid of . . . you know who."

"I think he should kill him and be done with it."

"Agreed. Why risk his escape again?"

The announcer extended his hand to Lia and raised his eyebrows. "How do you pronounce your name, miss?"

Lia forced a smile. "Kate Hellingham." She tuned her ear back to the other conversation.

"And he should burn that book. If he's so worried about it getting taken, then get rid of it."

"Instead he even brings it with him to a ball," Broderick scoffed.

Lia grinned at the news.

The announcer's chest puffed up before he bellowed to the room, "Kate Hellingham."

Turning her full attention to the ballroom, Lia stepped forward. Raiyn came alongside her and took her hand to pass between the stone lions. She watched her feet as she took the four steps down to the floor of the chamber. Her neck prickled before she even looked up. *What's wrong?* She raised her head.

Every head in the room looked her way. Men's mouths gaped. Women either raised their eyebrows or shot daggers with their gaze. The musicians had even stopped playing.

"Keep going," Raiyn whispered, releasing her hand and motioning for her to proceed.

Lia swallowed. She lowered her head and resumed her walk forward. Her cheeks burned. She clenched her jaw. Her dress swished, its folds rustling together. She heard the words, "gorgeous," and "exquisite," muttered as the crowd resumed speaking to each other.

Raiyn stepped next to her and bowed. "Is there anything I can help you with, miss?"

Lia looked at him then found herself stuck, unable to decide.

"Perhaps I can get you some food . . . or a drink?"

Lia blinked several times then looked around. People in the crowd looked away when she made eye contact. Most of them held a glass. "A drink, please." Her voice shook as she forced out the words.

Raiyn nodded then disappeared toward a bar, leaving her alone.

Her breath came rapidly. She clasped her hands in front of her as she waited, her eyes darting around the room.

A man materialized before her. "Kate, was it?"

She extended a gloved hand, and he bent over to kiss its back. His short, brown hair pressed to his head with a shine. He wore a brown suit with layer upon layer of shirt and vest and tie and another shirt. His posture was erect, and his jaw was sharp. His greasy smile put her on edge. She estimated his age was nearly thirty.

"I thought I'd met all the beautiful young ladies of Felting's high society. Clearly, I was wrong." The grin somehow grew even larger. He set his hand on his chest. "My name is Willoughby . . . Ralph Willoughby. My father owns the two largest banks in the city."

"It's a pleasure to meet you, Ralph," she forced.

"Are you from Felting?"

She paused while maintaining a polite smile. "No. I—my parents live in Lorranis. They run a string of shops near the port—dresses and jewelry mostly."

He gestured to her body. "That explains this lovely piece you're wearing." He chuckled. "I don't think I've ever seen something quite so striking."

"Thank you. My parents have great taste in choosing gowns."

He leaned forward, his oily expression taking on a new level. "I wasn't referring to the gown, Kate."

She fought back a groan.

Another young man stepped up. "Excuse me," he said. "Kate, I'm

Conrad Wynter. From the moment you stepped in the room, I knew I had to introduce myself."

"Can't you see I'm speaking with the young lady, Conrad?" Ralph said, staring pointedly at the new arrival.

"Yes, I can see. I'm just saying hello." He turned to Lia. "That's not a problem, is it?"

Lia opened her mouth to reply.

"Yes, it is a problem," Ralph interrupted. "You may speak with her once she's done with the conversation."

"I imagine she's capable of determining who she wants to speak with."

"Did I hear your name was Kate?" A third smiling young man butted his way past the other two.

"No, Walter!" Ralph turned. "I'm having a conversation with her."

"As am I," Conrad added.

Ralph raised his finger and pointed. "You *both* need to leave. I was here first!"

Lia took a step backward while the three young men bickered. Her heart leaped as Raiyn approached.

"Miss Kate." He handed her a glass. "You're needed over this way."

The three men didn't seem to notice as they snuck away.

"Thank you," she said when they were out of earshot. "Those boys were crazy."

Raiyn chuckled. "You might need to get used to it. I doubt that's the last of the attention you're going to receive."

She lifted her glass. It contained a clear liquid that wobbled as she walked. A slice of lime floated on the top. "What is this? It's probably a bad idea to have anything strong. I need my wits about me."

"It's water."

She smiled. "Good call."

"I had them add the lime to make it look fancy."

Heads continued to turn as Lia followed Raiyn through the crowd. She scanned the room, noting Cedric patrolling along the far wall. "Have you seen *him* yet?"

Raiyn angled his head back as he walked, then shook it. "I found someone else, though."

The imposing form of Geoffrey Bilton emerged as the crowd split. He wore his formal army uniform and engaged in conversation with another officer.

Raiyn touched the brim of his hat—their prearranged signal.

Bilton's serious expression melted into a friendly smile.

"I'll be over there." Raiyn pointed to the area where the other attendants congregated. "Wave me down if you need anything." He leaned closer and whispered, "Good luck."

Lia turned her attention to the high lord, who bowed. "I saw you enter." His voice resonated. "I'm Geoffrey Bilton, High Lord of Defense for Feldor, and this is Captain William Moulton. What was your name again?"

She extended her hand. "Kate Hellingham."

"Kate." He kissed the back of her hand. "It's a pleasure to meet you."

After nodding across the room, the captain matched Bilton in the same act. "It is my pleasure as well, Kate. Unfortunately, I must take your leave. My wife is petitioning the master of ceremonies to begin the dancing. She'll make me regret it if I don't join her." He nodded to Bilton. "Sir."

When the other man had left, Bilton stepped closer and lowered his voice. "Everything is arranged. My men should report back soon."

"And you think Danik will take the bait?"

Bilton nodded. "I'll give him the note just before. If he doesn't go for it, I can increase the pressure."

"If we take the book, but Veron isn't freed, Danik's reasons for keeping him alive will grow thin. The escape must be tonight."

The man didn't answer

"He's coming, right? The king?"

Bilton's head lifted to scan over her head. "Should be here soon. Great disguise, by the way. Had I not known you were coming, I would have thought you were the daughter of a city lord."

She smiled.

A trill of notes rang quickly through the air, then stopped. A man in a black suit with long tails stood before the musicians and raised his hands. "Ladies and gentlemen, please step forward as we kick off the dancing. The first dance will be . . . the Berrytrot."

Excitement rose in the crowd as men and women moved toward the center of the room and formed into lines. When the music started, they bounced in time, clapping and turning. The lines moved, and the dancers rotated throughout the floor.

Lia grew weary of trying to remember the pattern. *I won't need to know that anytime soon.*

Footsteps at her side drew her attention. She froze. Cedric stood next to her, glass in hand.

Don't recognize me. Don't recognize me.

"Not dancing?" His words slurred while he swayed.

"It appears not," she replied through much effort.

"Someone as pretty as you would be the star of the floor."

She managed a weak smile.

"You like men though, right? Are you just not a fan of dancing in general? Perhaps you prefer *other* activities?"

Her stomach turned as his insinuation. "I intend to dance, but . . ." She searched for an excuse, then held up her glass. "I thought I'd finish this first."

"What's your drink?"

Lia looked at the floating lime and considered ways to run the man off. "What I drink is my own business."

The man laughed, a harsh cackle.

Her eyes jumped to see if they drew any attention.

"I like that." He waved his own drink. "A girl of mystery." He leaned closer. His breath wafted noxious fumes across her nose. "I'd love to get to know you better."

She took a half step away to gain more space, cringing as the tip of his tongue ran across his lower lip.

A crescendo of music preceded a rousing applause from the dance floor. Lia turned as men and women clapped, breaking their rigid formations.

The master of ceremonies raised his hands as the applause faded. "Next up, please join us for the Lendlion!"

Lia's heart jumped. *Yes!*

She turned to Cedric and lifted her glass. "Would you hold this? It's time I stretched my legs."

Cedric took the drink and frowned. Before he could object, she had already turned and walked away.

The relief of getting away from the awful man was short lived. Her pulse beat faster when she arrived at the dance floor, having no idea how to start. Other couples held hands and moved naturally to form a large circle. She tried to insert herself but couldn't find a place with an unmatched man.

"Kate!"

She turned. *Ugh. Ralph.* He stood in the circle, motioning to an empty place at his side. She forced a smile and joined him.

"You looked like you could use a spot." He extended his hand.

She pushed back her aversion and held it. An older man with gray hair and a smile that hid behind his beard arrived on her other side. Lia took his extended hand and nodded.

"I apologize about earlier." Ralph squeezed her hand to get her attention. "That was not a pretty scene."

An apology, Lia thought. *Maybe he's not a possessive jerk after all.*

"Those men should *not* have interrupted us like that." He scoffed. "I can't believe how rude they were. I was there first, and they *clearly* should have realized that."

Or maybe he is.

The music began, rescuing her. The circle of alternating genders raised their hands in unison before stepping together toward the left.

Despite having no reason to doubt Raiyn's dancing knowledge, a relieved feeling rushed through her as each new move matched what she had learned. She spun and stepped, counting to four repeatedly in her head. She moved to the center circle on cue with the other ladies, taking the hand of a smiling olive-skinned woman with dark-brown hair and an older lady on the other side.

An unbidden smile grew. Caught up in the music, laughter, and rhythmic stepping, Lia forgot about the stakes of their mission. She lost herself in the joy of the moment. While dancing back to the outer circle, Raiyn caught her eye from across the room with a smile on his face.

The music eased into a final chord and sustained it while the dancers bowed. She released the men's hands and joined the others in applause. Her pulse felt slightly elevated, and a sheen of sweat prickled at her forehead.

"Thank you for joining me, Kate. That was a joy." Ralph's face was red. "Could I interest you in another?" He pointed toward the musicians and raised an eyebrow.

Lia waved her hand while managing a polite smile. "Thank you, but I should catch my breath."

"That's a great idea. I'll join you."

Lia's neck reddened as the young man followed her toward the bar. A glimpse of Cedric ahead, still holding her glass, turned her in the other direction. She pushed past a cluster of men until the sight before her caused her to freeze in her tracks.

Danik stood directly before her with a crown balanced on his head. A dark blue robe hung from his shoulders and draped to the floor. A sharp, gray jacket with a white shirt poked out from beneath the blue. Young women barely older than Lia stood on either of his sides. One had shocking red hair, tied up in a bun. Her deep-blue gown stood out from her fair skin. The other girl had dark skin and black hair and wore a lilac piece.

"I don't believe I've had the pleasure of meeting you," Danik said.

Lia's heart pounded. *He's going to recognize me. I know he will.* She stood still and silent while Ralph bowed next to her.

"My name is Danik, and as king, it's my job to learn everything about my kingdom. You name was . . . ?"

"Kate," she whispered, a catch in her throat making it sound garbled. "Kate Hellingham."

29

MAKING AN IMPRESSION

Raiyn perked up at Danik's arrival. The corner of the room where the wardmen and wardesses waited had not been particularly exciting. He had avoided conversation with the other attendants by standing to the side, and when the king showed, he drifted closer to the action. He lingered by a table of food and drink, keeping an eye on Lia.

She needs to get out of there. It's not time yet.

He scanned the room and found Bilton already drifting in his direction.

"Can you get things moving?" Raiyn whispered out of the side of his mouth when the high lord was within range.

"We need the guards to return," he replied. "The plan depends on it."

"When will they be here?"

Bilton glanced at the far end of the hall. The lines on his face grew more pronounced. "Soon . . . I hope."

"KATE," Danik said as if tasting the name on his tongue. "You realize, you've made a lot of enemies, don't you?"

Lia remained frozen. Her mouth needed to move, but her jaw wouldn't work.

Danik's eyes jumped around the room before returning to her. "Every woman in this room hates you." He leaned closer. "They didn't realize there was a young woman in Feldor as beautiful as you."

At another time, she may have enjoyed the compliment, but coming from his lips, it turned her stomach.

"Lisette and Dawn . . ." he said.

The girls on either side straightened.

"Take notes." He paused to wink at Lia. "Kate has raised the bar."

Ralph and his shiny, brown hair took a step backward. "I'll take my leave," he whispered as the music behind them kicked off another dance.

Danik turned to the red-haired girl. "Would you fetch me a drink please?" He glanced at the other. "Both of you. A brandy."

As the girls left, a bulge in Danik's inside coat pocket caught her eye. The red cover of a book peeked out.

"Bilton," Raiyn whispered. "You need to get over there."

The high lord sighed. "I can't. Not yet. The note on its own won't be enough."

"What if you distract him? You could pull him away to talk. I'm worried Lia's going to pounce before it's time."

"We'll draw enough suspicion as it is. We need to—" Bilton stopped.

Raiyn looked up and followed the man's eyes. A guard stood at the entrance, speaking with the man at the doors.

"They're back. It's time."

"Tell me about yourself," Danik said, turning back to Lia.

The origine simmered in her gut. Her desire to grab the book and push him down warred against her need to be patient. *Could I make it out? No. It's not time yet. I need to wait.*

"I, uh . . ." she searched for something to say, but nothing came.

"Who are your parents?"

To prevent him from recognizing the voice he knew so well, she kept her words to a whisper. "Shopkeepers in Lorranis."

"Your Majesty." Bilton's timely arrival saved her.

Finally.

"Something arrived I think you should see."

A flash of annoyance crossed Danik's face. "I'm at a ball, Geoffrey. Don't you think—"

Bilton held up a note with a broken wax seal—a familiar wax seal created by Matthew only hours before. "Trust me."

After a pause, the king's smile returned. He nodded to Lia. "I'm so sorry, Kate. Excuse me." He followed Bilton who stepped to the side of the room.

HE'S COMING, Raiyn thought. He averted his eyes and turned to the table of food.

"This had better be good," Danik said, barely loud enough for Raiyn to hear.

Paper crinkled. Raiyn imagined the king opening the note and creasing back the folds. He held his breath, straining his ears for any reaction.

"What is this?"

"The note was left with the castle guards," Bilton said.

"Who left it?"

"They don't know, but they said it was a hooded man. He ran off immediately after insisting it be sent to me."

"What's going on?"

Raiyn frowned at the arrival of the new voice—a Norshewan accent. He snuck a glance and found Nicolar standing with the other two men.

"'The prisoner will be freed during the ball.' What does that mean?" Nicolar asked.

"I . . . can only assume it refers to—" Bilton paused. "You know."

"That doesn't make any sense. Why would someone tell us this?" the king asked as the paper rustled. "There was nothing else with the note?"

"Nothing, Your Majesty. I thought it important enough to let you know."

Raiyn's ears strained during the silent moment that followed. He felt suddenly conspicuous, standing still, so near their conversation. A large bowl of punch caught his attention, and he selected an empty glass from the table.

"Who would be able to free him?" Bilton asked.

Raiyn cringed. *Don't push too hard, Bilton.*

"I can't imagine our men would be behind it," Danik said.

"Not the Knights of Power," Nicolar added. "We should kill the prisoner while we can."

"Or . . ." Bilton's voice lowered. "Do you think the note could be from . . . the other two?"

"If they were alive, possibly," Danik said. "But . . . it's probably a joke."

"We can't ignore this," Bilton pushed. "He's too valuable to risk it."

"You're right," the king said. "No need to risk. Add more guards to his cell."

Raiyn sloshed the ladle of punch, pouring over the side of his glass. *No!*

"Sir," Bilton said. "Do you think that might be what they want?"

"What do you mean?"

"What if the guards are part of the plan? They could be loyal to the old regime. If we load up on guards, and if *they* arrive, that could give them allies."

"What else would you do?"

Bilton paused, giving the illusion of thinking. "Might it make sense to . . . move the prisoner before they could get here?"

Raiyn raised his glass to his lips and sipped on the punch, taking care not to spill it on his false beard. His ears strained to catch any response.

The king thought out loud, "*If . . .* the other two are still alive . . ."

Raiyn's pulse pounded in his head as he listened to the interminable pause.

"Yes, it could be beneficial to move him where no one else knows."

"The east tower of the castle is barely used," Bilton said. "There is a locked room at the top where we could hide him."

"We'd need to keep the circle of who knows small. Bilton, you know where this tower room is?"

"I do."

The tight feeling in Raiyn's gut eased.

"Ah!" Bilton's voice carried a new inflection. "My man from the arena returns. Hopefully this will confirm what we suspect, and none of this will be needed."

Drinking his punch and turning toward the rest of the ballroom, Raiyn feigned his attention elsewhere. From the corner of his eye, he noted the arrival of a royal guard in full uniform.

"Dodson, were you able to confirm?"

"Yes, High Lord. Yes, Your Majesty. My team and I entered the animal's lair while it slept." The guard's voice wavered as he spoke. "We, uh . . . found the remains of the girl and the young man, as we expected."

"What?" Bilton exclaimed.

Raiyn nearly choked on his drink, turning back toward the table to avoid attention.

"They were there?" Bilton asked.

"Yes, High Lord."

"This is great," Danik said, hands hitting his sides. "That settles it."

"But-but—" Bilton stammered. "You're sure of it? Could it have been . . . someone else?"

"The bodies were nearly unidentifiable, but we were able to distinguish some of the clothes they wore the other night. Ask any of our team. It was clearly theirs."

"Thank you, guard, for your service." Danik dismissed the man.

Raiyn's arm shook while he tried to hold his glass steady.

"This solves our problem of the note," Danik said. "Nicolar, hurry to the dungeon and ensure the prisoner is taken care of as soon as possible."

"Taken care of, sir?" Bilton asked.

"As we discussed. Without the others, he's not needed anymore. Eliminate him."

"Of course." Nicolar nodded before turning and heading toward the closest door.

Danik clapped Bilton on the shoulder. "Thank you for bringing it to my attention, Geoffrey. Dispose of the note. There's no need to chase that any longer."

The king walked away, leaving Bilton frozen in place.

Raiyn hurried the few steps to the man's side. "What do we do?"

Bilton shook his head, his eyes vacant and staring toward the wall. "I-I-I don't know. I don't know what happened."

Raiyn pulled on his arm. "Bilton!" His whisper bordered on a yell.

The man remained stunned.

"Gah!" Raiyn turned away in a huff and scanned the room. *Where is she?*

Lia tensed at the sight of Raiyn cutting through the crowd. *Something is wrong.* Her smile hardened as he arrived. "What is it?"

Raiyn leaned to her ear. "They think we're dead."

Her head jerked. "What?"

"The guard reported they found our bodies in the lair. They're heading to execute your father now."

Her body tensed, and her breath grew shallow. "No. This can't be happening. We have to show Danik we're alive. So he can call off the execution."

Raiyn shook his head. "There's no time. Nicolar's heading there now. I'm going after him. You stay here and get the book."

He turned away, but she grabbed his arm. "I'm coming, too."

"I can do this," Raiyn said. "I've been down in the dungeons. I know where the passages lead. We don't just need your father. We need the book, too. You need to stay here and finish that."

Raiyn ducked his head and pulled away, his sleeve slipping through her fingers.

"No, we should—" Lia's words stuck in her throat.

Dressed in his royal garb, Danik stood before her. "Trouble with your wardman?"

She blinked several times, her mind spinning. *Father. The dungeons. The book. Raiyn. The ball.* The dancing crowd applauded the end of a song.

"Is everything all right?"

She forced herself to meet his eyes. "Yes," she managed. "It's nothing."

He stepped closer. "I hate seeing anyone at my Coronation Ball upset. I do have something that should cheer you up."

Lia waited, expecting him to finish the thought. Her eyebrows raised.

"I've made my choice." The king raised his hands higher.

Her gaze dropped. Danik had been holding his hands together, but she had failed to notice what they contained. Her heart plummeted. A long green stem contained thorns and leaves, and at the end, a white bud bloomed. A rose.

The crowd around them cheered, but Lia could only stare.

"Don't be so shocked," Danik said. "With beauty like yours, how could I not choose you for my Rose partner?" He extended the rose toward her.

Lia looked at the flower. It hung in the air, motionless. Past it, a red book spine peeked out from inside his jacket. She breathed in then out then in again. *I'm not prepared for this. I can't get that close to him. He'll recognize me. Should I take the book now?*

She glanced around. Every face in the ballroom stared at her. The applause had died, and the entire room waited on her response.

"Kate?" The friendly look on Danik's face developed an edge. The flower moved closer.

Holding her breath, Lia extended her hand. Her mind screamed.

She longed to lunge for the book, knock him down, and sprint for the door. Instead, her fingers wrapped around the stem.

FUELED BY THE ORIGINE, Raiyn ran in a crouch along the carpeted hall. Away from the ballroom, any unauthorized visitors would be questioned, so he hurried between corners, hoping the path remained clear. He stopped before the next intersection, leaning against the wall. His breath came quickly, and his sweaty clothes stuck to his body.

He poked his head around the corner and sucked in a breath. Nicolar took the last few steps to enter a staircase, the one Raiyn remembered that led deep under the castle. The man pulled a dagger from his belt the moment before he disappeared into the stairwell.

Raiyn turned the corner. He prepared to run, but a pair of approaching voices halted his sprint. Instead, he jumped across the hall to where a large column spiraled from the floor to the arched ceiling. A shadow of the column reflected on the wall from the lantern in the hall. He cringed at the sight of his two shoulder shadows sticking out on either side. He pulled in his arms, scrunching his chest.

"And he wasn't suspicious?" a voice asked. The hushed voice carried across the empty hall.

"Bilton asked questions," another voice said, "but the king was eager to accept it."

"Good. If he knew—"

"There's nothing to know."

"Yeah, but what if those two show up alive somewhere? It will be our heads."

"It would have been our heads had we gone in there—like those others who checked. But there's nothing to worry about. There's no way they got out of that lair alive."

Should I tell Bilton?

The footsteps passed the column, and Raiyn shuffled around the curve in the opposite direction. The door to the dungeons gaped ahead. *No. There's no time.*

The sound of the men rounded a corner. He peeked his head out from behind the obstacle to confirm. *Alone again.* He left his hiding place and ran.

The stairs spiraled counter-clockwise into the earth. Raiyn leaned into a decent amount of origine to speed his descent, while taking it slowly enough to ensure he didn't stumble into anyone.

The bottom of the stairs spilled into a familiar room, the beginning of the dungeon. Gloomy cells lined the right side, and a lone torch hung on the opposite wall. An empty chair leaned against the wall, and a club rested on the ground beneath it.

The isolation chamber! He grabbed the club and flew down the corridor.

His heart pounded. His lungs begged him to rest and bring in more oxygen. He paused before a corner. With his hands on the slick, stone wall, he held his breath and peeked around the edge.

His old cell waited at the end of a short passage. Six guards formed two lines of three in front of it. Their attention wasn't on him though. The heavy door had already been opened, and the guards peered inside. With torchlight dancing on his face, Veron kneeled in the center of the cell. His hands were pulled behind his back, and a gag tied across his mouth. He looked up to where Nicolar loomed over him, dagger ready.

No!

Raiyn didn't take time to think. He pulled what energy he could find and rounded the corner in a full sprint. His legs pumped. His hair flew back. The men looked frozen. He passed the guards and flew into the cell with his arm cocked.

Nicolar turned, no longer frozen like the others. The devion allowed the man to register the attack moments before it happened, but he was too late. The wooden club cracked against the side of his head in a hideous *thump*. The dagger flew from Nicolar's hand and clanged against the stone wall. The man collapsed, limp and quiet.

Raiyn sucked in air, standing firm. He stared to make sure, but the man on the floor didn't move. After a moment, he turned to Veron. The man's eyes were wide. He mumbled through the gag, but Raiyn couldn't understand the words.

Clang!

Raiyn spun. His heart seemed to stop. His breath didn't come when he tried. The cell door had closed.

30

TIME TO ACT

L ia's neck reddened as she followed where Danik led, pulling her by the hand. The other men and women had cleared the dance floor.

The master of ceremonies approached and plucked the flower from Lia's hand. "Thank you, miss." As if reciting a familiar speech, he turned to the crowd. "The flower is given. The gift accepted. Time stops for all while these two introduce us to . . . the Rose."

Polite applause filled the room. The musicians readied their instruments—fingers on strings and bows in hand. Their eyes turned to Lia.

"Kate?"

She looked at Danik. One arm held out with an open hand, inviting hers to join. The other reached toward her.

"Are you ready?" One of his eyebrows lifted.

Her stomach felt twisted in knots. Her heart pounded in fear rather than excitement. She stared at his chest, imaging the book behind the layer of wool.

Can I make it?

Her eyes flicked to the crowd. Regular men and women with eager expressions waited on them to dance. Between two heads, she recognized Cedric's leering gaze. The man crossed behind the onlookers and stopped next to Broderick. Lia swallowed.

Not yet. Once the others start dancing, there will be less eyes on me. She extended her gloved hand and placed it in Danik's.

His other hand reached around to her back and pulled her in.

Lia's chest constricted. Her entire body cringed at his touch. She inhaled as their chests pressed together. When her other arm finally rested on his, the musicians eased into a lilting tune.

Danik tightened his grip and led.

Lia tried to maintain even breathing, but her rigid arms and stiff back strained the attempt. Her feet followed his, their connected bodies stepping and swaying together.

She kept her eyes forward, her mind racing for an idea. Something rustled her hair. Her eyes flicked and caught him staring from a breath away.

"You're tense." His voice was low. "You can relax."

She forced a smile. "I'm sorry," she whispered. "I'm not used to . . . all of this."

"We got cut off before. You were talking about your parents and where you came from."

His eyes bore into her. She imagined him seeing past her disguise and calling his knights to attack. "I was?" She pulled her eyes away. A trickle of sweat creeped down from her hairline.

Danik adjusted his hand on her back, his pull against her strengthening. "You're from Lorranis, are you? What brings you into town?"

"I, uh, um . . ." She mumbled, unprepared for how to answer the question.

"Are you warm?" the king asked.

Her head turned back to him. "Huh?"

He released her hand and pulled a kerchief from a pocket in his coat. "Allow me."

It took her a moment to understand his intent. As his hand reached for her forehead, she jerked backwards.

Danik startled.

"I'm sorry," she whispered, her smile back. She took the cloth from his still hand. "I can do it. Thank you, though." She dabbed the line of sweat at her forehead, careful to not disturb the line where the wig met her skin.

"I am the one who should be sorry," Danik said. "I should not have presumed."

She handed the kerchief back, and he tucked it in his pocket. Taking hands, they resumed dancing.

Lia glanced at the musicians. They continued to plod along, oblivious to her urgent desire for them to speed up.

An unsettled feeling creeped into her gut. *What's wrong*, she thought. She turned her head and found Danik's smile gone, replaced by pinched eyes and a creased forehead.

"Is something the matter?" she asked, trying to keep her voice level.

The king's head tilted. "You seem familiar. Have we met?"

Her breath caught. She held a clenched smile, forcing herself to maintain calm. "I don't believe so. Have you been to Lorranis recently?"

"Not in years."

"Then I'm sure we haven't."

Danik continued to stare.

Lia swallowed around the lump in her throat. A few of the onlookers held hands, looking ready to join them on the floor.

Come on, song. Get to the second half!

"It's something else," Danik said.

Leaning away slightly, she looked back at his face.

"Your eyes. They're . . . familiar."

She blinked coyly and turned away. "I hear that a lot." Her neck reddened.

"It's not just your eyes though. It's your whole face." He laughed softly. "I know what it is. You have the look of someone I know."

She nodded. "That makes sense then."

"It's uncanny. Makes me wonder if you're related. You never did say who your parents were."

She opened her mouth, unsure of what was about to come out.

Thankfully, the master of ceremonies filled the silence. "Now we welcome all couples to the floor. Women, find your Rose partner, leave no one behind."

Lia glanced around, making a show of being aware of their space. The distraction was a great excuse to ignore his question.

Couples joined them on the floor, pressing close and swaying with the music as the tune started over from the top. With plenty of tall people in the crowd, she felt the eyes boring into her diminish. She scanned again—Cedric and Broderick walked toward the bar.

This is my shot!

She glanced at his chest to visualize the target, but the pull of his eyes raised her chin again.

Danik's mouth formed a tight line. His hand pulled firm against her back. "Your parents."

The slow drawl with which he spoke the words made a chill creep up her spine.

He leaned even closer, his lips almost touching her ear. "Who are your parents, Kate? Do they—" His words cut off. "What is this?" he asked.

Lia imagined his face nearly touching her hair. *My hair!* The line where blonde meets brown ran just behind her ear. *If he sees that . . .*

Her heart pounded. She took a larger step in the wrong direction, resulting in them bumping into another couple.

"Kate," Danik said, "what—"

"I'm sorry," she whispered, overcorrecting in the opposite direction. Lia wrapped her heel around the back of his. With their bodies touching, there was no room for him to catch himself when her momentum pushed backward.

The king's arms flailed in the air. He fell backward, the flap of his jacket open.

Humming with a flood of origine, Lia pounced. Her hand darted in his coat to remove the red book. It slid free, smooth and easy. Clutched in her fingers, she crouched and flung the edges of her dress to the side. In a hurried move, she stuffed the thin book into her garter.

How could I be so foolish? Raiyn thought.

He dropped the club and rushed to the bars. "No! Wait! Please!"

The wall of guards outside the cell took a step backward. No one spoke.

Raiyn's chest heaved as he sucked in air, holding on to the bars. "You must let me out! He was going to execute him. I had to stop him."

He stepped back, appraising the door. Tapping into the origine, he pounded against it. A resounding *boom* filled the cell, but the door barely moved. He returned to the window. With his stomach clenched and power flowing through his limbs, he pulled at the bars. A groan roared from his lips. The metal weakened. Slowly, the vertical bars dented, and the space between them widened.

Keep going! he told himself.

The bars pulled and pulled, stretching farther. His body screamed for rest. His lungs ached for air, but he wouldn't stop. When he could hold it no longer, he gasped and hung his head. His hands still gripped the metal, but his arms drooped. His shoulders lifted with desperate breaths.

After a minute to breathe and allow his heart to settle, he looked up to the window. His hope shattered. The progress he'd made in widening the bars barely extended the space more than a few fingers.

"Gah!" he yelled.

"Get another of the knights," a guard ordered. "We'll need their help."

A man at the back of the group turned away and hurried down the corridor.

"Don't! Please!" Raiyn said, his voice weak.

"Wait!" a lone voice called.

The fleeing man stopped and turned as another guard slid into view.

"Raiyn?"

An inkling of hope poured into him. "Brannon!"

His guard from days before was one of the six.

"Yes, it's me," Raiyn confirmed. "You must help!" He pointed behind him. "This is Veron Stormbridge in here. You can't let him be executed!"

All six guards glanced between each other with shifting eyes and mutters.

"He and I are two of the last shadow knights! We're the only people who can stop Danik."

Brannon didn't move.

"Please!" Raiyn dropped his head. The raw emotions of adrenaline mixed with hope that turned into despair swirled in his mind. Moisture pooled at the corners of his eyes. "We're trying to save the kingdom. We keep doing what we can, but every step has a new setback. We need help. We need—" He stopped, considering what it was he needed. "We need someone who wants it as much as we do."

A *click* sounded in the door.

Raiyn jumped back and wiped his eyes.

The door swung open, the creak of hinges deafening.

Brannon stood in the center of the passage with a key dangling from his hand. His jaw was set, and his head nodded slowly. "I want it."

"We all do," another of the guards added.

Danik shouted as he fell. The surrounding dancers gasped.

Lia took a step backward and raised her hand in mock surprise as the king hit the ground, flat on his back.

"I'm so sorry." Lia's words were lost in the tumult. "My feet—they're so clumsy."

Danik stared up at her, his eyes narrow, his smile gone.

"Let me get someone to help." She turned to leave.

"No, it's fine." He waved a hand and gathered himself to his feet. "Stay."

The tone with which he spoke gave little room to disobey. Her legs felt stuck in place.

"I believe I'm finished with this dance, though. Would you walk with me?" He extended an arm.

Lia breathed deeply then ran her arm through his. Her heart pounded while they walked. A glance at the bar showed Cedric and Broderick were nowhere to be found, and the exit door loomed not far past it. The book strapped to her leg made her want to run for it.

"Can I go get you a drink?" she asked.

Danik stared. "I'll come with you."

"You should take it easy," she said. "I can—"

"I insist."

Lia forced herself to breathe. Danik walked with her, step for step until they arrived at the rich wooden counter. "Take a seat, Your Majesty." She touched a stool by the bar.

He sat but never took his eyes off her.

A man behind the bar arrived. "Your Majesty. What would you like?"

Danik raised an eyebrow to Lia.

"A, uh . . . water for me, please," she said.

"Brandy," Danik said without turning.

"Right away," the man said.

"I noticed your hair while we danced," Danik said quietly. "You're not a blonde are you?"

Lia touched her hair and put on a nervous laugh.

"It's a wig, isn't it."

Her smile faltered. "Please don't tell anyone. I, uh—always wear this thing. My parents would be crushed if they knew the secret was out."

She looked past his shoulder, longing for the door. The exit was clear, waiting for her. *I should run for it. I could get a head start, and—*

Danik's eyes flicked around the room.

She checked over her shoulder. Alton converged from behind and Cedric and Broderick closed from the side.

"I think I figured it out," Danik said.

She pulled her eyes back to him. His words sounded thick in her ears, deadened by the deep pounding of her pulse. "Figured what out?" Her breathy words barely reached her own ears.

"About your parents."

Her heart felt like it would pound out of her chest. *I'm blown.*

A smirk covered the king's face. "I also figured out why you're here." He brought a hand to his chest. "You thought you could—" Danik stopped. His eyes widened as he pressed against his jacket in the place where the book used to be. The surprised look turned to amusement. "Well done. That is well done, *Kate*—or should I say . . . Lia?"

Her true name rang like a bell, clear as the sky on a cloudless day.

Lia shouted as she kicked, fueled by the origine that had been begging her to use it. Her blow pulverized Danik's stool. With nothing for him to push against, the king fell.

Lia ran. Her tapping of the origine gave her a moment's head start, but the knights of power were close. Before she broke free of the bar area, Danik's hand wrapped around her ankle, pulling her to the ground. She fell, colliding into the ballroom floor. Her hands smacked the marble surface, and her dress billowed around her. Caught between the ground and her shoulder, the blonde wig pulled askew, ruining any semblance of authenticity.

"Don't let her get away!" the king shouted.

Throwing the wig to the ground, Lia jumped to her feet at the same time as Danik.

The rest of the ballroom was in absolute bedlam. Men shouted, and women screamed. The faces that had revered her beauty when she had first arrived had changed to horror.

She turned to run, but two bodies blocked her way: Cedric and Broderick.

"Nice seeing you again, Lia," Cedric snarled.

She fished through the slit in her dress and pulled out the dagger with a flourish, but the motion of retrieving it sliced through part of her garter. The book tucked against her thigh shifted, and a watery feeling ran through her.

A hearty laugh issued from the men.

She spun, threatening each in turn with her short blade.

"There's no hope, Lia," Danik said. "Drop the knife."

"No!" She spun again. Alton had crept closer, but she backed him up with a vicious swing of a dagger.

"Give me the book, Lia," Danik said.

"Never!"

"Give it to me, and I'll let you live."

She chuckled. "Nice try."

Lia settled into a crouch and held out her hand with the knife. Every muscle was tense and ready to respond. She bared her teeth and growled, "Come and get it!"

None of the men moved. They stared back with incredulous looks that hinted of respect.

Cedric's step forward shattered the stalemate. "I'll get it," he said, raising his sword with both hands.

Crash!

Lia gasped as a massive stone lion collided with Cedric's body. The knight dropped to the ground, clutching the back of his leg and screaming.

What happened?

Another collision with a lion blasted Broderick off his feet. His sword clattered across the floor while he groaned.

Lia traced the source of the object's flights and stopped at the entrance to the room. Raiyn stood, his feet planted and puffed-out chest heaving.

"Lia! Run!" he shouted.

She stood in stupor while he placed his hands against the massive stone columns flanking the entrance to the room. Over his shoulder, her father stared back. *He did it! Father's free.*

"Get them!" Danik shouted.

Raiyn's arms shuddered and his face strained. A crack ran down the columns he pushed. His mouth gradually opened, a roar growing stronger by the second.

A rumble grew in the room, and debris fell from the ceiling.

"Liiiiiaaaaa!" Raiyn yelled, continuing to push.

It's going to collapse, she realized.

Lia snapped into action. With Cedric and Broderick indisposed, the path was clear. She pulled from her well of power and sprinted. Danik and Alton ran after her, matching her speed. Raiyn continued to push. Above him, chunks of stone fell in slow motion.

Almost there!

The columns ahead gave a final heave, cracks splintering in all directions. The ceiling crumbled completely. Raiyn stopped pushing. He tried to lunge backward, out of the way, but his body didn't respond with the speed he needed.

Lia pumped her legs, racing the falling debris. Over her shoulder, Danik and Alton closed in, but they were too far to reach her.

I can make it!

As her legs bolted, something tore. A pressure around her thigh loosened and something fell to the ground. She didn't have time to stop and inspect, although she had an idea of what it was.

Lia collided into Raiyn. She blasted him through the entryway, a pile of stone, dust, and rubble blocking the hall behind them.

"Quick!" Alton shouted. "The back exit!"

Danik stared at the debris, his mouth hanging open as the debris stopped falling. A cloud of dust filled the air, billowing into the room.

"Your Majesty!" The other knight pulled at his sleeve. "Should we pursue? We could still catch them."

Cedric and Broderick moaned, lost in the fog, and the ballroom of people squawked like a flock of geese behind him.

Something on the ground caught Danik's eye. He ignored Alton's insistent shouts and walked forward, waving the dust in the air away. Using his boot, he kicked over a stone, and a smile grew on his face.

"Don't bother pursuing." He crouched. "They'll be back."

He picked up a thin book with a red-leather cover off the ground then chuckled as he stood.

Geoffrey Bilton arrived at his side. "Your Majesty, are you all right?"

The king turned. "What happened to them being dead, Geoffrey?"

Bilton shook his head, his jaw tight. "The guards who reported back will be dealt with, sir. Incompetence like that will not stand."

"Is it their incompetence, or yours?"

Bilton started, but his chin only wavered.

"Make it right," the king ordered, waving him off with his hand. "And don't let it happen again."

The high lord scurried away.

With a groan, Cedric stumbled to his feet. "Whew!" he exclaimed, bending over with his hands on his knees. "Healing from that will take it out of you."

Broderick approached, his walk slow and cautious, but his posture upright. "Agreed."

Alton nodded toward the book. "They didn't get it, huh?"

Danik shook his head and chuckled. "They stopped me from killing her father, and they broke him out of the dungeon, but the object they needed from the very beginning still eludes them." He turned the book over. "We still get to hold on to—"

The words caught in his throat. His eyes grew wide as he stared at the cover where "*Felting Tax Codes*" was printed across the front.

"What?" He flung the cover back and flipped through the pages—page after page of tax figures and numbers. "No!"

Danik threw the book to the ground, causing a puff of dirt to rise. He stared at the pile of rubble in the entryway, fuming. His shoulders rose and fell.

This isn't over, Lia Stormbridge.

PART II

LOYALTY

31

VILLAGE RETURN

Lia ducked low, dodging as a branch passed over her body. The strong steps of Lucy, a chestnut mare, continued forward without pause. Her body ached. A full day of riding left her exhausted and with sore legs. The sun hung low in the sky, partially visible through the thick forest.

Raiyn's horse, Freckles, walked next to hers. The young man's face looked eager and excited, despite the awkward way he sat. Marcus followed on a smaller pony, and Veron led the way at the front.

Bilton had followed through with their plan, meeting them at the edge of the forest with the mounts, including food, basic supplies, and a small amount of money before he returned to the city.

"Should be soon," Veron said over his shoulder.

Lia blew out a long breath, a puff of fog pushing through the chilly air. "Should we pick up the pace?"

Veron pulled the reins on Ranger, his tall, black stallion, and allowed them to catch up before resuming beside them. "I want to rush there even more than you, but we have to be smart."

"But we have the book. We have the map. We can head straight there and rescue them in . . . two or three days, probably."

Veron shook his head. "You saw the map the same as I did. We may wander the mountains for weeks. It's going to be long and treacherous. Plus, what do we do when we arrive? We know nothing about where they live, how they're defended, or even how many marked ones there are."

"We know to watch out for bears," Raiyn said.

"That's right," Lia said. "Mother warned us with the note. We'll figure the rest out."

A fatherly smile grew on Veron's face. "I'm sure we will. But we also need to be able to fight when we get there, and right now, there are only three of us."

"*Four* of us!" Marcus called from the back.

"Four, counting Marcus." Veron leaned forward. "You saw their abilities, Lia. We can't do this without help."

"Tienn or Karondir aren't too far out of the way though."

"We went over this. Danik is the king now. The barons and armies there will have divided loyalties."

"But you *know* those people! I'm sure you could convince them—"

"I'm sure I probably could too, but . . . it would be a huge risk. Men in power want to stay in power. They may have been loyal to Darcius, but they could be swayed. If we put our trust in the wrong person, the consequences could be dire."

Lia huffed and turned to Raiyn.

"Don't look at me." Raiyn raised his hands. "I'm not choosing sides between you. I'm along for the ride."

Marcus chimed in, "And I'm for whichever option has the greatest chance of getting my father back."

Lia wanted to dive back into her original argument but stopped herself. "What about this village? You said you haven't been here in, what . . . ten years?"

"Longer than that," Veron said.

"How are they more likely to be loyal?"

Veron paused and looked ahead into the woods. "The people here are a different sort. I would trust them with my life. Plus, they love your mother."

"Thank you again for coming to the Glade to get me," Marcus

said. "I'm aware I don't have the skills of a shadow knight, but I can fight, and I want to help."

"Well, we're glad to have you with us," Lia said.

Raiyn pointed ahead. "I see it."

Lia looked up. Through the trees, a row of wooden homes stood in a line on top of a rise. The sun dropped behind them, leaving an orange glow in the sky.

Veron stopped Ranger. "Nasco." He exhaled a satisfied breath. "Forgotten to the world." He glanced at the others as he swung a leg over to dismount. "Let's walk."

The party of four touched their feet to the dirt path. Lia shook her legs out, and Raiyn arched his back in an audible stretch. They held the reins of their horses and climbed the hill that led to the houses.

"This really is in the middle of nowhere," Raiyn said as they arrived at a dirt path that ran past the houses.

A woman carrying a basket along the path jerked to attention.

"Hello," Veron said in a friendly voice. "Is Russell or Nevi Martin around?"

A white ring surrounded the woman's pupils as she backed up.

"We're friends," Lia added. "You don't need to be afraid."

Her basket fell, hitting the dirt and spilling a load of apples. The woman turned and ran, disappearing toward the center of town with no sound but the rapid padding of her feet.

"That's odd," Veron said.

Lia approached the basket and peered inside. "Does she think we're raiders or something?" She noted the sword at Veron's hip and the axe looming over Raiyn's shoulder.

"Last I was here, they were attacked by soldiers. People were killed. Homes were burned."

"That's reason to be skittish," Raiyn said.

"But that was seventeen years ago." Veron waved them forward. "Come on."

The group of four walked up the main street into the village. Houses bordered either side until they turned into shops.

"Strange," Veron said.

Lia turned to him. "What?"

"These shops look empty."

"Well . . . you did say it's been seventeen years."

"But this was a thriving area." He pointed ahead where the path opened into a large grassy space with a rectangular surrounding of buildings. "All of this would be packed with people playing and talking. Lanterns would already be out, glowing in the twilight."

Lia stopped at the edge of the grass, holding onto her horse. All the shops that lined the area looked abandoned. A building that looked like a school had a door hanging ajar. *He's right. Everything's dead.*

"And up there," Veron pointed up the hill to a large building with a wall of windows. "That was where—" He paused.

Lia squinted to make out a flickering light inside the building. "Someone's up there."

"Who are you?" a gruff voice barked.

They spun. A greasy-haired man with a rough beard hurried across the grass. Looking around forty years old, his shirt stopped midway down his portly belly, and his pants sagged. Behind him, four unkempt men with swords and crooked teeth followed. The woman who dropped the basket waited in the shadows.

"I asked who you are," the man repeated.

"We are . . ." Veron hesitated for a long pause. ". . . friends."

The man laughed. "You're not *my* friends."

A feeling of unease crept over Lia. *Something is very wrong here.*

"Friends of Nasco," Veron said. "I lived here many years ago. So did my wife and my father. I don't remember you from last time I was here. Who are you?"

"Genaro Malthus, but everyone calls me Malt."

"Can I speak with the Martins? Are they here?"

No response.

"How about Aleks Bellingsworth or Finley Sainsbury? Maybe Royce Black?"

An evil grin formed on Malt's face.

"Are you . . . one of the elders?" Lia asked.

Malt and his guards all burst into laughter. "Elders, ha! That's great. No, I'm not one of those Nasco bag of bones."

"You're not from Nasco?" Veron asked.

"Now you're getting it," Malt said. "Kyrdtown born and raised."

"What's Kyrdtown?" Lia asked.

Malt glanced back at her then pointed northeast toward the trees. "A miserable scrap of a village two days' travel in that direction, at the edge of the Kyrd Forest."

"What are you doing here?" Veron asked.

"The soil grew arid about five years ago. The trees died, and the animals migrated. Well . . . not all the animals. The swamp flies quadrupled in number. You should see them—as large as a thumb with a bite like a dagger."

"So you moved here," Veron said.

Malt raised his hands in a shrug. "We were good neighbors. We wanted to share. But the people from Nasco were mean and brutish. They created a bunch of rules of things we could and couldn't do. Finally, they tried to kick us out—told us to go and find our own village. Can you believe that? Some hospitality your *friends* had."

"Then you . . . what? Took over?"

"You ask a lot of questions," Malt said. "Do you have a name?"

"Yes, I do," Veron said. "But I haven't decided if you get to know it yet."

The man stared. A sniff curled his lip. "I can take you to your friends." He turned over his shoulder. "Guys, take their weapons."

Lia's hand flew to the hilt of her sword, and Raiyn reached for his axe.

Veron raised his hands. "Whoa. Slow down." He looked at Lia. "Stop, you two."

All parties froze, hands on weapons while Veron stepped into the middle.

"We didn't come here to fight you. We just want to speak to our friends."

"And I'm happy to take you there." Malt spoke slowly and pointed between them all. "After you three drop those weapons."

Veron turned to Lia, his eyes unsure.

"No," Lia mouthed. She shook her head for extra confirmation.

"Rangolt," Malt said. "Show these visitors what happens when they don't listen to us."

A guard with a pointed, black beard moved first.

Wrong decision, Lia thought.

Her sword scraped as it pulled from her scabbard. Raiyn's battle-axe slung clean of its holder, and Veron's blade pulled ready.

"Marcus and Veron, behind us." Lia's command left no room for discussion.

Marcus remained safely behind, but Veron stood at her side.

"Father," she scolded out of the side of her mouth.

"I'm not an invalid who needs his daughter to fight his battles for him," he muttered back.

Malt's men cackled as they approached. Their swords flicked in the air, showing off their undisciplined grasp of proper technique.

Lia rolled her eyes. *This is ridiculous.* She pulled from the origine and leaped into action. Spinning through the air in a flash, she knocked the blades from each of the four men's hands, sending the weapons skyward. Then, she directed powerful kicks at each man's chest in turn, knocking them toward a central point. When she released the origine, the four bodies crunched together in a massive heap, falling to the grass. After shouting and groaning, the swords fell to the earth. Two landed harmlessly on the ground, one stuck in the grass next to a man's leg, and the other conked one of them on the head with its hilt.

Malt jumped backward, landing frozen on one foot. His jaw hung limp.

"Do you want to try that again?" Lia asked.

"R-R-R-Red sky! Red sky!" Malt bellowed into the air.

"Stop it!" Lia shouted, extending her sword toward his neck.

The man quieted, his hands raised in surrender.

"What was that?" Veron asked. He glanced around the quiet town center.

Up the hill, multiple torches roared to life with flames dancing from the ends. The lights rushed around the perimeter of the large building above them.

"You might want to withdraw that blade, miss," Malt said.

Veron stared up the hill, his sword drooping. "What's going on?"

"Those torches are ready to light up that building, and if you care about your friends, you don't want that to happen."

"Is that where they are?"

"Call them off!" Lia pressed the tip of her sword against the flesh of his neck.

"Lia!" Veron shouted.

"Listen to your father, Lia," Malt said.

The torches' flames licked at the eaves of the building. Lia's arm trembled.

"Lia," Veron said softer. "Back off."

Lia lowered her sword.

Malt flashed a wicked grin. "That's better. Men, get up."

The soldiers on the ground groaned as they got to their feet. They stumbled around to find their lost weapons.

"You're shadow knights, aren't you?" Malt asked.

Lia set her jaw, refusing to answer. She glanced at her father who appeared equally firm in his resolve.

"You don't have to answer that. It's obvious. So you come to my village and want to upset the way things are."

"All I want is to see my friends," Veron said.

"Let us tie you up and you can see them."

"No," Lia growled.

"You're not tying us up." Veron's sword lifted again. "Call off the torches!"

"It seems we're at an impasse," Malt said. "I refuse to pull back the torches, but you refuse to be tied up."

"The torches aren't a threat," Veron said. "If you light that building, we'll be up there so fast, the wind from our movement will blow out the flames. Even if it didn't, we could kill all of your men and rescue everybody from the building before it spread across half a wall."

Malt shrugged. "All right then. Do it."

Lia swallowed hard. She stared at the flames tickling the edge of the wood. *With just Raiyn and I, we'd have to use too much origine. We couldn't do half of that before exhaustion caught us.*

Veron shifted his feet, glancing between the men.

"I didn't think so," Malt said. "If you attack us, your friends die. If you run out of here to attack in the night, they die, now. If we stand here staring at each other, we'll all die from starvation, eventually. But if you allow us to tie you up, we can trust you. We'll take you to speak with your friends, and—"

"And hold us prisoner," Veron said.

"No." Malt turned up his hands with an oily grin. "We would never do that to you."

Coiled strands of rope emerged from the night, draping from the arm of another guard.

"If you attempt to tie me up with that, you will lose at least one of your hands." Lia nodded toward the coil.

The man stopped walking, and the rope dangled back and forth. Everyone stared with weapons bared and bodies frozen. A bird cawed somewhere in the woods, piercing the still moment.

"If I may." Raiyn lowered his axe and lifted a hand. "I have a proposal."

"Raiyn," Lia muttered under her breath. "What are you doing?"

"Trust me."

He squatted and set his axe on the ground. Taking a step toward the guards, he held his hands forward, wrists together. "Tie me up."

"No!" Lia shouted.

He leaned closer to her and whispered, "Look at the rope."

She peered at the coils and noticed the thin strands and frayed edges. *With the origine, we could rip through that.* Her pulse eased.

"It's all right." Raiyn stood straight. "We don't want anyone to die. You can keep me under guard. They can go up to the building to talk with their friends. They won't do anything stupid because you'll have me down here. Then, after they understand the people's safety and know what's going on, we can all sit down and find a fair way forward for the people of Nasco."

"Raiyn," Veron said, "you don't have to do this."

Raiyn didn't respond.

After deliberation, Malt chuckled then nodded to his men. "Tie him."

Raiyn stepped away from his axe and kept his arms out.

The man with the rope looped it twice around his outstretched hands then pulled it tight with a knot.

"All right." Veron turned to Malt. "Take us to them."

The leader nodded toward the grass. "I'll allow you two to skip being tied, but I need you to leave your weapons here."

Lia frowned and only dropped her sword to the ground after her father did.

Malt stepped back and motioned for them to cross the grass. He turned to his guards and pointed to the newest arrival. "Stay with him. Slit his throat if anything happens."

Lia's eyes flicked to Raiyn, who only smirked at the threat.

Marcus stood some distance away, his eyes darting around.

"Stay over there," Lia said to Marcus. "If anything happens to us, run."

Malt led the way up the hill with his four men surrounding Lia and Veron.

Lia's senses remained on high alert. Her muscles twitched in expectation. Her ears trained for any sound. Her eyes scanned her view. At any moment, a whirlwind of destruction was ready to be unleashed.

The hill didn't take long to climb. Malt's men with torches glared at them when they arrived.

Lia glanced back. Down the hill, Raiyn stood in the middle of the clearing with his arms bound. The guard stood behind him with a dagger poised and ready.

"Snuff the torches," Veron said.

Malt shook his head. "I'm not stupid. They stay lit until I'm satisfied you're not a threat." He stopped at the corner of the building then gestured to the front doors. "Go ahead."

Veron's grim face gave Lia a chill, but she followed.

Two guards stood post on either side of the entrance. A lone lantern hung from a hook on the eaves. One of the men scowled as he threw a latch and pushed open the doors.

Lia took a step forward. The hair on the back of her neck stood on end. *Whatever is in there is not going to be good.*

32

LONG-LOST FRIENDS

Veron's hand flew to his nose at the rank smell of decay and waste that rushed through the opening. He wrestled away the gagging sensation. The room was dim, backlit by the far wall of windows letting in the waning light. Hay spread across the floor but was difficult to see around the mass of bodies. The guards followed them inside along with Malt.

"Talk to whomever you like," Malt said. "But don't try anything funny if you care about your friend down the hill. We'll be watching."

Veron stepped forward, dodging people sitting on the ground.

A man stared up at him, his eyes slightly sunken into his face. His skin was sallow and loose. "Help us," he uttered, his scratchy voice barely discernible.

The woman next to him coughed, a rattling, deep expulsion of air and phlegm. She winced after the effort, pressing a hand against her chest.

The temptation to panic itched at Veron's mind. His breath grew rapid. He scanned the room. While many of the people were malnourished and decaying, over half looked to be in decent health, despite the disrepair of their clothes and the grime covering their bodies.

The clean and organized image of the Academy's training center in his memory was nothing like its current state.

"This isn't human," Lia whispered behind him.

Veron wanted to respond but had no words.

"Russell Martin," he called, finally. "Are you here?"

A hushed moment settled in the room before a rustling drew his attention toward the far wall. A man struggled to his feet, using the wall as support. A woman rose next to him, supporting his arm with both of her hands.

"Who's there?" the man's weak voice answered.

Veron's heart ached at the sound. He moved gingerly across the room, dodging limbs. "Russell, it's me, Veron Stormbridge."

The woman gasped.

The man's chest grew as he took in a deep breath. His jaw dropped but only quivered as stuttering sounds came out. A sniffling sound developed into sobs. His head drooped forward as choking tears came out in bursts. The woman wrapped her arms around him.

Veron rushed forward and set a hand on his shoulder. He almost flinched at the bony touch but forced himself to suppress the instinct. Despite the years passed and the deterioration of his body, Veron recognized the man who had raised Chelci for six years.

"Veron," the woman said at last. "I can't believe it."

"Nevi, is that you?"

She nodded, tears running down her cheeks. Her hair was gray, and her skin held more wrinkles, but he remembered the smile.

"Is Chelci with you?" she asked.

Veron shook his head.

"Is she all right?"

"We don't know. We're trying to get to her, but it's a long story. What happened?"

Russell wiped at his face then nodded toward the door. "Malt showed up two years ago."

"We heard a bit. Their village grew barren and they wanted to share yours?"

Nevi scoffed, resulting in a fit of coughing.

"Share? Ha!" Russell shook his head. "They tried to take over from day one. We welcomed them in. We arranged for housing. We gave them food."

Nevi joined in. "They ate *most* of the food we'd harvested, and our people had to go without. When we asked them to agree to a rationing system, they refused. They wouldn't work at any of the village jobs. They were always drunk and insulting our people."

"We started getting complaints from the young ladies of Nasco." Russell's mouth formed a scowl. "Kyrdtown's men were aggressive . . . and inappropriate. They grew violent when they didn't get what they wanted." Russell looked at his wife. "Early last wiether, we asked them to leave."

Nevi shook her head. "That's when they revolted. They—" She raised her hand to her mouth.

"They gathered the kids of the village in the town center. The Village Guard was ready to fight and die for Nasco, but . . . when their kids were held at sword point . . ." His gaze drifted to the ground.

"So . . . they've kept you in here for a year?" Veron asked.

"Close to," Russell said. "Villagers who swore allegiance to Malt were allowed to stay in their homes, but the rest were imprisoned here."

Veron scanned the room, his mouth hanging open. "This looks like the entire village."

"Just about," Nevi said. "At least the ones still living."

"What do they want from you?"

"We're laborers," Russell said. "Farming, cooking, cleaning, construction—anything they don't want to do."

"How are you supposed to labor if they don't take care of you?"

"The healthy ones get enough food," Nevi said. "But as soon as you get a fever or a cough—" She shook her head. "You're cut off."

"They still give us scraps, but it's not enough to live off," Russell said. "The few who are able to get better are allowed full rations again, but that's rare."

Lia stepped forward. "Have you tried fighting back?"

Veron gestured to her. "This is my daughter, Lia."

A joyful sound escaped Nevi's lips. "Lia." A broad smile grew. "You weren't even walking when we saw you last."

Veron chuckled. "Yeah, she's grown a bit."

"We tried fighting," Russell said. "Mid-wiether. A dozen of us died, and every woman and child was whipped as punishment."

"Wrap it up!" Malt shouted from the doorway.

Nevi stepped closer, resting her hand on Veron's arm. "Can you help us? Can you use your powers?"

Veron took a deep breath, cringing at his lack of access to the origine. "We'll figure out something. When they learned who we were, they threatened to burn this building down."

Nevi gasped.

"That's enough!" Malt called. "Don't make us take it out on your young friend!"

Veron rested a hand on their shoulders. "Give us a bit. We'll see what we can do."

"Thank you," Nevi said.

Veron backed off. "We're coming!" he called toward the door.

People on the floor adjusted to allow him space to walk. Whispered sounds of his name and Chelci's drifted through the air.

A chill wind took Veron's breath away when they exited the building.

"Shall we return to your friend?" Malt asked, pointing down the path they'd followed to get there.

Veron nodded and followed the lead guard.

"What do we do, now?" Lia whispered, drawing close on the path.

Veron's mind rattled through ideas, but nothing seemed like a good plan. "I'm not sure. If I had the origine, too, we could probably succeed with a quick attack."

"I can do it," Lia said.

Veron shook his head. "There are too many of them."

"Trust me, Father. Raiyn can break his bonds, then we can take out Malt and his guards. The torches—" She glanced over her shoulder and frowned. The men with the fire had resumed their alert stances. "The torches are still a problem."

The steps ended on flat ground, and Veron followed the guard toward the grassy area. Raiyn waited as they had left him, and Marcus stood to the side. Their weapons were nowhere to be seen.

"Put out the torches," Veron said. "We've proven we're not a threat."

"Have you?" Malt raised an eyebrow. "I'll be the judge of that."

Lia nodded to Raiyn. "Untie him, at least."

After a nod from Malt, the man who had been guarding Raiyn undid the knot, then unraveled the strand from around his wrists.

"Where are our weapons?" Veron asked.

"We placed them with your gear," Malt said. "You shouldn't need them for now."

Veron tracked the man's eyes to where their horses had been tied to a post along the edge of the square.

"So you spoke with your friends. Did they confirm what I told you or make up lies?"

Veron ignored the question. A simmering anger rumbled in his chest, but he forced his words to sound as even-tempered as possible. "You need to let them go."

"If you hurt any of them, you and every one of your gang will die," Lia added.

Malt's mouth formed a thin line. "That sounds like something neither of us wants. But you can rest assured, if you attempt any heroic shadow-knight action to try and kill me or my men, I won't hesitate to torch that building. Is that what you want?"

Neither Lia nor Veron answered.

"I thought not. With that ugliness said, you'll be happy to know that we have no intention of hurting you or anyone. I'm sure we can come up with a solution that is amenable to all. Would you permit me some time to confer with my crew?"

Veron's eyes narrowed. "Sure."

Malt smiled and turned to his guards. "Rangolt, would you take these four to the house so they can be comfortable? I'm sure they'd love to rest after such a long journey."

The guard with the pointed beard stepped forward. "Of course." He pointed his sword down the street. "This way."

Lia turned to Veron, her wary eyes conveying a healthy level of suspicion.

"Stay alert," he whispered.

Veron followed first with Lia and Raiyn behind and Marcus at the rear. His mind raced through scenarios of how to rescue the villagers, but nothing great came to mind.

The guards led to a small house. One turned a knob and opened the door. "Make yourselves at home," he said. "We'll be out here if you need anything."

"I have a need," Lia said.

"Huh?" the guard grunted.

"My sword. So I can send your head rolling across the ground."

Veron rested a hand on his daughter's back, dispelling the tension. "Come on. We'll go in."

The house consisted of a single room. A bed of withered straw set against the far end, and a rough table contained two stools. Two cushioned seats angled toward the hearth where embers of a forgotten fire smoldered, giving the room a toasty, welcoming feeling. A pile of fresh wood stacked next to the hearth, filling the air with the scent of oak.

Click.

The door closed behind them. Veron spun. Touching the knob, he turned it gingerly.

"Locked?" Raiyn asked.

He shook his head. "Like a lock would keep us in, either way."

Lia sat on one of the stools. "What should we do?"

Veron shrugged. "For now, we wait."

Marcus crossed to the bed and sat, creating a puff of dust. "How long do you think we'll be here?"

"Hopefully, not long." Veron sat on one of the stools and took a deep breath to settle his nerves. "At least we won't freeze to death. It's warm in here."

Lia pulled her shirt away from her body and fanned it to bring air to her face. Raiyn crossed the room with a frown on his face.

"What is it?" Veron asked. "What are you thinking?"

"I don't like it," Raiyn said.

"Like what?"

"All of this. They clearly don't respect other people's lives and only care about themselves." Raiyn stopped and looked Veron in the eye. "They can't let us go. We could attack in the night when they least expected it and take them out. But they also can't keep us here. We're too dangerous."

"You think they're going to try to kill us?" Marcus asked.

"I do."

Veron nodded. "I think you're right."

33

CLEVER NEGOTIATIONS

Lia's eyes flicked open at footsteps and low conversation outside the room. Her neck was stiff. She leaned against the wall in the corner farthest from the hearth. As the embers had faded, the light in the room had dimmed. The heat in the room remained, despite them having opened the windows a while before.

She nudged Raiyn. "Hey." Her voice was dry.

Raiyn blinked awake and sat straighter. After glancing around the room, his eyes settled on the door. "Someone's coming?"

"Sounds like it." Lia wiped a sheen of sweat off her forehead with the palm of her hand.

The latch on the door rattled, and the hinges creaked open.

A gust of brisk air cut through the room, bringing a smile to Lia's face. She inhaled deeply, savoring the cool respite.

"Malt wants to see you," Rangolt said with his lip turned.

Lia pushed off the wall and rose to her feet. Her bones ached from hours of sitting uncomfortably in the hot room.

Rangolt pointed his sword to the door, giving them space to exit.

Lia smiled. *He's scared of us . . . as he should be.*

The night sky was pitch black when they exited. The chill air felt glorious on her toasted skin. Her muscles relaxed, and she sighed.

Four guards escorted them, keeping hands on their swords.

"Can we get our weapons back, now?" Veron asked.

"Talk to Malt first," Rangolt said.

Lia's eyes scanned as they walked. The village looked either dead or asleep—both were believable.

Back at the village green, Lia glanced up the hill. Men with torches remained vigilant, standing next to the building where the imprisoned villagers waited. She made eyes at Raiyn whose jaw clenched in a grim line.

He leaned in. "If we have to act . . . you and I can take it." He nodded toward the hill. "We knock away the torches then deal with the men."

Lia nodded and turned back to the men leading them. They approached a large building at one end of the green. Another guard already waited at a door and opened it as they approached.

Inside the meeting room, lanterns rested on hooks, filling the room with light. The open space contained circles of benches and a vaulted ceiling with wooden beams.

Malt stood at the front of the room with two guards on either side. The man held a goblet to his lips and drank in loud swallows. A trickle of water ran down his chest.

Her throat felt drier just by watching. Her body ached.

Malt lowered his cup and smacked his lips. He returned the goblet to a table where several other cups waited beside a large bowl. The basin wasn't large, but water filled it nearly to the brim.

Lia swallowed to try and relieve her swollen mouth.

Something on the wall caught her eye. A display of bones was mounted on a wooden plaque. Two long, thick white bones ended in what looked like a paw with two claws, each as long as her hand.

"You like my trophy?" Malt asked, looking up at where she did. "It's a valcor, believe it or not. It attacked the village not long after we arrived during a midday meal. The people from Nasco didn't know what to do. A few died, and the others ran. But we Kyrdtown men stood our ground." Malt took a step closer but didn't leave the range of his guards' swords. "I was the one who killed it—stabbed it through its side and stopped its heart."

Next to her, Veron muffled a chuckle.

"Even after we saved the village, they still turned on us," Malt added. "Ungrateful wretches is what they are."

"You sound very brave," Veron said, his face fighting to contain a smirk.

"You don't believe me?" Malt risked another half step toward them.

"No, I don't."

"Tell me then," Malt stepped toward the wall and pointed to the bones. "What other animal has bones like that?"

"It *is* a valcor," Veron said. "But you weren't the one to kill it."

Malt's eyes narrowed.

"First, valcor are afraid of light. They only come out at night—even a full moon will scare them off. Second, you surely didn't stab it through its side. Its hide is as hard as steel. And last of all . . ." Veron pointed toward the bones. "Those bones show two claws, but valcor have three on their back feet."

Malt blinked rapidly. His mouth sputtered as he searched for what to say.

"There was one with two claws, and I've met it." He pointed toward the wall. "It was killed just down that path out there around eighteen years ago . . . by my wife. Save your stories for someone else."

Malt's scowl could have caused a stick to burst into flames. The glare softened, and a forced smile came over him. "I guess you have been around for a while. Still, it's a good story." He chuckled. "I've spoken with my men, but first, what is it you want?"

Lia's eyes flicked to the bowl of water.

"I want you to free the people of Nasco," Veron said. "They're all underfed, and many are sick and dying."

"Why care for someone who is dying?" Malt asked. "It's a waste of resources."

Lia clenched her teeth together.

"Because they're humans," Veron said. "They deserve to live, free to make their own choices. And you care for them because until they exhale their last breath, they're still alive. Additionally, we want you gone."

"Ha!" Malt scoffed.

"This isn't your village. You can't take over and kick its residents out. You are the ones who need to find a new home."

Malt pursed his lips then looked at Rangolt. The other guard's steely gaze gave nothing away.

"Contrary to what you may think," Malt said. "We're not monsters. I care about people, but I think you're right—We've gotten carried away."

Lia frowned. *That's not what I was expecting.*

"We had recently been talking about how we wanted to start somewhere fresh. The ground here is overworked, and the game in the woods is thin. It's been on my mind to take our crew and leave, and I think this might be the sign that it's time."

"You'll free the villagers and leave?" Lia asked, unsure if she had understood him correctly.

Malt looked around at the guards in the room and nodded. Several of them followed suit. "We will."

Lia breathed out. The tension in her limbs softened.

"Prove you're serious," Veron said then pointed toward the wall. "Have your men put out the torches."

"I will," Malt said, "in time. But . . . I'm not sure I can trust you."

"What do you mean?"

"With abilities like the Shadow Knights have, how can I be sure you won't kill us the moment we lower our defenses?"

"If you're freeing the others and leaving the village, we have no reason to kill you."

"You may be right. Still . . . I haven't gotten to the position I'm in by being careless. Here's what I want—"

Lia held her breath, afraid of what was to come.

"You four leave the village, first. Once you're out of sight, we will lower the torches and prepare to depart, ourselves. We'll be gone at first light."

Lia's mouth dropped. She sputtered to begin shooting down the plan when her father set his hand on her arm.

"Give us time to speak." Veron stepped backward, pulling Lia with him.

"Does he think we're stupid," Lia whispered, leaning into his ear. "His plan is ridiculous. Why would he let them go only after we're gone. It's clearly a bluff."

"I agree," he replied. "But . . . once we're in the woods, they won't know where we are anymore. We can slip back around to the training center. We could even find Malt when he's asleep in his bed."

"But what's to stop him from killing some of the villagers as soon as we're gone? Or coming up with a new threat to them?"

Veron's forehead wrinkled.

"I'm giving you everything you want," Malt called. "What's to debate?"

"You could release the villagers right now if you're really serious," Veron said. "Why would we trust you to do it only after we've left?"

Malt stood tall with his chest out. "I give you my word."

Veron raised an eyebrow. "And what's that worth to me?"

Malt's face contorted in disgust. "A Kyrdtown man's word is like stone. Our honor is what we hold most dear. You insult me by—"

"I don't mean to insult you, but all I know of you is what I've seen so far." Veron nodded after a short pause. "We will accept you at your word. We will trust you to release them once we're gone."

"*We* are taking a risk by letting them go," Malt said. "What's to stop *you* from turning on *us*, huh?

"You have my word that we will leave Nasco peacefully."

No one in the room moved. The faint flicker of the flames in the lanterns was the only audible sound.

"I hear shadow knights value their honor. I will trust you to uphold your end."

Veron nodded deep and slow. "If you keep your word, we will as well."

Malt's jaw flinched. He stared back for another long moment. "Be off, then."

"What of our weapons?"

"They are with your horses." Malt glanced at the door where a guard nodded. "Do you need anything for your travels? Food? Supplies?"

Veron shook his head. "Nothing."

"Could we—" Lia's eyes jumped to the water. The dryness of her mouth felt suddenly worse. "Could we have some water?"

Malt smiled and chuckled softly. "Of course." He stepped back and motioned toward the bowl. "Help yourselves."

Lia hurried to the bowl, keeping her eyes up and her back to the wall. She selected a goblet and dunked it in the basin. The liquid rushing into the vessel made her throat ache in anticipation. Marcus joined her, panting as he submerged a cup of his own. Veron and Raiyn grabbed their own goblets.

At the door, a guard's eye twitched.

Lia held her breath. *What's going on?*

Her cup hovered in front of her lips. The cool liquid teased her. Her eyes danced between the guards. They all looked tense.

Rangolt's sword drooped, but the knuckles on the hand that held it were white.

The room grew still. None of the guards appeared to breathe.

Water sloshed in Marcus' cup as he raised it.

Lia felt her pulse pound in her ears.

"Stop." She touched Marcus' elbow before his drink reached his lips.

The boy stopped.

Veron's and Raiyn's bodies tensed, immediately alert.

Lia tipped her cup, letting a measured swallow pass her lips. Her throat rejoiced, but the small drink wasn't enough to satisfy. She swallowed.

"What's the matter?" Malt asked.

Veron leaned toward her. "What is it?"

"Is it okay?" Raiyn asked.

Lia looked at the table where Malt's discarded goblet rested. She took a hesitant step forward and peered inside. Her gasp shattered the silence. She looked in her own cup and noted the remaining liquid.

A tickle scratched at Lia's throat. The swallow she had taken continued to work its way down. She stepped toward Malt but pointed at his cup. "The water you drank, where did it come from?"

The man's forehead wrinkled. "From that basin—right there."

She shook her head. "No it didn't. The water in the basin is murky, but what's left in your goblet is as clear as a crystal. You didn't drink from this."

Malt opened his mouth but didn't reply.

"The heat in that house," Veron said. "The lack of water. It all makes sense." He flung the water from his cup forward, then threw the vessel on the ground.

Malt and the closest guards jumped aside but still took the brunt of the water. They cringed at its touch, recoiling as if it burned them.

"It's nothing," Malt said, wiping his dripping hand on his pants. His nervous laugh bounced through the room. "You're being paranoid."

The guards raised their weapons, their bodies poised and ready to fight.

A twinge of pain lanced through Lia's gut. She held her stomach and doubled over.

Raiyn rushed to her side and set his hand on her back. "Lia! What can I do?"

She winced, the pain spreading rapidly.

"Is it . . . ?"

She nodded. Her jaw quivered as she forced the words, "Poison. It's all right. I've got this." The warm tingling sensation of the origine rushed in but barely registered through the overwhelming agony that racked her body.

Lia fell to the ground. The pain in her stomach felt like it burned her from the inside. From her fuzzy vision, she registered an explosion of movement. Raiyn moved first, his blurred form rushing through the room while Malt's men shouted. The commotion sounded muddled in her ears.

Raiyn attacked in a flurry of steel. He twirled through the men, striking them down one after another. One of their swords shattered in half. Another man crashed through a wall after a kick to his ribs. The last thing Lia saw was Raiyn's sword piercing Malt's gut.

She rolled on her side and closed her eyes, pressing them tight to fight the pain. Her breath was nothing more than shuddering gasps. She allowed the power of the origine to focus her body into fighting the poison. Her limbs shook, and her hands clenched. Blinding lights seared into the backs of her eyelids. She yelled through gritted teeth, but the sound barely registered. She fought, draining her energy until there was nothing left to drain. Her vision darkened until everything went black.

34

KNIGHTS OF POWER

Danik's head pounded as he threw back the sheets. Sunlight filtered through the curtains at a high angle, indicating it was several hours after sunrise. His mouth felt sticky and dry. He groaned as he sat up and tossed his legs over the side of the bed.

After he had discovered the alcohol in the meeting room at the rear of the Hall of the King, the chamber had quickly become his favorite in the castle. He pressed against his head, unsuccessfully trying to remember how late he had stayed there with his knights the previous evening.

With his silk robe drifting against the floor, he stumbled across the room and splashed water on his face from the basin. The water was clean and clear, filled by servants at some point in the early morning. Next to the basin, clothes hung on a rod, chosen specifically for him.

He pressed his eyes together, trying to blot out the ache in his head. His stomach rumbled. *Am I nauseous or hungry?* he thought, staring in the mirror as water dripped off his chin.

He tugged on a velvet rope that rested against the wall. A dull chime sounded somewhere unseen. "Food!" he shouted.

A few seconds later, the door to his bedroom opened, and a young female servant entered. Her black dress hovered over the floor, while her white collar buttoned tight around her neck. She bowed straight and fast. "What can I get you, Your Majesty?"

"I'm hungry," he said. "Bring me some bread and cheese with some fruit."

She bowed again then turned to leave.

"Also." He raised a finger, stopping her. "A tonic. My head aches. Find me something to ease it."

"It will be done." The servant pulled the doors closed behind her.

Danik blew out a breath and stared in the mirror again. He cupped a fresh handful of water and splashed it over his face. He watched the water drip, wishing the cool liquid would somehow soothe his head.

He frowned then lifted his chin.

The water trickled down his neck, washing away the concealing powder and revealing the black stain that grew more pronounced every day.

He ran his finger down his neck, slowly wiping the water up and down. Everywhere he touched turned black, as if he painted on the rough, dark shape with his finger. He gritted his teeth, staring at the mark. The powder he applied daily could barely cover it up anymore.

It's worth it, he told himself. *It's only a mark. The power I receive makes up for it.*

A pull tugged at him. His sinuses cleared and he stood straight. He clamped a hand over his chest, but the action didn't lessen the power that pulled at him. He looked out the window and found the Straith Mountains standing in the distance. *What is this? What's drawing me?*

Again, the feeling evaporated in an instant. He placed both hands on the sides of the basin and stared in the mirror. *It's fine. It's nothing.* His breath settled.

A click announced the door to his room opening. Danik jumped and covered his neck. "What are you—" He stopped himself.

The servant had returned with a tray. "I'm so sorry, Your Majesty! I-I thought you wanted me to bring it in."

Danik turned away from the door. "I did." His anger cooled. "Leave it over there."

He heard the tray settle on the table next to the door.

"The tonic is being prepared now," the servant said, her voice meek. "I'll bring it as soon as it's ready."

"Thank you."

"Sir, did you want me to have Lisette or Dawn fetched?"

Danik's eyes flicked to the disheveled sheets of his bed. He pursed his lips then shook his head. "No, I'll be going out. That is all."

Her footsteps exited the room.

Alone again, he grabbed his container of concealer and brush from a shelf and went to work brushing the black spot away.

DANIK PUSHED OPEN the door of the old Shadow Knights facility. The smell of the hall took his mind back. He laughed that only a few weeks before, he had been the low knight in the pecking order. He smirked. *And now I'm king.*

The rooms along the hall were dusty and dark. He paused at the door to the common room. No food cooked over the hearth. No laughter reached his ears. He looked at the bench seats and remembered the last night he'd sat there with Lia, enjoying a meal.

"Everything all right?"

Danik turned as Nicolar approached, the sound of clacking swords in the distance behind him.

"You look . . . pensive."

"Just remembering." Danik turned back to the table. "It seems so long ago."

"Where do you think they went? Lia and the others."

Danik sighed. "Probably tromping after the Marked Ones."

"That book had a map, right?"

He nodded.

"But you're not . . . nervous?"

Danik shrugged. "The map directs them to a star in the middle of the Straith Mountains. What's going to happen is they're going to wander around in the snow looking for . . . whatever it is, until they all die."

"What if they find it?"

"I'm not worried. Talioth captured nearly all of them here. If three more show up on their doorstep, I'm sure they can finish them off."

Nicolar shuffled. "Is it possible they don't go after them?"

Danik turned. "What do you mean?"

"They could cause a lot of trouble around here if they go public. People know them, right? What if they start talking in the square? Remember how those guards in the dungeon turned on me? Imagine if the whole city did that."

Danik clenched his teeth. He pictured Veron and Lia speaking to a crowd, telling the truth about what happened to the previous king. "They won't," he said. "If there's any hope of saving his wife, he'll go after her." He straightened and looked back down the hall. "Now, do I get to see how these recruits are doing?"

Nicolar nodded and beckoned him forward. "Come on."

Danik followed down the curving hallway until it emptied into the courtyard. Nostalgia hit him at the sight of the men sparring with wooden swords. Broderick walked between the men, barking orders and correcting form.

"Line up!" Nicolar ordered.

Five men looked his way then hurriedly arranged in a row. Danik nodded toward Broderick who gathered with Nicolar.

"These recruits came from the Red Quarter, here in Felting," Nicolar said.

Danik scanned the row. "Are you trainees here to join the Knights of Power?"

Cries of affirmation rolled down the line.

"You think you have what it takes?"

The cries repeated, louder.

Danik turned to Nicolar. "What have they learned?"

Broderick stepped forward after Nicolar turned to him. "Sir, we started with basic sword forms and dagger drills, then moved to strength and conditioning. They've all done exceptionally with the rigorous routine."

"And what of the devion?"

"The basics, so far. They're adapting it for speed and strength but struggling with control still."

Danik pointed at the first man, a massive, bald specimen with arms as large as the average man's legs and a neck as thick as his head. "You there. What's your name?"

The man's shirtless chest stuck out while his abs rippled down to the hem of his loose brown pants. A tattoo of six stars ran down his side. He turned his head to Danik and lifted his chin, his black beard bouncing as he spoke. "Luc, Your Majesty."

His deep voice boomed off the courtyard walls.

"Luc, why are you here?"

"Because I want to serve you as a knight of power, sir."

"And what does that mean?"

The man's bald head wrinkled. "To, uh . . . do whatever you need me to."

Danik chuckled. "What did you do in the Red Quarter, Luc?"

"I was a, uh . . . collector—of sorts."

"Collector? What does that mean?"

"I worked with people if someone owed them payment but had trouble following through. Sometimes they needed convincing."

"You pounded on them until they paid."

Luc's smile was faint but discernible. "If needed."

"What do those stars represent?" He pointed at the tattoos.

The man's eyes flicked to the man standing next to him. "Those, um . . . they represent people who were, uh . . . difficult."

Danik stared into his eyes as sweat dripped down the man's face. "People you killed?"

Luc swallowed hard. "Um, I . . ."

"It's all right." Danik waved his hand. "I'm not a constable here to mete out justice. You're not afraid to do what needs to be done. That's good."

The large man's chest settled, and the tension on his face eased.

"Why do you think you can make it as a knight of power, Luc?"

A smug grin formed. He looked down at his body then chuckled as he glanced down the line at the other men. "Is it not obvious?"

Danik raised an eyebrow. "What's obvious to me is that you know nothing about what makes an effective knight of power."

The smug look vanished.

"Would you say you're stronger than I am, Luc?"

The man's eyes grew. He opened his mouth, but only a stuttering jumble of words came out.

Danik laughed. "Is it that difficult of a question? Look at me!"

"I, uh . . . if you mean with, um . . ."

"Of course you're stronger than me!" Danik laughed. He pointed down the line of men. "Do any of you think I'm stronger than you?"

The other four men chuckled and glanced at each other. Their heads shook.

Danik motioned for Broderick to toss him a wooden sword. He caught it and spun it through the air. The grip was familiar, used over years of training. He walked to a table where a small hourglass rested and flipped it over. Sand fell through the object, piling slowly in the bottom half.

"Work together—fight as one. Your goal is to strike me. Every one of you is stronger than I am, so it should be easy for you. If any one of you touches me with his sword, all five of you will sleep in the castle for a night."

The men stood straighter with grins growing on their faces.

"You will eat at my table and drink from my wine cellar, and the one who strikes me first will sleep in my own bed tonight." He pointed to the stairs at the edge of the courtyard. "I will take one of the old straw-filled piles of junk here. But you only have until that sand is gone to do it."

Danik dropped into a crouch and raised his weapon above his head. The five men stood, stunned. They glanced at each other, eyes shifting.

"The sand's moving," Danik said. "And you're not going to hit me while standing over there."

All five men moved at once, running and stomping to face off with the king.

Danik barely even had to try. His masterful control of the devion left him running circles around the men. They swept awkward blows in his direction, but Danik merely dodged. He followed with kicks to their chests and punches in their sides. Heavy blows rained on their arms.

The trainees flared their use of the devion, getting bursts of strength and speed, but the inconsistency made them easy to fight off. Luc yelled as he heaved his sword. The blow was significant, but Danik ducked, letting the whizzing attack pass harmlessly over his head. He cracked his own weapon against it, knocking the sword from the unsuspecting man's hand.

The men continued coming, but their arms drooped. Their mouths hung open as their breaths labored. Speed slowed down and feet dragged. Danik danced around them, striking their backs and causing them to twirl until they nearly fell.

The last of the sand dropped through the glass. "That's it!" The knight trainees fell to the ground. They groaned and sucked in air. Some panted on their hands and knees while others rolled from their backs to their sides, looking equally miserable no matter what they did.

One man pressed his hand against his side where a red welt already formed. Another held his back, massaging an area where Danik had laid a devion infused punch. Luc sat on the dirt with his chest bent over. Swollen spots on each arm sported an angry red color. He raised his head, dripping sweat from his beard.

Danik tossed his sword to the dirt. "You may all be stronger than me, but strength is not what makes the Knights of Power great. The devion is what powers us. Your strength comes from your control of that power, not from the size of your arms."

Luc's head retreated into his neck.

"You all show promise. You're tapping into the ability, but you're still raw and unrefined. We will teach you control. We will teach you instinct and how to react. And once you're ready . . ." He lifted his arms to indicate all five men. "You will each become one of my elite force."

The men's panting had lessened, and they nodded where they lay.

"When King Darcius was in power—when the Shadow Knights kept order, how were you treated?"

None of the men replied.

"You." Danik pointed. "What's your name?"

"Mirko, sir," a dark-skinned man with black hair and a beard said.

"Mirko, how did you live a few weeks ago?"

"Not well, sir."

"The Red Quarter, right?"

Mirko nodded.

"Did King Darcius lift you out of poverty?"

He shook his head.

"Did the Shadow Knights give you a nicer house or food to eat?"

"No."

Danik paced to speak to them all. "Once you become a knight of power, you will live in luxury. You will be given a place to live, food, and clothes."

The men nodded.

"As long as you serve me, you will be taken care of. Does this sound like something you would like?"

The cries of affirmation were enthusiastic and strong.

"Good. Keep training. You will be needed soon." He nodded to Broderick.

The knight stepped forward and roused the men. "No time to be tired! Up! Grab a sandbag from the pile. You're going on a run."

The men groaned as they struggled to their feet and followed Broderick to the supply room.

Danik motioned for Nicolar to step with him to the side.

"They still need work," Nicolar said. "I know."

"They're coming along," Danik admitted. "We need more though. The sooner the better."

"Tomorrow, a batch of twelve new ones begin. Plus, Cedric and Alton are out recruiting. They will hopefully be back with even more in a few days."

"Good." Danik paused, deciding whether or not to speak what had been on his mind.

"Is there something else?"

Danik pursed his lips. "Have you . . . felt anything recently?"

Nicolar's forehead scrunched. "What do you mean?"

"I've, uh . . ." Danik glanced up at the walls around the courtyard. "I've felt . . . a pull."

"A pull?"

"It feels like . . . a call or some force wanting me to go somewhere."

Nicolar raised an eyebrow but didn't reply.

"You haven't felt anything like that?"

The man shook his head. "I have not."

Danik nodded then moved to leave.

"I noticed something else, though," Nicolar said, stopping him.

The knight's eyes shifted around, then he pulled down the high collar around his neck and pointed to a faint mark.

Danik inhaled a deep breath.

"I first noticed it two days ago," Nicolar said. "Today, it seems a bit darker."

"I have the same mark." Danik touched his powdered neck. "It's nothing."

Nicolar leaned in and squinted his eyes.

"I have powder over it. I believe it's from the intense power we wield. It doesn't affect anything else, and it's easy to cover."

The tension in Nicolar's face eased.

"I'll send you some powder to help."

Danik stepped to the side as Broderick and the other trainees thundered out of the courtyard, passing into the hallway. He smirked, remembering his time with those same sandbags.

He followed at a walk and turned back to Nicolar. "Keep them training. The sooner we get our army, the better."

35

HELP FROM THE WOODS

"She's waking!"

The indistinct voice sounded muddled. Shuffling noises echoed vaguely in Lia's head. She slowly opened her eyes and blinked away fatigue to find three faces staring at her.

"Are you all right?" Raiyn asked. He leaned forward directly next to the unfamiliar bed she lay on.

Marcus waited next to him with eyebrows lifted, and Veron stood at the foot of the bed. His eyes looked red and puffy, but a relieved smile covered his face. He held on to her toe that hid under a blanket.

"I-I think I'm good," Lia croaked.

"Out of the way," a woman called, pushing Raiyn and Marcus to the side.

Nevi looked stronger than when Lia had last seen her. The woman moved with a limp and her voice rasped, but she ordered the young men around as if she were in prime shape.

"Here, take some water." She extended a cup.

Lia took the drink.

"I filled it myself," Raiyn said. "There's this basin of water I found in some building by the square last night. It looked so good that—"

Lia slung her free hand at him. "Funny."

He dodged with a peel of laughter from both him and Marcus.

"I filled this up directly from the well," Nevi said. "It should be clean."

Lia lifted the cup to her lips and sipped. The water brought relief to her parched throat. She started with a sip and soon found herself taking large gulps.

"Take it easy, Lia," Raiyn said.

The water tasted too good. She didn't want to stop but finally pulled the cup away and gasped for air.

"Don't worry about going easy," Nevi said, turning her head to expel a rattling cough. "Other than pembrake powder, the best cure for xolopyr root is to flush the system."

"Is that what it was?" Lia asked. "The poison? Xolopyr?"

Nevi glanced at Veron.

"We think so," Veron said. "We inspected the water. It had a cloudy tinge with a slightly higher viscosity."

"And there was no odor," Lia said. "Their old town was in the Kyrd Forest, right?"

Nevi nodded.

"It should be readily found there."

"It's amazing you survived," Nevi said. "That origine thing seems mighty handy."

"On the chance the water was poisoned, I figured I'd be able to flush a small swallow with the origine. I had no idea he'd use something as potent as xolopyr. I guess Malt wasn't taking any chances." Lia turned to her father. "What happened after I passed out?"

Veron nodded toward Raiyn. "Raiyn happened."

The young man blushed with a pained smile.

"You should have seen him," Marcus said. "He grabbed a sword and tore through the room before I could even blink. Then he ran up the hill and freed the villagers."

"That was a sight to see," Nevi said. "When we bolted out of that place, the people from Kyrdtown fled. They didn't even collect food or clothes, they just ran."

"What happened with Malt?" Lia asked.

Veron looked at Raiyn, whose eyes drifted to the floor.

"Dead," Veron said. "He and most of his guards."

Lia inhaled, her eyes on Raiyn.

"You did what was needed, son," Veron said. "You have nothing to be ashamed of."

Raiyn nodded. "I know, sir. And I'm glad the village is safe."

"As are we, dear." Nevi patted him on the shoulder. "Thank you."

Lia pushed herself up to a sitting position.

"Whoa!" Alert again, Raiyn held his hands out. "Take it easy."

"I'm fine," she said. She paused, giving her body a second to respond. A wave of dizziness rolled over her.

Am I fine?

She pivoted her legs, dangling them over the side of the bed. "We need to get going as soon as possible. I can't just lay around."

"You've been poisoned," her father said. "Don't push yourself."

Lia allowed her body to slide to the floor. Her bare feet hit the wood, and she waited, making sure she wouldn't fall over. She swung her arms then shook out her legs. A vague haze muddled her brain, but she felt lucid and able to move. "I should be good," she said tentatively. "Mother's waiting. Where are my boots? We need to go."

Veron chuckled. "All right, then."

Nevi brought her boots from the other room.

"I don't suppose we can take any helpers from Nasco anymore, huh?" Lia asked.

"They had a village meeting this morning," Veron said. "The sick and weak need time to recover and nourish their bodies, but there are many who are nearly at full strength."

"They need most of their healthy crew to stay around," Raiyn said. "They need to rebuild the village and take care of the others. But there were a few who wouldn't be held back that are going to come with us."

"I wish I could help," Nevi said. "I would do anything for Chelci. Did you know it was in this same room that I nursed her back to health after being attacked by that valcor?"

Lia raised her eyebrows.

"That was . . . eighteen years ago." Nevi smiled wistfully. "She's a tough one, too—like you."

Heat crept up Lia's neck at the compliment. "How's your husband?" she asked. "Russell? Was that his name?"

Nevi flashed a pained smile then nodded over her shoulder. "Yes, thanks for asking. He's resting in the other bedroom. He's going to need some time, but he should recover. He brightened up at the broth he ate earlier today."

"What about you?"

"Psshh!" Nevi waved the question away. "Nothing's going to slow me down. In fact, I need to go and check on him now." Nevi left the small bedroom and hobbled across the other room, her feet creating a limping rhythm on the floor.

Lia sat to put on her boots and turned to her father. "When do we leave?"

Veron glanced out the window and looked toward the sky. "We were planning to give you time to recover, but . . ."

"I'm good," Lia said.

He smiled. "In that case, we have some light left in the day. We can probably be off right away. Looks like it will rain soon, but I'd rather make ground while we can."

"The other guys are gathering their stuff now," Raiyn said.

"Marcus," Veron said. "Can you jog ahead to the village center and let the others know we're ready?"

Marcus grinned and nodded. He jumped into action and jogged out of the house.

"All right then." Lia tapped the straps on her fastened boots then stood. "Shall we go?"

It took a few steps for her to steady herself, but once she greeted the fresh air outside, her senses cleared. The haze that had enveloped her mind dissipated, and her body felt strong.

Veron led the way off the front porch and up a dirt path. Raiyn walked next to Lia. He set a light hand on her back and attentively watched her every move.

The clouds above were dark and heavy. A firm breeze blew in from the west, bringing what looked soon to be a storm.

"Father, you can walk faster," she said.

"I am aware." His stride seemed to shrink. "We'll be waiting on the others anyway. No need to push it, especially when you're still weak."

Lia rolled her eyes. "I'm not weak."

A chuckle from Raiyn turned her head.

"What?"

He grinned. "No, you're not weak."

"But you're still supporting me like I can't walk," she retorted playfully.

"I'm cautious," he said. "I've never been poisoned before, but I can't imagine it's an enjoyable experience."

When he removed his hand from her back, a wistful longing tugged at her heart. *Why did I have to act so confident?*

"How are you doing, by the way?" Lia asked. "It sounds like you had a lot of action."

Raiyn was quiet for a moment.

Lia leaned forward, unsure if he missed the question.

"It was terrifying."

Lia's eyes grew. "With so many men? And you being the only one able to fight with the origine?"

Raiyn turned to her with his brows pinched together. "What? No, it wasn't that."

"What do you mean, then?"

He paused again. "Killing them—all of them. I've never killed anyone before."

"You were defending yourself—all of us."

"I know, but—"

"They poisoned me," Lia said. "They tried to poison the rest of us, and you can be sure they would have finished us off with their blades."

"Yes, but—"

"It's normal to be afraid when it comes to death, Raiyn. Were you afraid of dying or that you had it in you to kill them?"

Raiyn shook his head. "Neither."

Her head cocked.

"It was . . . odd . . . to kill, but it was either us or them, and I know that." He inhaled then blew out a long breath. "I had an incredible source of power running through me, but at the same time I couldn't do anything to help you."

The corners of Lia's mouth turned up.

"You were writhing on the floor, and I couldn't help. All of my energy and strength and speed were useless. It terrified me."

Lia dropped her eyes to the path in front of her. Her smile threatened to take over her face and her pulse quickened.

"Every swing of my sword, every man I struck down—I could control those. That was something I *could* do. But I couldn't do anything for you. I watched over you, after it was done."

"You stayed with me?"

He nodded. "Except for during the village meeting, I've been by your bed the rest of the time."

The dirt crunching under their feet emphasized the awkward moment of silence. His hand swung by his side next to hers. *Take it,* she told herself. *Hold his hand while you walk.*

Her heart thumped. She rubbed her fingers against her palm, wiping away the sweat that formed. Her eyes stared straight ahead. She held her breath as her fingers stretched toward his.

Her father stopped ahead and turned. "You still doing all right?" he asked.

She jerked her hand back to her side. "Yes. I feel good—ready to ride."

"Good." Veron pointed ahead to where Marcus patted down a saddled horse while talking with a group of men. Lucy, Freckles, and Ranger waited next to them along with three other horses. "Looks like they're about ready."

Three men turned in their direction as they approached, and the tallest stepped forward. Slightly older than her father, the man had a clean-shaven face and groomed brown hair. His broad shoulders led to a thick pair of arms.

"Marcus says you're ready," the man said.

"That's right. Lia is up earlier than we expected," Veron said.

"That works." He smacked the saddle bags hanging from the nearest horse. "Supplies are loaded, and we're ready."

He turned to Lia and extended his hand to shake hers. "You must be Lia. It's an honor to meet you. I'm Aleks Bellingsworth, an old friend of your mother's."

"Me, too," the man next to him said, shaking her hand next. His hair fell ruffled and shaggy over his eyes. His toothy grin gave him a comical look. "Finley Sainsbury. Chelci was incredible, and all of us owe her our lives." He shook a finger at her and chuckled. "You look like her."

"Yeah, I get that a lot," Lia said. She glanced at the third man.

Short dark hair and a beard framed a severe face. His arms crossed over his chest.

"Are you an old friend of hers, too?"

The man frowned. "I wouldn't say friend."

His deep voice and scowl took her aback.

"Royce doesn't have friends," Finley joked.

Lia's eyes flitted between the others in the group, weighing their response to the surly man's presence.

"Don't let him fool you," Aleks said. "He likes to give the impression that he doesn't care."

"Of course I care," Royce muttered. "I'm here, aren't I."

"We're thankful to have you all," Raiyn said, rubbing his hand along the neck of his horse.

"And we're honored to ride with Raiyn the Slain!" Finley said.

Aleks groaned. "I told you, that name doesn't make sense."

"He destroyed them all with a snap of a finger. It was epic—so I hear."

"Yeah, but 'the Slain' implies he was killed, not the one doing the killing."

Finley shrugged. "It rhymes, and it's cool. I like it."

Aleks turned to Raiyn. "What's your actual name?"

Raiyn's eyes widened. "Uh, my name?"

"Yeah, your surname?"

"Um . . ." He sighed. "Raiyn Bale."

The three men froze, then glanced at each other.

Finley broke the silence. "Bale, as in . . ."

"Yes," Raiyn said. "As in Edmund Bale. The King of Norshewa was my father."

Finley's eyes grew enormous. A colorful curse snuck out of his mouth before he apologized.

"Don't worry," Veron said. "He's nothing like him."

"I think I'll stick with Raiyn the Slain," Aleks said.

The others laughed.

Veron held up his hands. "Again . . . as much as we welcome the help, I feel awful asking you all to leave your village, especially with what all will be needed and what just happened here."

"We owe much to Chelci," Aleks said. "If she's in danger and you need our help, we're by your side."

"The village will be all right, thanks to you all," Finley said, "especially thanks to Slayer here."

Raiyn shook his head and chuckled.

"But seriously, there are a lot of healthy men and women who are able to help get the village back on their feet."

"When do we go?" Royce asked, his arms still crossed over his chest.

Veron stepped up to inspect Ranger. He pulled on straps and patted bulging pockets. Appearing content, he turned to take in the group. "We go now."

A distant rumble shook the air, drawing Lia's gaze. The clouds drew near. *It's going to be a wet day.*

36

FORDING THE RIVER

Drops pattered on Raiyn's head. His hood kept the water from dripping in his face, but his clothes had become soaked hours before. He kept Freckles' reins in one hand and wrapped his other around it to keep it warm. The cool air and wet rain were a challenging combination.

Ahead of him, riding on Lucy, Lia passed a limb of a tree. Raiyn kept an eye on it as the branch bent farther and farther. He held a hand up, ready to catch it.

Whack!

The supple limb flung backward, smacking him in the arm and face, and flinging water over him.

"I'm so sorry!" Lia turned backward in her saddle. "Are you all right?"

Her words were quiet, muffled by the sound of the driving rain. Her wet, brown hair fell out of her hood on either side of her mostly hidden face.

"I'm fine." Raiyn bit back the sting and wiped away the water. He moved the branch past his head, ensuring it didn't sling behind him.

"My face thanks you, Slayer," Finley said at his back. "For the caution with the branch."

Raiyn chuckled. "This trail is a little tight." He spoke up to be heard over the rain.

"Yeah, we don't take it often. We typically head south from Nasco, toward Felting, or northwest, to Karad. Those trails are better worn. No one from Nasco's been this way in years."

"How long does this path take to get to Tienn?"

"Not long. If you start in the morning, less than a day. At the pace you all are setting, even faster."

"If Tienn is that close, why don't you go there more?"

Finley quieted.

Raiyn turned to make sure he was still there. "Don't you need supplies and stuff?"

"It's the ford," Finley said.

"The Kardolian Ford? What about it?"

"It's not the . . . *safest* route to take."

A peel of thunder shook the sky while Raiyn ran the words through his head again. "That's where we're heading, right?"

"It is."

He chuckled. "Sounds fun. What makes it unsafe?"

"A gang of bandits led by a guy named Flame used to patrol the ford. They'd wait until you were halfway across the river then cut you off on both ends. They'd collect a 'tax' of . . . whatever they wanted."

"Coins?"

"Coins. Food. Clothes . . . or worse."

His trailing words ended ominously. Curiosity pecked at Raiyn, but he decided not to pry.

"Could be nothing now, though." Finley's words brightened. "Like I said, it's been years. They may not even be there anymore."

Raiyn faced forward and peered through the trees, wondering when the sight of the river would break through. The path sloped steadily downward on a slight angle. He pushed against the wet saddle horn to keep his body straight. In all directions, thick trees and bushes blocked the way, and the river remained hidden.

When the slope flattened, the path widened, giving space for two horses to walk astride. Eager to talk with Lia, he prepared to prod his horse forward until he noticed the one ahead of her slow, taking the spot.

Aleks.

The man wore his hood down. His brown hair and broad shoulders taunted Raiyn from where he sat on his horse, embracing the rain. Lia and Aleks turned to each other, and Lia lowered her hood. Raiyn couldn't make out what they said, but he noticed the smile on her face and the laugh that followed.

An itch in his mind made him eager for the path to widen more so that he could join. He looked over their shoulders and frowned. The space ahead remained the same.

Rather than grow annoyed at his inability to travel next to Lia, he pulled his reins back and drifted next to Finley.

"So, what's his deal," Raiyn asked, nodding ahead.

"Aleks?" Finley asked, his mouth turning up. "Not sure what you mean by 'deal,' but he's a good man."

"Did he have a thing for Chelci?"

Finley stared at him, his crooked smile causing Raiyn to shift in his seat.

"The way he looked when he mentioned her made me wonder."

"He did, actually," Finley said. "But it didn't work out. Don't worry, he's not going to make a move on your girl."

Raiyn scoffed. "What? She's not—" Flustered, his words petered out.

Finley grinned. "I've got an eye for things like that. So, are you two . . . together?"

"Yes—well . . . no, not exactly. We—" He sighed. "I'm not sure what we are."

Ahead, engaged in conversation, Lia reached across the space between her and Aleks and felt the hood of his cloak as if testing the fabric. Whatever the man said, it sent her into another round of laughter.

Raiyn's frown grew. "What about you?" He turned to Finley. "Are you married?"

Finley shook his head. "I almost was. When I was young—

younger than you—I had a huge crush on Kyla, the village teacher. She was a couple years older than me, and somehow I got her to like me back."

"It didn't work out?"

Finley shook his head.

"What happened?"

"We grew up. More specifically, *she* grew up. Most people say I still haven't." He laughed. "She set her sights on Captain Honorpants."

Raiyn followed the direction of his eyes. "Who? Aleks?"

Finley nodded. "It stung for a while, but that faded." A genuine smile covered his face. "Aleks has always been my closest friend, and they were a great pair. I was happy for them when they got married. I never found anyone else after that."

Lia's and Aleks' horses stopped suddenly, and Raiyn's followed suit.

Raiyn craned his neck ahead. "What is it?"

Aleks held up a fisted hand. The rain had lightened, and a few sounds of the forest broke through. A squirrel chittered in a tree. A garront called from somewhere on the ground. A mild wind rustled the leaves at the top of the canopy, and a faint, continuous gurgle reached their ears.

"We're at the ford," Aleks called over his shoulder. "Dismount and walk. Have your weapons ready and look alert."

Raiyn spotted the line of water through the trees. He slung his leg over the side and dropped to the earth, splashing mud. He stepped forward, holding on to his horse's reins.

"Lia, how are you holding up?"

She turned and held a finger to her lips.

He dropped his hood and lowered his voice. "Sorry."

"I'm fine," she whispered back.

The line of horses moved forward at a slow walk. Raiyn's eyes darted around the woods but found nothing of significance. The gurgling of the river grew more pronounced, interrupted by the patter of rain on leaves. After a few minutes of silent travel, the trees thinned to where all travelers were able to gather in a group. Raiyn sidled up next to Lia and flashed her a smile.

Aleks moved to the center. "The Kardolian Ford is a treacherous crossing. We're here because you requested speed, and this cuts off over a day when compared to the road. Night will fall soon, so we'll make camp after we cross. There's a cave thirty minutes east of the river that will be dry."

Raiyn lifted his eyes, noticing how dim it had grown. The entire trip had been gloomy and wet, but the sky seemed noticeably darker.

"What should we expect?" Veron asked.

"With this rain, the water level will be high. Watch your footing, be aware of the current, and lead your horses slow and easy. We don't want any twisted ankles."

Raiyn petted Freckles' neck.

"That doesn't sound too bad," Lia whispered to him.

"If there are bandits," Aleks continued. "They will show themselves when we're exposed in the river. Expect bows in the trees and spears on the banks. Could be on either side."

"All right," Lia added. "That's less good."

"Do you think bandits are likely?" Veron asked.

Aleks' jaw formed a hard line as he paused. He glanced toward the river. "I don't know. I try never to come here. I'm hoping for the best, but we should be prepared for the worst."

"I suggest putting Lia and Raiyn on opposite ends of the line," Veron said. "They can defend if we're attacked and make sure we're not surrounded. Are you two all right with that?"

"Of course," Lia said as Raiyn nodded.

"They're the best suited to fight off any threats that may come at us."

"Very good," Aleks said. "Raiyn, can you take the front? I'll stick with you."

"Will do," Raiyn replied.

"And Lia, why don't you take the back." Aleks looked at his village mates. "Finley and Royce, have bows ready."

They nodded.

"I'll ride at the front as well," Veron said. "Marcus, stick behind me."

The young boy nodded, holding on to the reins of his horse.

Raiyn wished Lia, "Good luck," then joined Aleks.

The man held his sword as his eyes scanned the woods. Raiyn didn't hear anything other than the river.

"Where do we go?"

Seeming content with his visual appraisal, Aleks finally turned to him. He nodded his head forward. "This way."

Raiyn walked Freckles forward, dodging bushes and trees. Soon, they broke out of the cover of the foliage, and the footing turned to rock.

The Felavorre River stretched wider than anywhere Raiyn had seen before. Instead of the deep, flowing current he was used to, the water rippled over rocks, capped with white. On the far side of the river, trees grew in a thick line, blocking any sight into the dark woods beyond.

After a short travel, they arrived at a small, rocky beach of smooth stones. The river lapped at the stone, gurgling past. Aleks stopped and allowed Raiyn to come next to him.

"This is the shallowest portion." Aleks motioned ahead with his arm. "Take it slow and steady. We'll travel side by side. You take downstream."

Raiyn nodded. He felt over his shoulder and touched the haft of his battle-axe. He gave it a tug, making sure the tension was right. Behind him, a line of horses and men followed close. Lia emerged from the woods on the bank, the last in line.

"Let's move," Aleks said.

Raiyn stepped forward, his foot sinking into the river. Water poured through every seam of his boot. His foot had long been wet and nearly numb, but immersing it in cold water caused him to gasp. His other leg sank deeper, up to mid-calf. Freckles seemed unperturbed by the water or the temperature. She stepped forward, her feet gliding through the current.

"If bandits were to attack," Raiyn said. "When do you think they'd come out?"

Aleks kept his eyes up while his feet continued onward. "When we're close to the far bank. That's the deepest part of the river, and where we'll be the most vulnerable."

"So, you've run into them before? What happened?"

Aleks' face hardened. Water splashed as he sloshed ahead. "I have," he said finally. "We killed four before the rest ran."

"Nice. So, they didn't take anything from you?"

Aleks inhaled a deep breath, his eyes smoldering. "They took."

Splash. Splash.

"They took enough." His voice shook with a labored tension.

Raiyn averted his eyes, wishing he'd not asked.

Halfway across the river, the water reached his knees. The rocks at the bottom of the river were uneven and lumpy. One of his arms held on to Freckles' bridle, and the other extended for balance.

Raiyn kept scanning the trees. Other than rain and wind pushing the leaves, nothing moved on the far bank. Gradually, the intensity of the rain picked back up.

"Thank you for coming with us," Raiyn said, loud enough to be heard over the shower.

Aleks glanced his way and nodded. "All of Nasco owes the Stormbridge family. If they ask for help, I'll be there."

"When you return home, tell your wife thank you from us as well."

"Actually, it's just me. I'm not married."

Raiyn frowned. "I thought you were married. Kyla was it? Finley said—" Raiyn cut himself off at Aleks' pale expression. "I'm sorry. I didn't mean to—"

"It's fine." Aleks paused, the river flowing around his trunks of legs. "I *was* married. Kyla and I had just celebrated ten years together when she passed."

Raiyn's heart fell. "Illness?"

Aleks shook his head. "Killed by bandits."

It was Raiyn's turn to turn pale.

"Shot through the neck with an arrow"—he pointed ahead— "about ten paces from where you stand."

Raiyn swallowed the lump in his throat.

"That was the last time I attempted to cross this ford."

Raiyn wanted to say something comforting or apologetic, but nothing came out. When Aleks continued forward, he fell in stride.

A fresh boom of thunder rippled the sky, and the rain picked up. Raiyn pulled the axe from over his shoulder to be prepared for anything that came.

"Here's where it gets deep," Aleks said. "Be ready."

Raiyn glanced behind him to check on the progress of the team. The line of horses and people stretched through the water nearly back to the opposite shore. Lia gave him a nod from the end of the line. He turned and tightened his grip on the axe. Simmering in his gut, the origine waited, ready for action. Water dripped from his hair down his face. He wiped it with the back of his hand and took a step forward.

The riverbed dropped again. Soon the surface reached his thigh and then his waist. The pelting rain both drummed on his head and splashed up from the river. He slogged forward on numb legs, pulling his horse.

Aleks kept his arm with the sword up, his elbow hovering over the water. His rapid breath was even louder than the driving rain and rushing river.

Movement on the shore caught Raiyn's eye. *What was that?* He squinted, trying to find it again. His eyes jumped from tree to tree, trying to confirm any potential danger. *Nothing.* He stepped forward again. A loose rock threw him off balance, and the weight of the current tried to push him over. He pulled at his horse to maintain balance. Freckles' strong neck strained against him, keeping him from plunging completely under.

"Careful," Aleks said, slow and deliberate. "We're almost there. Don't lose it now."

Twenty steps more would get them on the shore.

Raiyn creeped his feet forward, making sure each step was solid.

Any deeper—any misstep, and he could be swept away. With each move, he anticipated the depth shrinking. The hope of a safe crossing grew. He shuffled his leg forward and the river bottom angled up. A smile grew. *We're going to make it.*

Keeping his eyes forward, he spoke to Aleks. "Maybe those bandits aren't here anymore. I think we're about through the—"

A *thwang* drew his attention. Another immediately followed.

Raiyn pulled the origine into his body and flashed into action. Releasing his horse's reins, he gripped the axe with both hands and twirled through the air. In a blink of an eye, he swung the weapon, slicing the air just ahead of Aleks' chest. An arrow zipped through the air until the head of his weapon cleaved it in two.

The follow-through of his swing plunged the weapon into the river. Raiyn followed the momentum through the water and pulled the axe up, near where he stood. The blade bit into the air, slicing the shaft of another arrow just behind the tip.

When he released the origine, an explosion of water shot into the air, and bits of arrows scattered across the river.

Aleks flinched, then froze, holding his sword higher. The horses neighed and pawed at the river. Raiyn gripped the axe, trying to find the source of the danger. His head jerked in each direction until a man emerged from the shadow of the trees.

Wet, brown hair plastered down the sides of the man's face to cover his ears, and a graying beard dripped water. His thick cloak was dark brown, and a fire tattoo crawled up the side of his neck.

"Well that was something you don't see every day," the man said.

Four bowmen rushed forward, spreading out on either of his sides.

"I guess they're still here," Raiyn said.

37

DEALING WITH OBSTACLES

"Drop your weapons!" the man shouted. "Toss them in the river unless you want to try your luck with another move like that."

"We need our weapons," Veron called back. "We're on an urgent mission for King Danik."

A round of laughter sounded from the men.

Raiyn's eyes darted between each of them, looking for any sign of attack. He tried to steady his breath, heavy from the sudden use of origine.

"Sure you are." The leader held his sword casually in front of his chest. "Drop them, then we'll let you out of the river."

"Who are you?" Veron asked.

The man on the shore smiled. "You're looking at the Felavorre Raiders, and I am their leader, Lorenzo Flame. We own this passage and require a toll for you to cross."

Aleks' hand creaked over the leather grip of his sword. His knuckles grew white.

"What sort of toll?" Veron said.

Flame smiled. "Your *stuff*, of course. You seem to have plenty of horses, loaded with gear. We will content ourselves with only taking half."

Aleks spoke slowly and deliberately with his jaw tight. "Like he said, we're on a mission. We need our weapons, we need our horses, and we need our . . . stuff."

"If you *don't* lose the weapons, we will fill you with arrows, one by one. If you run, we'll put the arrows in your backs instead of your chests. We will wave at your bodies floating down the river as we retrieve your horses and the cargo they're packed with. In that scenario, we'd take everything. So if you *listen*, you can skip the bloody, floating part."

Raiyn tensed. He leaned forward on the balls of his feet, ready to snap into action. The water still reached his waist, bogging down his potential for movement, but his axe was ready.

"Finley," Raiyn said, turning halfway around. "Are you ready?"

"I am," Finley replied, barely audible over the rain and the river. He stood motionless with his bow taut.

"Take out the leader."

The pause lasted a moment. "A-are you sure?"

"Don't worry about the others. I'm watching. Shoot him."

An arrow zipped over his head. Raiyn used the origine while watching its flight. The arrow drew closer and closer. The men on the shore seemed frozen while his mind processed. The projectile struck the flat blade of Flame's sword.

A *clang* filled the air, and the man jumped. He patted his chest and glanced around before zeroing his eyes on Finley. "Kill that archer!" he ordered.

Raiyn raised his axe handle with both hands as the arrows were loosed. Watching them in slow motion gave him time to swing his weapon back and forth, blocking the shots. Four arrows *pinged* against the metal cheek before falling harmlessly into the river.

The silent bandits stared with open mouths.

Flame's eyes widened as he took a step back. "Shoot again!"

Raiyn extended his weapon again, knocking more projectiles from the air.

"Incredible," Finley gasped.

Raiyn took deep breaths. He barely kept his hands above the surface of the river as his body shook from use of the origine. His eyes jumped between the bandits.

"Target this one!" Flame shouted.

Bows turned in Raiyn's direction, and a gasp escaped his throat.

"Are you all right?" Aleks asked.

Raiyn panted, his limbs fatigued and breath growing more rapid.

The *twang* of strings perked his ears as arrows flew toward his chest.

Raiyn lunged to the side. The water impeded his movement, and an arrow narrowly missed him, tearing through the hem of his tunic. He spun, knocking the next one with the head of his axe. Before he turned, his arm flung through the air and grasped the shaft of an arrow headed for his head. He stopped it dead, preventing it from reaching his unguarded face.

The last arrow was a moment behind, and he almost missed it. The shaft cut the air, streaming toward his chest. He pulled from the origine, but the well of energy grew thin. His speed slowed, and the strength in his limbs weakened. He lunged to the side, fighting the current, but his strength wasn't enough. The arrow arrived before he moved out of the way. The tip bit into his arm, slicing through skin and muscle, then stopped when it protruded out the other side.

"Argh!" He dropped his axe. The weapon splashed as it fell into the river.

Pain ripped through his body, singeing his nerves. He squeezed his eyes shut, trying to quell the pain.

Laughter brought him back. He opened his eyes. The bandits wore smug looks as they stepped closer and casually nocked more arrows.

"Hit him again," Flame said.

I can't go like this, Raiyn thought. His eyes darted to his horse and to Aleks, but his mind came up with nothing. He pulled what origine he could to prepare himself to respond.

A tingle ran down his arm, and the pain around the protruding arrow eased. The sensation was incredible. Like water pouring from a pail, agony streamed out of his body. He gave into it, his muscles relaxing.

No!

Suddenly alert, he realized what was happening. *There's not enough!* He tried to block the origine and keep it from healing. The tingling in his arm subsided, but his body slumped over. He tried to rise, but his muscles wouldn't respond.

Stand up! Come on!

Raiyn willed himself to face his attackers, but he couldn't. His chest felt heavy. His arms dragged in the water. Rain relentlessly pelted his head, unable to rise. Pulling what energy he could summon, his muscles slowly responded. He groaned as his head rose.

On the bank, the archers drew back. Strings stretched taut, waiting to release.

Like drinking from an empty vessel, Raiyn's body ached for more. He wanted to dodge, but his body wouldn't respond.

"Fire!" Flame shouted.

Raiyn held his breath and tensed.

The archers released their bowstrings, but the arrows never arrived. In an instant, all four weapons were cut in two, sliced through the lower limb of the bow. The arrows flew, shooting harmlessly into trees and across the river.

Raiyn blinked rapidly, struggling to understand what happened.

The archers reeled backward, dropping their broken bows. In front of them, a dark cloak spun. A young woman crouched, her hair flinging with motion, spraying water from the tips. A sword lifted above her head, elbows up, tip pointed at the men.

Lia! Raiyn beamed.

Aleks jumped into action. He surged forward, lunging through the deep water with his sword raised.

Flame backed up, his weapon held shaking before him. "Who-who are you?"

"What should I do with them?" Lia shouted over her shoulder. Her sword remained solid, fixed as stone.

"I've got this one," Aleks growled, dripping as he rushed onto the shore.

Flame turned with wide eyes toward the man from Nasco. Aleks met him with a raised sword and eyes of fire.

Veron hurried through the river. "Are you all right?" He paused at Raiyn.

Raiyn managed a nod. "Go ahead," he rasped, struggling to breathe.

Lia held the unarmed archers at bay while Aleks and the bandit leader traded blows. Swords clanged and grunts filled the air. A shout resulted in Flame's sword being knocked to the riverbank. He lunged for it, but Aleks ran his weapon through the man's chest.

"That's for Kyla!" His words were nearly lost in the rain.

Flame fell to his knees, his eyes rolling back. As if in slow motion, his body dropped forward, plunging from the waist up into the river. The strong current pulled an arm forward, and soon the entire body whisked away.

"Have mercy," one of the archers pleaded with hands raised. "Lorenzo made us do it. He wouldn't feed our families unless he helped him."

Veron stood next to Lia, his sword pointed toward the men. "What do you think, Aleks?"

It took the man from Nasco a moment to snap out of his fury. When he finally turned, his shoulders loosened. "Let them go."

The archers sighed and dropped their hands. Relieved smiles covered their faces. "Thank you! Thank you!"

Aleks held up his blade, pointing at their chests. "If I hear of you back at this ford, I will track you down and kill every one of you."

"As will I," Lia said.

Their eyes grew even wider.

"Go!" Aleks shouted. "Now!"

The men ran, colliding into each other as they hurried to leave. Their feet tramped over wet leaves as they disappeared into the brush.

Raiyn was nearly to shore. He had fished his axe out of the river and used it to help balance as he struggled forward.

"Raiyn!" Lia hurried to his side. She took his axe and ran an arm around his back while Veron took the reins of his horse. "Does it hurt?" she asked.

"A bit." He followed the words with a deep breath. "I accidentally . . . used . . . origine."

"Save your breath." Lia stepped with him as the water grew shallow.

"Great work, Raiyn the Slain." Finley waved from dry ground. "You saved my life back there. You too, Lia."

When they reached the shore, Lia helped him to sit by a tree. The rain had slowed to a trickle, making it easier to talk.

"Where did you . . ." He paused to breathe. ". . . come from?"

A sly grin came across her face, and she nodded downriver. "I hopped across when they weren't looking." She shrugged. "It wasn't hard."

He laughed then winced, moving his free hand to his injured arm.

"Rest a bit," Lia said. "We'll get that out soon."

RAIYN LOOKED AWAY at the cave wall. Firelight danced across the rock while a drizzle continued to fall outside the cave's mouth. He leaned against the stone, taking deep breaths to calm his mind and ignore the protruding arrow in his arm.

Lia crouched beside him while Veron and Aleks braced his limb. He gritted his teeth and flexed.

Veron rested a hand on his shoulder. "Relax."

Raiyn forced his muscles to ease.

"Here's what's going to happen," Veron said. "We're going to hold your arm like this. When you—"

A rough jerk pulled at his arm.

"Argh!" Raiyn yelled. Aleks had pulled the shaft through when he least expected it. Raiyn breathed fast and sharp.

"Use the origine." Lia rested a gentle hand on his good arm. "It's clear now."

"Nice work." Veron stood. "Heal up, then take it easy."

Raiyn closed his eyes and allowed the power to flood his arm. The prickling, soothing sensation was like water on a fire. It immediately doused the heat, leaving him sighing. "That's better," he said.

He looked at his arm. The hole over his bicep had closed, leaving a faint mark.

"Looks good," Lia said.

"Yeah," Raiyn agreed. "All things considered, things could have gone worse. Thanks for being there."

"Of course. We've got to watch each other's backs." Lia's eyes drifted around the cave. "I'm glad this place was here."

Raiyn followed her gaze. The rocky chamber was large enough for all seven travelers with horses and room to spare. A fire crackled in the center of the space, and wet clothes dripped, hanging on every surface.

"I'm glad there was dry wood," Raiyn said.

"Oof!" Marcus yelled from the other side of the fire.

Finley stepped closer, his sword angled away. "Are you all right?"

The boy waved him off. "It's fine. Just knocked the breath out of me." He pressed against his side then raised his sword. "Again."

"Elbows up, Marcus!" Lia shouted.

The boy's elbows lifted higher before he and Finley met, trading a series of blows.

"He's pretty good," Raiyn said.

"Yeah. Gavin must have been working with him for a while."

On the other side of the fire, Aleks and Veron practiced throwing metal bolos at a stalagmite.

Lia and Raiyn sat, staring in silence while the others trained in the firelight.

"Do you think the knights will be all right?" Lia asked. "When we get there?"

"I think so." Raiyn wasn't about to admit the doubts he held. "Those marked ones seemed to want them alive, so that's a good sign.

Give them time, and I'm sure Chelci and the others can figure out some way to escape. I bet once we get up in the mountains, we'll run into them coming out safely before we even find where they're held."

A smile creeped over Lia's face. As if suddenly thinking of something, she jumped up and walked to her father's saddlebags.

"Need help?" Veron asked, a bolo dangling from his hand.

She shook her head and pulled out the red book. "Just wanted to check this map out again."

Veron tossed his weapon to Aleks and joined her in returning to Raiyn.

After sitting, Lia flipped open the cover and rustled through pages until she found the hand drawn map. A large area of scribbled, jagged peaks dominated the center of the page, running almost the entire length. On either side of the mountains were dots, roads, rivers, and a few roughly scratched names. In the center of the jagged peaks, a star marked a point with *"Devion"* scratched beside it.

"We need to get to this star, and this range is clearly the Straith Mountains," Lia said. "There's nothing else in Terrenor that it could be."

"We're assuming this is a map of Terrenor," Veron commented.

Lia frowned at him.

Raiyn pointed at a wavy line. "This would be the Felavorre River, putting us somewhere around . . ." He tapped the page. "Here."

"That's assuming that Tienn is this . . ." Veron leaned close and squinted to read the label on a small dot. "Mortghin."

"It has to be." Lia pointed southwest to a large dot. "Paraghan should be Felting, and *this* on the other side of the mountain, Maraghill, is likely Bromhill. The geography is correct, the names are just strange."

"You've never seen any names or words like this before?" Raiyn asked.

Veron shook his head. "I know of Common Norshic and Tarphic, but I'm not aware of any other forgotten languages."

"So, assuming this is Tienn," Raiyn said. "That puts this point a day or two southeast, through the mountains?"

"It's difficult to judge the time from here," Veron said. "Mountain travel can be slow and treacherous."

Lia pointed just above the star on the map. "What about this oval shape here? I've never seen that landmark on a map before.

Veron took the book. He brought it closer to his face and squinted before shaking his head. "Nor have I, but if it's there, it should make the search easier."

Lia breathed in quickly. "We should stop by Tienn on the way."

"Why?"

"Benjamin Edkins."

Raiyn's forehead creased. "The mine owner?"

Lia nodded. "His mine sits on the edge of the mountains. The men talk constantly about looking for new locations. I'll bet he knows more of the mountains around Tienn than anyone. And he's a good man. He'll talk to me."

"That's a good idea," Veron said. "And it's on the way. Maybe we'll get lucky."

Lia flipped through the book.

"Do you remember the book talking about the oval landmark anywhere?" Raiyn asked.

Veron shook his head.

After another flip, the headline *Devion* filled the center of the page. "What about the devion?" Lia asked.

"I read it multiple times," Veron said. "It's nearly identical to what the Shadow Knights book had on the origine. It even has the same issue with metal. It impedes the flow of their power just like in us."

"Just like in *some* of us," Lia corrected.

"Right," Veron chuckled, "except us *alloshifters*."

"There's nothing about that in the book?" Raiyn asked.

Veron shook his head. "Nothing about the crystals either, or the black marks on their throat. The only other notable thing mentioned is something called the *Gharator Nilden*. It's described as a life magnet —whatever that means—but very little is said about it."

"Gharator Nilden." Lia shook her head. "Such strange words." She closed the book and handed it to her father.

Veron tucked it under his arm and rose to his feet. "You two get some sleep. Tomorrow will be another long day, and we'll all need our energy." He turned to the rest of the cave and projected his voice. "That goes for all of you. Get some sleep while you can."

A sweaty Finley clapped Marcus on the shoulder as they put up their swords. Aleks headed toward where his bags lay on the ground.

Veron took a few steps toward the cave's mouth and lifted a hand. "Royce!"

Raiyn glanced down the cave and saw the faint silhouette of a man waving back.

"Wake me for the second shift!"

Lia remained by Raiyn's side. His heart beat faster as she set her hand on his arm. "How's the wound?" she asked.

He gulped. "Good. It's good. The pain is gone, and, uh—" He let his vision drift around the cave. "Fatigue seems manageable."

She gave a gentle squeeze and smiled. "You'll be as good as new by morning."

38

RETURN TO TIENN

I t felt both strange and familiar to pass through the streets of Tienn. Lia imagined a lifetime had passed since she'd left, but it had only been a few weeks. She led the way. The train of men followed with their horses' hooves clopping along. The sun had only climbed half its distance into the sky, and the air retained its chill from the night. Thankfully, the sky was clear.

The sights and smells brought back memories of Danik and the ups and downs of the time she'd spent in the city. Ahead, the building where she'd lived for a brief stint came into view. A stain of black crept down the stone walls, and the ceiling had collapsed in a pile of charred debris. She shuddered, the memory of being left for dead pricking her brain.

Raiyn trotted up next to her, glancing over with plaintive eyes. "How are you?"

She straightened her shoulders. "I'm fine." She forced a smile. "Eager to speak with Ben and see if he knows anything."

He nodded toward the husk of a building. "You've been through a lot. It's all right to have feelings about it."

She looked at the building, her eyes tracing the scorch stains. She inhaled deeply. "It was a time I'd rather not relive." She turned to him with a weak smile. "Except for the last part, where you showed up."

His genuine smile soothed her nerves.

"How are we doing?" Veron called from behind.

She turned and called over her shoulder, "We'll take a right up here. His mine is just past the edge of town." A memory of the burned office rushed into her mind. *At least, I hope it's still there.*

Progress was quick on horseback, and the sloped path leading toward the mountains was easy to travel. They passed the edge of the city and followed the path into the foothills. When they rounded the final corner, her jaw dropped.

Most of the charred rubble had been cleared away from the old office, and a new building rose between it and the entrance to the mine. Walls had already been erected, and part of a roof topped it. A dozen or more workers chopped, sawed, and lugged beams of wood.

Past the building, a miner rolled a cart down the hill toward the sluices where Karlson waited to check in his load. At the far end of the yard, the tired form of Bones Hopking pushed a cart of rubble to the slurry pile.

"What is it?" Raiyn asked.

"Only a few weeks ago, this was all a pile of charred firewood after Danik burned it down."

"Looks like they've been busy."

Lia kicked her horse into a trot to close the rest of the distance. She stopped in front of the new structure, and the group dismounted.

"Veron and Raiyn," Lia said. "Why don't you two come with me?" She turned to the others. "You all wait here. We shouldn't be long."

Lia nodded at two unfamiliar workers who walked past, carrying a large beam. Then, she climbed the steps to the open doorway and poked her head in.

One man worked on a table in the center of the room while another constructed a row of shelves against the wall. The room smelled like freshly cut wood, and a grit rubbed under her boots.

On the far wall, Ben Edkins stared out an unframed window with his hands on his hips.

"You miss me?" Lia said, approaching him from behind.

Ben turned, his eyebrows raised and face lit up. "Lia! My baltham magnet, of course I've missed you. Where have you been?"

"I had to leave town and didn't get a chance to tell you." She turned to the others. "This is my father, Veron, and my, uh . . . friend, Raiyn."

The men shook hands.

"What's happening? I've only been gone a few weeks and you already have this rebuilt?

"I thought I was ruined," Ben said. "The office had burned. The baltham was gone." A grin grew on his face.

Lia fought back her smile, knowing what happened next.

"Someone left a pouch of coins on the doorstep of my house." He leaned closer and whispered, "Fifteen gold sol."

"Wow!" She feigned surprise by lifting her eyebrows. "That's incredible."

"I may have lost the baltham, but those coins sure made it easier. I made a payment to the bank, hired this crew, and immediately began to rebuild."

She looked around, nodding as she inspected. "Quick work."

"Quality, too," Raiyn added, running his hand along a wooden board. "These are well done."

"So . . . are you back?" Ben asked. "Judging from your company and those travelers outside, it doesn't look like you're here to chip at rock."

"Unfortunately not," Lia said. "Although I'm glad things are going well. We could use your help." She turned to her father.

After looking over his shoulder, Veron pulled the red book out of a pocket. He flipped through the pages. "You've traveled in the mountains, haven't you?"

Ben nodded. "Not everywhere, but . . . yes, I've gotten around. A mine boss has to be on lookout for potential sites."

Veron stopped flipping, folding the pages open to the map. "Does anything on this look familiar to you?"

Ben accepted the book and turned it around. He held it close to his face. Lines creased on his forehead. "What are these names? Mortghin? Paraghan?"

"We believe Mortghin may be another name for Tienn," Veron said. "What we're interested in is this place." He pointed to the star.

"Is this the Straith Mountains?"

"We think so."

"So this would be . . . southeast of Tienn." He pursed his lips and frowned. "There's nothing in that direction except snowy peaks and endless chasms."

"What about legends or rumors?" Lia suggested. "Stories from a long time ago. Anything come to mind?"

Ben shook his head slowly then stopped. He squinted, bringing the page closer. As if an idea washed over him, his wrinkles shifted. He opened his mouth and tapped the oval shape as if wanting to say something but unsure of what it should be.

Lia's heart beat faster. "You recognize that?"

"The Window of Terrenor," Ben said in an awed voice.

Lia's eyes grew. "You know it?"

"I've not seen it but I've heard rumors. It's supposed to be an oval-shaped arch deep in the mountain range."

"What's there?" Veron asked.

Ben shrugged. "Nothing."

Lia felt like the air had been sucked out of her.

"It's just an arch, high on a ridge. Are you wanting to get there?"

"If we *did* want to . . ." Veron said. "Do you know where it is?"

"I could draw you a map—at least something close. But like I said, I've never seen it, so it's just a general idea."

"That would be great," Lia said. "Thank you Ben."

"How do you know there's nothing there then?" Veron asked.

Ben shrugged again. "I guess there *could* be. I've never known anyone who's been there. It's all hearsay. I'm not even sure you *can* get there, to be honest. It's supposed to be high up in the range. At that elevation, the elements will be brutal. You'd need to be prepared and make sure you didn't get lost." He returned the book to Veron. "I've got some paper around here. Give me a moment and I'll draw out something for you."

Lia glanced out the window as Ben left. A familiar man with tufts of hair peeking out of his tunic rolled a heavy load past her view. Her jaw tightened.

"You know him?" Raiyn asked.

She nodded. "Rankin. He's a piece of scum. I only worked here for two days, and in that time, he stole from me twice and tried to kill me once. I can't believe he's still working here." With a huff, she turned away.

"This could be what we need." Veron tucked the book back in his pocket. "A map. If we can find the arch, the point that marks the devion should be just past it."

"We need to hope that point is where they took the knights," Lia said.

A rumble of hooves sounded outside the front door.

Lia turned to find two horses stop in front of the building. She stepped closer, looking through the open window space. The new arrivals dismounted on the far side of her crew.

Muttered words exchanged. Standing taller than the others, Aleks shrugged then pointed at the building.

Raiyn set his hand on her back. "Who's there?"

His touch sent a warm feeling through her body, relaxing her muscles. She smiled and leaned into him.

A man rounded the far end of Aleks' horse, and Lia jerked. Raiyn's hand squeezed against her back. She stepped reflexively backward, but there was nowhere to go as the knight of power, Cedric, walked toward the office door.

Lia turned, hoping to find some place to hide, but the room was bare. Her hand reached over her shoulder, and her stomach dropped —Farrathan remained tucked with her saddle bags.

"Quick," Veron said. "Out the back."

They hurried across the room to the back door. When Lia was about to step through the open doorway, she noticed Alton through a window. The other knight of power walked around back, heading toward the sluices. Lia extended her arms and skidded to a halt. "We're surrounded."

"Should we run for it?" Raiyn asked.

Lia shook her head. "That would leave them with my father and the others."

Her breath came quickly. She stood in the office, spinning, having no idea of what to do next.

"I found him!" Alton called from outside.

Lia stopped spinning then creeped to the window.

The man leaned around the side of the building and yelled in the direction of the horses, "He's back at the sluices!"

The boots that were heading to the front door turned to travel the side of the office. Lia held her breath when Cedric passed the window, heading away from them.

The two men walked to the sluices and stopped when they met Rankin, who had set down his loaded cart.

"They're recruiting," Veron said.

Lia groaned. "Rankin. Perfect."

Footsteps approached from behind. "Here you go."

They turned.

Ben held out a piece of paper. "It's not the best, but it should move you in the right direction . . . if you're really serious about heading there."

The sheet contained a zig-zag line drawn from a dot labeled "Tienn" to an oval shape. It curved around large triangles and passed a couple of lakes.

He pointed out the front of the building. "If you keep following this path, after about thirty minutes, the trail narrows and veers uphill. That's where this map starts."

"Thank you." Veron took the sheet. "We appreciate the help."

Ben pursed his lips then sighed. "You sure I can't talk you into staying?"

Lia grinned. "In case you forgot, you didn't even *want* me around at first."

He chuckled. "I remember."

"Ben!" an unmistakable raspy voice called from outside.

Lia froze.

"I'll meet you out front," Rankin muttered before he arrived at the back door.

Lia turned away from the window as Alton and Cedric obliviously walked past.

Rankin's boots clunked on the wooden floor. Lia lifted her eyes to meet him, and the man froze.

"What are *you* doing here?" he asked, his words brimming with vitriol.

The vile smell of his breath wafted across Lia's nose.

"She's none of your concern," Ben said. "What is it?"

Rankin held Lia's stare for a long moment before finally turning toward the mine boss. "I'm leaving."

Ben frowned. "What do you mean?"

"I mean, I quit. I'm done mining. Something else has come up."

Ben's frown faded, and he nodded. "Very well then. Be off."

"As soon as I get my pay, I will."

"Ha!" Ben scoffed. "After what you did?" His eyes flicked to Lia before turning back. "You're lucky I didn't fire you or turn you in to the constable, three weeks ago."

"But I haven't made a fuss since then, as agreed."

"What you *agreed* to was four weeks of probation. And if you worked four weeks with no incident, you'd receive half pay for that time before being fully reinstated. At this point—one week shy—your pay is zero."

"I brought in a vial of powder all by myself!" Rankin shouted. "In that three weeks, I made you more money than the rest of the team combined!"

"And yet it was only a fraction of what *she* brought in the two days she worked."

Rankin's eyes flicked to Lia.

"But, of course, you know this. That's why you stole it and claimed it was your own."

A low growl came from Rankin's throat as he stared at Lia.

"Your pay is zero," Ben said firmly. "If you work through the fourth week, you'll receive half pay, as agreed."

Rankin's lip flared, his eyes maintaining contact with Lia's. He stepped toward her with his chest puffed. "It's a pity the mountain didn't finish you off. You would have made a great-looking corpse."

Raiyn and Veron stepped closer in unison.

"If you have a problem with her, then you have a problem with me, too," Raiyn said. He stood tall, looking down on the scraggly miner. His toned arms looked ready to strike at a moment's notice.

Rankin stepped back, raising his hands at his waist. "No problem." He turned to Ben and scowled before turning and crossing the room.

When he exited the front door, Lia and Raiyn both exhaled.

"Sorry about that," Ben said. "I wanted to give him another chance, but . . ." He shook his head. "It's good that he's gone."

"Thank you again," Lia said, "for your help."

Ben smiled. "It's no trouble. And when you finish your adventure, if you change your mind about coming back, I'd be happy to take you at any time."

39

PROMISING RECRUITS

D anik twirled the mug of ale on the table, turning it slowly and listening to it scrape against the wooden surface. His back pressed against the booth, and the deep hood blocked the rest of Fetzer's Tavern from his sight.

He lifted the mug and took a deep drink, tipping the bottom back and gulping until the contents drained. He glanced out to the tavern and caught the eye of Clara, the server he'd known for years. He shook his empty mug until she nodded. With his hood up and only having spoken in a whisper, he was sure she hadn't recognized him yet.

Why am I here?

He rubbed his fingers on the wooden surface and thought through the countless times he'd sat there with Lia. The memories warmed him and brought a wistful smile to his face. The Shadow Knights were frustrating and pretentious, but . . . the group had been his home for so long. *Home*—something he'd never known until they chose him.

In the corner of the room, the circles on the knife target caught his eye. Six knives with red and blue handles stuck out, spread out around the circles. He smiled at the memory of time with Lia.

I'm here because I miss it.

Even his parents' house had never felt like a home. Days getting picked on in the streets. Meals with little to satisfy his stomach. His father spending nights carving gourds into miniature houses by firelight. He resented the time, the poverty, and his father's lack of attention, but he would still do anything to have it back—to have had his abilities and been at home the night the thief killed his parents.

A fresh mug clunked on the table. "Here you go," Clara said.

He nodded, keeping his hooded face away.

The fresh ale foamed over the top of the mug, spilling down the side. He brought it close and stared into it.

A sudden pull tugged at his chest. *No! Not again!* His arms tensed, gripping the table as his body felt dragged toward the wall. He clenched his teeth together and noticed his body didn't actually move. As quickly as it arrived, the pull disappeared. He took in deep breaths, staring at the wall in the direction where the pressure came from.

A bell over the door to the tavern snapped him back to the present. He turned and startled at the sight of Cedric and Nicolar entering with a string of three men behind them.

Nicolar scanned the room.

Danik pulled his hood back slightly and raised a hand until the man's eyes fell on him.

The crew crossed the tavern until they arrived at his booth.

"You weren't easy to track down," Nicolar said. "This was the fourth tavern we checked."

Danik nodded to the three unfamiliar men. His breath gradually settled from the increasingly unnerving experience of feeling pulled by an invisible power. "Who's this?"

"New recruits, sir," Cedric said.

Nicolar leaned closer. "We have some . . . urgent things to speak about, but I also thought you'd want to meet them before we began their training."

Danik slid to the wall and motioned for the rest to join him. Nicolar and Cedric sat on the same side as him, and the other three men hesitantly took the opposite bench. Their bodies were stiff and their eyes wide as they slid in.

"Where are you from?" Danik asked.

"I picked them up in Tienn," Cedric said.

Danik glared down the table. "I'd like to hear from them."

The man at the end spoke first. "In Tienn, Your Majes—"

"Ah!" Danik's raised hand and short rebuke stopped him. He glanced out of the booth to see if anyone turned their way. "Not here."

"I'm sorry," the man said. He appeared in his mid-thirties with thinning brown hair and a matching beard.

Danik waved the apology away. "What's your name?"

"Ambrose, sir. I worked security for the baron."

"Baron Shepley? What do you think of him?"

Ambrose frowned. His eyes shifted between the three men across from him.

"Speak your mind," Cedric said.

"We, uh, had our differences," Ambrose said in a calculated cadence.

"How so?" Danik asked.

"He fawned over the Shadow Knights. For years, he insisted they were the greatest protectors the kingdom had even known. It was nauseating."

"You do realize I was one of those knights." Danik said.

Ambrose's eyes grew. "I'm sorry. I don't mean disrespect."

Danik chuckled. "It's all right. I'm messing with you. Why did it bother you?"

"Well . . . we were his security. We worked day and night to do our job, and all we heard about was how much better the Knights were."

Cedric leaned forward to be seen down the table. "I've known Ambrose since we were young. He's a good fighter and will serve well."

"Very good," Danik said. "How about you, two?"

The other two men straightened. One was bald with dark-brown skin and a shaved face. The other's pale skin looked permanently stained by dirt.

"We're miners," the pale one said in a raspy voice that reminded him of Nicolar. His skin looked almost leathery. Shaggy-brown hair topped his head and sprouted from the top of his tunic. His beard was short but still unkempt. "I'm Rankin, and this is Cross."

"Do you have any experience with combat?" Danik asked.

"We know our way around weapons," Cross said.

Rankin nodded. "And we're not afraid to get our hands dirty."

"I worked with Rankin on some jobs in the city when we were younger," Nicolar said. "We both did."

Cedric nodded. "He knows his way around a crossbow."

Rankin gestured toward Cross. "He's been my right-hand man in the mines. He's deadly with a pickaxe, and I'm sure he'll learn anything else you need."

Danik scanned down the line. "All three of you are ready to serve me?"

They nodded.

"We'll teach you the skills you need. You'll be part of an elite fighting unit that will put the Shadow Knights and their abilities to shame.

Rankin smirked.

"You'll live well, and you'll be rewarded for your service, but I expect loyalty. If you waver in this, you'll find yourselves no longer useful."

"We'll fit them in with the others immediately," Nicolar said. "This brings us up to twenty recruits."

Danik grinned. "Excellent. I think that's enough for the moment. Let's get them up to speed then see what we're able to accomplish with a trained group of this size."

Nicolar smiled. "Let's see Lia and the others show up and challenge us, then."

Danik pictured his line of knights, vastly outnumbering her, Veron, and Raiyn. *They'd still be foolish enough to try.* He chuckled at the thought.

"Did you say, Lia?" Rankin leaned forward and spoke softly.

Cross straightened and leaned in as well.

Danik took in a breath and glanced at Nicolar before turning back. "You know a Lia?"

Rankin nodded. "In Tienn." His eyes narrowed. "Who are you talking about?"

"A girl—late teens, straight brown hair."

Rankin lifted his chin.

"You know her?"

"I did. She gave us . . ." He glanced at Cross before turning back. ". . . trouble—in the mines."

Danik's mind flashed. "You were at Benjamin Edkins' mine."

Rankin's eyes flared. "Yes. What does she have to do with all of this?"

Danik folded his hands on the table and pursed his lips. "Lia Stormbridge wants to stop what we're trying to accomplish."

"Stormbridge!" Rankin sat up straight. "That's right!"

Cross nodded. "She mentioned it, but we didn't think anything of it."

"She's a shadow knight," Rankin said. "Isn't she?"

Danik sniffed then nodded after a pause. "Along with her father and another young man, they want to destroy the Knights of Power."

A crooked grin came over Rankin.

"What?" Danik asked. "You know something?"

"I know it's not just those three."

Danik's eyes narrowed. "What do you mean?"

"Lia, her father—Veron I assume—and another young man were in Tienn only a day ago.

"What?" Cedric leaned in.

Danik's arms tensed. "How do you know this?"

"I saw them." Rankin nodded to Cedric. "Before we left the mine. They were talking with the mine boss, but it wasn't just them. They had others."

"The group outside the mine office." Cedric groaned. "I should have gone in the building," He shook his head then turned to Danik. "There were four others with them: three men and one barely into his teens. Based on the horses and supplies they had loaded, I'm guessing they were about to head into the mountains."

"They're searching for it," Nicolar whispered.

Danik clenched his teeth. Ideas sped through his mind so fast his mug of ale spun. He pressed his palms down on the table. "Would you men like to try out the tavern's knife board?" He nodded toward the corner. "Why don't you test your skills against each other?"

Rankin shrugged. "I'd just as soon stay—"

"Go to the corner." Nicolar cut him off with a direct approach.

Rankin's eyes grew. The three recruits slid out of the booth quickly and left to go to the corner of the room. Cedric moved to the opposite bench, and the three men leaned in.

"They're on their way to the Marked Ones," Nicolar said. "Seven of them."

Danik looked at Cedric and lowered his voice. "What do you know of the others? Could they have been shadow knights?"

Cedric shrugged. "I don't know. I guess they *could* have. They looked . . . rough, like they lived in the woods or something."

Nicolar whispered, "Is it possible there were other knights you didn't know about?"

Danik took a deep breath as he pondered the question. "Maybe. I don't know."

"Either way, Talioth and his group can block the origine with their crystal power, right?"

Danik frowned but nodded. "Right."

The group of three sat in silence. The foam on Danik's ale had long settled while the drink waited, untouched.

"Maybe we should go," Nicolar suggested.

Danik raised an eyebrow. "Go and, what . . . help them?"

Nicolar shrugged. "Sure. If they need it." He scratched at his beard as his eyes jumped around on the table. "Also . . . uh, I felt a sort of . . . pull."

Danik tensed. "Like a force trying to drag you away, but your body doesn't actually move?"

"Yes. I felt it this morning."

"Where is it pulling you toward?"

Nicolar leaned in. "It feels like . . . the mountains."

"I felt it again today, too," Danik said. "I imagine it's the place on the map."

"The place where *they're* going?"

Danik nodded and drummed his fingers on the table.

"Also . . ." Nicolar began, then looked at Cedric.

Cedric glanced around before raising his chin and touching his neck. "A spot is forming."

"I gave him the powder," Nicolar said.

Danik sighed. "I guess it's all of us." He glanced over the booth at the men in the corner.

"Should we tell the knights and the other recruits?" Nicolar asked.

"Alton was rubbing his neck this morning," Cedric said. "We all learned at the same time, so I'm guessing Broderick and he are feeling it already."

"We should tell them," Danik said. "But . . . we need to understand it better, first."

Nicolar raised an eyebrow.

A plan formed in Danik's mind, the foggy cloud of uncertainty evaporating. "We will go to the mountains, and we will find what draws us there."

Nicolar nodded, and Cedric sported an evil grin.

"Take these recruits to the training center." Danik nodded to the corner. "Have Alton and Broderick stay behind to train. You two, go and pack. We'll leave within the hour."

"What do you think we'll find?" Nicolar asked, scooting out of the bench.

"We'll find answers—I hope. I want to speak with Talioth and learn from him. And while we're there . . . maybe we can take care of the remaining shadow knights once and for all."

40

SCOUTING

A gust of wind sent a blast of cool air through Raiyn's multiple layers. He shivered. His legs continued forward, stepping over the crunchy top layer of snow. He pulled his wool hat lower to tuck in his ears.

In all directions, jagged mountains filled his view. Sheer cliffs of rock gave way to white slopes of ice and snow. Valleys led to distant crags, and every turn of the path revealed a precipitous drop or a daunting climb.

Freckles whinnied and shook her head, her hooves stepping through the frozen ground covering.

"It's all right, girl." Raiyn patted her neck. He looked at her body and adjusted the blanket that draped over her. "Is that helping keep you warm?"

The horse didn't reply.

"How are you doing, Marcus?" Raiyn called.

The boy turned from where he sat on his horse. A thick blanket wrapped around him, and a warm woolen hat pulled low over his hair. "I'm good, b-b-but a bit cold."

"It's time to walk again," Veron called from behind Raiyn. "You're lighter than the rest of us, but Arrow still needs plenty of rest, especially with this slick ground."

Marcus nodded then grabbed the horn to swing his leg over.

"Hold up." Raiyn jogged ahead to put his hands on the boy's waist. "You don't want to slip."

Marcus dropped lightly to the ground while Raiyn helped him keep his balance. "Thanks."

Raiyn returned to grab Freckles' reins. "What do you think, Veron? Sometime tomorrow?"

The older man lifted his eyes to the land ahead. "It's tough to say."

"It's been two days already. The map doesn't look *that* far. We must be close."

"Travel through the mountains is slow." Veron glanced west. "And this storm is not going to help our progress."

Raiyn turned to look. The darkening view grew more ominous with every minute they walked. Visibility had dropped, and now a thick blanket of clouds covered the sky. "I wish we had another cave."

"That would be nice. It's possible we may find something still, but . . . we're running out of time, today. It looks like our canvas tents will have to do."

"Aleks returns," Royce called from the front of the line where he led two horses by the reins.

Raiyn looked up to see Aleks jogging toward them. His breath fogged in rapid puffs as he returned down the snowy slope. His inscrutable face revealed nothing.

"Hopefully he found something," Raiyn said.

The group paused where the path widened. Aleks gave time for those at the back of the line to catch up. Raiyn smiled at Lia as she led Lucy and stopped next to him.

"You staying warm?" he asked.

She smiled and shrugged, her cheeks a bright red that almost matched her crimson scarf. "Eh . . . warm enough, I guess."

"What'd you find?" Veron asked after Finley arrived.

"No sign of the arch yet," Aleks said.

A disappointed sigh rolled through the crowd.

"And . . . the path forks ahead."

Veron frowned and pulled the map from his cloak.

"It splits around a mountain, and it's not clear which route is best."

"There's no fork on this." Veron stared at the map.

Lia chimed in, "Ben did say it was a rough estimate, and that he'd never actually been there."

"I think we're on the right path though." Veron pointed to the paper. "We passed the second lake this morning, which means . . ." He looked up and turned in each direction. "It's tough to tell with these clouds, but we should still be heading south."

"There's space at the fork to camp," Aleks said. "I say we stop there and dig in for the night. If we're lucky, we'll make it before this storm, but it looks like it's going to dump on us any minute."

Veron looked around the group. "Anyone need anything? Are we good to push forward?"

Nodding heads answered him.

Aleks took the reins of his horse from Royce. "All right then, follow me."

A light snow began as they moved forward. Raiyn kept his head down and his feet moving. The harsh cold left his toes numb, so he tried to wriggle them between each step.

Thirty minutes of uphill climbing later, their path ended at a wall of stone, where the trail split. The track to the right hugged the side of the mountain until it disappeared in the gloom. The one to the left led over a ridge and vanished from sight. Where they met, a lone tree spread bare limbs in an attempt at shelter, although the only true refuge was provided by the slight overhang in the vertical rock.

The crew dismounted. Snow gathered on the people's hats and dusted the backs of their horses.

"Unpack quickly," Veron ordered. "The storm's getting worse, and we need these tents up."

Saddle bags were untied and gear was brought out. A flurry of activity over ten minutes saw two four-man tents erected and rations brought inside. Raiyn helped lug the gear, then tied the horses as far out of the elements as he could. Before entering the tent, he glanced to the sky. The fading light grew even dimmer as the storm intensified. He ducked through the flap.

"Whew! That's cold," Marcus said, rubbing his hands together, standing in the tight quarters. Veron, Raiyn, Marcus, and Lia shared one tent, while the men from Nasco took the other.

The flap to their tent opened again, and Aleks entered. "You good for now?" he asked. "You have enough food?"

Veron nodded. "We should be good for tonight. I'm worried about the trail though."

"What do you mean?" Lia asked.

"All this snow is going to make travel difficult. Fresh powder can hide dangers."

"How will we know which route to take?" Raiyn asked, his stomach turning at the thought of being lost. "The path to the right looks easier, but the one to the left heads more toward the center of the range."

The group was silent.

Veron pursed his lips. "Hopefully we'll be able to tell better after the storm's gone."

"When the trails are covered with snow?" Lia asked. "What if the storm lasts for days?"

Veron sighed. "We can't control the weather."

"I'll scout it out," Raiyn said.

All heads turned to him.

"Now?" Veron asked.

Raiyn nodded. "There's still some light. The storm's not *too* bad and the ground isn't covered yet."

"It's too dangerous."

"If I get into trouble, I can use the origine. I won't go far."

Raiyn glanced between the group, but no one said anything.

"It could be helpful," Lia said after a long moment. "I'll go with him."

Veron took a deep breath then finally nodded. "Stay close. And stay together. If the storm strengthens, get back as soon as possible."

. . .

A WINDY GUST of snow blasted Raiyn in the face as he exited the tent. He held the flap open for Lia. Her face was barely visible in the layers of hat, hood, and bright-red scarf that wrapped around her.

"You sure about this?" he asked.

"Are *you* sure about this?" Her crooked grin peeked out from the scarf. After glancing in each direction, she turned to him. "Which way?"

"As nice as the path to the right looks . . ." He spun toward the trail leading up. "This one feels more promising."

"Agreed."

The fresh powder sank under each step. The snow continued to fall in a slant as the wind blew it sideways. They took the trail up toward the ridge.

"Earlier this suether, if you had come to the lumber yard and told me I would join you in an expedition into the Straith Mountains to save the Shadow Knights, I would have laughed at you."

"You didn't see this coming?" Lia teased. "What's the most unbelievable part? The snow?

"Haha, no. Don't forget, I'm the lost heir to the throne of Norshewa. I may have spent most of my life in hot and sandy Tarphan, but snow runs through my veins."

"What is it then?"

He paused, listening to the rhythm of the crunching snow. "Purpose."

"What do you mean?"

"My mother and I lived to survive. We moved to stay alive and hide who we were. I worked in a *lumber yard*, and that didn't even earn enough to pay our bills. I wanted something bigger—something that drove me to wake up every day knowing what I did mattered. I found that in the Knights."

"Until my father kicked you out."

"Yeah."

They shared a laugh.

"Being here is the most purposeful thing I've ever done. Rescuing your mother and the other knights. Returning to Felting and stopping Danik from his coup. This matters. I matter." His eyes drifted as if staring at a far-off object. "'Make your moments count.'"

"What's that?"

"Something my mother always said—'Make your moments count.' I feel like I'm finally doing it. I've never felt as alive as I do now."

Lia's scarf flapped in the wind, her grin on full display.

"What?"

She turned to him and shrugged. "I feel the same way."

"How so?"

"I've been in the Shadow Knights all my life. I learned the code, I practiced the moves, and I wore the cloak. But—" She stopped as they arrived at the crest of the ridge. "I've never truly believed in what we do until these past few weeks."

Raiyn's attention turned from her to the view. With the clouds hanging low, visibility didn't stretch far, but what he saw brought a fresh chill to his bones.

The ridge dropped precipitously on the other side. A valley below filled with jagged spires and crevasses. Deep shades of blue and purple painted a scene that disappeared into haze the farther he looked. Above them, mountains rose taller on all sides. The trail they'd taken to get there continued around a cliff, biting into the side of an icy slope with a chasm yawning below.

Lia whistled. "What a sight!"

"It's beautiful." Raiyn's voice was filled with awe. "But terrifying at the same time."

He crept closer to the edge, but Lia grabbed his arm. "Don't get too close," she warned.

"I'll be careful."

"If you fall here, you're dead—origine or not. And I'm not going to follow you to pull out your broken corpse."

"You sure origine doesn't allow you to fly?"

"Ha ha." She pulled again. "Come on."

Raiyn stepped away from the edge and turned back toward camp.

"I guess this route is out." Lia sighed. "I thought this direction was the right one though."

Raiyn glanced up the slope where the trail narrowed and wound around the cliff.

"Don't even think about it."

"What if that's the way?" Raiyn said.

Lia looked along the cliff, her eyes solemn. "If that's the way . . . the others are going to have a *really* tough time."

He pointed to where the trail rounded the corner. "We could probably tell if we got to that point. It might level out past that." Raiyn's heart pounded as he stared. A gust of wind sent a flurry of snow into his face. "I'll check."

Lia was silent until she finally nodded.

Raiyn went first. On the right of the cut-out trail, the packed snow slope of the mountain rose at a steep angle. He could press his right hand against it for balance if he leaned the slightest bit. He kept his feet on the far right of the narrow trail. A step to the left would plummet him to the abyss below.

Raiyn stopped and turned. Lia creeped along behind him, following in his footsteps. "You all right?" he asked.

Her voice wavered. "I'm good."

He turned back to the trail. He gazed ahead to where the path curved to the left. A watery feeling rumbled through his stomach at the sheer drop.

His steps were short and choppy. He kicked his boots into the snow against the slope to create a flat area to step. The chasm yawned a breath away, but he kept his eyes on the trail. As he walked, the falling snow grew stronger, but he continued forward.

"Raiyn? I think the storm's getting worse."

He stopped walking and looked up. The dim light trickled through the clouds and snow. The corner they had set as their goal was only a few more steps. He checked behind them and couldn't even see the ridge where they were moments before.

"I agree," he said. "We're almost there though. You wait here. I'll check then be right back."

He moved forward, eager to inspect the trail ahead then get them both out of danger. His foot turned on an icy step. His arms jumped out for balance, and his sinuses cleared to take in a sharp breath.

"Careful!" Lia shouted.

That was stupid, Raiyn. Don't rush.

After a dozen more steps, he arrived at the corner. The ledge was small but appeared solid. He leaned against the slope of the mountain to round the last few steps. Thankfully, the turn of direction afforded protection from the elements. The snow lessened, and the howling wind settled to a whisper.

Despite the reprieve from the storm, when Raiyn looked ahead, his heart fell. The narrow trail they had followed dwindled to nothing, disappearing against a sheer vertical rock face.

"Nothing?" Lia touched him on the back, her question a conversational tone.

Raiyn jumped. "Lia! You scared me."

"I'm sorry."

"I thought you were waiting back there."

She shrugged. "I couldn't leave you alone. Plus, it's like we're protected from the storm here. Also—" She turned to the chasm around them. "What an incredible view!"

Pushing away the disappointment of the dead-end path, Raiyn took a moment to appreciate the setting. The backside of the mountain held an even more spectacular sight. A break in the clouds allowed a ray of sun to shine into the valley, cutting through the fog. The pit below them seemed to stretch endlessly. Wisps of snow puffed off rocky pinnacles like milled flour caught in a breeze. Across the nothingness, on the far side of the mountain, a flat path led south.

"That's it," Lia said, pointing. "That's the trail we need."

Raiyn chuckled. "Looks like it. And I bet it's accessible from the trail on the opposite side of camp."

"I think you're right."

"Good thing we came all the way out here," Raiyn said sarcastically. "Now we can freeze to death with a beautiful view."

Lia stepped closer and wrapped one arm around his back. She leaned into him. "I'm not sad we came."

Raiyn warmed, partly from the heat of her body and partly from the rapid flow of blood through his veins. His heart thudded to keep up. He leaned into her, not daring to breathe.

"What changed?" Raiyn said after a long moment of silence.

Lia turned to him while sliding her hand to his arm. Her face scrunched up. "What do you mean?"

"You said you've felt a difference these past few weeks—more purpose. What happened?"

"I, uh . . ." Her cheeks grew even redder than they already were. She lowered her face. "It started when I met you."

Over the faint wind, her words sounded like a whisper. She raised her head, her tender eyes gazing as if looking into his soul. "When Father put me in charge of your training, I felt alive. What the Knights did made sense, and I had the chance to instill it in someone else."

Raiyn swallowed the lump in his throat and nodded. "So . . . my presence helped you do your job better, as a knight. That was the purpose you found?"

"It was more than that, though. When you left, I—" Her words caught, and a tear formed in the corner of her eye. She rubbed her hands up his arm. "I missed you."

His heart felt like it would pound out of his chest. "I missed you, too." His words were barely a whisper.

"I didn't realize it until you came to me in Tienn—when you rescued me. That's when I truly felt it."

He cleared his throat. "Felt what?"

"What I wanted became clear. All along, I was missing something." Her hand slid down his arm and worked its way into his. "And that something . . . was you."

Bumps ran up his arms and along the back of his neck. He tried to breathe, but his body didn't seem to work. He didn't dare move his fingers in case she would pull away.

"Over the last few weeks, I figured something out, and it's only grown clearer with each day that passes."

"What's that?" he whispered, leaning forward. He wanted to reach for her, but his limbs wouldn't work. He couldn't hear a thing except the thudding of his pulse.

She stared at him with a soft expression. "Make your moments count." Lines formed at the corners of her eyes as her face lifted. She stepped closer, then drew both arms around his back and pulled him to her. Her bundled face was a breath away.

Raiyn leaned in.

Lia lifted her scarf away, and her mouth curled in a mischievous smile.

Their lips met.

A surge of energy rushed through Raiyn, lighting up his senses as if he were alive for the first time. A wave of heat blossomed through his body. He wrapped his arms around Lia and held her tenderly. The kiss was sweet. He closed his eyes and lost himself in the warm caress. His worries and the rest of the world faded. The snow and wind disappeared. Soon, his smile was so strong that it broke their kiss.

He looked again. Her eyes held him in their gaze, and they both giggled.

Raiyn rubbed his hands up and down the back of her thick cloak. "Well . . . that was unexpected," he said.

She cocked her head, continuing to grin. "Was it? Hmm. I've expected it for a while."

Somehow, his smile grew even larger.

Breaking the moment of bliss, a deep, rumbling crack sounded above them, like a frozen river preparing to split. Raiyn looked up. His heart, that had felt light and airy, plummeted in his chest. A torrent of ice and rock fell with nothing to stop its path.

He pulled from the origine and lunged, bracing to push Lia along with him. What would have normally resulted in him speeding off in a flash of movement, left his feet sliding out from under him on the icy path. His chest hit the ground, knocking his breath away. "Lia! Run!"

She lunged at him instead of toward safety.

He brought up his knees and tried again to sprint, but his efforts were too frantic. Nothing happened except his legs slipping.

The rumble grew louder. The ledge shook.

Lia grabbed his hand and pulled, but her feet slipped, leaving her flailing to maintain her balance.

"Just go!" Raiyn shouted, his words lost in the tumult.

His heart pounded. Any second, he expected the mountain to collapse onto them. He pushed against Lia's arm to move her away, but she continued to turn toward him, slipping and sliding on the narrow path.

A gut-wrenching terror gripped him. *Calm down, Raiyn. Take it slow. Then move.*

He stopped sliding, trying to ignore the impending wall of death coming for them. One foot gripped the path, then the other became steady. He locked eyes with Lia and they turned to flee.

The mountain arrived.

With a monumental impact, the snow and rock pummeled Raiyn, knocking him to the path. He dug his fingers into the icy ground, gripping with all the strength he could muster. The impact was brutal, pounding his back and legs with an unending force.

He clenched his teeth and closed his eyes. Sound became muffled, and the force beating on him lessened. He lay still, taking in breaths that seemed to surround him. He couldn't feel anything. His face was numb, and his limbs didn't move.

Lia!

The thought struck him like a punch in the gut. "Lia!" he shouted, but the muffled sound didn't travel. He opened his eyes but only blackness greeted him. His breath quickened.

He pulled the origine through his body and arched his back. The massive weight above him shifted. He managed to get his hands down and pushed with his arms. Snow and rock fell off him as his body lifted. Through much effort, he emerged from the pile of snow and rested back on his knees. Tumbling debris piled on the path they had traveled. He pulled his legs free and stood.

Able to finally see ahead, his mouth dropped open. He tried to breathe, but his lungs didn't work. Just before him, where Lia stood moments before, the path was gone. A chunk of the trail had been knocked away by the falling debris.

He spun in all directions, frantically hoping to find her, but there was nowhere to hide. He crept to the edge. "Lia!" he shouted into the abyss.

Nothing answered but the roar of the wind. Wisps of snow twirled in the air until they disappeared into the cloudy nothingness below.

Tears formed in his eyes. His sight grew blurry, and his heart felt like it would shatter. He gasped to take a deep breath then bellowed with all his strength, "Lia!"

41

LOST IN THE MOUNTAINS

Raiyn could barely see the tents when he stumbled into camp. The storm had intensified and filled his vision with a wall of blowing snow. The light was practically gone, but the white blanket across the ground reflected what little made it through the clouds. Frozen tears crackled around his eyes. His chest felt like a shell, as if his heart had been ripped out, while his body lumbered mindlessly forward.

He pulled the flap of the tent back, and stumbled in. A lamp hung from the roof, and all five men jerked their heads in his direction.

"There you are!" Veron's shoulders relaxed. "This storm is as bad as I've ever seen."

"We were worried you got lost," Aleks added.

Raiyn wanted to reply but couldn't form the words. Tears formed again, running over the frozen patina on his face.

Veron's eyes focused, and his body grew rigid. "What's wrong?" His eyes drifted past Raiyn's shoulder. "Where's Lia?"

Raiyn hung his head. "Sh-she—" His words died in his throat.

"Raiyn." Veron dodged the other men to get to him. He placed both hands on the young man's shoulders and stared.

Raiyn lifted his chin and sniffed back tears.

"Where is she?"

"She fell," Raiyn whispered.

The hands on his shoulders clenched.

"We were on a ledge, and the mountain above us collapsed. It-it —" He shook his head. "There was nowhere to go."

Veron's body shook. His chin quivered. "Where is she?" he whispered.

"I-I tried to save her, but I couldn't."

"Where is she?" The voice grew stronger.

"It was my fault, sir. I'm sorry." Tears ran freely down his face. "I was trying to find the path, but I shouldn't have put her in danger."

Veron shook against him. "Raiyn! Where is she!"

Raiyn wiped at his face and blinked. He looked around the tent, taking in the faces one at a time. Eyes filled with sorrow stared back. Heads looked to the ground. He brought his gaze back to Veron and took a deep, shuddering breath. Finally he nodded. "I'll show you."

Aleks stepped forward. "You can't go back out there!"

Raiyn's mind agreed with the man from Nasco, but his heart wouldn't accept it. He turned to leave, and Veron moved with him.

"Veron, Raiyn." Aleks pulled on each of their shoulders.

They stopped.

"It's a white-out blizzard out there. You won't see a thing, and you'll end up lost, yourselves!"

Veron ducked out of the tent without a word.

Raiyn looked at the men inside. "Stay here, all of you. We'll be back."

When he stepped outside, the wind hit him fresh in the face. He pulled down on his hat and tightened his cloak. He looked in each direction. *Where's Veron?*

Lia's father returned from around the corner of the tent where the horses were sheltered. A coil of rope wrapped over his shoulder. His eyes were piercing, focused. "Show me."

Raiyn trudged up the hill. His steps felt like iron lined his boots. The snow had grown deeper, but the sorrow filling his heart weighed him down even more. He looked over his shoulder to make sure

Veron was with him and stopped. Barely visible through the blinding snow, bodies exited the tent, one by one.

When the others arrived, Aleks nodded and shouted over the wind, "We're with you!"

Raiyn waved them ahead, his hope surging. "This way!"

The slope rose steadily. His legs pushed hard, moving fast. He forced himself to slow, to allow the men without the origine the chance to keep up. His blood pumped hard, working up a sweat.

"There's a trail that cuts across the cliff." Raiyn leaned toward Veron and spoke loudly while they climbed. "It's at the top of this ridge. We'll have to navigate it to get to where she fell."

"Could you see her?"

Raiyn shook his head. "It was too far down and too dark."

"Lower me with the rope," Veron said. "If it reaches, I'll search for her."

"No," Raiyn said. "You lower me. I have a better idea of where she'll be."

"You have the origine for strength to hold my weight."

Raiyn pointed over his shoulder. "You have five men. Plus, I might need the origine at the bottom."

After several silent steps, Veron nodded.

They arrived at the top of the ridge, and Raiyn pointed along the cliff trail.

"You went out there?" Aleks yelled to be heard over the wind.

Raiyn swallowed. *I should never have put her in danger.*

"We wanted to check what was around the corner, in case the path opened." His weak words blew away. "The trail is slick. Take short, choppy steps and dig into the slope."

Traversing the path was agonizingly slow. Raiyn longed to run forward but forced himself to hold back. Not only did he need the others, but he would likely slip off the edge and fall himself.

When he finally turned the corner, his stomach sank at the sight of the gaping hole where Lia had fallen.

"Down there?" Veron asked.

Blocked by the mountain, the wind settled to a modest level, although the snow continued to fall.

Raiyn nodded quickly. "The rope. Come on."

Veron sloughed the rope off his shoulders. Raiyn and Finley worked to unfurl it while Veron creeped to the edge of the gap.

"Don't get too close," Raiyn said.

Veron stood at the edge and leaned over while Aleks extended a stabilizing hand.

Raiyn worked the end of the rope into a loop and pulled the knot tight. He slid the coil over his body and pulled it taut around his waist. "I'm ready! Lower me down."

Veron backed away from the edge and stood before him. "It looks far. I'm not sure the rope will reach."

"It will reach," Raiyn said. "It must."

Veron took the front position, then called for the other four men to line up along the trail and stretch the rope back. He blew out a deep breath. "We won't be able to hear you down there. When you get down, give two hard tugs on the rope to let us know you're safe. When you're ready to be pulled up, give it three."

"Three pulls. Got it."

"If we run out of rope and you're not down . . . we're pulling you back up."

Raiyn nodded.

The men pulled gently against the rope to take out the slack. They all braced themselves, feet forward and bodies leaning away.

"Ready when you are," Veron said.

Raiyn glanced behind him. The blackness of the drop-off yawned to swallow him. He gulped. His pulse raced. He took several breaths.

Lia. I'm coming for you.

TUMBLING, rolling, sliding. White, black, white. Falling, bouncing, crashing.

Crack!

An acute pain seared Lia's leg. She screamed, her shrill cry lost in the wind.

She wanted to lay still, as if refusing to move would keep her body from suffering, but the agony was there, nonetheless.

Her red scarf wrapped around her face, blocking her view. She pawed it away and sat up. The movement radiated shooting pains up the right side of her body. Sitting halfway up, she braced an elbow to lean on. Her back and arms felt pummeled and bruised.

A pile of white snow and rocky debris littered around her. She lifted her head, tracing her eyes up the sheer wall of the mountain. The clouds from the storm were so thick she couldn't even see where she had fallen from.

A spasm of pain turned her attention back to her leg. She touched it tenderly below the knee, then winced and sucked in rapid breaths. The tumble down the mountain had sapped a decent amount of origine to keep her from dying, but she still had some left to use.

Leaning back on both elbows, she pulled the waiting power from where it rested inside. Her limbs tingled, sending a soothing warm gush through her body. The pain in her leg subsided. After a moment, the shooting sensation was gone.

Lia gasped. She leaned back against the snow and breathed deeply.

I'm all right, she thought. *I fell off the mountain, but I'm safe.*

Her thoughts turned suddenly to Raiyn, and she struggled to her feet.

"Raiyn!" she shouted. "Are you all right?"

The wind batted down her words. She took a step forward, but exhaustion made the ground spin. She crouched and set her hand against the snow to keep from falling.

"Raiyn?" she called again, quieter.

There was no sign of him. The valley where she landed extended away from the cliff, passing a group of trees. Another steep slope dropped off a few steps from where she had come to a halt. She leaned toward the chasm, squinting. Nothing revealed itself from its depths except for jagged rocks and more pits of darkness. Another bout of dizziness made her wave her arms for balance and step away.

How am I going to get back up? Even in the best conditions, with a full supply of origine, a climb up that cliff would be impossible. *Will someone come and look for me?* She shook her head. There was no way to safely get down. *I need to get myself out of here, and for now, I need shelter.*

Lia stood and turned to the trees. She gave her body time to steady itself. Her vision spun, the trees dancing in a slow pattern as they gradually settled into their fixed positions. When her sight no longer wavered, she blinked, unsure if her eyes played tricks on her. A chorus of growls filled the air, confirming that her eyes were not lying.

She gasped.

A pack of mountain wolves had emerged from the trees and pawed across the snow toward her.

Lia reached into her cloak and pulled out a knife. She stared at it, gulping at its length. Barely as long as the width of her hand, it was all she had. Her heart thumped in her chest.

The wolves drew closer, fanning out.

Lia cleared her mind and sought the origine. The power that was usually ready for anything existed as only a trickle after the healing. She paled.

The rumbling growls drew closer as the wolves closed in.

She glanced over her shoulder, but there was nowhere to run. A cliff blocked one side, a slide into an abyss stopped her from heading in another, and the wolves penned her in from the last direction.

White teeth bared at her as the animals crouched toward the ground, slinking toward her. She held the knife forward, waiting to call on whatever dregs of energy she could muster.

Two of the animals lunged. One reached for her leg, and the other jumped at her chest. Their movement slowed as the origine sped up her reactions. She dodged the flying animal and raked her knife along its flank. The sharp blade bit through the skin, sending a spray of blood through the air. The second animal received a sharp kick to the muzzle before she released her burst of energy.

The flying wolf fell in a heap on the edge of the slope with its limbs twitching. Blood spurted across the snow, marring the pristine white with a macabre scene. The other animal yelped. Lia's hard kick caused it to dance away, circling back behind the other waiting wolves.

Lia crouched and extended her knife again. She shouted, baring her teeth, trying to match the animals' fierce looks. Her scarf caught in the wind, blowing in her face and blocking her view. She ripped it from around her neck and threw it to the ground.

A wave of dizziness washed over her. Her feet caught against the limp body on the snow. One wolf feigned a lunge at her until she waved her knife.

"Back!" she yelled. "Stay back!"

Keeping her eyes on the wolves, she nudged the one on the snow toward the edge until gravity pulled the carcass. It moved down the frozen slope, scraping and sliding until it disappeared into darkness.

Free of obstacles, her legs continued to wobble. She blinked furiously, but the trees danced in circles again. "Stay back," she breathed. She tried to shout but could barely hear her words.

Her eyes wouldn't stay open. Her arm grew weak, and the knife rolled out of her shaky hand. Her swaying form fell forward, landing in the stained snow with a crash.

Lia thought of the wolves about to attack. They would shake her neck until it broke, then tear her body to shreds. She wanted to care, but the blackness of her mind couldn't bring her to do anything about it.

Where's that pure connection? I couldn't be more spent and in need than I am now.

The snarling sounded distant and muffled. She flopped her face over to see. While she expected to see a snapping view of teeth and fur, the sight of a man with a wild beard and layers of pelts took her by surprise. The figure waved a torch and shouted something indecipherable at the animals. The wolves snapped and lunged, but the torch held them at bay.

Raiyn? No. Who is that?

With her mind spinning, her eyes closed. Soon, everything went black.

RAIYN LEANED TOWARD THE DROP, but the rope around his waist kept him upright. The men on the side of the cliff stood strong and steady. Veron nodded.

A step backward brought his feet to the edge. He continued to lean back. The pit loomed below, waiting to swallow him. He stepped farther, onto the side of the drop. His body swayed awkwardly. He held on to the rope that pulled taut before him. His brow beaded sweat. He stepped again.

Loose rock gave way under his boot. His foot slipped, and he fell. His stomach jumped for a quick moment. His body slipped past the lip and then slammed into the cliff.

Oof!

"Raiyn!" Veron shouted from above.

Raiyn clutched the rope. He dangled in the air, his side pressed against the mountain while his body spun. "I'm fine!" he shouted back then took several rapid breaths. "Let me down!"

The rock wall seemed to slide upward as his body lowered. Raiyn turned around and set his feet against the wall, using them to control his spin while he dropped. He glanced down, peering into the gloom.

Nothing yet.

Before long, the overhang of the mountain took him away from the wall, and he dangled in midair, continuing to lower. Exposed to the elements, the wind picked up. The rope creaked as it twisted, but thankfully the knot held.

He scanned the scene as he continued down, looking for any sign of Lia, but all he found was gloomy darkness. The likelihood of running out of rope before arriving on the ground weighed on his mind. He glanced up. The rope climbed, straight as an arrow, until it vanished in the haze above.

There can't be too much more length to go.

The bite of the loop tied around him pinched his waist. He longed to get out of it. He looked down and squinted. A white reflective surface emerged from the darkness.

That's it! Almost there!

His body continued down, slowly but surely. The ground drew closer but remained just out of reach. Down. Down ... Stop.

Raiyn gasped. The ground was a body length below him, but he stopped descending.

That can't be it! I'm so close!

He wriggled his legs, trying to will the rope to descend a bit more, but his height didn't change. After a moment of dangling in the air, he moved higher.

"No!" he shouted, craning his neck up. "It's right there! Don't bring me up!"

He continued to rise.

They can't hear me.

He looked down. The ground was still visible but grew smaller every second.

I can't leave her behind.

Pulling with both hands on the rope above him, he took his weight off the loop and wriggled his body. The coil moved back and forth around his waist until it slid free. Raiyn dangled, his legs free and body swinging in the air. He glanced down and sighted the white snowbank.

This may be a bad idea. He let go.

His arms flailed as he fell through the air. The wind rushed against him, and in a moment, he was down. He braced his legs with origine to absorb the fall, but the soft landing of deep snow made it unnecessary. He sank to his waist in the powder.

Exhilarated, he breathed quickly then spun around. He'd landed in a valley between the mountains. The blowing snow had lessened, and a glowing light reflected off all the white surfaces. Ahead of him, flat ground continued forward with rubble of rock and snow from the mountain littering the ground. To his side, the path dropped precipitously again. An icy slope stretched down toward another pit of nothingness.

"Lia!" he shouted. He cupped his hands around his mouth. "Lia!"

He strained to catch any sound but heard nothing over the wind.

The rope above him had been dropped back to its lowest point. Raiyn scrambled out of the deep snow to tread lightly, giving him higher ground. Stretching his arm, he was able to barely reach the end of the loop. He tugged twice on the end to give them the signal that he was safe.

"Lia!" he shouted again.

Not wasting a moment, he scrambled across the snowy surface. He lifted rocks and moved hardened chunks of ice. He stomped through the powder. His hands soon grew red and numb, but he didn't stop.

She could have survived, he told himself, hoping a positive attitude would make it true. *With the origine, she could have made it.*

Something caught his eye, and he froze. While most of the snow was pristine white, a large section was covered with red—wet, bright, blood-colored crimson, splattered with streaks and speckles. The stain of red continued to the right, lightening as it streaked down a pitched slope. His legs wouldn't move. His lungs wouldn't work. Only through much effort, he snapped out of his trance and rushed forward.

"Lia." He tried to shout, but only a faint whisper came out.

He ran toward the precipitous slope, desperate to find a gentle area at the bottom where her body may have stopped. A wave of nausea came over him as he discovered the reality—an incline dropping into a bottomless pit broken up by glimpses of jagged rocks.

She's gone. No one could survive that.

He fell to his knees in the red snow, fresh tears springing to his eyes. He had dared to hope, only to have it crushed once more.

Maybe . . . the stain wasn't her. Maybe—

Fabric pressed into the stained powder caught his eye. At first, he had thought it was merely a stained portion of the snow, but as he lifted the familiar red scarf, any vestiges of hope were dashed. Blood spattered across it, and rips tore at the fabric. A tightness grew in his chest.

Something moved ahead. *What was that?*

He scanned the snow, looking for a sign of life. A copse of trees nestled against a rock face with snow weighing down the branches. A gust of wind picked up a drift of powder, flinging it through the air. The ground seemed to shift from the blowing snow—except in one place. An object stood, unmoving. Two eyes stared at him, unblinking.

A low growl cut through the air as the animal's lips pulled back to bare its teeth. It moved. Gray fur undulated as it stepped forward, light across the surface of the snow.

Raiyn held his breath. He stepped backward, keeping his eyes on the wolf while his hand moved to his hip.

No! He had left his knife with his gear back at the tent.

His eyes flitted in each direction. *If it's only one, I should be able to take it. I'm fast. I'm strong.*

He stopped backpedaling and reached for the origine. His limbs tingled in anticipation. His muscles readied to spring into action.

The wolf paused and lowered its head. The growl halted.

Raiyn smiled. *It's scared of me. Maybe it senses that I could—*

His stomach dropped as five more wolves emerged from the trees. A thick lump formed in his throat. The growl returned, but from the entire pack.

The wolf close to him opened its mouth and reared back its head. A howl pierced the night. The other wolves joined in, their chorus of noise filling the air.

Raiyn stood frozen, feeling gutted. The horror of the scene and the loss of Lia left his body unable to respond. He stared at the scarf as it flapped in his hand. A gust ripped it from him. The red scarf drifted through the air, blown over the edge. It fell into the depths, disappearing from sight.

One by one, the howls faded.

Raiyn's instincts overrode his grief. He stepped backward, slowly at first. When the closest wolf sprinted forward, he turned and ran.

The snow made sprinting difficult, but he didn't have far to go. He pictured the animal closing on him from behind. The snarl grew louder, but the rope drew closer. His feet pumped through the deep powder, flinging white in all directions. When he arrived at the dangling rope, he stretched on the tips of his toes to reach. His hand grasped the loop. He pulled down hard in three quick bursts, giving the men above the signal to lift.

A raging snarl turned him around. The arriving wolf flew toward him with teeth bared and claws extended. With no time for Veron and the others to lift him out of the way, Raiyn released the rope and ducked. When the wolf's body reached him, he pushed up, driving with his legs.

The animal flew into the air. Its claws lashed in all directions as it tumbled end over end, flipping through the air. The snarl faded as its body flopped into a snow drift.

Raiyn reached back up. *No!* The rope had raised just out of his reach and continued higher.

He readied his legs and leaped with excess power. Shooting out of the snow, he rose into the air. His hand found the loop of the rope.

Got it!

Both hands held the rope while his body dangled below. He creeped higher—too slowly. Snarling and lunging, the other wolves arrived. Raiyn brought up his knees, tucking his feet away from the animals below. They swiped and growled, but he kept out of their reach. Soon, he was high enough to let his legs down.

The rope crept upward in smooth, steady pulls. The animals below circled but soon faded into the gloom.

Raiyn's sight grew blurry as tears pooled in his eyes. He sniffed but couldn't wipe his face. The longer he dangled, the more his fingers ached. He pulled a steady stream of origine to hold on.

While moving upward, a strained snapping sound preceded a short drop. He craned his neck and paled. Above the knot tying the loop, the rope contained several claw slashes where the wolf had flown by. The tight coils of the rope had split, unwinding as he watched.

Raiyn lunged up, pulling hand-over-hand. His gut tingled from the origine surging through him. He held his breath. The rope jerked and snapped, dropping him more with every movement.

Come on, Raiyn! Almost there!

He grunted as he lunged the last bit, grabbing the end of the rope just above the tears. His second hand solidified his grip. He gritted his teeth, holding on with both hands as he slowly continued up. His eyes were eye level with the frayed portion of rope. He watched as it twirled and twirled until the knotted loop dropped, falling silently into the fog below.

"Almost there!"

The shouted words above sounded distant. Raiyn looked up and sighed at the approaching ledge. The tingling power in his gut lessened. The rock wall ahead of him turned blurry as his vision spun. His grip on the rope strained.

He moved higher. Then higher. His feet rested against the rock wall to keep him straight. Veron's head peered over the edge—then an arm.

"Grab my hand!" Veron shouted.

After another surge upward, Raiyn released the rope and grasped Veron's hand. The other men helped, and Raiyn collapsed onto the snowy cliffside trail.

He sucked in air, staring at the icy ground on his hands and knees. His chest heaved, and dizziness threatened to knock him over.

"What'd you find?" Veron asked.

Raiyn took a few more breaths before he sat back on his haunches. He looked up at the men, gathered together with expectant eyes.

His own grief mingled with the disappointing fact that he'd let Veron and the others down. The image of the scarf and the blood wouldn't leave his mind.

"I'm sorry." He shook his head, sucking in another deep breath. Finally, he dropped his eyes to the ground. "I'm sorry, but she's dead."

42

SHELTER

Disoriented and confused, Lia's mind worked through its haze.

Where am I?

Her eyes shot open. She lay on something firm. While her face was cool, her body remained warm, covered with a layer of animal skins. Directly above her, a curved stone ceiling looked pocked with holes and crevasses. A mildewy, earthy smell filled her nose. Her body ached as she lifted her head, but the room around her caused her to forget her pains.

It looked like a cave. The ceiling remained low in all but a few places, and the uneven floor dipped and rose in jutting levels. A rocky shelf held canisters of some sort. A small table with three stools and a sloped surface sat against the wall while an unlit lantern hung above it.

A fire burned in a rudimentary hearth. Instead of stacked stones or clay bricks, the hearth appeared to be a natural rock formation. Over the flames, a large pot rested on a pole with a ladle hanging from the side. A meaty smell wafted through the air, making her stomach rumble. On the far side of the hearth, wind whistled through a passageway.

What is this place?

Shuffling feet perked up her ears. She watched the passage, suddenly tense. Instinctively, she felt at her hip but found no weapon there.

A stack of wood with legs walked around the corner.

Lia frowned and cocked her head.

The legs headed toward the hearth then bent down. When turned sideways, the wood carrier revealed himself.

The boy looked ready for a growth spurt. Short and wiry, he wore clothes of rough-looking skins with fur sticking out of the sleeves and neckline. Blond hair fell across his face. Lia guessed his age around twelve. Apart from his skin and hair color, he reminded her a lot of Marcus in the shape of his body and how he walked.

After setting the wood gently next to the fire, he stood and turned. His eyes widened when they fell on her.

"Hello." Lia's scratchy voice took her by surprise.

The boy gaped, frozen for a long moment.

Lia glanced around, curious if something else was going on she needed to be aware of, but she found nothing to explain his pause. "Where am I?"

"The-The Straith Mountains," the boy spluttered after another pause.

"Yes, I know that. Who are you?"

"Cecil. Cecil Gregson."

Lia smiled. "It's nice to meet you, Cecil. I'm Lia. Are your parents here?"

He shook his head.

"Where are they?"

His shoulders dropped. "They're—they're gone."

"Gone, as in . . . they're coming back?"

The boy shook his head again.

Lia frowned. "I saw someone—with the wolves in the snow. Someone arrived." She raised an eyebrow. "Was that your father?"

Another tight shake of the boy's head. "That was the man who lives here."

"Who is he?"

"He's a mountain man—an odd sort."

"Is he here?"

"He's out checking the traps."

While the boy stared, she sat straighter, arching her back. She groaned with soreness, but no sharp pains warned her of anything serious. She folded back the animal skins and found the blood splattered across her clothes had dried in a rust color.

"Can you help me get back to my people?" she asked. "They were up the mountain from the place with the wolves."

Cecil's head shook. "I don't know how to get there."

Lia sighed and dropped her head.

"I do have food though. Are you hungry?"

Her head jerked up.

A smile creeped over the boy's face. "I guess that's a 'yes.'" He walked to the rock shelf and picked up two bowls before returning to the pot over the hearth.

Lia eyed an empty stool at the table. Pushing back the rest of the coverings, she scooted to the end of the narrow bed, noting two similar beds to the side. She gave her sight a moment to stop swaying before she stood. The ceiling was just high enough that she didn't have to duck, but the rocky patterns made her take caution, lest her head smack into a sharp edge. With a slight stoop, she stumbled the few steps it took to get to the table. The stool wobbled when she sat.

After filling two bowls, Cecil draped the ladle where it had previously rested and set a lid back over the pot. He crossed the room, holding two steaming bowls in his hands. He set one down before her, and the other on his side. Another ledge held two rough-carved wooden spoons. Cecil handed one to her.

Lia's mouth watered. The bowl was filled with broth but contained some sort of mashed vegetables and chunks of meat. It had been days since she'd had a warm meal. She cupped one hand around the edge of the dish and let the warmth seep into her fingers. She sighed then picked up the spoon.

The stew steamed as she lifted it in the air. The smell teased her nose. When she spooned a bit into her mouth, her tastebuds danced with excitement. She groaned out loud.

Cecil chewed on his mouthful as he spoke, "I hear you almost froze out there."

Lia shrugged. "It wasn't the cold that almost got me as much as it was the wolves' teeth."

His eyes brightened. "You got one of them though. Thank you. We're always having to keep an eye out for that pack."

"Do they give you much trouble?"

"Some . . . but it's worth it when they keep our bellies full."

Lia cocked her head in question.

Cecil chuckled. He lifted his bowl slightly. "Thanks to you."

"Oh!" She looked down at her bowl and noted the chunk of meat with fresh appreciation. "I'm, uh . . . glad I could help."

She took another bite.

"How long have I been here?" she asked after swallowing.

"A day," Cecil said. "You were out cold all last night. Today, you started tossing and mumbling around midday. Now, the sun's about to set again."

"A full day," she whispered to herself. "They're going to think I'm dead."

"Who are you with?"

An instinct of caution pricked her mind. "My father," she said, "and some friends. We were heading through the mountains when I got separated in the storm." She glanced around the cave. "Where are we, by the way? Is this part of a village or some sort of outpost?"

Cecil shook his head. "We're on our own."

Lia paused then set down her spoon. "You *live* here? In the middle of the mountains? What do you—" She stopped, unsure of what she wanted to ask.

"I was from the village of Piryd." Cecil's voice filled with melancholy.

Lia frowned. *Why does that sound familiar?*

"I came up here earlier this suether. I was looking for my father. A snow bridge broke. I fell into a crevasse and broke my leg. The man heard me yelling and rescued me."

"Is your leg still . . ."

"Oh, no. It's fine now."

"But you stay?"

Cecil nodded. "I haven't found my father yet."

Lia took another spoonful of stew as she mulled things over.

"Tell me about him," she said.

A faint smile formed on Cecil's face. "He was the strongest man in the village. Titus was his name. Everyone looked up to him."

"You most of all, huh?" Lia asked.

His smile brightened.

"What happened to him?"

His smile faded and his head dropped. He opened his mouth, but a distant rustle cut him off. A gust of wind cut into the room, chilling the air. The fire flickered, and feet stomped down the hall.

Lia turned in the direction of the sound. "Is that the mountain man?"

Cecil nodded.

Heavy clumps thudded closer, slow but deliberate. A man rounded the hearth. Thick furs covered his body, forming a bulky shape. A wolf-pelt hat covered his head. Dirty-blond hair spilled out the sides, reaching to his shoulders. An untrimmed beard parted around his mouth and drooped well below his chin in a tangled mess. A cord over his shoulder tied the legs of two white hares, one dangling upside down limply on each side of his body.

He stared at Lia. His eyes held neither anger nor kindness nor curiosity.

Apathy, Lia thought. *Interesting.*

"Traps were full?" Cecil asked.

The man nodded.

"You must be the one who saved me." Lia jumped up. The quick movement made her dizzy. She grabbed the table to counter the blurred vision while the other hand extended out straight for balance. "I can't thank you enough."

"It seems I've made a habit of it," the man said, glancing at the boy.

He walked to a side of the room where a flat stone area rested next to a basin. He flopped the rabbits onto the stone and pulled a knife out from an unseen pocket.

"I'm serious," Lia said. "Those wolves were going to tear me up. You arrived just in time."

The man ignored her words and went to work skinning the rabbits.

Despite his grizzled appearance, his cuts with the knife were precise. Although he looked much older, she guessed his age to be around forty.

"I'm eager to get back to my group," she said. "There was a ridge up the mountain from where you found me."

He glanced over his shoulder while blood drained from the animals into the basin.

"I need to get back there. I need to find a way up the mountain."

He chuckled then turned back to his work.

"Can you take me there?"

"No," he replied, terse and gruff.

Her brows pinched together. "No? But—is it far?"

"It's a ways."

"Please! They're probably out looking for me. I need to get back as soon as I can."

He shook his head. "They're not looking for you."

Her jaw dropped, and a scoff escaped. "Excuse me?"

He stabbed the knife down into something out of sight. It stuck handle-first into the air, and he turned. His eyebrows raised in wait.

"You don't know them," she argued. "Raiyn will look for me. My father cares. The others—" She groaned in frustration. "Who are you to say they're not looking?"

He nodded his head slowly. "You want to go?"

She breathed in quickly. "Yes!"

He beckoned for her to come, then turned toward the passage that left the room.

Lia glanced around to make sure she wasn't leaving anything important, then remembered she had nothing—a terrifying reminder of her dangerous predicament. While the man rounded the corner, she tossed another large bite of stew into her mouth. She wiped her lips with the back of her hand and hurried after him.

By the time she'd crossed the room, her vision already spun. She extended both hands to keep her balance. Pocked rough stone covered the walls, scraping lightly against her fingers while she hurried up the passage. She caught up in short order where the man had stopped by a wooden door.

"Are you sure you want to go, *now*?" he asked.

Her heart pounded in her chest. "Yes, I need to." She stepped forward.

He pulled the door open, and a voracious wind cut into the passage. Lia lifted her arm to block the driving snow from her face.

"You see that couloir leading up that slope?" he yelled over the wind.

Lia moved her hand, squinting to see. He pointed into the whiteness, but Lia couldn't see a thing.

"Follow that up for about thirty minutes. Then, there's a precarious bridge you need to cross. Don't wander too far to either side or you'll fall on the jagged rocks below. At the end of that, there's a maze of stone towers. You'll want to keep to the right because the path to the left leads to a sudden drop-off. Then, you'll be back where I found you. But if you want to get up to the ridge you speak of, you'll need to learn to fly because there's no path leading up that cliff."

With her hand blocking what wind and snow she could, she crept forward. Her hair flew behind her. Icy pellets stung her face.

"Weren't you just out in this?" she shouted.

He waved his hand in the other direction. "I barely traveled more than a stone's throw from the cave."

Lia's mouth hung loose. Her gaze drifted up in the direction he pointed.

"Good luck." He gestured toward the opened door.

Her heart sank. She stood rooted for a long moment until he finally closed the door, killing the deafening wind.

"Like I said," he continued at a normal volume, "your friends are *not* looking for you. If they were yesterday, they've given up. If they haven't given up, they're dead. And if *you* want to try and get back to them, you'll be dead, shortly."

She clenched her jaw, wanting to argue his point but afraid he was right. "I'm tougher than you think," she muttered before turning around and returning back down the passage.

Cecil looked up with his spoon in his mouth as she entered the room. "You don't want to be out there in this," he said with a full mouth. "Trust me."

Lia held her tongue. She sat roughly back on the stool she'd left, thankful to put her teetering body on a solid surface again.

The man clumped into the room and returned to his rabbits.

"What's your name?" Lia asked. She waited, but no answer came. "All right then. Why do you live in the mountains?"

The cutting continued.

Her mouth curled up. "Maybe you're up here to rescue people like Cecil and me?"

The knife stopped moving. The man's head lifted. After a pause, he turned back to his task. "That's not why I'm here." The words were barely above a whisper.

Shivers ran down Lia's spine.

"Why are you up here?" the man asked, keeping his back turned.

Lia perked up at the initiation of conversation. "I'm here with some others. We're—" She wanted to talk but didn't want to reveal too much. "We're looking for something."

He chuckled. "Snow? Wolves?"

"Have you ever seen an oval shaped arch high in the mountains?"

His jaw twitched, then he stopped moving.

Lia held her breath. *He knows something!*

The man turned, his eyes piercing into her. "What do you know about it?"

"I need to find it," she said, a twinge of desperation coming through. "We're looking for something, and we *must* get to it."

He continued to stare, his jaw rolling as if he worked something around in his mouth.

"You know where it is, don't you?"

A slow nod confirmed her theory.

"Can you take me there?" Her heart pounded in her chest. "That's where we're heading. If my friends think I'm dead, that's where they'll go, and maybe I can catch them. Once the storm dies, will you take me?"

The man took in a deep breath while drips of blood rolled down his knife onto his hand. "Once the storm settles . . . and it's safe to travel . . ." He stopped to glance at Cecil before turning back to her. "That oval arch is the last place you want to go. You're welcome to leave here at any time in any direction, but I will *not* lead you there."

43

DECIDING TO LEAVE

Lia peeked through the crack in the wooden door that covered the cave opening. The wind buffeted against it, singeing her forehead with a fierce cold. She gazed up the slope where the man pointed the day before, wishing the blizzard would lighten.

She had barely slept the previous night. Despite still being exhausted from her ordeal with the wolves, her mind was on edge—trapped in a cave, lost in the mountains while her friends assumed she was dead.

The faint light of day that had pushed through the storm was all but gone. She sighed, closed the door, and trudged back down the passage, preparing herself for another night stuck in the cave.

In addition to the ever-present smell of stew, the tantalizing scent of baking bread filled the air as she stepped into the room.

Cecil looked up as she entered the room. "Any change?"

She shook her head.

The boy frowned. "Maybe tomorrow then. Sometimes these storms last for days, but then one morning you wake up, and every-thing is clear." He returned his attention to a stick he'd been whittling. He scraped a knife down the shaft, flicking off strips of wood into a pile of shavings on the ground.

"Tomorrow morning, I'm leaving, storm or not," Lia said.

A chuckle rumbled from the surly bearded man in front of the fire. He stared into an alcove adjacent to the fire, where a metal pan sat.

"You find that funny?" Lia's patience ran short.

"I do," he said. "Good luck to you."

"Thank you." She chose to ignore his sarcasm. "If you won't go with me, maybe Cecil would be kind enough to lead me back."

Cecil's eyebrows raised, and he glanced at the man.

"I don't doubt he would." The man spun, bringing his legs around to face her. "But here's what's going to happen. You wake up and find the weather is clear, so you bundle up and head out. It takes you hours of trudging through the snow to get back to where the wolf attack happened. But because you can't climb that cliff, you'll have to take the long route, going around the mountain and taking the trail up the eastern slope. That will set you back another half a day. Then, by the time you finally arrive where you left your friends, you'll discover they've been gone for nearly the entire day."

Lia lifted her hands. "What am I supposed to do then?"

He shrugged and turned back to the fire.

Lia shook her head then paced across the room. It only took five strides to reach the opposite wall, then she turned around and continued.

"What do you do with your time up here in the mountains?"

Cecil's knife stopped after stripping off a fresh cut. "There's not a lot to do during storms like this. Basically, we wait it out."

"What about when it's clear?"

"Hunting. Gathering mountain berries. A few weeks back, we took a trip down the mountain to load up on supplies."

Lia cocked her head. "Really?"

"You may not believe it, but it's tough to grow wheat up here." Cecil laughed at himself. "Then, every few days, I'll go out on a search, combing a new section of the mountains."

"Searching for your father? What was his name? Titus?"

He nodded.

Lia stopped pacing. "What happened? You said he ran away, to the mountains?"

"He didn't run away."

"He got lost?"

"He was taken."

Lia frowned. "Taken? And brought up here? Are you sure?"

She glanced at the man by the fire, but he didn't look at them.

"You don't believe me," Cecil said.

"No," she protested. "It's not that. It's just—Why would someone do that? There's nothing up here. There's no one—" She stopped, a picture of the Marked Ones forming in her head.

"What is it?" the boy asked.

She sighed. "I'm not sure. It's just a crazy thought." A realization hit her. "Piryd!"

The others jumped at her outburst.

"That's the village with the—" She stopped, conscious of Cecil staring, then lowered her voice. "That's the village that was destroyed."

The boy nodded, his face somber. "I'm the only one who lived."

"Who was it? The people who took your father—what were they like?"

"There were nine of them—some men and some women. They all wore gray robes."

Lia inhaled sharply. "Gray robes," she breathed to herself.

"I'd never seen them before. It didn't seem like anyone else in the village had either."

"Did they have anything else unique?"

"They were strong and fast—exceptionally so."

"What else?"

Cecil frowned. "They had these . . ." He mimed a curved shape in front of his chest.

"Necklaces?"

Cecil brightened. "That's it. They had some sort of dull red objects."

"Crystals?"

He nodded. "Yes, and what was most odd was—this is going to sound crazy, but . . . on their necks, there was some sort of—I guess I would call it—"

"A black mark," Lia said.

The room was silent as she and Cecil stared at each other. Her heart thudded, and her breath grew rapid.

"Yes," he said, finally. "How did you know?"

"I know because they visited us too—in Felting."

"Felting?" The bearded man turned.

Cecil stood with his eyes wide, the whittled stick and knife set aside.

"You're looking for your father," Lia said. "Well, I'm looking for my mother."

Cecil stepped forward. "And you know where they are?"

"I believe so." With renewed hope, Lia turned to the man. "We're looking for our parents, and I'm pretty sure I know where they are. Now, will you agree to take us to the oval arch?"

"No!"

His refusal made her jump. Her eyebrows pinched together. "What? Why not?"

The man scrambled to his feet and pointed in her face. "That arch brings nothing but death. I will not take you there."

Her mouth hung open. She sputtered a few times. "I have friends there, too!"

"You're welcome to venture on your own, but I will not help you." The man turned away and stared into the fire. "I've had enough death on my hands."

"I see your problem." Lia stepped close. "You don't care about anyone but yourself."

The man's shoulders raised as he inhaled.

"That's right," Lia continued, her blood heating up. "You live in your secluded snow world, doing whatever you want, not having to care about anything."

"You're right," he said, laced with sarcasm. "I pulled Cecil out of the crevasse because I *didn't* care what happened to him. I rescued you from the wolves just for fun."

"Then take us to the arch!" Lia shouted. "That's what we need."

"It's because I care that I *won't* take you to the arch. I'm sorry Cecil, but your father is dead. And you . . ." He turned to Lia. "Your mother and your friends are dead. And if you two want to trudge through the mountains to find that place, you'll end up just like them. So don't tell me I don't care about anyone else. I'm *trying* to save your lives!"

Lia narrowed her eyes and stepped directly in his face. "You don't care about other people. You don't care about me. I've been awake for a full day, staying with you in this one-room cave, and you've never even asked my name."

He scoffed then glanced between her and the boy. "Your name. That's the definition of caring about someone—asking their name? Tell me your name."

"Forget it," Lia turned around.

Cecil raised a hand. "Her name is—"

Lia silenced him with a raised hand. "He doesn't deserve to know."

"Aah," the man waved her away and stomped past the hearth to disappear around the corner.

"Good riddance," Lia muttered once he'd left.

"He knew, all this time." Cecil's eyes stared vacantly into the fire. "I could have been there ages ago."

"We don't need him. Tomorrow, you and I will leave. It may take a while, but we can get back up to the trail where my friends were. If they're gone, we can follow their tracks."

She rubbed her hands together, standing by the fire. Invigorated, blood raced through her veins.

"He doesn't talk a lot," Cecil said, "and he's pretty gruff, but he's been good to me."

Lia sniffed, refusing to accept it.

"I'd be dead if it weren't for him," he added.

"And now your father might be too," Lia said. "All because he was too afraid to take you somewhere."

Cecil quieted.

"I'm sorry. That was harsh," Lia said. "I'm just frustrated. I'm stuck here away from my group, who probably think I'm dead. And this guy knows where I'm trying to go but won't help."

She joined him, staring into the fire. The flames were low, but the heat given off by the bed of coals succeeded in fighting back the cold of the world outside.

"Tell me about your father," she said.

Cecil glanced her way then smiled as he turned back to the fire. "When I was little, he used to walk around Piryd with me on his shoulders. He was already a head taller than everyone else, and that put me towering over them. He'd greet people, and when they said hello to me, he acted confused as if he didn't know I was up there." He chuckled. "He'd say, 'Cecil? What? No, he's not here. Who are you talking to?' And he'd spin around as if he tried to find me."

Lia smiled along. "He was a . . . farmer?"

"A miner. But if someone found a boulder when clearing a field, they'd call him. He'd lumber off to their land with this pickaxe of his." He shook his head with a nostalgic smile. "He was incredible."

Footsteps approached up the passage. Lia's smile turned into a frown as the bearded man arrived.

He pulled a scarf off, pausing at the sight of them before continuing and dusting off snow that had collected. "Your luck is turning," he said. "The storm's lightening."

Lia breathed in quickly.

He grabbed a piece of cloth then used it to pull the metal pan out from the alcove. A yeasty smell intensified as he carried it across the room then turned the pan over. A golden brown loaf of bread flopped onto the table.

"The wisps off the bluff are curling down, which is a sign that we're in the tail of the storm. Should clear sometime in the night. At first light tomorrow, I expect clear skies."

Lia turned to Cecil. "We should pack tonight, so we can leave first thing."

The boy's chest expanded. His face lightened with an excited yet nervous energy.

"If you insist on going, take food with you." The man pointed over his shoulder. "I have a salt cellar with dried meat and fruit. You can fill up water skins at the spring next to it." He pointed to the table. "And you can have that loaf."

Lia opened her mouth to speak, but only a smile reflected back at him.

He lowered his head. "I still wish you'd reconsider—both of you —about wanting to go to the arch."

"What are you not saying?" Lia asked. "What do you know about that place?"

He took a deep breath. "I wasn't the first person here"—he gestured to the room—"in this cave. I was traveling the mountains about to starve and freeze when I ran across Josef and Myrtena. They took me in."

"When was that?" Lia asked.

"Years ago," he said, turning to gaze at the fire. "They were a reclusive couple—ten years older than me. They liked being away from the world and its troubles, which is exactly what I was looking to do. We instantly hit it off, and they let me stay. For years, we had our tiny community of three."

"What happened to them?"

"Josef always had a bad feeling about the place around the arch, but he couldn't pinpoint why. He said it felt like death and insisted we all stay away. Myrtena laughed it off, though. She had a more adventurous spirit, always pushing the limits. It made her feel alive. One morning, she was gone, leaving a note behind. Since Josef had refused to go with her, she headed there on her own. He rushed after her before I'd even gotten out of bed." A crackle in the fire filled the long silence that followed. "Neither of them ever came back."

He turned to look at Lia. "I may appear rude at times, and I may seem like I don't care . . . but I do."

"I have to go," Lia whispered.

"I understand," he said, "but I still won't take you."

Her shoulders fell.

"Will you tell me your name?" the man asked.

She smiled, nodding faintly. "Lia."

His eye twitched.

Lia's brows pinched together. "What is it?"

He turned, a rough swallow bulging his throat. "Lia. From Felting."

She stepped closer. "That's right."

"Your mother. She's from Felting, too?"

"Yes. Her name's Chelci."

His chest puffed out as he sucked in a deeper breath.

"And my father is—"

"Veron," the man breathed. "Veron Stormbridge."

Her eyes grew wide. "How'd you know?"

He stared into the fire. His jaw ground in a circle.

Lia glanced at Cecil who only turned up his hands.

The man continued to stand, frozen, lost in unknown thoughts. When he spun toward her, Lia jumped. "You're sure you want to go there?"

"I am," Lia replied.

He nodded, his mouth tight. "Your friends will be gone by the time you would make the ridge, so I'll take you to the arch."

Her eyes opened wide. "You will? Thank you!" She glanced at Cecil, who smiled back.

The man turned to face the room. "We'll need extra-warm skins and supplies to dig out a shelter at night. I've got two packs to divide the load. It should take close to a day to get there."

He knelt next to one of the beds and pulled out a longsword with a sheath.

Lia's head whirled at the sudden adjustment. "I don't understand. What changed?"

He stood and looked at her. "You look like your mother."

"You know her?"

He nodded then turned back to the fire. "Many years ago, I used her to curry political favor and advance my career. I framed your father for murder and sold him into slavery. I tried to have him killed, multiple times."

Lia stepped back, her jaw hanging loose and her mind reeling. "I don't understand. Are you wanting to . . . kill them?"

He laughed through his nose and shook his head. "They're also the closest people I consider to be friends." He turned to Lia. "And Brixton Fiero will never turn on his friends again."

44

DECIPHERING THE PULL

Danik's eyes shifted in all directions as they traveled the cavern passage. In the wide areas, the marked ones walked on either side, leading their group through the rocky corridors, but when the passages grew narrow, they resorted to single file.

Nicolar stepped close as they walked. "So far, so good," he whispered. "They're leading us in and they didn't disarm us."

Danik set his hand on the hilt of his sword. "Yes, that's a good sign. We may rely on the same power source, but I'm far from interested in placing my full trust in them, yet."

A woman in gray with a prominent black stain glanced over her shoulder just ahead of them. She carried a torch that outshone the sporadic red glow running down the passage walls.

Danik flashed a smile and nodded. "These caverns are incredible." He projected for her to hear.

Her flat expression didn't change. She turned back around and continued walking.

Danik glanced over his shoulder to where Cedric walked just behind. "Do you still feel it?"

"The pull?" Cedric shook his head. "The whole way here I did, like we were following an invisible rope that led us directly to these caverns. I haven't felt anything since we entered, though."

"Me neither," Nicolar said by his side.

"What do you think that means?"

Danik mulled the question over and considered the implications of some unseen power forcing him to do something. His stomach turned.

"I think it means we found the right place," Nicolar answered.

"We're here," the gray-robed woman said as they exited the narrow passage into a larger chamber. She turned to the side and hung the torch in a holder on the wall.

Danik's jaw dropped. Hundreds of people could fit in the massive oval chamber. The support column in the center contained shapes and symbols extending to the ceiling, high above. Light poured in from shafts dug deep into the roof.

"And our Feldorian friends finally arrive!" The voice boomed from a raised area with three stone chairs in a line.

Danik recognized the man who spoke. Talioth sat in the middle chair with his hands draped over the armrests. The man on the left looked familiar. *Centol? Was it?* But the woman on the right was new to him. Older with thin-gray hair, she was not part of the group they met in Tienn. On the flat ground, another six men and women dressed in gray stood facing them. Each of them sported an inky stain on their necks.

Talioth's words registered in Danik's mind as they crossed the room. "You knew we were coming?" His brows pulled together as he stopped at the base of the dais.

"One can only put off the Call for so long," Talioth said.

"The Call?"

"It's what led you here, isn't it?"

Danik leaned forward. "I felt—" He gestured to the other two with him. "We felt a . . . pull of sorts. It was the strongest for me, but we all sensed it."

"And it got stronger the closer you got, leading you directly to this place, didn't it?"

Danik nodded. "Until we entered the cavern."

A broad smile came over Talioth's face. "We refer to it as 'the Call.'" He extended his arms out, taking in the broad expanse of the room. "No matter where you are, it will lead you home."

Home?

Danik's eyes shifted, but the people of the room maintained pleasant smiles. "What happens when we leave?" he asked. "Will we, uh . . . feel the Call again when we step outside?"

Talioth waved the question away. "We have time to discuss that. First, I'm curious . . . were there not others with you? I thought you had seven?"

"We did," Danik said. "But we're down to five, now—us three plus two more back in Felting, training more."

"Training more, huh?" Talioth chuckled softly, his eyes crinkling at the edges. He glanced back at the older woman, who laughed along.

Danik rankled the longer they laughed.

"I wish they'd let us in on their secrets," Nicolar muttered, leaning close.

"What happened in Felting?" Danik projected his voice. "You were supposed to take out the Shadow Knights."

Talioth's laugh stopped. "We were *supposed* to?"

"That's what you said you were going to do."

"You speak as if we owed you something."

"Don't forget, we were the ones who told you where they were to begin with."

Talioth pursed his lips then nodded. "Yes, you did. And for that, we are appreciative. It was our intention to take all the knights, but . . . circumstances changed."

"Our plan hinged on you doing your part," Danik said.

"Were you not successful?"

Danik lifted his chin.

"Did you not take the crown?" Talioth rephrased.

"I did," Danik replied after a pause. "But the three you left have been causing us trouble."

"Nothing you couldn't handle, I trust?"

"They killed two of our group, and now—" He stopped and chuckled. "It looks like they may cause you trouble soon."

Talioth paused and tilted his head. "What do you mean?"

"What did you think would happen when you took their fellow knights and waved goodbye as you skipped town? Did you think they were going to say, 'Oh well,' and let it be?"

"How would they know where we are?"

"They found a map," Danik said. "An ancient book in the king's library about the devion points right to this place. And the last place they were seen was on the doorstep of the Straith Mountains, headed this way."

Talioth made knowing eyes toward Centol, then his other men below.

"Where were they last seen?" Talioth asked.

"In Tienn, three days ago."

"That should put them close," Talioth said. "Was the storm still going as you approached?"

Danik shook his head. "It stopped this morning. It didn't slow our travel, but I imagine they will have struggled. There were seven of them."

Talioth raised an eyebrow. "Seven?"

"Three men, one boy, and the three knights you left. There could have been more we weren't aware of, though. The skies are clear now, and I'm sure they're coming."

Talioth turned to his right with a broad grin. "You, Centol, are brilliant."

The other man in gray beamed back. "Thank you. It was a hunch, but I guess it played out."

"Gralow, move the two troublemakers, just in case."

"I'm sorry." Danik raised a hand. "A hunch? What are we missing?"

Talioth turned back to him with a placating smile. "You're missing years of knowledge and experience, but don't worry . . . there is time for you to gain both."

The other marked ones laughed quietly.

Talioth stood and opened his arms. "We thank you for coming to warn us, and we welcome you into our home. We will find living quarters for you shortly."

Danik frowned. "We don't need"—he glanced at Nicolar and Cedric and noted their confused expressions—"living quarters. That's not why we're here."

"Why are you here?" Talioth stepped forward and stopped behind a large, rectangular, stone box where he rested his hands.

"We felt—the Call, I guess. And we wanted to stop the Shadow Knights. And . . . I would love some answers."

"Ah!" Talioth said. "There it is. The truth comes out. You want to know how this power works. You want to understand everything." His eyes dropped to the box, and he pressed into it with his hands. "I remember that feeling." His hand lightly rubbed along the length of the box while his eyes seemed to drift. "I've been where you are." His eyes lifted. "What questions do you have?"

Danik's eyes widened. "Uh—" His words left him. His mouth hung open, but he couldn't think of where to begin.

"Our necks," Nicolar said. He touched his neck where the black stain showed through the powder that had mostly wiped away. "What is this stain, and how do we get rid of it?"

Talioth and the others burst into laughter. "If you figure out how to get rid of it, let me know."

Danik sucked in a breath.

Nicolar leaned toward him. "You mean we're stuck with this?" His voice carried an edge.

"Power comes at a cost," Talioth said. "Both the devion and the origine need fuel. The devion manifests itself in one centralized area as it pulls from your body."

"Our necks," Danik breathed.

"That's right. Don't worry, soon you won't even notice it anymore."

Cedric and Nicolar grumbled.

"What about 'the Call?'" Danik asked. "We live in Felting. We *can* return there, can't we?"

"As you are *now* . . . " Talioth paused and turned up his hands. "No."

Danik tensed. "What?"

Nicolar stepped forward, a rumbling sound in his throat, and his hand on his sword hilt.

Danik held his arm up to stop him. "Wait. That can't be. Why didn't you tell us this in Tienn when we met?"

Talioth chuckled. "You didn't ask. Plus, you were already using the devion when we found you. There's much you have yet to learn, but some things are easier to learn by experiencing them yourself."

"So we're stuck here in this mountain?"

Talioth shook his head with a wry smile. "I never said you were stuck. I said you're not *ready* to leave. Are you three prepared to join the ranks of the Marked Ones?"

Danik took a step back.

"What does that mean?" Nicolar asked.

"Take them to the Siphon Chamber," Talioth declared.

Danik swallowed hard. *This may have been a bad idea.*

DANIK BLANCHED when they entered the circular room. The surrounding red crystals in the walls lit the room with an eerie glow, but the center of the room held his attention. A hole as wide as a man's height gaped in the floor. Directly above the hole, a massive crystal hummed, glowing and pulsing. The light seemed to warm the room.

"Where does that hole go?" Nicolar whispered.

Cedric leaned in. "I'm not sure what this place is, but I don't like it."

Danik stared at the pit, the blackness making his stomach churn.

A dozen of the marked ones filled the room, standing at their sides as well as behind them.

Danik tried to watch everyone. A sheen of sweat lined his palms.

They still haven't taken my sword. That's a good sign.

Talioth stepped to the center of the room. His feet stopped a hair from the pit, and he set his hand against the pulsing large center object. The man's eyes closed, and a smile covered his face. "Ahh, that feeling. The power. The comfort." He turned to Danik. "Can you sense it?"

Danik's eyes flicked to the large crystal. *What should I feel?* He released his clenched hand and let down his defenses. A sensation crept across his chest, like invisible tendrils pulling at him. *What is that?* His heart slowed, its beat syncing with the pulse of the room. The fear and uncertainty he'd felt smoothed out until they disappeared.

"What is this?" Nicolar asked.

Cedric chuckled. "I like it."

A rush of warmth flooded through Danik. The desire to return to Felting vanished. *I am home. This place is all that matters.*

As suddenly as it arrived, the warmth dissipated, leaving a tingling coolness behind. His muscles felt both tight and relaxed. His store of energy seemed unlimited.

"This crystal is what supplies our power," Talioth said.

Danik opened his eyes, present once again. *What did that do to me? I can't lose myself like that!*

"It pulls us, draws us in. This is what you felt calling to you from Felting."

"Where'd it come from?" Danik asked, his voice weak. "The crystal."

Talioth shrugged. "None of us know. We were all drawn here, like you were. The power of both the origine and the devion is fueled by our bodies. It uses who we are and allows us to do incredible things. And this crystal is where it originates."

Still leery of everything, Danik's mouth hung open. "Incredible."

"The more you rely upon the power, the more you crave the presence of this place. And that is why you can't leave. Your desire to be here will be too great; it will allow you no peace."

"How can we leave, then?" Nicolar asked.

Talioth raised his eyes, and the crowd around the room began to chant.

The hair on Danik's arms stood on end. He took a step back and fingered his sword hilt, ready to jump into action.

The men and women in gray cloaks with black stains on their necks uttered words in unison that sounded like gibberish. The noise had a deep, rhythmic feel, like a drum in a distant room.

The old woman appeared. She approached the center of the room, staring at the pit with something in her hand.

Cedric leaned closer and whispered, "What is she doing?"

Danik focused.

She stopped next to the pit and crouched, her back facing him.

The pulse of the room tried to draw his eyes to the central crystal, but Danik wouldn't take them away from her. His heart pounded. The marked ones behind him closed in, their boots scuffling nearer as their chants grew louder.

"Be ready for anything." Danik's whisper was lost as soon as it left his lips.

The pulsing light brightened. The oppressive sound grew deafening. Sweat pricked his skin as his pulse raced.

A new light filled the room. This time, it came up from the pit, leaving the blackness and spilling over the side like water over the lip of a basin.

Danik grasped the hilt of his sword. His sweaty hand slid along the grip as his eyes flitted in all directions.

The chorus of people reached a fevered pitch.

He pulled at his sword but halted as soon as the motion began.

The pulsing light diminished to a steady glow, and the chanting stopped. Silence filled the room, broken only by the throbbing noise of the pulse thumping in his head.

Danik's breath labored. He released his sword. Next to him, Nicolar did the same.

The woman stood. Something lay on the ground, but her body blocked his view.

"What is it?" Cedric whispered.

"There is more to learn about what we do and our powers,"

Talioth said. "But we want to start with a gift—something for each of you, as well as for the two you left behind."

The woman stepped aside.

Danik's eyes grew. His pounding heart settled quickly. The tension in his hand relaxed, and a smile crept across his face.

"Now we're talking," Nicolar said.

45

THE ARCH

L ia poked her head out of the cave opening and gawked at the scene before her. Sunlight peeked over the mountains, illuminating a clear, blue sky without a cloud to be seen. The wind had settled to a whisper. Fresh snow created a pristine blanket of white across the landscape. Peaks and ridges sprang up in each direction, creating impenetrable walls of rock, and a grove of trees lay just down the slope from the cave.

"Beautiful," she breathed, then moved out of the way to give Brixton and Cecil room to exit.

Cecil helped her strap oversized wooden devices to the bottom of her boots. Supposedly they spread out the weight and allowed her to walk on top of the snow without sinking. With a pack weighing her down, she stepped onto the fresh powder and marveled at how well they worked. Brixton carried the other pack with a crossbow slung loosely over the top. Young Cecil remained unburdened to help offset the disadvantage of his short legs.

Brixton hadn't exaggerated the difficulty of travel. Their path ran up and down hills. They scrambled up rocks and steep couloirs. Lia used a trickle of the origine to keep up and made good use of the times they rested.

The sun traveled across the sky, warming the air as the day progressed. Despite the chill in the air, Lia remained comfortable, even taking off layers on the steeper portions of their journey.

"Need a rest?" Brixton asked, waiting at the top of a ridge as Lia mounted the last few steps.

She panted, her back bowed under the weight of the pack. Sweat dripped down her forehead into her eyes. "Need to keep . . . going." She spoke between breaths. "Father could . . . be there."

"I'm up for a quick rest." Cecil arrived a few steps behind her. Even without a pack, his body slumped in exhaustion. He collapsed onto a flat rock.

Lia nodded, glad to have an excuse to stop. She sloughed the pack off her shoulders and sat next to him.

The view from the ridge took her breath away. Snow-capped peaks towered in each direction. A chasm yawned down the far side of the ridge, dropping to nasty-looking crevasses below. Through a narrow break in the mountains, she spied the green forests of Feldor. They seemed so close yet so far away at the same time.

Brixton extended a skin of water, which she took with relish. She gulped a long draught to replenish all she had sweated out. She smacked her lips then passed the skin to Cecil.

"My parents spoke about you." Lia eyed Brixton. "They miss you."

Brixton raised his eyebrows.

"Why'd you leave?"

He chuckled. "That's a long and sad story."

She shrugged. "Try me."

He pursed his lips and looked down at the snow. "Feldor pardoned me for my crimes."

"What did you—?"

"I don't want to talk about it. I can't believe I wasn't executed, and a lot of that was due to Veron and your grandfather, Darcius." He kicked at the snow with his foot, digging a hole in the powder. "I had a second chance. I worked at a bakery, which I loved. I earned money. I had a place of my own to live. With each change of season, people forgot more and more about my past."

"That's good, right?" Lia asked. "If people didn't remember?"

His face turned down. "I remembered. Everyone else moved on as if I was this regular person who simply baked rolls and pastries. But all I could think about was who I was . . . before. And that person didn't deserve the grace he was given."

"Have you changed?" Lia asked.

Brixton pursed his lips. "I think so."

"So maybe that grace was effective."

"But I was never truly punished for what I did," Brixton blurted. "I was on probation. I had limits, but then it was all forgotten."

"You don't have to be punished in order to change."

"It's what I deserved."

Lia stared at him. "Isn't that the definition of grace? Undeserved forgiveness?"

He frowned and turned back to the snow. "It was too much. Anyway, I couldn't take it anymore. I couldn't live in a kingdom I'd almost ruined—being friends with people I'd betrayed. So I fled."

"You came here."

He nodded. "I wanted to get away from cities and villages. I didn't want to come in contact with anyone whose life I'd messed up." He laughed a short puff of air. "And here you come again, falling into my lap."

"You never messed up my life," Lia said.

He turned to her, his eyes tender and heavy with sorrow.

"You saved me from wolves, and you saved him, too." She pointed to Cecil then rose to her feet and stepped closer, peering into Brixton's eyes with an intense focus. "Don't write off your potential because you made mistakes in your past. Your impact on the world isn't finished until you take your last breath."

"Whoa!" Cecil rustled his clothes as he rubbed his hands along his arms. "That gave me chills."

Brixton's steely demeanor cracked with a partial smile. "Thanks, Lia. I'm working on it."

"Why now?" Cecil interrupted again.

"Why what?"

"Why help now? You ran away from them before. What made you decide to help?"

Brixton looked into the distance, appearing to ponder the question. "I've let Veron and Chelci down enough," he said at last. "I'm not sure how much purpose my life has left, but if they need me, I'll be there."

Lia smiled.

"We should get moving." Brixton nodded toward the west. "We don't have too much light left."

Lia noticed the position of the sun for the first time in a while. It rested low in the sky, partly tucked behind another peak.

"Do we need to look for a place to camp?" Cecil asked.

Brixton shook his head. "No." He nodded over Lia's shoulder. "We're there."

Lia spun and traced her eyes up a long, snowy incline. At the top of the rise, two peaks rested on either side of the trail, and a stone arch spanned the gap. "We made it," she breathed.

Brixton pointed to several steps of footsteps in the snowy incline. "And it looks like we weren't the first ones."

LIA PRESSED her hands on her knees as she pushed herself higher. The pack felt heavier than ever. Her legs and back ached from the strain. From the ridge below, the slope to the arch didn't look too bad, but the farther she walked, the farther away the goal seemed.

"Do you . . . know what's on . . . other side?" Lia asked through her breaths, glancing over her shoulder.

Brixton glanced up from two paces behind. He lifted his feet one at a time. "No, but we'll need to be careful when we get up there. If we run into trouble, leave it to me. All right?" His sword hung from his hip in a leather sheath.

"I'm quite the fighter myself," Lia said. "I'm sure I can be of use."

Brixton chuckled. "Your parents may not have told you, but I'm actually a skilled swordsman."

Lia rolled her eyes and wished she hadn't left her blade in the tent when she and Raiyn had gone scouting.

"If I had a second sword, I'd be happy to let you borrow it," he said.

Lia called up the slope. "How are you doing, Cecil?"

The boy kept his head down and legs driving until he paused. He rested his hands on his knees and blew out a loud breath. "Ugh, this hill is tough!"

"Shh," Brixton scolded. "Not so loud. We're getting close."

The arch appeared closer than when Lia'd last checked. She closed her mouth and picked up her feet, tuning her senses in to her surroundings.

Shadowy areas marked the cliff walls on either side. The higher they climbed, the longer the shadows grew. Her mind turned to her mother. *Did she come this way? Did she pass under this arch? Is she nearby right now? Hopefully the bears didn't get her.*

The rock bridge loomed ahead, high above the snow. She looked up, gaping at the massive structure. A light breeze pushed at her back, blowing up the trail. Her footsteps crunched in the snow. The top of the saddle between the peaks approached. She craned her neck forward, eager to see what lay beyond.

Lia's ear perked at a new sound. The hair on her neck stood on end.

"Don't move," a voice said.

A raw blade rested against Lia's neck. *How did they—* Her mind whirled until she realized what was happening. *The devion.*

She turned her head slowly. A woman in a thick gray cloak and hood stood in the snow. One arm held a sword to her neck while her second blade pointed at Cecil.

Lia's eyes darted around, noticing the dark protected area against the stone, where the guard had likely been hiding.

"Hands away from your weapon," another voice ordered.

The second guard held a sword to Brixton. Dressed in matching gray attire, his necklace swung free of his cloak with a red crystal at the end—a *dull* red crystal.

Lia fought not to smirk.

"Who are you?" the guard asked.

"We're travelers." Brixton kept his hands up. His head turned on a swivel. "Where did you come from?"

"Quiet," the woman said. "We'll ask the questions. Why are you here?"

"We, uh . . . we—"

"We're surveyors from Bromhill," Lia said. "King Tomas wants updated maps of the Straith range. We only needed to summit this ridge, and then we're heading back down."

"Surveyors?" the woman said. Her eyes jumped to the other guard.

A gust of wind blew through the pass, flapping open the top of the woman's cloak. Her bare neck showed, revealing the deep black stain marking it. Over her chest, a dull, red crystal, matching the other guard's, peeked from her cloak.

"It's them," Cecil whispered.

"Quiet!" the guard shouted, pressing her sword tighter against his chest. She stepped closer to the boy. "What's *us*?"

Neither Lia nor Brixton answered.

After a silent moment, the male guard spoke up. "Let's take them in. Either workers or fuel, we can always use more."

He flicked his sword tip toward the top of the ridge. "This way. All of you."

"And don't even think about trying anything." The woman reached to take Brixton's sword. "Trust us when we say that any attempt to escape will result in—"

Lia pulled a torrent of origine from her well, and time seemed to stand still. She grabbed the hilt of Brixton's sword before the woman reached it. Moving as fast as possible, she spun, slicing the weapon across the woman's neck. The blade bit, cutting through skin and bone in a smooth stroke, separating the woman's head from her body.

Fast! Move fast!

Without hesitating, she turned to the other guard and stepped once. The man's eyes grew. Lia stabbed, lunging with all the speed she could muster. Her sword was reaching for his chest when the red crystal sprang to life.

Like water doused on a fire, her ability evaporated in a puff. The man sped up, lifting his own blade in defense.

Her mind raced in an instant. She anticipated him overpowering her like the others in the Shadow Knights' courtyard. *We're so close. We can't lose it now!* She pushed, relying on her own non-enhanced strength.

His sword continued to rise in defense, but it was late. *Too late.*

The tip of her blade entered his chest, tearing through fabric, then skin. The guard's body jerked. His lifted sword lost steam and tumbled from his limp fingers. He looked at the weapon stuck in his chest with his jaw dropped. The red crystal faded, allowing the warm tingle to return to Lia's body.

Staring at the sword, the guard's mouth closed. His eyes narrowed, then his teeth bared as a growl reverberated from his chest. He grabbed the bare blade and pulled.

Lia fought him, pressing forward to keep the sword embedded, but the weapon gradually slid out while blood trickled down the gray fabric.

He's stronger than me!

Changing tactics, Lia lifted a boot. In one smooth motion, she kicked against him and pulled the blade out herself. The guard wasn't prepared. The sword slid free, back into Lia's capable arms.

The man's crystal sparked, but the full glow didn't return. Keeping her speed, Lia thrust the blade once more.

The strike to the neck was more than the man could handle. He fell to his knees, gurgling blood before his body keeled over and dropped to the snow.

Adrenaline coursed through Lia's body while her pulse thudded in her head. She panted, taking as deep of breaths as she could manage.

"I should have known," Brixton breathed.

Lia spun, remembering she wasn't alone.

"The daughter of Veron and Chelci, of course you'd share the ability. That was amazing."

Cecil took a hesitant step toward her. "What. Was. That?"

She chuckled. "That's what a shadow knight can do."

The boy's eyes grew. "I had no idea."

Brixton cocked his head. "Wait . . . so this group . . . How'd they capture Chelci and—" He cocked his head as if thinking of something. "Were all the people taken, shadow knights?"

Lia nodded.

"How did that happen? Who are these people?"

"They have a similar power—the origine's evil twin, so to speak. And these crystals . . ." Lia nudged the woman's recently freed necklace. "They inhibit our abilities—or something like that. That's how they captured everyone. We don't really understand it."

Brixton glanced back down the hill they'd come up. "The others in your group of seven . . . Can they use the origine, too?"

She frowned. "Only one of them."

"Veron?"

"Actually, no. A guy named Raiyn."

His forehead creased.

"This group did something to Father. We don't know what, but he can't use the origine."

Brixton nodded for a long moment. "With abilities like that, it's going to make getting your mother—" He nodded toward Cecil. "—and your father, difficult."

"We have to try," Cecil said. "I have no one else. The rest of my village is dead."

"I must find them," Lia said.

Brixton exhaled. "All right, then. I'm with you."

Lia extended the sword, handle first, toward Brixton. He lifted his arm then paused. "You know what? I think you might be able to use that better than me."

A grin covered her face. She lifted the handle higher. "Thanks, but—" She nodded toward the dead bodies and their fallen blades. "I've got three others to choose from."

46

THE FINAL PUSH

After unlashing the ties, Veron pushed against the tent flap, slowly moving the pile of snow out of the way. The morning sun reflecting off the white forced him to squint while a pile of powder tumbled in. The clear sky should have given hope and filled him with excitement, but inside, he remained gutted.

"Everyone pack up," Aleks called, standing outside of the other tent. "We need to be moving soon."

Veron stumbled outside, fogging breath puffing from his mouth. His body shivered, not entirely from the cold.

Aleks walked to him. Without speaking, he leaned inside the tent and emerged with a thick wool hat. "Forget this?"

Veron accepted the hat, then placed it on his head.

"How are you?"

Veron wanted to frown but didn't think his face responded. He felt empty, drained of purpose. "I'm fine."

"You're lying."

Veron shrugged. "What does it matter?"

"Chelci and the rest of the knights need you. They're waiting somewhere very close to here. Think of how excited they'll be when you show up."

Veron managed a weak smile.

Behind him, Raiyn and Marcus emerged from the tent. Marcus scurried about, packing supplies, but Raiyn, with his pale face and morose expression, looked even worse than Veron felt.

Finley rounded the corner of the tent where the snow-covered tree rested against the rock wall. "Horses are good," he said. "A bit cold, but nothing a steady walk won't cure."

Aleks lifted his chin. "Finley, can you help Marcus with their tent?"

The man nodded and Marcus perked up.

"Raiyn," Aleks said.

The young man stumbled a few steps to join them. His eyes were red and held a vacant expression.

Aleks set a hand on each of their shoulders. "If we're going to complete this mission—If we're going to rescue the Shadow Knights —If you want any hope of taking the throne back from Danik—We need you two here."

Veron's mind drifted to the edge of the cliff. He pictured his daughter's torn body somewhere below, ravaged by wolves with her remains buried, lost under a pile of snow.

Aleks squeezed gently. "Are you with us?"

Veron blinked several times, trying to bring his mind back to the present. He looked at Raiyn then back to Aleks. Finally, he nodded.

"I should never have gone out there," Raiyn said in a weak voice, his head dropping. "I should never have taken her with me."

"You did what you thought was best," Aleks said. "You tried to keep us all safe by finding the route we should take while it was still possible. And you were successful in that."

Raiyn lifted his eyes.

"Lia falling was an accident, and it wasn't your fault."

Raiyn nodded vacantly then turned to the sight of the others breaking down and loading supplies. "I need to pack." He left to return to the tent.

"Thank you for your kind words, Aleks," Veron said. "You're right.

Chelci's still out there, and she needs us. Saving her won't bring Lia back, but that's all we can do."

VERON PICKED UP HIS FOOT, moved it forward, then let it sink into the snow. He picked up the next foot, moved it forward, then crunched into the snow. The process had gone on all day since they left camp.

The day's travel wearied him. The physical demands of the high-altitude trail—combined with the emotional toil of loss—left Veron exhausted. Normally alert and motivating others, it was all he could do to keep placing the next foot in front of the other. With evening approaching, his body didn't have much left in it.

Taking a moment to breathe, he turned around. The rest of the group trailed behind, men walking through the snow, leading their packed-down horses by the reins. Directly behind him, Raiyn led Lucy in addition to Freckles.

Raiyn seemed to fare the same as Veron. Quiet, he walked with his head down. Marcus peppered him with questions much of the morning, saying it was good for him to talk, but the older boy didn't take the bait.

"Whoa," Aleks said. "What's the matter, girl?"

Veron turned to see the man ahead of him patting his horse on the neck. Moments later, Ranger pulled the reins in his own hand and exhaled a snort. "Something's got them spooked," Veron called.

He looked ahead. The ridge they traveled dropped off on either side, and ahead, the slope angled sharply up to where it disappeared around a peak.

"Should we set up camp?" Veron asked. His eyes scanned, but there didn't seem to be a sheltered area fit for setting up. "Maybe up that path, between those peaks?"

Aleks nodded and pulled on his horse's reins. They made it another few steps until the animal snorted loudly and reared up on its hind legs.

Ranger followed suit and tossed his head from side to side,

digging his hooves into the snowy path. Veron struggled against the reins then finally released them in a huff. Ranger stopped fighting and stood still, planted firmly where he stood.

Veron shook his head, walking ahead to join Aleks. "Probably an animal in the area. Hopefully it will clear by morning." He took a few steps forward to peer up the path between the peaks. "If we could get the horses down here, we could set up the tents right where—"

His jaw hung loose as he stared up the slope, his eyes fixed on the oval-shaped, stone formation at the top of the ridge.

"What is it?" Aleks jogged to join him. He gasped when he arrived. "The arch. We're there."

A nervous smile came to Veron's face, and his heart pounded. The fog that filled his brain over the previous two days vanished in an instant. *Chelci*, he thought. *We're here!*

Aleks pointed toward the snow ahead. "Tracks, too. A half dozen of them."

Veron nodded. He stepped back to where the others congregated. "We're at the arch," he began, turning heads in his direction. "We don't know what to expect here. We don't know how many people they have or the true extent of their power, but we *do* know that power is great. They're fast, and they're strong. They can suck away the origine with their crystals. This is a disadvantage for Raiyn but shouldn't affect the rest of us. If you stab one of them, remember they can heal, so twist the blade after you strike."

Royce stepped up with an armload of metal bolos and held them out.

"Perfect," Veron said. "Take one. If you can sling it around any part of their body, it will wipe their ability as long as the metal surrounds them.

He turned to Marcus. "Stay here with the horses."

"No," Marcus protested. "I can fight, and you need everyone you can get."

"The horses are skittish and won't go any farther. We need someone—"

"It's my father." Marcus' words choked. "I need to help." A tear ran down his cheek.

A wave of compassion ran through Veron. He stepped in front of the boy and lifted his chin. "Your father has taught you well, and you're growing to be a great fighter. The other five of us are all here to rescue him, but we can't all go because our horses and our gear will run off. If we're going to get out of here safely, *with* your father, we need someone to protect them." He bent his knees to get closer to the boy's eye level. "Will you stay here and watch over them?"

After a pause, Marcus sniffed and wiped his nose, then nodded.

Veron stepped to Lucy and pulled Farrathan from Lia's saddle-bags. The sword gleamed in the fading light, catching the ruby in the hilt. "Grab your weapons and gear, but only what you need. We'll travel light and fast."

AT THE TOP of the rise, the peaks grew closer, and the stone arch loomed overhead. Veron's head swiveled, inspecting the shadows behind every rock. The men panted after the endless uphill slog.

At the crest of the saddle, an incredible sight opened before them. A bowl of lush green filled the backside of the ridge. A ring of cliffs and towering mountain slopes protected the area from prying eyes or wanderers.

"This is unbelievable," Finley said. "How is everything green?"

"Geothermic activity," Veron said. He pointed to a puff of smoke coming up from a bare area. "See that steam? Heat from the earth must pool here and warm it."

"This was the star on your map, right?" Aleks said. "What do you think it marks?"

Veron scanned the valley until his eyes settled on a cave against the far cliff where a red glow spilled out of the opening. "That's it." He pointed. "That's where we need to go. Look alert, everyone. They could be waiting anywhere."

"Veron," Royce called, quiet from behind.

Veron spun. The Nasco man looked at the ground where he stood and gingerly stepped away. A red stain marred the disturbed snow.

Veron yanked the sword from over his shoulder and tensed. The other men did the same, turning and looking in each direction. Content that no attack was imminent, Veron kicked at the stain, revealing a larger area of bloody snow.

"That much blood . . ." Aleks said, "Something died here."

Veron clenched his jaw. "And it's fresh."

"Could it have been an animal?" Finley asked.

"Bears, maybe?" Raiyn prompted.

Veron pointed to a nearby disturbed section of snow. "These are footprints," he said. "Someone attempted to hide it."

"What does that mean?" Finley asked.

"It means people could be nearby," Aleks replied.

"Don't forget bears," Raiyn added.

Everyone was quiet for a long moment.

"Let's move," Veron said. "But keep your eyes up."

The air warmed quickly as they descended into the valley. All the men loosened layers. Finley and Royce even tossed some aside. The group soon passed through a grove of trees. Veron enjoyed the shelter until he imagined marked ones hiding behind each one they passed. He instinctively reached for the origine to heighten his senses and chided himself when it came back empty.

The sun completely disappeared once they dropped into the valley. Residual light spilled over the tops of the mountains, but it wouldn't be long before night bathed the entire area. A bird fluttered from the bough of a tree, causing several of them to jump.

Veron paused at a large, cleared section of the trees. A flat, rectangular area of tilled earth lay before them.

"Is this a garden?" Raiyn asked.

Veron walked forward and stepped down a row of green plants reaching his waist. "This is verquash." He ran his hand along the stalks. "And that row looks like beans, then cabbage."

"I can't believe they can grow up here," Finley said.

Veron stared, calculating the size of the space and the food it could produce.

"Is something wrong?" Aleks said after a moment of silence. "Should we go?"

Veron held up a finger, and the rest of the men waited. "Sixty to seventy people," he said.

"What?" Aleks started. "Who lives here?"

"That's my guess, based on the size of this garden and the food it could produce."

"How many did you say came to Felting?"

"There were nine," Raiyn said.

Finley gasped. "Nine were enough to capture all the shadow knights, but there are seventy of them here?"

Veron turned. "Like I said in Nasco, this will be dangerous, and I can't guarantee your safety. If you wish to turn around now, there will be no hard feelings."

Royce tapped against his sword. "We're not going anywhere."

Veron scanned the faces of the men who stood resolutely and nodded. A smile washed over him. "Thank you."

"We did take out three of those nine," Raiyn added. "So . . . that makes it a bit better."

Veron chuckled. "More specifically, *you* and Lia took out three."

"How'd you do it?" Aleks asked. "Is there a secret?"

"We had surprise at our advantage."

"Which we will hopefully have here," Veron added.

A wistful smile crossed Raiyn's face. "And we had Lia."

Veron nodded. "Let's do this for her."

Veron led back into the trees, keeping behind trunks and limbs whenever possible. At the far end of the grove, he stopped and peered out from a branch.

"Anything there?" Aleks whispered.

The cave lay up a short slope. Veron scanned the front but saw nothing of concern. He turned to the group of men. "Are you ready?"

They nodded.

"Our cover is gone after we leave these trees. Keep your eyes open and weapons ready."

Raiyn touched his shoulder. "Wait."

Veron turned as a man in gray exited the cave.

The group shuffled farther behind any nearby cover.

"Varlod!" the man in gray called. He took a few steps toward the valley and scanned the scene.

Veron kept his breath even as he peeked around the trunk.

"Someone else is here too," Raiyn whispered.

"Someone else *was* here," Veron said.

"Varlod?" The man in gray shook his head and turned back to the cave.

"We need him alive." Veron turned to Raiyn. "Can you do it?"

Raiyn inhaled sharply and stared at the cave. "I can." He held his sword in a tight grip and glanced around in the trees. "I'll hit him from the side."

"Take this." Veron held up a metal bolo. "You may get the jump on him, but if you're going to keep him alive and restrained, you must suppress his ability."

Raiyn took the object and nodded. After a last glance at the guard, he sped along the edge of the trees, moving out of sight.

Veron watched and waited.

The guard in gray called out again, and still nothing responded. The man's body fidgeted, as if he wrestled with what to do.

"Something's bothering him," Aleks whispered. "He's agitated."

"Come on, Raiyn," Veron whispered. "Where are you?"

With a definitive turn, the guard faced the cave and jogged toward the red glow.

"We can't let him go." Veron readied his legs. "We need to—"

A blur rushed toward the mouth of the cave.

"That's him," Veron said, louder. "Let's go."

He led the charge, leaving the cover of the trees and sprinting across the exposed ground. A brief scuffle ahead consisted of blurred limbs and a strangled cry. He slowed the last few steps and arrived where Raiyn held the guard from behind.

A hand wrapped around the man's mouth, and the bolo wrapped around his neck. He tried to yell, but only muffled sounds came out.

"Quiet," Raiyn hissed.

The man moaned.

"Quiet!" Raiyn punched with his free hand into the man's side.

The man in gray groaned and tried to bend to the side, but Raiyn held him up. Around his neck, a red crystal glowed, throbbing in bright pulses.

"Do any of you have a gag?" Raiyn asked.

"Here." Aleks held up a strip of cloth.

Finley and Royce held the man at sword point while Raiyn tied the fabric tight around his mouth. With the gag in place and Raiyn's hands free, he grasped the crystal necklace and yanked. The necklace broke, and the red glow instantly dimmed.

Raiyn sighed. "That's better." He tossed it to the rocky ground. The crystal bounced and clattered but didn't break.

Veron stepped into the guard's face. "Do you know where the shadow knights are?"

The guard stopped fighting. His shoulders drooped, but his wide eyes flitted between the group.

"Do you?"

The guard took a deep breath and his eyes narrowed. Finally, he nodded.

Veron's balled hand flew through the air and struck the man across the face with weeks of pent-up anger. The bones of the guard's cheek crunched under his fist. He followed through, knocking the man nearly to the ground.

Veron shook his hand. It ached with a throbbing pain, but the sight of the guard groaning and holding his face made it worth it.

Aleks stepped between them and lowered his voice. "Let me handle it, Veron."

Veron clenched his teeth and exhaled, shaking his fist again. The grin wouldn't leave his face. He stayed back.

Aleks turned to the guard. "I'm sorry about that. We don't need to hurt you as long as you cooperate."

The guard held his hand against his cheek and glanced between them.

"Where are the knights being held?"

The guard's shoulders bounced as he snorted. He mumbled words that were lost in the gag.

"Take that off." Aleks nodded to Raiyn.

While Raiyn pulled the cloth and dropped it below the man's chin, Aleks stepped closer. "If you call out or refuse to cooperate, that fist will be the least of your worries."

A sharp metal sound preceded Royce stepping forward with a raised dagger. "Don't mess with us on this."

Veron smiled at the passion of the Nasco men.

The guard's mouth was free, but he didn't raise an alarm. He only stared at the dagger.

"Again," Aleks said. "Where are the knights?"

"What happened to Varlod?" the guard asked. "Did you kill him?"

"We haven't killed anyone . . . yet," Aleks said. "But if you test our patience, you will become the first. Where are they?"

"They're in the hold," the guard said.

Veron's brows pinched together.

"What's that?" Aleks asked.

The guard's eyes narrowed. "You'll never get there. You have to pass through the Hub, and we have people everywhere."

"Is there another way?"

He shook his head.

Aleks pointed into his face. "You're going to take us there."

The guard chuckled. "You want me to turn on my people? Not a chance."

Royce whirled. His dagger plunged through the man's gray robe and stuck into his arm. A cry began but was stifled as Royce covered the guard's mouth.

He groaned for a long moment, writhing and shaking his head. When he finally calmed down, he stared at the group.

"That's only the beginning." Royce tapped at the end of the knife's handle. "Do you want me to twist this?"

The guard sucked in air through his nose and whimpered.

"What will it be?" Aleks asked. "Take us to our people, or let Royce carve you up some more?"

Royce removed his hand, and the man remained quiet. Sweat dripped down his face. After a long moment, he nodded. "I can take you."

47

REUNIONS

A mildewy smell mixed with sulphur and earth hit them when they crossed the threshold of the cave. Crystals embedded in the walls glowed with a faint red light, not bright enough to see well, but enough to keep them from stumbling in darkness. The glow cast the group in an eerie light as they left the fresh air behind.

The rocky and uneven ground made them watch their feet as they walked. For a while, the main tunnel was the only passage.

"Raiyn, how's the origine?" Veron whispered.

"It's light," the young man replied after a brief pause.

"I was worried these glowing red walls might affect it."

"They are. And the closer I get to the walls, the worse it is."

A narrow passage branched on the left of the main shaft, and Veron halted.

"Do you know anything about this place?" Aleks whispered. "Or where we need to go?"

Veron shook his head. "They took the knights as prisoners, so they're likely to be kept in a cell somewhere." He turned to the bound and gagged guard that Royce dragged with him. "Which way?"

With pained eyes, the gray-clothed man nodded down the main passage.

Veron resumed walking.

"We can't trust him," Aleks whispered. "He could be leading us into a trap."

Veron nodded. "He likely is, which is why we need to stay alert, but we don't have any other choice."

Raiyn's arm flung in front of his chest, stopping him in his tracks. Veron's hand jumped to his sword hilt, and his muscles tensed, ready for action. He looked forward then spun around, but he saw nothing. "What is it?" he finally asked.

Raiyn pulled his arm off Veron's chest and pointed to the wall.

A faint red light revealed a curve in the rocky wall of the tunnel. The curve rose from the floor and outlined an object that stood in relief. The carved body had strong arms, a large chest, and a wide-open mouth. Chiseled marks in the stone gave the illusion of fur across the statue. Paws held up with claws pressing out of the rock. Each of the two eyes held a glowing red stone.

"It's a bear," Veron whispered.

"Watch out for the bears," Raiyn breathed.

"Over here, too." Aleks pointed to the right wall of the cave where an identical carved bear faced the other from the opposite side.

Veron spun toward the guard. The man in gray had shrunk back several steps until Royce stopped him with a knife.

"Where do you think you're going?" Royce asked.

"What do the bears do?" Veron asked, pulling down the gag.

The guard lifted his shoulders. "What do you mean?" His nervous laugh bounced off the walls.

"We were told to watch out for the bears. Are they a trap of some sort? What do they do?"

Royce's knife appeared in front of the man's face. His eyes crossed, watching the blade. "They don't do anything." His confidence faded.

Veron approached one of the bears, making sure not to touch it or cross its path. The gaping mouth seemed to disappear into darkness. The glowing eyes protruded from the stone.

"Have him go first," Raiyn said.

Veron nodded. "Good idea." He pointed at the guard. "Show us how safe it is."

The guard shook his head while his jaw clenched.

"Shove him across it," Royce said. "Then we'll find out what happens."

Veron grabbed the man with both hands. The guard's legs were useless to resist the strength with which Veron manhandled him. Despite his struggles, he drew closer.

"No, no!" The guard waved his hands. "It's the mouth. If you cross its path without deactivating it, an acid fog sprays across the tunnel."

Veron stopped pushing. The group was quiet. "How do you get past?" Veron asked. "Show us."

The guard sighed. Veron stepped back and left two strides between him and the bear.

The man in gray stepped forward and stopped just before the bears.

"Go on," Raiyn urged.

The man lifted a shaking arm but didn't move any farther. After a heavy exhale, he crossed to the bear and set two fingers against the red eyes. He pressed. The crystals sank back into the statue, and the glow faded. The red from the bear on the opposite side followed suit. With slumping shoulders, the man stepped past the bear.

Veron followed, holding his breath and ready to sprint. He passed without incident.

The rest of the group crossed a moment later.

"That was fun." Veron nodded toward Raiyn. "Good catch."

Raiyn smiled.

"Keep your eyes open for more." Veron waved forward. "Let's keep going."

Raiyn stepped closer as they resumed their journey. "Have you thought about what will happen when we escape?"

Veron looked at the young man and took a deep breath. "I've thought about it some."

"I'm wondering . . ." He lowered his voice. "Assuming we find everyone and break them out, we're still in the middle of a snowy wilderness. And only some of us can use the origine. What's to stop them from running us down and dragging us back?"

Veron sighed. "That's the part I haven't figured out yet."

Raiyn frowned. "Maybe we can sneak out without them knowing we were here."

Veron chuckled. "That would be nice, but somehow I doubt that's going to be our reality."

"Maybe we could hide as soon as we get out."

"We'd need a well-timed storm to cover our tracks."

"Hmm." Raiyn's eyes drifted to the ceiling as he walked. He stopped with a jerk, his eyes wide.

"What?" Veron followed Raiyn's eyes to a double beam of wood, bracing the ceiling of the tunnel. "You think these beams are bearing the roof?"

Raiyn ran his hand along one and nodded. "Eastern Perryvine wood. Used in construction to support great loads." He leaned closer. "You think this tunnel is the only way out?"

Veron shrugged. "Either way, collapsing this on our way out will buy us time."

A loose rock in the passage behind them made Veron spin. He pulled his sword and stepped forward, putting himself between his group and the glowing-red void. The tip of his sword extended into the passage. "Show yourself."

The group was silent for a long moment. All Veron heard was his own breath. He stepped farther, grit scraping under his foot.

"Don't be mad," a weak voice replied. A boy with dark skin stepped into the glow with his hands up and a grimace on his face. A sword hung on his hip.

"Marcus!" Veron lowered his weapon. "You were supposed to stay with the horses."

"I know. I'm sorry, but . . . my father. I just—I couldn't do *nothing*! I tied the horses up."

Veron lowered his head and sighed. "It's too dangerous to wander back alone, now."

A smile grew on the boy's face.

"Stay close."

He nodded vigorously. "I will."

Veron led the group forward with Raiyn next to him. They paused at each corner and peered around with swords up. They passed two more small passages before they halted at the edge of a large room. Veron pressed against the wall with Raiyn on his left. He leaned his head forward, peeking from just behind a rocky edge.

From where they stood, only a portion of the room was visible. Red crystals gave a small amount of light, but it barely penetrated the large space. Large columns, glowing in red, emerged from the gloom. In the roof, a large hole cut into the ceiling with a faint red glow. Somewhere in the darkness, water gurgled.

Veron turned to the guard. "Is this 'the Hub?'"

The man paused before nodding.

"You have people everywhere, huh?" Raiyn said. "Looks deserted to me."

The man in gray continued to stare forward without reacting to the comment.

"I don't like it," Veron said after scanning his surroundings. "It's too exposed. There are too many places for ambush, and we need to catch them by surprise." He turned back to the guard. "Give us another way."

The man shook his head until a gasp preceded him arching his back.

Royce stood behind him with an impassive look on his face. His arm was pressed against the man's back. The guard whimpered until Royce backed off. A dagger in his hand glowed in the red light.

Raiyn pulled down the man's gag. "Another way?"

Still whimpering, the man nodded then tossed his head as if motioning back the way they came. "The corridor we just passed," he said. "It takes longer, but it will get us there."

Veron exhaled. "All right. Back up. Let's try it."

It only took a few minutes to arrive at the previous route. The walls were narrow, and the low ceiling made Veron stoop, but the frequent crystals gave it enough light. Having enough width for one, Raiyn took the lead with Veron just behind.

"The power is even fainter here," Raiyn whispered after traveling a ways down the new passage. "These crystals are closer together and seem to have more of an impact. There's some origine left but not much. Do you think that was the guard's plan?"

His words gave voice to the fear Veron mulled over. "I don't know. I don't think there is a safe way to go."

They continued. With each dark branch of the tunnel they passed, they looked to the bound guard, but he kept pointing them forward. Raiyn kept his sword up at the lead. Veron's gut grew more and more hesitant the farther they traveled. Eventually, their passage opened into a larger room with three junctions leading in different directions.

"Bring him up here." Veron motioned behind him.

Royce dragged the guard forward with a dagger held to his neck.

"Where do we go to find the shadow knights?" Veron asked.

The guard's forehead creased. His eyes bounced between the different exits to the room. Eventually he shrugged and mumbled something indecipherable.

Veron pulled down roughly on his gag and got in his face. "Where are they?"

"I don't know. I don't remember this place."

"Liar!"

"Veron," Raiyn said.

The waver in his voice caught Veron's attention. He turned and followed Raiyn's eyes as they looked at the walls—walls filled with glowing red crystals.

"I can't access the origine at all."

Veron held his breath as he turned, lost, powerless, and deep in the enemy's lair. His eyes stopped. A bright red glow drew closer up one of the passages. The next passage caught his eye as it lit up as well.

A deep laugh filled the chamber as two marked ones rounded the corners.

"It's a trap," Aleks gasped.

The two men held swords casually in front of them while glowing red necklaces drooped in front of their gray clothes. "Thanks for bringing them, Barolt," one of the men said, nodding toward the bound guard.

"Now, release him," the other man ordered.

"No." Royce's dagger pressed tighter against Barolt's neck.

Veron and Raiyn stood in the front with swords raised.

"Let's play this out, shall we? You kill Barolt with that small knife. Then, using the devion, we kill all of you before you even blink. How does that sound?"

"The power doesn't make you that fast," Veron said. "With our numbers, we'll take out one—possibly both—of you before you can get to us all. Is that a risk you're willing to take?"

The man smirked. "You may know the origine, but you don't know the power of the devion."

"Show me, then." Veron leaned forward. The tip of his weapon hovered in the air as he stood in dragon stance.

The marked ones sneered back but didn't move. "The alternative is . . . you release Barolt, and we *don't* kill you. We take you to your friends, and you have a joyous reunion, together. Which sounds better?"

Veron gripped tighter on his weapon's handle. A drop of sweat trickled down his forehead, running into his eyebrow. *They'll be fast.* His muscles tensed.

"Release him!" the man shouted, the black stain on his neck shaking.

Veron counted three breaths before he answered. "No."

The man's face turned down. "Hmm . . . that's too bad."

Veron readied to attack. His arms twitched when a *thump* filled the chamber and a crossbow bolt stuck through the man's head.

The other marked one jerked his head and stared at his partner, who fell to his knees.

Raiyn pounced at the remaining man in gray before he overcame his shock. His sword thrusted into the man's chest and twisted in a fluid motion.

Painful cries bounced off the walls in all directions. The stabbed man dropped to the ground, clutching his chest as blood spurted freely.

Behind Veron, another body fell. He spun to find Barolt's body flopping against the ground with a red slash across his throat. Royce stared over him with his dagger dripping.

"Gah!" Raiyn shouted, spinning and panting. "Is that it? How did they—? What is—?"

He turned to the passage on the left at the same time as Veron. A crossbow lowered, and the unmistakable face of a young woman with brown hair waited behind it. A face Veron had known for sixteen years.

"Lia!" Raiyn ran to her.

Veron gasped. His legs trembled. "You're alive." Tears sprung and fell down his cheeks. He took lumbering steps forward then wrapped his arms around the locked forms of his daughter and Raiyn. "I can't believe it."

She pulled back, her smile beaming. "Yes, I'm alive."

Raiyn backed away, keeping a hand on her arm. "What happened? How did you survive?"

"I had some help." She looked to her side. A young boy around Marcus' age waved. "This is Cecil, and *this*—" She paused conspicuously and pointed to a man against the wall. "Is someone you may recognize."

Veron wiped the blurriness from his eyes and cocked his head. The grizzled man had more hair than face. His weathered skin looked chapped and tough, but beneath the blond tangles, an oddly familiar look stared back. The corner of the man's mouth quirked up, pulling his beard with it.

Veron gasped. "No." His eyes widened, and he stepped forward. "Is it you?"

The man flashed a reluctant smile.

"Brixton?"

"Hello, Veron."

He hadn't seen his friend in many years, but the voice was unmistakable. "I can't believe it." He stepped forward and squeezed him in a hug. "How-how—?"

"He saved my life," Lia said.

"You can all catch up later," Aleks said, dousing the moment of joy and bringing everyone back to the tension they'd just left. "We can't stand here waiting to be caught. Lia, do you know where to go?"

Still smiling, she pointed ahead. "The one on the right. We've been wandering these tunnels for what seems like hours, but we haven't tried that one yet."

"Let's go then, quickly. Leave the bodies."

Aleks took the lead with the rest of the group filing in behind him.

"It's good to see you, Brixton," Veron said before he fell in line behind his daughter and ahead of his old friend.

The group of nine jogged through the tunnels. They meandered through the red glowing passage until it emptied into a large, open room. The men from Nasco parted, letting Veron push through.

"Is this them?" Aleks sported a hopeful grin.

Over a glowing chasm, five familiar faces stared back from a square platform.

"Veron!" Dayna called from across the pit. "I can't believe it!"

Veron's eyes flicked through the stranded group, and his stomach turned. *Where is she?*

"Lia! Lower that bridge!" Dayna shouted.

"Wh-where's Chelci?" Veron stammered.

Bradley pointed in the distance. "They took her and Gavin earlier. They didn't say why or where."

Veron's heart pounded.

A wooden bridge dropped from its vertical position to smack the stone platform. The five knights hurried across.

"I'll save the introductions for later." Veron waved to the rest of the group he arrived with. "We've still got people to rescue, then we need to get us all out of here. Do any of you have an idea of where they might be?"

"Chelci mentioned something about a large oval chamber with a single column they took her to a few days ago," Dayna said. "Maybe they went to the same place."

"Do you know where it is?"

She lifted her shoulders. "I've got a vague idea, but none of us have been there."

"All right. We can start with that."

"What about a group of villagers?" Lia said, pointing to Cecil. "We need to find Cecil's father and the people from his village. They were taken."

"We passed a barred cage when we first arrived," Bradley said. "There were other people kept in there. It was straight up this corridor, halfway before you get to the large room."

Cecil's eyes lit up. "That might be them."

"Don't worry," Lia said. "We'll get them."

"I think we should split up," Aleks said. "This group is too large to stay secret."

Veron nodded. "Agreed. I'll lead the group for Chelci and Gavin."

After a pause, Lia spoke up. "And I'll take a group with Cecil to find his father. Bradley, can you take us there?"

The man nodded.

"I'm with Lia," Raiyn said.

"The rest of you, split up, and if you've got more than one weapon, share them." Veron sloughed the straps off his shoulder and extended Farrathan with its sheath. "Lia, I had a hunch I should bring this. Take it."

Lia beamed as she slid her arms through the straps.

"Marcus?" Veron craned his neck but didn't see the boy. "Marcus?"

"Here, sir," Marcus said, pushing around Royce from the back of the group.

"Stick with me. We'll get your father back."

48

TWISTING PASSAGES

Lia rushed up the passageway, stepping lightly and peering around each corner. "Have you figured out how to stop the red crystals from killing the origine?" she whispered.

"Unfortunately, not," Bradley replied. "We've been in that room with the pit pretty much since we arrived. We haven't learned anything."

"In rooms where there weren't many crystals, it wasn't too bad," Raiyn said, his breath heavy as he jogged to keep up.

Lia nodded. "Yeah, I found a few passages where it worked." She frowned, gazing at the bright red glow of the walls as they hurried past.

"It should be soon." Bradley pointed ahead. "I remember this dark section."

The passage immediately ahead was darker than the rest. Lia hurried to the next corner. She peered around and tensed. Two men in gray stood outside of a barred cell door. She turned to the others behind her as a line of five people formed in the shadows.

Lia reached inside to test the connection to the origine.

Nothing.

She leaned back and whispered, "We're there. It's about ten paces until the cell door, but we can't close that distance without the origine."

"Without them being ready, at least," Raiyn added.

"Did you see the people in the cell?" Cecil asked.

She shook her head.

Finley held up a bolo. "Do you want to try these?"

Bradley inspected the metal device. "Nice. Do we know if metal works on them though?"

Lia nodded. "It should, but I don't think we'd have a shot. Where they're standing, they'd both see it coming and could easily dodge.

The group grew quiet. Lia kept checking over her shoulder, as if someone could round the corner at any time.

"I've got an idea." Finley turned to Raiyn. "You up for something?"

Raiyn raised his eyebrows. "Uh . . . what?"

"Just play along." Finley turned to the others. "You wait here and stay in the shadows. We'll be right back."

Lia's mouth hung open. She intended to protest but had trouble processing what he meant. "The . . . shadows?"

"You idiot!" Finley said, pushing Raiyn in the chest.

Raiyn's eyes widened.

Lia sucked in air at the volume of his words. "What are you—"

Finley's wink made her stop. He stepped toward the corner, beckoning Raiyn, who eventually followed. "You said it would work, but it didn't!"

"Um . . ." Raiyn paused until Finley motioned for him to keep going. "I didn't say it would work."

They rounded the corner with Finley wagging a finger in the air before they both disappeared. "You see, that's your problem. You think—"

The words stopped. Lia pressed her back against the dark wall and raised her crossbow.

"Who are you?" echoed down the hall from a gruff voice.

After a hurried scuffling sound, Finley and Raiyn rounded the corner at full speed, blasting past her down the dark hallway.

A moment later, two guards followed suit. Their steps slowed as they entered the dark section, but their caution was too late. Bradley and Salina pounced with deadly accuracy using their borrowed swords. The guards' cries were quick and shrill.

Finley and Raiyn jogged back. "No sweat." Finley smiled.

"Good work." Lia rifled through the fallen guards' pockets. A jingle announced a ring of keys. "Got it!"

The cell contained thick, metal bars, crusted and slick to the touch. After rattling a few keys, she found one that worked, and the door pivoted open with a creak.

The odor of sweat and dirt hit Lia as she entered. With no crystals to give the cell light, the dimensions were difficult to discern, but a faint outline showed it was larger than she expected.

"Who are you?" a trembling voice asked.

"I'm Lia, and we're here to help. Who are you?"

The body of the shaking voice stepped forward. His massive form towered over her. "I'm Titus."

"Father?" Cecil's high-pitched voice cut into the room.

"Cecil?" The man breathed. "Is that you?"

Cecil ran forward and wrapped his arms around the man. Muffled cries filled the room while the other dark shapes lumbered closer.

"What is this?" Titus mumbled into his son's shoulder. "How are you here?"

"We're here to rescue you," Lia said. "How many of you are there?"

"Fifteen," another man answered.

Lia frowned. *Too many to wander the tunnels.* She motioned to the room. "Come on. We need to move."

The prisoners rushed from the cell as fast as the malnourished group was able. The large group hurried past the fallen guards, down the passage they knew. Raiyn led the way, twisting and turning in the vaguely familiar passage. Before long, they came to a halt in the junction room.

Lia grabbed Finley's shoulder when he stumbled in. "Can you lead them out however you got in?"

"Sure." He glanced at the tunnel they first arrived through. "As long as we don't run into anyone."

"Take this." Lia handed him the crossbow.

"Are you searching for the others?" Finley asked.

She nodded.

Titus stepped up. "Where are you going?"

"To find my mother," Lia replied.

"I'm with you," Raiyn said.

"Us, too." Bradley and Salina stepped forward.

Lia smiled. "They might need some shadow knights on the way out. Could you two go with them?"

Bradley glanced at Salina then at the group they'd rescued. He nodded.

"Do you know where your mother is?" Titus asked.

Lia lifted her shoulders. "I heard about a large room with a single column. I'm not sure where it is though."

"That's the Chamber Room." Titus pointed down one of the passages. "Take this for about four hundred paces. When it branches, take the left fork. You'll be close."

A rush of adrenaline surged through Lia, and a nervous smile tugged at her mouth. "Thank you."

Raiyn nodded. "We'll get them."

"The rest of you, with us." Finley raised a hand from across the room. "Good luck, you two!" He disappeared into the glowing red tunnel with Bradley on his heels.

Lia took a deep breath then extended her hand. Raiyn grasped it, firm yet tender. "Thank you for being here," she said.

He smiled.

She turned to the glowing-red passage. "You ready?"

"Ready."

Lia ran.

VERON STOPPED short at the intersection, nearly skidding into Dayna.

"I don't think this is where we're supposed to be." Dayna glanced down the tunnels continuing in each direction.

Veron took deep breaths, his pulse thudding in his head. "Does anything look familiar?"

"We've never *been* here. I'm only going by what Chelci said, but . . . I don't think it was this far."

"We've got to move."

Dayna glanced back and forth, but her legs remained planted. "I-I don't know."

Veron sighed then ran to the left. "This way, then."

Footsteps followed behind him. The glowing red passage twisted and turned until it spilled into a chamber.

All aspects of the round room pointed toward an enormous red crystal hanging from the center of the ceiling. A faint hum filled the room. A pulsing glow illuminated the black pit that yawned beneath it.

Veron's eyes grew. "This is interesting."

In eerie, red light, Bradley followed closely behind the unfamiliar man who had arrived with Veron. He seemed to know where to go, so Bradley hurried after him. He kept the tip of his sword up to prevent it from running into anyone in the dark.

"Slow down," a voice called from over his shoulder.

Bradley turned. The large man they rescued lumbered to keep up, and the people from his cell lagged even more.

"They don't have a lot of strength," Salina said as the three people in the lead slowed. "We need to take it easy."

Bradley turned to the man he didn't know. "How much farther?"

"The main tunnel should be close. I'm Finley, by the way."

"Thanks for coming for us. I'm Bradley, and this is Salina."

"You're shadow knights?"

Bradley nodded. He reached inside to test, but still found the origine unresponsive. "I hope we can get to an area where the power isn't blocked—at least before we run into any of their people."

Titus arrived, panting. "All right. Keep going."

Finley led the way, and Bradley moved next. After only a short run, space seemed to open up ahead.

"This is it," Finley said. "Once we enter the main tunnel, it will be a quick run to get outside."

Bradley grinned. He'd nearly given up all hope of rescue, and the thought of breathing free air again filled him with joy.

When he spilled out of the tight passage, Finley's frozen form made him look up. He skidded to a halt. Three men in gray with black necks and swords barred the new passage. The red crystals around their necks glowed bright, illuminating their faces from below.

"Were you thinking of going somewhere?" one of the men asked.

Bradley pulled from inside, but nothing responded. No tingle. No strength rushing through his limbs. He lifted his sword along with Salina. He raised it out of instinct, but hope was nowhere to be found.

VERON STEPPED CLOSER to the glowing object, his eyes transfixed.

"What is that?" Brixton asked.

"We never came here," Bridgette said. "It reminds me of their necklaces. Just . . . bigger."

Aleks stopped at the edge of the pit. He peered down and whistled. "Don't want to fall in there."

Veron cocked his head. "What makes it work, I wonder?" He took another step. The pulsing red light seemed to vibrate his chest.

"Watch that edge," Dayna warned.

Veron stopped moving. His toes crested the edge of the drop, and his hand reached forward. "In Felting, they sucked the origine out of me, and it entered their crystal." He waved his arm. "I've been powerless since then. I wonder . . ."

Veron set his hand against the object's smooth, hard facet. His fingers curled, sliding along the grain. His nails tapped the surface. After taking a deep breath, he closed his eyes and pressed his palm flat. He exhaled long and slow. Then he pulled from inside him.

Power flooded into him like a raging torrent, and his eyes flew open. Light shone through his pores, and his body shook while a metallic hum filled the air.

"Veron!" Dayna shouted. "What are you—"

He held up his other hand, stopping her. "It's all right," he managed through gritted teeth.

He kept his hand on the crystal, and vibrations rolled through his arm. As the light raged through him, his vision grew dim.

What is happening?

His other hand balled in a tight fist. He groaned behind a clenched jaw. When he felt he couldn't take any more, Veron pulled his arm away.

Why can't I see?

He gasped for air and blinked.

No . . . it's not me.

His eyesight was fine. It was the room that had grown dark. The hum in the air faded as the main crystal steadily grew brighter from the dull, faded form it had momentarily taken.

"What did you do?" Dayna asked.

Brixton, Aleks, and Royce had taken large steps back from him.

Veron spun toward the others, holding his hands up. He laughed, hesitant but giddy.

Brixton looked at the walls. "Is it me or is it dimmer in here now."

"It's not you," Aleks said. "The crystal lost something."

Dayna looked down at her body and gasped. "I feel it! It's back—the origine!"

Bridgette's eyes widened. "You're right!"

Ruby nodded.

Veron held his breath and lifted his hands. He turned them over, marveling with his mouth hanging open.

"What is it, Veron?" Dayna asked.

He looked at her, and an enormous grin covered his mouth. "I feel it, too."

.   .   .

LIA'S panting breath filled the corridor. *Run faster. Run faster.* The dim light and tight passages forced her to slow. They had angled down the left fork minutes before. *We should be there by now!* Her eyes scoured the walls, making sure she didn't miss anything.

The red glow dimmed.

"Whoa!" Lia stopped running and set her hands against the walls.

"What'd you do?" Raiyn asked.

"I didn't do anything. It just—"

The light dimmed nearly to full blackness while a faint hum ran through the walls.

"This isn't good," Raiyn said. "If we lose this light . . ."

She waited, her heart pounding. After a moment of terror, the light gradually returned.

Raiyn sighed. "That could have been trouble."

"Let's go." Lia resumed running. She pressed off the wall and frowned. "Something's wrong," she called over her shoulder.

"I agree, but . . . I can't tell what."

"It's the light," Raiyn said. "It's dimmer."

Lia squinted, continuing to run. "It is dimmer, but . . . it's something else."

Rounding a corner, the passage opened into an enormous room with a single column in the center. Two lone torches hung on either side of the doorway, casting a small amount of light through the space. Lia brightened when she found what she sought—two people tied to chairs on a raised stage. One of them—a woman—lifted her head.

Her heart surged.

"Mother!"

FINLEY RAISED the crossbow with one hand and pulled out his bolo with the other. The metal object dangled loosely while his mind raced for how to engage.

"Step aside!" His voice was firm, but his legs wobbled.

The marked ones laughed. "Nice try," one of them said. "Drop your weapons if you don't want to die."

"You drop yours!" Bradley shouted, taking a step forward. "We outnumber you."

A man in gray spit on the ground. "You could have twenty armed men for every one of us, and we'd still defeat you with one arm behind our backs."

Finley shot a look at Bradley. "Got any ideas?"

The shadow knight stood tall, but his delay in responding revealed his hesitance.

Finley sighted down the shaft of the crossbow. *Maybe I can take one out with a bit of luck.*

The red light dimmed, and a hum filled the air.

The men in gray's eyes shifted. "What's happening?" one of them asked. All three looked unstable on their feet.

The light grew so dim, Finley could barely see their group. After a brief moment, the red gradually returned. His heart pounded. *This is our only shot. We need to use the distraction.* He sighted the crossbow again, aiming at the black stain of a man with a scraggly brown beard. His finger wrapped around the trigger. The man continued to stare at the walls, his eyebrows quirked in a confused pose.

"Salina," Bradley whispered to the side. "It's back."

Finley frowned. *What do they mean?*

"You're right . . ." she replied.

With his eyes trained on the man in gray, Finley could still hear the smile in her voice.

". . . the origine is back."

Finley gasped then pulled the trigger.

Lia and Raiyn sprinted across the chamber. The room felt like it grew larger the farther she ran. Her footsteps echoed in the grand space.

Chelci and Gavin squirmed in their seats as they approached.

Gags muffled their words. Their wide eyes held a mixture of shock and fear.

"We're here!" Lia rushed onto the raised platform. Tears tugged at her eyes as she fumbled at the ropes binding her mother's arms and chest. "I'm so sorry, Mother—for everything." She pulled a rope end through a knot. "I should never have abandoned my duty that night. I should never have left. We made it, though. Father is here. We found the other knights." Her eyes flicked up. "We're going to get you all out of here."

Chelci mumbled into the gag around her mouth.

"Hold on." Lia pulled another rope end, tugging and tugging as the loose section unraveled. The rope fell limp.

Chelci pulled her arms free then went to work on the tied end of her gag.

Lia moved to the rope around her legs. The knot slipped easily, and she pulled against the loose rope.

"Lia!" Free from the gag, Chelci's voice contained a mixture of love and terror. "You can't be here."

"It's all right. We've got a team." Lia looked over her shoulder. "Father and Brixton were supposed to be here—"

"Brixton?"

Lia dropped the rest of the ropes. "Yeah, we ran into him, too."

Gavin freed his mouth. "She's right. We need to go, *now!*"

"It's all right, we're going. Gavin, you'll never guess who else we have with us."

Free from her ropes, Chelci stood and grabbed Lia's shoulders. "It's *not* all right. It's a trap!"

Lia's brow furrowed. "What's a trap?"

Chelci gestured her arm across the room. "All of this. They knew you were coming!"

"Who's with you?" Gavin asked as he stood.

"I'm not sure how happy you'll be that he's here, but . . . we have Marcus with us."

Gavin's face twisted in confusion. "Marcus?"

"Chelci!"

The sound of her father calling from across the room made Lia's heart surge. She spun to find him and his crew racing in their direction.

"Veron!" Chelci cried. She jumped off the platform and wrapped him in her arms, squeezing in a brief hug.

Gavin grasped Lia and looked intently into her eyes. "What do you mean you 'have Marcus'?"

Grinning, Lia craned her neck to glance through the arriving crowd.

"Brixton! Aleks! Royce! Raiyn! What—" Chelci shook her head. "No. There's no time. We have to go . . . *now*!"

"Where are the others?" Veron asked, drawing Lia's attention from her search.

"Oh!" She blinked. "We found Cecil's father and rescued the villagers. Finley is leading them out along with Bradley and Salina."

"Great!" Veron's beaming smile encompassed his entire face.

"Where's Marcus?" Lia asked.

Veron's eyes brightened as they flicked to Gavin. "That's right. We have a surprise for you, Gavin."

"Marcus?"

"I don't see him," Lia said.

"He was with us." Veron spun. His smile faded to a frown. "Marcus?"

"I haven't seen him in a while," Aleks said.

Royce shook his head. "I don't remember him in that crystal chamber."

"What are you all talking about?" Gavin yelled.

Lia sighed. "Marcus was here with us, but . . . he might have gotten lost."

"Marcus who?"

Lia glanced at her father.

Veron blew out a deep breath then set his hand on Gavin's shoulder. "We found Marcus, your son."

Gavin's brows pinched tight. He looked between Lia and Veron with his mouth open. "I-I-I—"

"I know we shouldn't have brought him here," Veron said. "But he—"

"I don't have a son," Gavin blurted.

Veron's face scrunched up, his mouth remaining open.

"We met him in Felting." A feeling of unease grew in Lia's stomach. "Thirteen years old, dark skin, you've been training him, mother was Harmony."

Gavin shook his head, slow and deliberate. "I don't have a son . . . and I've never known anyone named Marcus or Harmony in my life."

Lia stood, stunned. His words shook Lia to her core. Her gut dropped.

"If he wasn't your son," Veron muttered, "then who was he?"

Glowing red objects surged to life around the perimeter of the room.

Lia's jaw dropped as her eyes traced the line of people in gray. She counted fifteen in a row, each with a glowing red crystal. A man grabbed one of the torches off the wall then touched it to a ridge. The flame jumped, sputtering to life and running along an unseen line that circled the room.

With a shaking arm, she ripped Farrathan from its holder.

She recognized Talioth. His long gray hair waved gently as he stepped forward, holding his curved blade casually.

"How kind of the rest of you to join us," he said. "It pained me to leave you behind in Felting, but now you've made my job easy."

The fighters on either side of him held a dragon stance pose, their swords high, the tips toward her, their elbows up.

She frowned. *Their elbows are too low.* She gasped. "Just like Marcus."

Her eyes scanned the line until they stopped on a young man with dark skin. He wore a gray cloak and red crystal like the others. His hand gripped a war hammer that looked too large for the size of his arms.

"Marcus, you traitor!" she shouted.

The young man didn't flinch.

Talioth erupted in laughter. "You shadow knights are far too trusting. You fell quite willingly for our ruse. Marcilith has spent his entire life in these caverns. This was his first mission in the world, and I couldn't be prouder of how he pulled it off."

Lia's chest heaved as anger surged through her.

"Let it go, Lia," Raiyn whispered at her side. "He fooled all of us."

She breathed out, trying to calm down by blowing a steady stream of air.

Talioth's gaze swept down their group. "I'm surprised he's the only one here who's caught your attention." Lines formed at the corners of his eyes as his face lifted.

What does he mean?

She scanned the line of people again until her breath caught. Cedric's leering gaze stared at her. Nicolar's goatee and shaggy black hair glowed red in the light of the crystals. Continuing down the line, her eyes stopped.

No!

Wearing a gray cloak with a red crystal dangling from his neck, the young man shuffled his feet and held a sword loosely. A faint stain marked the base of his neck.

"Danik?" she gasped.

Her former friend clenched his jaw and looked everywhere but at her.

"Your ranks have grown, but so have ours," Talioth said. "You can't hope to defeat us."

Lia's eyes flitted to the door behind the marked ones.

"How do we get out of this?" she whispered.

Veron whispered back. "You haven't noticed it yet, have you?"

She snuck a look at her father. He wore a crooked grin as he held his sword forward.

"Noticed, what?"

"It's back."

Her forehead pinched. "What's back?"

"The origine."

Lia tested her connection to the power, then gasped as she found the tingling sensation waiting to be used. She stared at the line of glowing red crystals before them, her mouth agape. "I can use it."

Veron chuckled. "So can I."

49

SACRIFICE

"I don't think he realizes." Lia kept her eyes on Talioth as the man walked toward Veron.

"No." Veron stepped forward with Lia. "He doesn't."

"What happened?"

"I'm not sure," Veron said. "There's this room with a huge crystal. I touched it and . . . I don't know what happened."

"Veron," Talioth called. "Do you wish to lead all your people to death?"

"Is that not what I would have done had I left them here? Or were you intending to release them soon?"

Talioth came to a stop just outside striking distance. He raised his long, curved knife, showing off the jagged edges along the back. Gralow stepped next to him, holding his sword at the ready.

A smirk formed on Talioth's face. "While Shawn may have met his fate weeks ago, you'll notice the rest of your group is alive and well. I'm offering to allow you all to live, at least for a time. But if you don't like that prospect and are determined to resist, we can cut those lives short."

Lia tightened her grip on Farrathan. Her legs were taut, her muscles poised and ready to spring into action.

"Thank you for the generous offer," Veron said. "But I'm afraid we must decline."

The leader's face hardened. "You can't use the origine. You're outnumbered. Some of you don't even have weapons. What can you possibly hope to gain?"

Veron whispered toward Lia. "You ready?"

"Ready," she answered.

"There's one thing you're missing, Talioth," Veron said.

"What's that?"

Lia rushed forward with her father. She swung Farrathan with a vice grip. Her speed and power severed the air and crashed into the flat side of Talioth's curved weapon. His metal blade exploded into useless pieces that flung into the air.

Veron flashed his sword at Gralow, knocking the blade from the man's unsuspecting grip. The length of steel tumbled through the air as the marked one stared with an open mouth, lunging to recapture it.

Chelci sprung from nowhere, leaping, twisting, and flipping with her feet over her head. She grabbed the handle of the sword before it fell into Gralow's extended hand. She continued her flip and landed on the ground with bent knees, pointing her newly acquired sword at the man in gray in a move to match her husband.

"Those red crystals you love . . ." Veron continued. "They're not working."

Talioth and Gralow took tottering steps backward with loose jaws and the whites of their eyes showing.

Veron, Chelci, and Lia lunged in unison but the two marked ones spun away, retreating to their line of fighters in a flash of devion-powered energy.

"Kill them!" Talioth yelled.

An explosion of shouting erupted at once. Shadow knights rushed forward. Marked ones sprang into action. Lia pulled from her tingling well of energy and met a gray-clothed female in a fierce display of amplified combat. Farrathan clanged against the woman's sword. Lia ducked under a thrust. She spun and parried a rapid exchange of steel before leaping out of range.

The trio of Brixton, Aleks, and Royce caught her eye. All three stood together with lifted swords. Outmatched on their own, they moved as one, running toward a lone marked one.

The man in gray's crystal glowed brighter as they approached, but it had no effect on their un-enhanced bodies. They attacked with ferocity and precision. The marked one was fast, but they were fierce. Aleks missed a parry but Royce was there to block while Brixton lunged. The man moved to his heels, backing away from the relentless group. He blocked two strikes but missed the bolo that wrapped around his leg. His movement slowed. He yelled moments before Aleks plunged a blade into his chest and twisted.

A sword flash grabbed Lia's attention as an unfamiliar man in gray sprung before her. The origine kept her core tingling. Her sword crashed back and forth, sending sparks into the air. The man she fought looked fresh. He moved like lightning, and his blows pummeled against her sword. She parried over and over until finally, she dodged, slipping to the side and swiping against his chest. Farrathan tore a gash across his gray cloak. The man yelled, clutching his wound. He turned and ran before Lia had a chance to deliver a killing blow.

Temporarily alone, Lia scanned the room. Bodies and steel tangled together everywhere she looked. Her father faced off against Cedric. Dayna fought some tall man in gray. Her mother pivoted around Talioth as they both stared with weapons raised. The light from the surrounding flames and glowing crystals threw shadows in multiple directions. Clanging steel filled the air. Lia pushed her hair back, wiping off a sheen of sweat from her face.

A yell turned her head. Aleks stumbled away from his trio with Royce and Brixton, clutching his arm.

Preparing to duck back into the fray, she pulled at the origine. Her eyes widened. The waiting power was there, but it felt fainter, as if it drifted away from her. The red crystals around the room pulsed.

A few steps away, Veron placed a kick in Cedric's chest and

blasted him off his feet. The man flew through the air, crashing into the cavern wall. As soon as Veron finished the move, he slumped forward with a hand on his knees.

Lia hurried to him. "Father!"

Veron turned, his sword up and eyes wide.

"It's all right. It's just me. Is the origine still working?"

"Something's wrong," he said. "It feels like it's only partly working."

"I think whatever saved us from those crystals is wearing off."

Veron nodded.

Lia glanced at the door. "We need to get out of here. We're not going to win."

Veron stepped forward. "Chelci! Gavin! Everyone!"

A few heads turned toward him.

"To the door!" Veron pointed his sword in the direction of the lone exit.

Lia rushed forward, pushing people in gray down. The shadow knights followed her example, and the room converged on the passage. She and Veron pushed back the marked ones, keeping them from the door. They allowed Ruby, then Brixton, then a stumbling Aleks to make it through.

Veron turned to Lia and yelled, "Go! Lead them out."

"Not without you!"

He shook his head. "They'll run us down in the tunnels. I'll stay behind and hold them at the door."

A pang of terror rushed through her. *He can't hold them all off.*

Running toward them, Dayna screamed and arched her back. She dropped to the ground after Nicolar pulled his sword out.

"No!" Lia yelled.

To the right, a woman in gray yelled in triumph. Lia traced where her flung arm pointed and found a thrown dagger stuck in Royce's chest. The man from Nasco fell to his knees and stared vacantly ahead. Another marked one ran a sword into his side. Royce fell across Dayna's limp body.

Chelci was the last standing member of their group to arrive at the door, followed in hot pursuit by Talioth himself. Veron raised his sword and growled, baring his teeth. The leader of the Marked Ones halted.

"Get out of here, all of you!" Veron shouted. "I'll stay!"

Bridgette ducked through the door with Ruby on her heels. Chelci didn't follow. She lifted her weapon and stepped forward, standing next to her husband. Brixton stepped past Lia, taking her father's right side.

"I'm with you." Raiyn raised his sword next to Lia.

She glanced over her shoulder.

"The others are on their way out," he confirmed. "We can give them time."

"The origine is nearly blocked." She panted. "You should go."

Raiyn nodded. "We both should . . . but we won't."

"We may not survive this."

His mouth formed a tight line. "Like I said, I'm with you."

Lia's heart surged as his display of commitment.

"Fools, all of you!" Talioth's group formed a wall pressing in on them. "Those tunnels are a maze, and we'll run your people down soon after we kill you."

"You'll have to get past us first!" Lia shouted.

Chelci glanced over her shoulder and flashed a proud smile.

The red crystals seemed to intensify. The smell of sweat and blood filled the air.

Talioth raised his sword and advanced. Veron met him head-on, the clang from their swords ringing in the air.

The rest of the marked ones converged, but the space to attack was narrow. Chelci, Brixton, and Veron pushed forward, their twirling blades cutting the air.

Lia and Raiyn stood together, blocking the door while the other three kept the marked ones occupied. A body leaped around the edge of the fight. Danik's blond hair bounced as he landed before her. His scowl, combined with the growing stain on his neck, turned her stomach.

"Enjoying the time with your friends?" Lia asked.

"You could have had this power, too," he said, "but you turned it down."

"And I would again." Her mouth pulled up on one side. "Nice design on your neck."

Danik sneered then lunged.

Lia parried the weapon away then dug her fist into his ribs.

"Oof!" He reeled, stepping back and rubbing his chest. His teeth showed as he roared and attacked.

Lia gasped at his ferocity. She moved her sword as fast as possible, barely fending off the steely edge. Raiyn joined the fray, filling in the gaps as Lia slowed, but soon Cedric arrived, taking his attention.

Lia's hold on the origine grew fainter. The strain to fight off the power of the crystals intensified. Trapping Danik's sword with her own, she pressed toward the ground, taking both weapons out of play. Both arms strained. A roar bellowed from Lia's mouth as she pushed with all she had.

Danik's fist came as a shock when it crashed onto her hand. Lia jerked, releasing Farrathan's hilt. She gasped as both swords clattered to the ground.

Weaponless, Lia lunged at him, her speed amplified by the fizzling power she could barely find. Danik's eyes grew. He tried to shuffle away but caught a rock and fell backward. Her hands grasped for his throat as she leaped onto his prone body. She eyed the stained flesh, longing to choke the life from him, but her hands never found their mark. His raised feet met her chest, springing with immense power and sending her body flailing upside down through the air.

Weightless and helpless, Lia soared through the air, far past the other fighters. Her arms beat futilely, and her body rotated before she finally hit the ground on the back of her neck. She rolled over and slid across the rough ground before stopping at the base of the central column.

"Argh!" she yelled, her scraped skin burning.

Bright-red lines marred her flesh. Drops of blood dribbled down her arms.

Don't use the origine. Wait before healing.

She scrambled to her feet. The dais of chairs was to her right, and the crowd of fighters were a distance away. She took a moment to rest her hands on her knees, panting and wheezing. As she gulped in breaths, a tingling sensation of the origine returned.

It's working again! I must be far enough away.

As soon as she got her hopes up, the power faded—not completely gone, but very weak. She lifted her head and froze. Two glowing crystals approached. A boy jogged toward her with a war hammer as wide as his body swinging from his grip. Danik walked with him.

"Danik. Marcus." Lia shook her head and panted. "It doesn't have to be like this."

"Sorry, Lia." Marcus' impassive face didn't reflect the apology. "We have to do what we have to do."

Danik's arm flexed, and his sword blurred through the air, heading for her body.

Lia jumped backward, narrowly missing the weapon as it *wooshed* in front of her chest. She backpedaled until she smacked against the stone column.

Her eyes grew as the hammer sped toward her face. She ducked, leaving the object to crash into the column directly over her. A *boom* resounded in the chamber.

Lia peeled away and rushed around the backside of the column. Dust rained from the ceiling of the chamber as she circled the obstacle.

A sword emerged from nowhere. She ducked, leaving it to clang harmlessly off the stone. She checked the other direction and jumped to the side as the hammer crashed next to her.

I've got to do something. I can't keep this up!

She lunged at Danik, trying to immobilize his arm before he could rear back, but he was too fast.

Slam!

A force jolted her from the direction she wasn't watching, crushing her arm into her body. The room blurred as she spun, twirling until she fell to the ground, crashing against the side of the raised dais. She jumped to her feet, but the ground tilted. Her arms extended to keep her from falling. As her sight settled, Marcus and Danik both arrived.

Danik took a deep breath then lifted his sword. The weapon swung in a furious attack, aiming for her head.

Grasping at any remaining ability to touch the origine, Lia ducked forward and rolled. Danik's strike went long, catching nothing but the rocky floor. The legs of both foes stopped her momentum. They stared down at her with curious expressions. Danik's eyes morphed from curiosity to shock in the time it took her to reach up both hands. Lia grasped each of their glowing crystals and yanked the necklaces. The leather cords popped from around their neck, and the hard objects dug into her hands.

Marcus raised the hammer, preparing for another strike. While he heaved it through the air, Lia flung the crystals across the stone floor of the cavern. Already dimming, they skittered away into the distance.

The effect was instantaneous—like an anvil had been removed from her chest. The hampering barrier was gone, and the warm sensation of the origine flooded into her limbs at full strength.

Lia dodged the falling hammer and kicked hard into Marcus' stomach. He expelled his breath and crumpled forward. Lia chopped his hand and knocked the hammer free. It bounced once off the ground before she scooped the weapon up and deflected Danik's hurtling sword. She followed with an origine-infused punch into his side.

The boy looked up first. He raised his hands as Lia slammed the hammer into his chest. The sound of cracking ribs filled the air as his small body flew to the ground. Danik turned as her blow arrived, catching him in the side. His body twirled then collapsed to the ground.

Lia panted, staring between the fallen foes. Her chest heaved, but her limbs felt strong, buoyed by the sustaining power inside her. She glanced across the room and blanched. A dozen more marked ones bore down on their sad excuse for what was left of the rescue team.

Red crystals surrounded them, pressing Veron, Chelci, Brixton, and Raiyn toward the exit door.

Raiyn's eyes caught her. He beckoned with an urgent hand. "Lia! Come on! We need to run!"

Lia's mouth hung open. Her pulse thundered.

We'll never make it. They'll just come after us.

Danik rustled on the ground. He groaned as he struggled to stand.

Lia turned back to Raiyn. She opened her mouth to speak but had no plan.

How can we stop them?

More dust drifted down from the ceiling, and Lia looked up. She traced the wispy puffs up to see cracks running along the ceiling from the top of the column—the one she stood next to. She placed her hand on the column, feeling the coarse rock under her fingers. Her other hand gripped the hammer, spinning its heft.

"Lia!"

The call turned her back to Raiyn where Veron and Chelci had joined him in staring.

Veron waved her forward. Her father mouthed something, but the words turned to mush in her head.

"No," she whispered, the word lost in the cavern. "Go."

Her hand flexed. She pulled the origine through her core and swung the war hammer into the stone column. The room shook. The deep thud echoed off the distant walls.

The crowd of marked ones all stopped fighting and turned in her direction.

The room was silent. Dust tickled Lia's neck as it drifted down on top of her. She sucked in a lungful of air and shouted, "Go!"

Boom!

The crash was louder, and the room shook again.

"Lia!" Veron yelled. "Don't do it! Come with us!"

"We can't make it!" Lia shouted back.

Boom!

Danik arrived on his feet, dazed and stumbling.

"We have to try, Lia," Raiyn cried. "We can lose them!"

Boom!

She tried not to look at Raiyn, but her eyes forced her head to turn. "I'm sorry," she mouthed, tears spilling down her cheeks.

Raiyn shook his head. His sword drooped by his side. "Don't," he mouthed back.

She choked on the raw emotion.

Boom!

The shaking of the room intensified and didn't stop when the hit was done. Falling rocks joined in with the dust.

Talioth peeled away from the other stunned members of his group and rushed toward her. "No!" he shouted.

Keep them alive.

Lia put her body into it. She leaned forward, flexing her muscles with all the origine she could muster. Her vision blurred from the tears. Her energy was nearly gone. Her body shook. She grasped at any residue of strength she could find. The hammer slammed into the column, shaking the stone.

A crack ran up its length.

"Lia!"

She ignored the cry.

Come on origine, don't run out on me. It's not for me; it's for them.

"Stop her!"

Boom!

With the final hit, the column crumbled. Stone shattered into pieces, falling onto the ground with resounding booms. Cracks splintered out from the ceiling, running across the roof. Chunks fell, raining enormous boulders into the room, crashing and rumbling in a deafening roar.

Lia dropped the hammer. Her lungs heaved. Her legs were too weak to even walk. Debris fell around her. She barely managed a wince when a massive chunk of rock crushed Marcus' unmoving body.

Danik stared at Lia, tottering on uneven legs before he turned and stumbled in the opposite direction.

By the door, Raiyn, Veron, and Chelci stared helplessly. Brixton attempted to pull them into the doorway, but they remained rooted while the ceiling collapsed around them.

"Go." Lia waved a weak hand, her voice lost in the tumult.

I'm doing this so you can live.

Her sinuses cleared. A thought flashed through her mind. *Father had almost died when fighting Bale. He didn't want the power to save himself. It was all for Mother.* Ideas swirled in her mind. *He was willing to die for her when the pure connection showed up.*

"Is sacrifice the key?" she whispered.

Raiyn gave in to Brixton's pull and took a step toward the door. Veron and Chelci followed just before a boulder crashed to the ground where they'd stood. They paused in the doorway and looked one last time.

A fresh tear ran down Lia's face, but her limbs were too weak to wipe it away. A smile pulled at her face.

They're going to make it.

A loud rumble sounded directly above her. She looked up. The remainder of the ceiling gave out. Rocks and debris fell in a wave, raining down with unrelenting force. Stone struck Lia's back, throwing her to the ground. It continued to pile, more and more. And then . . .

Darkness.

50

NUMB

Veron trudged up the snowy slope. His legs felt numb, his heart callused and dead. The stone arch loomed above him as he took the last few steps to crest the saddle that led out of the hidden valley.

"Veron, we need a rest," Brixton's voice puffed over his shoulder.

Veron turned.

Brixton looked fatigued with his arms pushing against his knees. Behind him, Bridgette and Ruby puffed, watching where they set their feet. Out of the group, Aleks looked the worst. The man from Nasco grimaced as he climbed the slope with a stained-red rag tied over his arm. He huffed and wheezed. Sweat beaded on his red face.

"We can take a quick break," Gavin said, already standing on the ridge. He stared across the valley toward the cavern entrance.

Chelci arrived on the ridge and came to Veron. Her eyes were red and puffy. She wrapped her arms around him and buried her head into the crook of his neck. The squeeze of her arms comforted him. He returned the embrace.

"Thank you for coming for me," she said.

A fresh tear fell from his eye. "Lia was even more insistent than I was. We both knew it was a near-impossible task."

She lifted her head to look in his eyes, and a weak smile came to her face.

Raiyn caught Veron's eye, standing next to them with a forlorn stare toward the caverns.

"She cared about you," Veron said.

Raiyn glanced his way then nodded. "You would think it would be easier after the storm. But seeing her die for the second time is no less difficult."

"I know. I feel the same."

Veron extended his arm, and Raiyn joined their embrace. Tears fell. Hearts ached. Time seemed to freeze as they held each other.

Brixton clearing his throat made Veron open his eyes.

"Sorry to disturb your moment." Brixton nodded toward the cavern. "Do you think those marked ones will live through that?"

Veron sighed, releasing Chelci and Raiyn. "Unfortunately, so. Lia's sacrifice will have killed some—I saw Marcus crushed. Many of them were near the edges of the room though, and the devion is powerful. They'll find their way out. Our additional cave-in from those support beams will slow them for a while, but they'll dig out. They'll be on our trail soon."

"It *is* them," a voice called.

Veron spun with his hand on his sword.

"Finley!" Aleks called.

The other man from Nasco emerged from a shadowy outcropping in the rocky walls of the path. Salina and Bradley came next, followed by a large group of men and women.

Finley pointed over his shoulder. "We took shelter while we waited. I can't believe you made it. Looks like you found them!" He scanned the newly arrived crowd then frowned. "Where's Royce . . . and Lia?"

A fresh stab of pain dug into Veron's chest.

"They didn't make it. Along with . . ." Aleks turned to Veron.

"Dayna," Veron whispered.

Finley's face fell. His eyes flicked to Chelci. "I'm sorry."

Veron pushed away the thought and looked at the new group.

An enormous man approached with a small boy. "You must be Veron," he said.

"Oof!" Veron's lungs expelled air as the man grabbed him in a huge embrace.

"I can never thank you enough for rescuing me and my group."

Veron nodded in return, patting the man on the back until he finally released him.

"Where do we go from here?" Gavin asked. "We need to make fast time, but . . . we need a destination."

"We can't go back to Felting," Bridgette said. "They'll find us again."

"You'd all be welcome in Nasco." Aleks' voice was weak, but he nodded enthusiastically. "We have a lot of rebuilding to do, and our location in the woods should keep you hidden."

Veron smiled weakly. "Thank you Aleks. We can't stay hidden though. We have a lot of work to do, and we have a place near Felting that will work."

The large villager gestured to his group. "We're going to head back to Piryd. It's probably not safe to stay there, but we'll salvage what we can from the village, then find a new home—maybe another village along the Relavorre River, or maybe all the way to Kandis, on the coast."

"What work?" Finley faced Veron. "What do you need to do in Felting?"

Veron looked at his wife, then at Gavin and Raiyn. "Last I saw Danik, he was running toward safety. I'm guessing we haven't seen the last of him and his knights of power. If they're going to continue to grow their ranks, we may be the only people in Terrenor who can stop them. We could easily have another Bale on our hands."

Raiyn flinched.

Veron held up a hand. "Sorry. You know what I mean. Plus . . . something tells me we haven't had our last run in with the Marked Ones."

"If you can use me, I'd love to help," Brixton said.

Veron sucked in a breath as his eyes jumped to his old friend.

"I've hidden in the mountains for too long. I ran to punish myself for all the wrongs I'd committed, but . . . I'd rather *do* something about it than hide."

Veron nodded, a pained smile on his face. "I'd love to have you, Brix."

"I see horses down there." Gavin squinted as he gazed ahead, down the slope.

"Those are ours," Raiyn said. "We should probably keep moving."

Veron raised an eyebrow and looked at Aleks. The injured man gave a pained nod.

"Let's move," Veron said. "We have supplies with the horses: blankets, food, water, even a few warm cloaks. Let's get out of these mountains as fast as we can. Then . . . we'll make a plan to save Terrenor."

DARKNESS. Pressure. Dust. Lia's mind scrambled. Her lungs fought to breathe. Her legs and arms were pinned as a weight pushed on her back.

What happened?

The collapse of the cavern flooded into her memory. Her pulse quickened.

Raiyn! Father! Mother!

The image of them leaving the room flashed into her mind.

They must be safe. They had to escape.

An odd sensation pricked her mind.

Something's wrong. What's off?

Despite being trapped under a mountain, unlike her time in the mine shaft, her heart rate settled. A calm sensation washed over her.

Why am I not in pain?

The reason hit her like a battering ram. Tingling ran through her entire body, so complete she hadn't even noticed it. Her limbs shook as if itching to come alive. The power was beyond anything she'd ever experienced, despite having used all of her origine to destroy the column.

She pushed with her arms. Her back lifted, sloughing off piles of rocks and boulders as if they were pebbles. She planted her legs, as strong and firm as trunks of trees, then stood. Debris continued to shift, until light finally reached through the rubble.

The pure connection!

Lia smiled, her lungs taking in the fresh air. Her body felt invincible, as if nothing could stop her and the energy would never end.

She climbed free, pushing a last boulder off her leg before taking in the scene. The Chamber Room had mostly collapsed. Massive chunks of rock and dirt littered the space in every direction. Some of the roof remain intact, but much of it was pocked with gaping holes where sections had fallen. The ring of flame lighting the room persisted in portions where the wall remained undisturbed.

Two of the chairs on the dais had broken backs, and the lid of the stone, rectangular box was cracked into pieces.

She laughed out loud. *I can't believe I'm alive! I can't believe I was able to—*

Her stomach felt like it turned to water. The unbridled power waiting to be used faded like a candle snuffed by wind.

What happened? She spun. *Where did it—*

Lia froze.

Rips and holes littered Talioth's cloak, now more black than gray. His long hair fell on either side of his face, and wide, blue eyes felt like they pierced her soul. The red crystal around his neck glowed as brightly as she'd ever seen.

Lia reached inside to find the power, but it was inaccessible once more.

"Was that it?" Talioth's voice was nearly hoarse.

Lia's brows pinched together. "Was that . . . what?"

Danik stumbled forward to join him, equally dirty and disheveled.

Lia's eyes flashed to him as a scowl took over her face.

"The ceiling crushed you. You should have died." Talioth stepped closer. "Was that . . . the pure connection?"

Lia stopped breathing then shuddered.

What if—What if he gained that power?

A curious look on his face caused her to have another frightening thought.

How does he know? That was only in the Shadow Knights' book.

His mouth quirked.

Lia's heart pounded.

Danik watched the leader of the Marked Ones with equal curiosity.

Talioth raised a sword. A ruby in the hilt glinted against the flames running around the room.

"My sword," she blurted.

Talioth cocked his head. "*Your* sword? It's curious how you can feel ownership after having something for such a short amount of time." He held up the blade and grinned while his eyes ran down it. "Farrathan is *my* sword."

Lia's hands felt clammy. She forced herself to breathe, but the inkling that she was missing something wouldn't go away.

Talioth's eyes flicked to the broken box on the dais. He frowned as he stepped toward it. "You feel cocky because you follow a code. You think you're doing the right thing because hundreds of years ago someone wrote down silly rules that you blindly live by." He stopped at the box and peered into it.

"They're not silly!" Lia shouted. "The code of the Shadow Knights is what makes us great. I live by them because I want to make a difference in this world. It's what separates us from people like you!"

His frown faded until a laugh bubbled to the surface. It began small but quickly grew in intensity. He leaned forward and pushed a broken chunk of stone off the top of the box.

Lia glanced at Danik, who looked equally uneasy as he stood silently.

Talioth's laugh died. "The code separates you from me, does it?" He leaned forward and rummaged in the box.

What am I missing?

"Do you know the reason why I don't have to follow the code?" Talioth straightened, lifting a black object out of the box. "Why I can do whatever I want without worrying if I'm breaking the rules or not?" Holding on to one edge, fabric unfurled from his fingers, falling to the ground in the form of a thick, black cloak. "Because I'm the one who wrote them."

Lia gasped. On the chest of the cloak, the emblem of the Shadow Knights stared back at her.

"I figured naming the group after myself would build more respect, but I see that admiration is long gone." He raised an eyebrow. "Are you putting it together, finally?"

The Shadow Knights. Talioth.

Lia's eyes grew wide. "Are you Talon Shadow?"

THE EPIC STORY of the Shadow Knights concludes in Shadow of Hope. Purchase today at mybook.to/shadowofhope.

"I THOUGHT my dad's book was doggaly-amazing! I just went online to leave a review, but then I found this ball. Now, all I can think about is ball. Since I'm busy, could you go online and BALL for me. Wait...that wasn't it. What did I want them to do again?" - Charlie

PLEASE leave an honest review on Amazon or wherever you got the book from. Do it for Charlie.

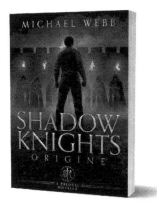

Get a FREE prequel novella to the Shadow Knights series - Shadow Knights: Origine - by signing up for my mailing list at www.subscribepage.com/michaelwebbnovels or scan this QR code

ACKNOWLEDGMENTS

This book was so much fun to write. I couldn't have done it without the help of several people who I'd like to recognize.

First, my beta readers: Eli, Nicholas, Manton, David, Johnny, Debbie, Aden, Don, Tara, and Andreas. You all do a fantastic job picking out things I miss—plot points, character weaknesses, grammar, holes. Some of them seem so glaring after you point it out that it makes me laugh. I may start with a decent story on my own, but it's you that make it great. Thank you so much!

Thank you to the Lair (my writers group). You all provide great wisdom and insight from your years of publishing. Having your collective knowledge to lean on makes the process so much easier.

Thank you Sarah for your editing skills. It's shocking how many times I misplace a comma or still miss a quotation mark.

Thank you Julia for believing in my dream and being proud of me. Without your support I couldn't do it at all.